MOONRISE

D0050812

Also by Sarah Crossan

The Weight of Water
Apple and Rain

With Brian Conaghan
We Come Apart

MOONRISE

SARAH CROSSAN

WITHDRAWN

BLOOMSBURY

NEW YORK   LONDON   OXFORD   NEW DELHI   SYDNEY

BLOOMSBURY YA
Bloomsbury Publishing Inc., part of Bloomsbury Publishing Plc
1385 Broadway, New York, NY 10018

BLOOMSBURY and the Diana logo are trademarks of Bloomsbury Publishing Plc

First published in Great Britain in September 2017 by Bloomsbury Publishing Plc
Published in the United States of America in May 2018
by Bloomsbury YA

Text copyright © 2017 by Sarah Crossan

All rights reserved. No part of this publication may be reproduced or transmitted
in any form or by any means, electronic or mechanical, including photocopying,
recording, or any information storage or retrieval system, without prior permission
in writing from the publisher.

Bloomsbury books may be purchased for business or promotional use. For information
on bulk purchases please contact Macmillan Corporate and Premium Sales Department at
specialmarkets@macmillan.com

Library of Congress Cataloging-in-Publication Data
Names: Crossan, Sarah, author.
Title: Moonrise / by Sarah Crossan.
Description: New York : Bloomsbury, 2018.
Summary: With little money or support, Joe Moon, seventeen, travels to Texas to help the older
brother he barely knows through his last few weeks before being executed for murder.
Identifiers: LCCN 2017025085 (print) • LCCN 2017038987 (e-book)
ISBN 978-1-68119-366-3 (hardcover) • ISBN 978-1-68119-367-0 (e-book)
Subjects: | CYAC: Novels in verse. | Brothers—Fiction. | Prisoners families—Fiction. |
Death row—Fiction. | Capital punishment—Fiction. | Family problems—Fiction.
Classification: LCC PZ7.5.C76 Moo 2018 (print) | LCC PZ7.5.C76 (e-book) | DDC [Fic]—dc23
LC record available at https://lccn.loc.gov/2017025085

Typeset by RefineCatch Limited, Bungay, Suffolk
Printed and bound in the U.S.A. by Berryville Graphics Inc., Berryville, Virginia
2 4 6 8 10 9 7 5 3

All papers used by Bloomsbury Publishing Plc are natural, recyclable products made
from wood grown in well-managed forests. The manufacturing processes conform to the
environmental regulations of the country of origin.

To find out more about our authors and books visit www.bloomsbury.com and sign up for
our newsletters.

For Jimmy Fox

MOONRISE

THE FIRST CALL

The green phone
on the wall in the hall
hardly ever rang.
Anyone who wanted to speak to Mom called her cell.
Same with Angela.

I listened to the jangle for a few seconds
before picking it up.
"Hello?"

"Joe?" It was Ed.
He hadn't been in touch for weeks.
I'd started to worry,
wondered if he was ever coming home.
"Is Angela there?" he asked.
He was breathing fast
as though someone was chasing him.
In the background
        hard voices,
        a door slamming.

"Angela's at soccer practice," I said.

"And Mom?"

"No idea.
Hey, Ed,
I found a baseball glove at the park.
Will you be back soon to play?"

Ed sighed heavily. "I dunno, Joe."

"Oh." I picked at some peeling paint on the wall.

Another sigh from my big brother.
"I got arrested, Joe.
They think I done something real bad."

I pressed the receiver tight
            against my ear.
"What do they think you done?"

"They think I hurt someone.
But I didn't. You hear?"

"Yeah."

"I mean it. You hear me?
'Cause people are gonna be telling you
all kinds of lies.
I need you to know the truth."

The front door opened and Mom stormed in
carrying a bag of groceries
for my sister to conjure into dinner.

"The police got Ed!" I shouted.

I held out the phone.
She snatched it from me,
dropping the bag.

A tangerine rolled across the rug.
I picked it up,
the skin cold and rough.

"Ed? What's going on? . . .
But how can they make that sort of mistake? . . .
Don't shout at me, I'm just . . .
No, I know, but . . .
I don't have the money for . . .
Ed, stay calm . . .
I'll call Karen. I said I'll call Karen . . .
Stop shouting at me . . .
Ed, for Christ's sake . . .
I'm just not able to . . . Ed? Ed?"

She held the phone away
       from her ear and scowled
       like it had bitten her.
"The cops are charging him with murder," she said.

I was seven.
I didn't know what that meant.
Did he owe someone money?
We didn't have any cash to pay the electricity bill.
My sneakers were so small
they made the tips of my toes white.
"Can I call him back?" I asked.
The tangerine was still in my hand.
I wanted to throw it in Mom's face and hurt her.

"No," she said.
"And don't expect to speak to him for a long time."

I didn't believe her.
I thought Ed would call.
I thought he'd come home.

But he never did.

SLUM LANDLORD

Aunt Karen told me not to come here.
She said Ed didn't deserve an entourage
after the pain he'd caused our family.

Even after ten long years
she blames him for everything.
            She points to Ed and says,
            "See what he did to us."

And maybe she's right.
Everything turned to shit
when Ed got put away;
nothing worked anymore.

So maybe this *is* a stupid idea.

I'm already pining for home, Staten Island,
anything that isn't Wakeling, Texas,
in the broiling heat.

It's not as if I *want* to be here,
checking out some slummy apartment.
But I can't afford to keep staying at
the Wakeling Motorstop Motel,
not for the whole time I'm in Texas, anyway.

"Six hundred for the month," the landlord croaks,
coughing up something wet and
spitting it into a Kleenex.

Judging by the dishes in the sink,
the apartment hasn't been lived in for months, and
he'd be lucky to get a dime for this hole—
roaches in the closets,
rodents in the kitchen.

"I need it until mid-August.
I'll give you four hundred," I say.

He snorts. "Five hundred. Cash."
And I can tell by the way he's
        backing out of the apartment
        that it's as low as he'll go.
Well, I guess he's the one with the keys;
he can afford to play hardball.
"If I find out you been selling weed,
I'll send my men around.
You don't wanna meet my men."

But his men don't bother me.
I got bigger worries
        than getting bashed in with a baseball bat
by his hired goons.

I got Ed to worry about.
        Ed.

So here I am.
        Stuck.

And it's going to be the worst time of my life.
The worst time of everyone's lives.

        For those who get to live.

TEXTS

In the parking lot of my motel
a gang of bikers is slugging booze from paper bags,
hellfire rock music filling up the lot.

As I pass them, my cell phone pings in my
back pocket.
I don't bother checking the message.
I know it's Angela pestering me:
>   Where r u?
>   Did u go 2 the prison?
>   U seen Ed??
>   Hows Ed???
>   Karens still srsly pissed off.
>   Eds new lawyer emailed. He seems smart.
>   Where R U???

I have to call my sister.
And I will.
>   Later.
Right now, I'm starving.

And I have to get away from this music.

BOB'S DINER

The diner is all beat-up outside,
paint crumbling, half the neon sign unlit,
and inside it's the same:
broken floor tiles,
posters pale and torn.
A middle-aged waitress in a
pink bowling shirt smiles.
Her name—"Sue"—is embroidered into
her front pocket,
the black thread unraveling itself,
      snaking down the shirt like a
      little vine.

"You okay, hon?" she asks,
raising her hand to her mouth,
dragging on a cigarette right there
behind the counter
like it's totally normal—
      a waitress smoking in a restaurant.
And it might be.   Around here.

I pull out my remaining cash and wave it at her.
"What would four bucks buy me?" I say.

"I guess you could get a BLT
and a coffee.
Would that work, hon?"

"Great," I say, inhaling the
        tail of her cigarette smoke.

She shouts my order through a swinging door,
turns back to slosh coffee into a stained mug,
        and pushes it across the counter.

It's thick and bitter, nothing like you get in
New York,
but I don't complain.
        I tear open a Splenda
                tip it in to disguise the taste.
"Any jobs available?" I ask.

        "Wait there, hon."
        Sue vanishes
                through the
        swinging doors.

I grab a muffin in plastic wrap from a basket
on the counter, stuff it into my bag before
        a man appears,

a thick mustache hiding his mouth,
a belly that bulges over his waistband.

He reaches across the counter, shakes my hand.
"I'm Bob. I believe you're lookin' for work."
His accent is drawn out and totally Texan.

"Joe Moon," I say.

He nods.
"I need a delivery guy.
Someone with a car, 'cause the junker
out back won't run.
Or someone real fast on a bike.
The fast person would also need a bike."

"I fix cars," I say quickly.
"If I get it to run, could I have the job?"

Sue has reappeared, a fresh cigarette limp
	between her twiggy fingers.
She spits bits of tobacco onto the floor.
"Just so's you know, hon, my boyfriend Lenny's
good with motors. Even he couldn't get that
crap heap to turn over."

She uses a sour rag
to wipe coffee stains from the countertop.

"I could try," I say,
not wanting to sound too desperate.

"Okay. You can *try*," Bob says.
He reaches into the basket and
hands me a blueberry muffin.
"Dessert's on me, son," he says.

NO SHORE

All last week
Reed tried to cheer me up.
Sitting in his car drinking warm beer,
he tried to make me believe Ed would get off,
that I'd be back in Arlington before
the summer track meet
began.
"I'll win bronze for the four-hundred-meter hurdles,
you'll get a gold for the five thousand meters.
Then we'll go to the shore
and show off our medals.
We can stay at my cousin's beach house
as long as we want.
We'll get tans,
        smoke dope,
                hit on hot girls.
So many hot girls at the shore."

"Sounds good," I said,
knowing it was never gonna happen,
knowing I'd miss out on my entire
summer,
including the New York City
track meet.

It was the one thing that had kept me going
in school—
        knowing that at the end of the year,
        no matter how low my grades were,
        I'd have the meet to prove
        I wasn't some layabout loser.

But instead of running,
I was coming to Texas
to count down the days until
my brother's execution;
trying to make me feel better about that
was pointless.

THE SECOND CALL

I liked cheese sandwiches with a truckload of ketchup
and had a plate of them in my lap.
I was watching *Spider-Man* on TV,
        cross-legged on the carpet
        wearing scuffed-up sneakers—
laces undone, feet sticky inside them.

I was eight by then,
a year after that first call that had turned
        everything
        inside out.

Mom shouted at me, as she always did.
"Turn the goddamn TV down!"

She had her cell to her ear,
was squinting like she was trying to see
whatever it was she was being told.

And then,
        like a rock into a river,
        she fell
        and began to howl.

It wasn't like you see in movies,
someone collapsing but so beautiful
      and
        tragic.
She was a person possessed,
smashing into pieces,
and I was afraid to get too close.
"No!" she screamed.

I knew right away the words she was hearing.
Anyone could have guessed.

We were kind of expecting it.

And not expecting it at all.

Aunt Karen had been at some of the short trial,
came home and
told us things weren't going Ed's way—
for starters, there was his confession
      the day after he got arrested.
She said that if she'd been on the jury,
she'd have locked him up and
      thrown away the key herself.

"He didn't do it," Angela told her.

"I don't know anymore," Aunt Karen said.
"He looked pretty guilty to me."

And the day that second call came,
I was the only other person at home,
alone again with Mom in the house,
and
I didn't know what to do.
I mean,
Mom was always freaking out, but not like that:
       an animal caught in wire.

I went to her,
       tried to get her to stand,
       but
       she wouldn't.
       She couldn't.

       Mom stayed
       down for a
       really
       long
       time.

AUNT KAREN

Three hours after the bad news
our aunt Karen came to stay.
"I'm all you've got," she told us.

She stared at the ketchup stains on my white T-shirt,
like that was proof our family
couldn't take care of itself.
I wiped my nose with the back of my hand
and she flinched.

"We don't have space," Angela explained.

Aunt Karen scratched her nose with her
thumbnail.
"I'll take your room. You can share with Joe
for a while.
Ed's old bed is still in there."

Angela stood up as tall as she could.
"I need my privacy," she said.

"Yeah, well," Mom mumbled, cradling a gin.

"But I have finals," Angela tried again.

"I know you do," Aunt Karen said.
"And you'll pass them. I won't have you go down
the same road as Ed."

It didn't matter how hard we stamped our feet,
Aunt Karen had made up her mind,
and Mom was in no state to argue:
Aunt Karen was staying, and
we would start going to church,
not just on Sundays but after school too.
TV was
    out
and Bible study was
    in.
Karen knew how to save our souls
from falling into the darkness
that had carried off our brother,
and the first part of her plan was
             to never mention Ed again.

HOW MOM HANDLED IT

Mom stopped going out.
     She littered the house with empty pill bottles.
     She watched infomercials,
     shopped through the TV,
     said she was waiting until people forgot,
     that she'd get her act together and
     go back to work
     once the worst blew over.

But
     she never returned to work and
     when she finally ventured out,

     she didn't come back.

AUTO SHOP

When I told Reed's uncle at the auto shop last week
that I was headed to Texas for the whole summer,
he didn't take it well either.
"I don't know if I can keep your job open, Joe,"
he said.
"I got guys lining up to apprentice here
and you're taking off?"

I hadn't explained to anyone apart from Reed
the real reason I'd be gone.
I was ashamed and Reed must have guessed it.
"Give him a break, Uncle Sammy.
        Joe's got some girl knocked up
        and needs to get out of Arlington
        before her brothers do him in," Reed said.

Sammy rubbed his greasy hands against
his blue overalls and frowned.
        "You're lyin'."

        "He's lyin'," I said.
                "But I gotta go.
        I'll be back though."

21

Sammy sighed. "Okay. Okay.
You're a hell of a lot better than
Reed at getting dirty under a hood
anyway,
I'll give you that."

Reed grunted and reached for a wrench.
"I prefer to get dirty in other ways."

Sammy watched me.
"You're still standing there, Joe.
What do you want?"

I didn't like to ask.
It felt like begging.
"I'm owed two weekends."

Reed snickered.

Sammy rolled his eyes, reached into
his pocket, and pulled out a roll
of twenties.
"How much?" he asked.

TEAM WRONG

Back at the motel, I call Angela.
Her voice is high-pitched and
something is buzzing in the background.
"I can't hear you, Ange!" I shout.

The buzzing stops.

"I'm at the bar making mojitos," she says. "You okay?"

I want to tell the truth, say,
No, I'm not okay.
It's hot.
I don't have any more money for food.
I'm solo doing this,
which isn't how it should be.
I'm seventeen years old, for Christ's sake.
Why aren't you here?
Why isn't Aunt Karen? Mom?

"I found an apartment," I say,
leaving out the part about the bugs.
"Will the cash have cleared in my account yet?"

She coughs into the phone.
"Should have," she says.
"But then that's it.
The boss won't give me an advance
so it'll be next month before I've got
cash to come down there."

"Aunt Karen?" I ask hopefully.

"No way. She's still super pissed.
She picked up more stuff,
said she isn't moving back in.
I don't even know how we'll make the rent
unless she changes her mind.
And how the hell are you gonna eat?"

"I'm looking for work."

"I wish I could get more cash, Joe."

I half laugh.
            How exactly?
            Ask strangers for handouts?
We could never get away with that—
begging for loans to be with our brother.

See, we aren't the people anyone pities.
No one cares whether or not we get to be with
Ed at the end,
how poor or hungry we are.
The cop's widow though?
        If she set up a crowdfunding account
        to buy a black dress and matching hat,
        you'd have people donating
        big-time.
                The widow of a murdered guy?
                Do you take Mastercard?
But we aren't her—we're not the victims here.

Instead we're on the other side of right—
                players for Team Wrong.

"Have you seen Ed?" Angela whispers.

I go to the bathroom,
run cold water into the shower.
"No," I admit.

I haven't even tried.

CHICKENSHIT

Ed wrote to me last month
asking for help.
I'm the one he thought he could rely on.

He probably imagined his baby brother
had grown into a
      man.

But I'm too chickenshit
to even call the prison
and inquire about visits,
let alone
        drag my sorry ass
up to the gates
and try to get in.

LETTER FROM ED

Hey Joe,

How you doing man?
You best be studying hard or I'll kick your ass!
       Nah, I'm just playing.

Thing is,
       I didn't write Angela this week.
       Tell her it's my bad,
       but
       I need you to break something to her.

       I got my date through.
       Guys here telling me it's nothing to panic about.
       Just a date.
       But if I'm honest
       it makes me rattle like old bones,
       'cause it means they
       made up their minds
       and wanna do me in.
       And for what?
             For nothing.
             For something I never did.

The date they settled on is August 18, Joe,
but I got another appeal to go in the state courts
before then
and
we could go to federal for a couple more
I think.
Also there's a chance the governor will stop it
(or the president!)
so August 18's what they're planning on—
but if I convince them of the truth,
it might come and go
and I'll still be standing, you know.

Thing is,

    I got no lawyer to advise me
    and explain how everything works,
    'cause the state don't pay for lawyers until
    eternity, right?
    Anyway, the prison's priest is doing
    some detective work
    and finding out what's what for me.

Thing is,

    I'm wondering if you could come visit.
    Father Matthew says that even though
    you're not eighteen,

they might let you come if Angela can't,
on special request.
I wrote the warden, and I'm waiting to hear.
In the nine years I been locked up in Wakeling
I only seen him a handful of times on the row.
No one comes down to see
us deadbeats unless they have to, I guess.
But
he seems like a regular kind of guy.
Worth asking.

Anyway,
   I'll mail this now and write again when I know more.
   Don't freak out, okay?
   Let me do the sweating.
   I got plenty of time for it.

Be cool, little brother,
Ed x

WHAT IT MEANT

I got that letter two weeks ago,
read it,
then
threw it on the floor.

I couldn't touch it.
      Those words.
      What they meant.
      What I *guessed* they meant,
'cause even Ed didn't seem too sure.

I was standing in my bedroom and
when I looked up
      Angela was in the doorway,
      purse under her arm.
She pointed at the rug,
the letter lying
      faceup,
Ed's scrawl all over it.
"How is he?" she asked.

I wanted to tell her everything
but couldn't figure out what I knew.
"He's busy," I said,

which was stupid—he's in prison—
how busy could it get?

"Did he like my card?"
                    She smiled,
                    scratched her belly.

"He didn't mention it."
But he did mention an execution date.
He said I shouldn't worry,
but for the first time in ten years
Ed asked to see me,
sort of said he needed me,
which he'd never done before—
he'd always known the deal with Karen,
didn't want to mess up
things for Angela or me in Arlington.
"You guys get on with your lives,"
he said in a letter once.
So we tried.
We tried really hard to pretend Ed was okay—
that his death sentence was mythical
and not something that would ever really happen.

I closed my eyes. Rubbed my face.
"What time did you get in last night?" Angela asked.

"About one," Karen snapped, appearing behind her.
"If you want to graduate next year, Joe,
you have to study.
Where were you?"

"The year's almost over, Karen," I told her.
I wasn't going to admit I was with Reed,
smoking weed,
figuring out how to cheat on our Spanish test
the next day instead
of just studying for it.

I closed the door on both of them and
picked up the letter.
            I read it again just to be sure.

And I was.

It was true:
my only brother would be dead within two months,
and there was

                nothing
I could say or
            do to
            stop it.

A DECISION

When I finally told Angela,
she shook and twitched,
wouldn't eat the eggs I'd scrambled.

She said she'd go to the bank
for a loan, get him a lawyer,
said she wanted to go down to Wakeling
to help.

But then Aunt Karen got home
from her night shift at the hospital
and tried to shake sense into my sister.
"There's nothing you can do,
and I won't have you
wasting your money or your life
fighting for someone
who's not even sorry."

"Without a lawyer, he has no chance," Angela argued.

"That isn't our fault," Aunt Karen snapped back.

"He's my *brother*."

"But not a good one."

        I stood between them.
        "*I'm* going to Wakeling," I announced,
        not knowing before the words
        were out
        whether or not I really wanted to see Ed.

But someone has to be here.

Angela's got a full-time job,
Aunt Karen hates him,
and no one knows where the hell Mom is.

That was decided two weeks ago
and nothing's changed except one thing:
Ed now has even less time to live.

MUG SHOT

The only TV channel in the motel that isn't pure static
is the early-morning local news.
I watch the muted screen,
pulling on my sneakers,
when Ed's mug shot pops up.

He looks mean:
      chin raised,
      eyes small,
      face bruised.

I stare,
      scared.

What if Ed's like the guy
in that mug shot
and my memories of him aren't real at all?

And then his picture vanishes
and photos of Frank Pheelan flash up—
blue-eyed on a beach somewhere,
sand in his toes,
another of him in police uniform,
and then a family portrait with his wife and kids,

strawberry blonds, all of them,
with ripening smiles.
I've seen these faces before:
newscasters love revealing the beauty of the victims—
like they're the only ones who got slammed.

Reporters don't give a damn about our family.
We're not a story. We're dirt.
Although,
I guess that's a lot easier than having to admit
that by killing our brother
they're just pummeling more people.

The feature about Ed's looming execution ends
and a weather map replaces it.
Texas is covered in blazing yellow suns.

I lace up my sneakers;
      I'm going for a run regardless.

MORNING RUN

The traffic lights click and change,
though Wakeling's streets are still mostly empty of cars.

I run fast,
measuring my splits on my watch.
      I'm slower than usual.

I run and run,
try to get my speed up
and don't see anyone, which
is exactly why I go out first thing—
      for the quiet,
        the feeling of being the only person alive.

I pound the sidewalks,
my heart beating a million miles an hour,
and all I can focus on is breathing,
on not keeling over.

Which suits me.

Suits me just fine.

IN WALMART

Mr. Porter stopped me in Walmart.
He had his son in the cart,
         brown goo around the kid's mouth.
"Joe.
I saw Reed last night at practice.
He told me you ain't going to the summer track meet
in the city."

"No, sir. I can't."

He bit the insides of his cheeks.
"I had to apply for funding for the meet.
You didn't get the place by accident."
His kid stood up in the cart,
tried to climb over the side
         and make an escape.
Mr. Porter pulled him out, let the boy
waddle up the cereal aisle.

"Something came up, sir. I'm sorry."

"And you've missed a week of practice.
I'm kind of disappointed.

You know my thoughts on your performances.
But I can't force anyone to want something
and talent isn't enough.
You have to work hard."

I'd come into the store for toothpaste.
I hadn't planned on getting grilled
by a teacher.
He meant well, but it was summer vacation—
he had no right to nag me.

"I gotta go, sir," I said.

"Is something going on?" he asked.

"Nah. Everything's cool," I said.

I don't want anyone's pity.

HOME SWEET HOME

The landlord kicks a pile of junk mail
from the doormat,
leads the way into the kitchen, and
rips open the envelope I handed him.
He counts out the cash and
holds a fifty-dollar bill to the light.
Flies hum around us.
"No late checkouts. You got that?"
He dangles the keys in front of me.
I snatch them and he sucks his teeth.
"What are you in Wakeling for anyway?
You know someone at the farm?"

I turn on the cold faucet.
Yellow water dribbles onto the moldy dishes
piled up
        then abandoned
          by the previous tenant.

He shuts off the water.
"It'll run clear in a couple minutes."
He glances around like he might have forgotten
        something,
then takes off,
slamming the door behind him.

I flick a switch.
Nothing happens.

I try another.
    No light.

I dart to the door,
    holler into the hallway.
"The electricity is out! Hey, there's no light!"

    But I'm alone
    and the hallway
    is in darkness too.

LITTLE MURDERS

I murder close to twenty cockroaches
with the base of a rusty pan.
Their backs crack and crunch.
"Dirty bastards."

The apartment smells worse than I remember,
like whoever lived here
let their cat
or kid
piss all over the carpets.

In the living room
     I try opening a window
     but it's painted shut.
Grime and grease cake the pane.

I check my phone.
No one's texted or called since yesterday.
Not Reed, Karen, not even Angela,
which is sort of surprising and a little shitty.
Do they think I'm here
soaking up sun and scratching my ass?

I'm here for Ed. That's it.

I'm here 'cause he's my blood.
He needs me.
It's what I have to do.
But if I had a choice?
I'd be on a plane home—
      I'd be gone.

A single roach scuttles out from
      underneath the spongy sofa.
I stomp on it,
then look up
and realize
the damn things are crawling
      up the walls.

NO REPLY

I text Reed:
Hot as hell here, man!
SHIIIIIT! Whats happenin????

After a moment
I see he's read the message.
I watch my screen, wait for his smart-ass reply.
But nothing comes through, and then
he's offline.

      So I put my phone into my
      back pocket and
      head out.

STAR WARS

We used to play on the sidewalk,
brandishing long sticks as lightsabers,
smacking each other and
really feeling the force of it.

Then Ed got a real lightsaber,
gave it to me grinning.
"*Join me*," he said,
Darth Vader croaky.
But the dark side
never really appealed to me,
so I lit up my green sword
and used it to
      slice him
      to pieces.
He groaned, rolled on the ground,
while the kids in the neighborhood watched,
jealous for a brother like mine.

We watched *Stars Wars* obsessively,
and during a bad storm,
when school closed,
saw every movie back-to-back,

only stopping
to grab bags of chips for nourishment.

"Can't we watch *anything* else?" Angela groaned.

Ed turned to her, horrified.
"I feel like we shouldn't be family anymore."
He threw a pillow at her
and she laughed,
slumped on the couch next to us.
"Seriously, Ange, you're missing out."

"Angela doesn't like fighting," I said
to defend my sister,
and Ed nodded sympathetically,
then sucked on the back of his hand.
"Yeah. She prefers kissing."

Angela covered her eyes with her forearm.
"You're grossing me out.
That must be how *you* kiss your girlfriends."

We were laughing hysterically but hushed as
Mom slithered into the living room.

"I'm ordering takeout," she said.
Her eyes were black-rimmed,
sweatpants and hoodie creased.
She coughed and coughed
until she had to leave the room,
then called in from the kitchen.
"Angela, can you phone for pizza?
My voice is cut to crap."

"Sure, Mom!" Angela said,
her tone like sunshine,
as though Mom wasn't a complete screwup.

"Can we get plain cheese?" I asked.

"Course we can, little man," Ed said, pulling me close,
turning up the TV.
R2-D2 slid across a spaceship.

Angela dialed for dinner
and we watched *Star Wars*
into the night
while Mom threw up in the bathroom.

She said she had a bug,
told us not to come close
in case we caught what she had.

And even though none of us bought the bug story,
we all kept out of Mom's way.

WHEN THE COP GOT SHOT

After the first call came through from Ed,
Angela tried to explain
what he had been accused of
and what might happen next.
But I never really got my head around it.

When kids in my class asked
for the details,
I couldn't think of what to say.
Ed had taken off months before,
right after his big fight with Mom.
I had no idea where he was
the day Frank Pheelan got shot.

The day it happened
I was on a field trip to
the Liberty Science Center,
eating a bologna sandwich,
thinking about space,
Mars mostly,
a planet so close but so completely inhospitable.
I wasn't thinking about cops or death.

And until Angela explained it,
I didn't know that to be accused of murder
in the wrong state was
                    fatal.

ICE AND FLAME

Aunt Karen took me into the city
the Christmas after Ed was convicted
so we could skate in Central Park,
something I hadn't done before.
She held my mittened hand,
stopped me from slipping on the ice.
All I was thinking was
how much
funnier the trip would have been with Ed.
He'd have made Karen lighten up, laugh,
instead of worrying about
the other skaters' blades
chopping off our fingers if we fell.

Afterward we walked down Fifth Avenue
to St. Patrick's Cathedral,
where Karen lit red candles
and in front of the tiny flickering flames,
prayed for our family on her knees.
I lit a candle for Ed,
thought about him alone during the holidays
in a cell with no tinsel or twinkling lights,

no chance of seeing a full moon
or any moon
for that matter.

"Did you pray?" Aunt Karen asked on our
        way out,
dipping her fingers into the stone font
and crossing herself with holy water.

In the street I admitted,
"I prayed for the cops to send Ed home."

Karen knelt again, in the middle of the sidewalk,
this time to look me straight in the eye.
"I've read the reports and spoken to the lawyers, Joe.
Forget about Ed.
He isn't ever coming home, okay?
Ever."

People nudged me with the corners of their
fancy shopping bags.
"He told me he didn't do it," I said.

"He's lying," she said.

"*You're* lying," I never said.

Instead I decided right then
never to defend Ed again,
and
let my aunt
believe I didn't love him anymore.

MIRACLES

Sue is outside Bob's Diner,
    smoking and
      blinking at the sun.
"You're here," she says.
"I thought you was full of bullcrap."

"Where's the car?" I ask.

She uses her hand as a visor,
looks me up and down.
"You gonna fix it with superpowers, hon?"

I lift my baseball cap,
scratch the hair beneath it—
I hadn't thought about tools.

Sue snickers.
"Bob don't got a needle and thread,
but lucky for you
I borrowed my Lenny's toolbox.
He sees something missing, I'm screwed,
so you give it back how you found it, okay?"
She wags a bejeweled finger at me.

"You'll also need a miracle,
but Lenny didn't have none of those.
You looking for a miracle, hon?"

I shrug.
      Try to look tough.

"Who's at the farm?" she asks.

"Huh?"
First the landlord, now her?
Is it written on my face?

She sucks deeply on the cigarette.
"Look, no one shows up around here
unless they got business at the farm."

I hesitate. Do I trust her?
Even if I don't,
      I can't keep Ed a secret for long—
not in a town this size.
"My brother's scheduled to die next month."

Sue raises her eyebrows.
"And you're in Texas alone?"

"I don't mind," I lie.

                I kick the dirt.

"Is he guilty?" she asks.

What am I supposed to say?
Well, Ed says he isn't
and he's never lied to me before
but who knows?
Guys on the row must lie all the time.

She drops the glowing butt of her cigarette,
grinds it into the ground
with the heel of her rubber-soled shoe.
"You want a hot breakfast, hon?"

I nod.

Why the hell is she being so nice?
She doesn't know me and
what she *does* know is the bad stuff—
the stuff I usually keep to myself.

"Junker's open out back. Good luck."

THE FARM

When dogs get put down
parents tell their kids
the mutts got sent to a farm
to live out their last days
with peppy ducks and rabbits.

And it's as though the state of Texas thinks
we're all just as stupid as kids,
calling the state penitentiary
       "Wakeling Farm"—
like inmates lie around on hay bales
and spend their afternoons milking cows.

But just like the dogs,
most guys who go to this farm
don't ever come home.

THE JUNKER

It really is a junker:
dried-out grass growing around the wheels;
hubcaps gone or stolen;
the hood infected with rusty scabs;
not a drop of oil in the worn-out engine;
no gas in the tank.

I have no idea where to start.

But if I want to eat,
I've got to get this crap heap running.

Soon.

INSIDE OUT

When Ed got his driver's license,
Aunt Karen acted like he'd made the honor roll.
"Look at you! Driving!
Soon you'll be married
and how old will that make me?"
She smacked him playfully.

Ed grinned.
"Ah, Karen, you got good genes.
You're gonna outlive us all.
Anyway, it's about time . . .
      I should've got my license last year."

Angela looked up from her book.
"He's being cute 'cause he wants your wheels, Aunt Karen."

"What? That's real suspicious of you, Angela," Ed said.
"But . . . if our very cool aunt wants to lend me her car,
I won't say no."
He jabbed at Karen's coat pocket.
Keys clinked.

She backed away.
"Oh no. Borrow someone else's car."

Karen was tough, but that day
      Ed was persistent;
      he spent twenty minutes
      wearing her down
      until she handed over the keys
      to her twelve-year-old Mitsubishi.
"Be *careful*," she pleaded.

Ed said,
"I won't go over a hundred, I promise,"
and wrapped his arm around my shoulder.
He smelled of spicy deodorant and spearmint gum.
"You coming, copilot?"

Aunt Karen slumped onto the sofa next to Angela,
who put down her book and
      pushed her feet into a pair of purple Converse.
"I'll go with them, Aunt Karen."
She turned on the TV.
"You enjoy *Ellen*. We'll be back soon."

"Where's your mom?" Karen asked.

"Work," Angela said,
when we all knew she was probably at a bar
or with some guy she'd just met.

Ed was in charge of the driving,
Angela of the music,
and I was in the back seat feeding them snacks
after we stopped at a bodega and
bought a whole bag of candy.

"No *way*," Ed groaned as Angela turned the radio
to a station playing pop.

"Oh, what would you prefer, DJ Badass?"

"Anything, dude. *Anything.*"

Angela fiddled with the dials, then stopped.

"Elvis!" Ed cheered.
        "Jesus," Angela said.
"The King," Ed replied. "Turn it up!"
        "Oh, come on, Ed.
        Want a blanket for your knees too?"
He smacked the steering wheel.
"Turn it *up*!"

And   she did.
And   the windows were down.
And   Ed was singing.
And   then Angela was singing.
And   the song wasn't too difficult to learn.
And   I started singing.

After Elvis
it was Johnny Cash,
then the Supremes
and more singers and songs that I didn't know
but I sang along anyway,
     screeching out the windows
         as we boomed along Third Avenue.

Aunt Karen was waiting on the stoop,
wringing her hands on a dishcloth.

Angela turned off the music.
"Cool drive. Thanks, Ed," she said
and jumped out of the car,
practically skipping into the house.

Ed sat speechless behind the wheel.

"You coming?" I asked.

"When you're my age, screw Driver's Ed.
I'm gonna teach you to drive.
And then you, me, and Ange'll go for another ride.
Deal?"

"Deal," I said.
    I climbed out,
        stood on the sidewalk.

He stayed where he was, staring out the
        windshield.

I knocked on the passenger window. "Ed?"

He turned to me and winked.
"Tell Karen I went to get milk," he said, and
pulled away again slowly.

Karen squealed. I smirked.
But while we waited for him to return
I got to thinking,
even way back then

when I was too young to understand much:
you can know all the facts you want about
                    a person
—height, weight, the way they like their eggs—
but you'll never know for sure what's
                    driving his heart.

ED NEVER CAME BACK

Ed didn't return with the milk
or Aunt Karen's car.
We waited all evening, night,
        the next day
                and the rest of the week,
but by Sunday
it was clear—
            he was gone.

"You owe me the price of a car," Aunt Karen told Mom.

"It's your own fault—you gave him the keys.
I wouldn't trust Ed with a toothbrush."

They argued.
Screamed and shouted,
        Mom swearing at the top of her lungs
that she was fed up with the whole damn bunch of us,
Aunt Karen storming home,
riding the bus since she had nothing to drive.

"You won't go too, will you?" I asked Angela,
tucked up next to her in an armchair,
eating nachos.

"Don't worry," she told me.
"Everything's gonna blow over,
go back to normal.
        You'll see."

But since when had our family been "normal"?

Since
    never.

WHY HE LEFT . . .

I was in the next room making a space rocket from
two cardboard boxes Ed had brought home.
Their voices came through from the kitchen,
quiet at first then louder and louder
until I couldn't ignore them.

"You forgot to get bread for Joe's lunch," Ed said.
"So go to the store. You have money," Mom told him.
"Yeah, but I'm not his parent."
"Well, no, but you sure as hell act like mine."

Silence.

"You know,
        it's about time you got your own place,"
Mom said.
"You're kicking me out?" Ed asked.
"You're like your father,
        and he wasn't very likable."
"Well, thank God I'm not like *you*."
"Excuse me?"
"Oh, come on, Mom. Look at you. You're a joke."
"What?"

"A. Joke. Everyone knows it. Even Joe."
"Take that back."
"No. You're either drunk or hungover."
"So get out."
"No."
"I said get out! It's my house."

More silence.
A smack.
      Ed tumbled out of the kitchen,
      one cheek
      flashing pink.

"I can't take this anymore," he said.

It was a few days later that
      he took off in Karen's car.

NELL

"For you. From Sue," a voice says,
making me jump.
I knock my head against the hood and
drop the car battery.

A girl is standing with a
        tray balanced between two hands.
She places a plate of eggs, a bottle of water,
on the roof of the car,
pulls a plastic fork from the
        pocket of her apron,
        hands it to me.
She's wearing a bowling shirt like Sue's,
the name "Nell" embroidered in black.

She turns and struts off.
        But I don't want her to leave.
I want to talk to someone,
have a regular conversation
where I'm not begging for something or
having to explain what I'm doing here.
"You work at the diner?"
It's the only question I've got.

She stops. Turns.
"Do you have an above-average IQ?
You're *very* sharp.
You should be on a game show."

I call out.
"Wanna share my water?"
I hold it aloft,
jiggle it around,
try to be funny,
pretty sure I look and sound like an idiot.

She grins.
"I hear that stuff can kill you."
She marches off.
The laces of her sneakers trail on the ground;
her hair is tied haphazardly on top of her head
            and wobbles when she walks.

I'm about to shout again,
a third-time-lucky kind of thing,
but don't.
Sweat has pooled at the base of my back;
my head hammers from the heat.
I need to eat.

Still standing,
I gorge on the almost-cold scrambled eggs
in a few greedy bites,
guzzle down the water too,
and I'm about to get back to rooting around
      under the hood
when my phone rings.

A PRIZE

"Al Mitchell here. Is that Joe?"
Ed's lawyer sounds breezy,
not at all as serious as I'd imagined he would be,
and for a second I wonder
if Ed is
      off the hook,
if we can fly back to New York together and
pretend none of this happened.
I know we'll never be the Brady Bunch,
but maybe we could be a messed-up family again.

"Hello, Mr. Mitchell," I say.

"Nice to speak to you finally, Joe.
Angela's told me a lot about you.
I've already called her.
I have good news."

        He pauses.
        Takes a breath.
        And I do too.

"We got you full visitation rights to the row, Joe.
The warden's secretary called my office,

said you can visit today.
And every day after that at two."

I don't reply.
This is good news?
That I can see my brother,
talk about girls and cookouts,
do my best to haul his mind
away from the truth?

This isn't something to celebrate:
this is just bad news turned upside down,
bad news inflated and painted
to twinkle like a prize.

"I've lost you, Joe," Mr. Mitchell says.
"I think the connection's bad."

"Thank you," I say.
And then, "I'll visit this afternoon."

The lawyer detects my disappointment,
tries again.
"We still have one round left at the state level.
Then we've got the US Supreme Court
and the governor.

I believe we can do this.
It's not the end.
We save men all the time.
Oh,
    and Joe?"

"Yeah?"

"Please call me Al."

THE CHECKLIST

I look for a scrap of paper and the nub of a pencil
on the back seat of the car
so I can
scribble down
the three parts of the process left:
    the state court,
    the Supreme Court,
    the governor.
I want to remember
what we are waiting for,
what to expect.
But I can't find anything to write with.
And I guess it's unlikely I'll forget
Ed's three slim chances
of getting out of here.

POOR JUSTICE

Ed didn't have a lawyer for years.
After a few rounds in court
he was no longer entitled to a public defender
and we couldn't afford to pay anyone
        to represent him.

Ed was just left in Texas to rot
and we didn't know what to do about it.

Wasn't until he got his date through
that Angela wrote to every nonprofit
in the country
and eventually found Al Mitchell,
        who agreed to take on the case
        for free
        as charity.

And for the first time someone listened
and
made us think a different outcome was possible.

Al also explained to Angela
that most guys on the row don't have a lawyer
and

spend half their time
begging for representation
or
studying the law themselves.
"Like your brother did," he'd told her,
though we hadn't known Ed
was educating himself in the law from his cell.

"God. It's better to be guilty and rich,
        I reckon," I'd told Angela.
It was a couple of nights before I flew down to Texas.
We were eating noodles from boxes.

"No doubt!" Angela agreed.
"But now we've got Al, we've got hope.
He said the whole case was based on bullshit."

I chewed on chow mein
but didn't respond.
Hope wasn't really
        my area of expertise.

DISTRACTION

I poke and pull at the car,
hands covered in oil,
and don't stop until one o'clock,
when the sun has cooked me through.

Then I take off without telling anyone.

I don't want to go to the prison.

But I can't be late either.

WHO IS EDWARD MOON?

A text comes through from Aunt Karen:
> A lawyer by the name of
> Alan Mitchell called.
> Said you're visiting Ed today.
> Are you sure about this, Joe?

And of course the answer is
> no.

I mean, who the hell is Edward Moon?
He was my brother
> but I hardly know him now.

Last time I saw him I was seven years old.
What if I don't like him?
And he might hate me.
We could sit there gaping,
wondering what the fuck to discuss and
counting down every awkward minute,
a little like those parent-teacher conferences
where everyone is so frickin' polite
and you can't even make eye contact
with a person who's been teaching
you every day for two semesters.

I'm not sure about any of this.
But I'm here now.
             And seeing Ed
             is why I've come.

PARENT-TEACHER CONFERENCE

Ed showed up for my parent-teacher conference in
ripped jeans.
I sat opposite my first-grade teacher,
watched her features as she yammered,
noted Ed listening,
wondered how much he understood,
'cause I couldn't follow any of it:
"tardiness, achievement, literacy."

Afterward
Ed conjured up a candy bar from his denim jacket.
"I swiped that, so please enjoy," he said,
not a hint of shame,
maybe even a slice of pride.
He never usually admitted to stealing stuff
even though I knew he couldn't afford
the sneakers he wore
or the phone he used.

At home,
Mom was in bed.
"It was parent-teacher night," Ed explained
from her bedroom doorway.

She groaned.
"God, I forgot. Do they think you'll graduate?"

"It was *mine*," I corrected her.

                              Ed walked away.

Mom pulled back her blanket,
gestured for me to join her.

"I have homework," I lied.

Mom didn't protest. "Close the door."

My hands were coated in candy bar chocolate and
Ed stood behind me while
I washed them in the sink,
one hand on my shoulder.

"Mom cares more than she shows," he said.

"Does she?" I asked.

I was six.

Six years old, still wetting the bed,
no parent to walk me to school
or
make my bagged lunch.

And even then
I knew better
than to believe him.

SECTION A

"The row's apart from the rest of the prison,"
a guard says,
                    leading me out of the main building
                    into the heat.
He points the way to Section A
          where Ed's
          locked up with the other death-row inmates,
          the damned safely separated
          from the merely bad.

The Section A office is smaller, stuffier,
gray walls instead of green.
A massive guard, built like a marine,
          looks up
          from his desk.

"I'm here to see Edward Moon," I say.

He stands slowly, sighing,
palm against his lower back.
"You're the brother."

"Yeah. Joseph Moon."
I feel really young suddenly,

like I'm about to get grilled by the principal,
like I'm here 'cause I've done something dishonest myself.

"ID," he says.

I hand over my driver's license,
and he points to my backpack.
"No bags."

I open the top pocket,
        take out a bottle of water.

The guard shakes his head.
"Did you read the conditions of visitation?"
He licks his lips,
surprises me by speaking softly.
"Got anything else, son? Penknife? Recording device?"
I hand over my phone and
he crams everything into a locker,
gives me a ticket like a cloakroom clerk and says,
"This way."

I'm led through a
                sliding door,

a floor-to-ceiling metal gate
then
another entryway
that squeals as it
      opens,
      clangs as it
      shuts.
So many doors and bars, but no windows,
      not even high up,
      out of reach,
      to let natural daylight strain into the hall.
It's all fluorescent lighting,
flickering and humming,
like the building itself is
              strung out.

From somewhere close by comes a holler—
a laugh, barbed and desperate.

      The concrete walls press in on me,
      my chest tightens.

Another gate,
opened and closed—
        more clanging, crashing,
        slamming, squealing.

The marine-guard studies my expression.
"You'll get used to it. We all do," he says,
like he could possibly know
how I feel.

I want to tell him to go
                suck it
                but
I think I might be sick.

I'm led
        along a hallway,
                a sign above it:
                DEATH ROW,
                words printed in sloping
                red capitals
                like a vicious warning.

"I can't let you see him if you're gonna lose it.
Understand?" the marine-guard asks.

"Yes," I say,
understanding that despite

where I am and why I'm here,
I have to pretend I'm cool;
I have to pretend that visiting Ed
isn't making me feel like someone's
     grabbing,
          pulling at my guts with their
          bare hands.
Maybe I should whistle too.
Would that help everyone feel better?

He taps a ton of numbers into
a keypad on the wall
before elbowing open the final door—
the door to the
visiting room.

THE VISITING ROOM

A row of five booths,
hard chairs in each of them and
black telephones.

      The other side of the booth the same
           and
           separating them
      some pretty tough-looking Plexiglas.

There's no air-conditioning,
though it must be close to ninety degrees.
I think about asking for water,
but I won't take anything from these people.

Ever.

NOT A HOSPITAL

Everyone mouths off about
how much they hate the smell of hospitals,
but have any of them been to a prison?

IT'S ED

I don't look at the Plexiglas.
I study the floor,
my dusty sneakers,
then my hands, engine grease under the nails
to prove I haven't wasted my morning.

Something slams behind me.
     I don't turn.
I'm scared to look anywhere
     except
     down.

So I sit stiff in the chair.
I don't look at the Plexiglas.
I study the floor,
and finally a shadow
     falls.

     I look up.

     It's Ed.

COCO

The Ed I knew
didn't have the balls to kill a cat,
let alone a cop.

When our cat, Coco, got real sick
but the vet was out of town for the weekend,
Mom said, "For Christ's sake, take that thing
down to the bay and do it a favor."

Coco was cradled in his arms,
mewling like a newborn.
She couldn't move her own limbs,
hadn't eaten anything for days.
Her black fur was falling out.
      She was as light as a kitten.

Still, Ed held on.
"You want me to take Coco to the bay and *drown* her?"

We were in the backyard.
Mom was smoking a cigarette.
Ed and I were playing I Spy.
He wasn't letting me win;
he never did, just 'cause I was younger,
and I liked that.

"It would be the kindest thing to do," Mom said.

"Since when have *you* cared about the kindest thing?"
he murmured,
not wanting to upset the cat.

Mom rose, pushed her chair back.
"That thing's a goner.
Only difference doing it on Monday will be that
Dr. Death takes a hundred bucks off us
for the privilege of letting her suffer.
I've got a bag in the closet—
we could do it for free."

Ed glanced at me, kept his voice low.
"I'm not putting Coco into a *fucking* bag."

Mom slung
        her burning cigarette
        into the dry grass.
"I'll get someone else to do it. Give her here."

Ed recoiled,
eyes blazing,
the muscles in his neck tightening.

"I'm not paying for the vet," Mom insisted.

Coco mewled again,
thinner this time,
begging to be saved from our mother.

"Come on, Joe," Ed said.
He marched into the house,
knocking Mom out of the way
as he charged through the
        back door.

In our room, Ed passed the cat to me and
spread out a fleece on his bed.
I flattened my face against her bony head, and
she licked me with a gravelly tongue.
She hissed.
"Maybe it hurts to be held," he suggested.
I put her down gently and Coco lay still,
                closed her eyes.
"I'll go to the drugstore and buy a baby bottle,
get her to drink some milk."

I nodded.
"Do you think Coco might get better?" I asked.

"No, Joe. Coco's gonna die," he said
with certainty.

"You think she knows that?"

"I sure as hell hope not."
He grabbed his cell phone from his desk.
"Call me if Mom tries to touch her."

I curled up on the bed next to Coco,
watched as her tiny body
     moved
     up and
     down
     with her shallow breath.
I wasn't one for praying but
I asked Jesus to save Coco,
stop her from being eaten alive
from the inside by a massive tumor.

My prayer didn't work though,
and by morning,
when I woke up next to her,
Ed asleep in the other bed,
     Coco was cold.

THE PRISONER

White jumpsuit,
hair shaved close,
a bolt and crossbow tattooed on
one side
of his neck—
sloppily done, by another inmate maybe.

    Ed smiles,
    lips stretched thin,
      revealing every bad tooth in his head.

And I smile back,
'cause I'm not sure what else to do.

I was right to be nervous:
I don't know this person
shifting in his seat,
hunched like an old man,
a person in his own right
and not
just carefully constructed memories
and half-baked stories.

He's your brother, I tell myself.
He's your blood.
Be cool for fuck's sake.

Ed flexes his fingers.

Sure, he *is* my brother
but he's also a grown man
I haven't seen for more than a decade
with a whole life
that hasn't included me.

This Ed is a stranger.

MARINER'S MARSH

He was loitering outside the school gates,
hood up,
coat zipped to his chin,
    looking shifty.
"Ed," I said,
and skipped toward him.

I followed him up the street
and we walked and walked,
    finally reaching Mariner's Marsh
    about a mile away.
"We're not allowed to go in there," I said,
    knowing the park had been
    closed off to the public since
    before I was born.

Ed grinned and took my hand,
    led me into a place very few
people in Staten Island dared to go—
    an industrial wasteland,
    a perfect wilderness,
a place filled with burned-out cars,
old ship parts,
and dotted with ponds, marshes, swamps.

Every kid in the neighborhood knew
that a guy named Dempsey Hawkins
brought his girlfriend here in the seventies
and killed her.
       It's the perfect place for it—
       deserted, quiet,
       old barrels and tunnels
       where you could easily hide a body.

Ed led me to one of the yellow-bricked
passageways,
icicles clinging to the roof of the tunnel.
"Why are we here?" I asked.
Ed opened up his backpack,
took out a carton of milk,
and handed it to me.
"I don't wanna go home yet.
I flunked out of school," he said.

"Why?"

"'Cause I'm a loser."

I slurped milk through the straw.
It was so cold it made my brain ache.
"You're not a loser, Ed."

"I gotta get outta Arlington.
I gotta get out
and make something of myself."

I'd heard it before.
It was Ed's refrain—
        "I gotta go,
        I'm leaving,
        I can't stay."

"Will you be okay if I'm not around?" he asked.

"Sure," I said,
but I didn't mean it.
Ed was my brother but also
sort of like
my dad
and my best friend too.

It grew dark and we stayed right where we were—
huddled together beneath the cloudless sky
and a full moon that rose slowly
and lit up the wilderness
with yellow light.

"It almost makes you gasp to look at it," Ed said,
pointing to the sky.
"Or makes you want to hide."

I put my head on his shoulder.
"I could come with you," I said.
I always said this and Ed always agreed.

"Sure," he replied,
and ruffled my hair.
"Definitely."

THE FIRST VISIT

"He can't hear you, kid," the marine-guard says
  as I start to speak.
  "Use the phone."

I put the handset to my ear.
Ed does the same
once the guard has yanked off his handcuffs.
His breath whistles down the line.
"Jesus, man, you look thirty years old," he says.
His voice is scratchy,
like he's spent the years smoking,
and doesn't sound like the home videos Angela's kept
or even the guy I spoke to on the phone
a couple years ago
when Karen was away for a few days.
No trace of an Arlington accent.

I run a hand through my hair.
"The puberty troll turned up.
Said she couldn't wait any longer and
gave me facial hair.
Bitch."

Ed laughs, bangs the desk
  between us.

His guard glowers.
My marine clears his throat.

"So, how you getting on, Joe?"
        He leans forward to listen.
But what am I supposed to say?
I'd prefer to crack jokes for an hour
than talk about stuff that matters.
Then again, what *does* matter?

I sit up straighter.
"I'm doing good. Got an apartment,
and if I can fix a junker, I'll get a job too."

He smiles. "You're here for how long?"

I pause.
"For as long as you need me," I say.

He raises an eyebrow.
"And you got an apartment?
Shit.
When I first came to Texas,
I loafed around for months.
Here half a second and got yourself set up?
You aren't like me, Joe, that's for sure."

He rubs one eye with the heel of his hand,
holds the handset under his chin for a second.
"So . . ." he says eventually.

"Yeah. So."
I wait for him to say something
but he's struggling as much as I am.

"Are you . . . Is your . . ." I begin,
wondering about his case.
But before I've formed a question,
I change my mind,
ask something meaningless.
"How's the food?"

Ed sticks one finger into his mouth and
makes a gagging noise.
"It's lousy, man. Farm can't spend more than
a couple dollars on any meal,
so it's biscuits and barf most days."
He pauses, embarrassed.
"Don't suppose you could stick a few bucks
into my account for snacks?
        I hate to ask.
I guess Karen decided to stop sending cash.
I did wonder when that would happen."

"Karen was sending cash?"

"A few dollars a month, yeah.
Rarely answered letters though.
As I said, I hate to ask, but . . ."

I hold up a hand,
         stop him speaking.
"No problem," I say, even though I've spent
my last dime on rent and don't even have the fare
         for a bus ride back into town.

He sighs. "How's Angela?"

I shrug.
"She's okay. Works a lot."

He scratches his scalp
starts to bite what's left of a thumbnail.
"She got her head around this?"

"She's got Karen," I lie,
'cause Ed still doesn't know
         our aunt left last week
         on account of me being here, and
that Angela and I are pretty much
fending for ourselves.

In a flash, he brightens.
"So the job? You gonna be a drug dealer's wheels?"

I laugh,
and we talk about my running,
school,
the price of gas,
sports and
then *Star Wars*,
me trying to convince him that
Rey's way cooler than Princess Leia
ever was,
because, of course, he hasn't seen the new ones.

It's all
unimportant things
and never
                    The Thing.

And then, time's up.

"Three o'clock," the marine shouts
to no one in particular,
though I'm the only one in the room.

"I'll come tomorrow," I tell Ed.

"Have you heard from Mom?"
    he asks quickly.

I don't get a chance to answer.

    Already they've taken the phone from him,
    shackled his wrists and ankles,
    and are roughly leading him away.

UP AGAINST A COOKIE JAR

Angela thought the note
    propped up
    against an empty cookie jar
    was a joke.
"Why would Mom go to Minnesota on a bus?"

I didn't understand either.
She was gone? Like never coming back?
Like Dad was dead and Ed was in prison?

Aunt Karen rushed out to work,
cursing Mom for making us worry.

Angela and I ditched school.
We watched TV, waited for Mom to call
or come home.

We thought by the time it got dark
she would stagger in
carrying a stuffed-crust pizza.
Maybe she'd smell of beer or be
woozy from pills,
but that would be all right.

Better home
and
    out of it
than on a Greyhound to the Midwest.

Only it didn't happen.
Mom never came home
and Aunt Karen took over completely,
raging with Ed for what he'd done to us.

I was nine by then.

A week after Mom took off
we got a letter from Ed,
dropping onto the mat with a considered huff.
He wanted to know when we were heading
      down to Texas
      to see him.
"I wouldn't visit that lowlife
if he was tied to a tree in the yard," Karen yelled.
"He destroyed this family.
He destroyed two families."
She wasn't interested in his innocence.
Guilty by judge and jury was enough,
and she made sure we knew it.

"He killed a police officer
and finished off your mother."

Mom didn't vanish entirely though.
She sent postcards sometimes.

I never bothered to keep them.

EVERYONE WALKED

I	never had a dad
but	I had a big brother
and	then I didn't
and	then I didn't have a mother
and	I spent a lot of time wondering
when	I would lose
my	sister
my	aunt,
until	everyone I loved walked out the front door

leaving me alone.

THE GAS STATION

The girl from the diner, Nell,
studies a display of DVDs
along the back wall of the gas station.
I move toward her,
open a packet of gum without paying for it.
"I met you earlier," I say,
offering her a piece.

Nell's face is stony.
"You're new to town."
It's not a question.
She takes the gum from my hands,
pops a piece into her mouth and
puts the pack in her pocket.
"Your dad at the farm for robbery? Drugs?"

"My brother. His name's Ed. I'm Joe."

She holds up a copy of *Die Hard*.
"Bruce Willis used to be so hot."
She points to his picture on the box,
            tilts her head to one side.

"But he's not hot now?" I ask.

"He might be.
I haven't seen him since the restraining order."
Her mouth is straight—a wiseass.

She takes the DVD to the counter,
pays,
leaves
and stomps through the gas station parking lot,
along the sidewalk
        to an empty bench.

I drop down next to her.
"So DVDs. Bruce Willis. What else?"

She considers this.
"I just think old stuff is underrated.
Like Cyndi Lauper.
She's awesome.
Why the hell isn't she on the radio *all* the time?"

"Cyndi Lauper?" I snicker.

"Yeah, Cyndi Lauper.
And Dusty Springfield.
Do you even know Dusty Springfield?"

"Oh, sure, Dusty and I go *way* back."
I wink at her but her expression is unreadable.
I struggle to find something else to say.
"You wanna grab some pizza?" I ask.

She waves the DVD case in my face.
"I have a date with Bruce."

I'm not sure I like her,
but after the day I've had, I don't wanna be alone,
not for a third consecutive evening
with a bag of chips, my phone, and the internet;
that sort of night can only go one way.
"Hang with me for an hour," I beg.

"You might be a murderer," she says.

"Do murderers take their victims for pizza?"

"*You'd* know."

I swallow hard. Maybe I do know.
Maybe murderers look like the rest of us.
Maybe one looks a lot like me.

"You know, when I said let's go for pizza,
I meant would you buy me pizza 'cause I'm broke."

"You must be if you can't afford gum," she says.
So she noticed.

I wink at her again, hoping she'll find me
cute, not criminal.
She doesn't give anything away,
puts her hand into the pocket of her denim shorts,
pulls out some crumpled dollar bills.
"Don't go spending that on liquor and loose women."

    I push her hand away.
    Yes, I'm starving,
    but for conversation.
    I want to talk to her,
    forget why I'm in Wakeling,
    be seventeen instead of a grown-up—
    serious and sensible.
    And hell, if I make her laugh
    maybe she'll let me kiss her,
    help me forget everything
    for a while.

Her phone beeps.
"I have to go."
          Across the street, a truck jumps the curb.
"Enjoy the pizza."
          She throws the cash onto the bench.
"And wear something revealing next time."

I laugh. And it's real.
"I'll dig out my purple hot pants," I say.

She smirks. "I'm Nell, by the way."

"What sort of stalker would I be
if I didn't already know that?"

She nods, smiles, and
rushes off to meet the waiting truck.

SCRATCH-OFF

I should put the pity cash Nell gave me
into Ed's account
so he can get a snack.

I don't.
I return to the gas station,
buy a scratch-off,
take it back to the apartment and
scrape away silver foil
        with the edge of a dime.

I think about Nell in her shorts and baggy T-shirt,
not Ed in his jumpsuit.

I try really hard not to think about Ed.

And I don't beat the odds:
no matching numbers
beneath the panel of clover.

I think of Nell.
I think of her
        and I scratch.

UNLUCKY FOR SOME

Ed was convicted of shooting a cop,
a pretty ugly thing to do.
But you don't see every killer getting the gurney.
Some guys get fifteen years,
      others get life.

So death for Ed
but not for everyone.

'Cause it all depends on
who you kill
and
where you kill them
too.

Like,
don't shoot a white cop in Walker County, Texas.
If that's your plan, do it in Arlington, New York—
no needles or electric chairs there.

Just doesn't seem fair to me.

Just seems a little fucking random.

GOLD

Reed sends me a photo of the glossy gold medal
he won for the hurdles.
He gets a medal every year,
even though hundreds of city kids do the meet,
but he rarely comes first—
that's my job:
      gold for the five thousand meters.

      Just not this year.

Congrats, man!!!!!
I reply.
But I'm not noble enough
to be genuinely pleased.

A DIFFERENCE

Ed waves widely—Ronald McDonald–style.
"Did Al call you today?"
He's almost bouncing in his chair.

I shake my head
      but my body
      lightens,
      untightens.
Did the judge have a
      change of heart?

"So the biggest thing happened.
The cop who died and got me locked up,
Frank Pheelan,
his wife told the judge she didn't wanna see me die.
She asked him to change the sentence.
Al's gonna make it part of the appeal
in Houston next week. What d'ya think?"

I think about how much
I need water.
I didn't drink enough today
while I worked on the car,

and the minestrone soup Sue made for lunch
was too salty.

"Does this stuff make a difference?" I ask.
And can Al even mention Pheelan's wife
at a state-level appeal?
When Al explained the process he didn't tell me,
but I'm sure
Angela told me a long time ago
that they have rules about what can be raised
at each stage.

Ed's expression stiffens.
I've said something wrong.
"Sorry, I don't get the system. I don't . . ." I trail off,
'cause what I'm thinking is,
> I don't know what to say to you, Ed,
> or how to say it.
> I shout at Angela
> 'cause I've known her my whole life.
> But I don't know what makes you tick
> or what would even happen if I shouted.

Ed sniffs.
"I think it's *gotta* make a difference.

No way they can kill a man
when the victim's family says stop.
You know?"

I nod, eagerly this time.
"I see what you mean."

Ed sits back in his chair. Sighs.
"Look, I know it's a long shot,
but Al says it can't hurt."
He grins like a kid who's been
promised a chocolate dessert,
and it dawns on me that Ed
doesn't believe he's going to die;
he thinks Al will convince the judges
he never deserved any of this.

Water gurgles through a pipe on the wall.
I wipe my mouth with the back of my hand,
clear my throat.
It's hotter in here than out in the sun,
and that's saying something.

"You okay?" Ed asks.

"I'm thirsty is all," I tell him.

He laughs. "Oh, get used to that feeling, man.
You know they got air-conditioning in the main prison?
Air-conditioning and strawberry soap.
But you know what I'd love?
A Coke."

I lower my gaze.
"I forgot to put money into your account," I lie.

"Nah, that isn't what I meant.
Just gets to be a furnace in this place
and they don't go giving extras 'cause it's summer.
But I could destroy a cold Coke.
When it gets over a hundred,
I spend whole afternoons salivating
over soda cans and vending machines.
Like, you put your coins in,
the machine gobbles them—*clunk, clunk*—
and then—*bang*—
the can drops to the bottom
all cold and sweaty.
        Wet.
Thinking about that's like porn to me, man."
He licks the air with his tongue.

I laugh loudly.

He laughs too,
and after a couple minutes we can't stop,
tears on our faces.

When the hour is up,
    I feel a whole lot better.

Ed's happy.
The cop's wife
could make a difference.

So maybe things will turn around.
I mean they could.

        It's not impossible.
        Not totally.

PHILIP MILLER

A fat guy in a tight shirt
smiles from behind an office window.
"Who's that?" I ask
as the guard retrieves my belongings from the locker.

She glances over her shoulder.
"That's Philip Miller, the warden."

Mr. Philip Miller,
father to a whole farm of lowlifes,
responsible for keeping them
chained down,
      locked up,
           sealed in,
so the rest of the state can sleep easy.

And he stands there
grinning.

The jackass.

THAT'S WHO

My face is in my phone,
distracting myself with Mets news,
        their win against Toronto.

But Ed is always there,
        in the corner of my mind,
        fidgeting.

What does he do to pass the time?
How can he stand it?
If that were me on the row,
I'd lie awake listening to killers snore,
imagining my walk to the death chamber,
        the length of the gurney,
        the smell and feel of the leather straps,
        the last faces I'd see—
the team doing the dirty work
and the guests in the gallery.

        What sort of asshole buys scratch-offs
        instead of a soda for his dying brother?

Me,
that's who.

NIGHT RUN

I pull on my shorts and sprint full tilt
out of the building and
along Main Street,
past the gas station, motels,
pizza and fried-chicken places,
until I reach the diner.

I couldn't run five thousand meters at this speed
but I'm not training.
I'm not running to strengthen my performance.
I even forgot to wear my watch.

I slow and peek through a side window to
see if Nell's at work.

She's not.

She's probably at home
watching TV or
eating ice cream.

Something normal,
     I guess.

Which is how I'd like my life to turn out.
Eventually.

—

TAILGATING

I slow my pace on my run home
when I come across a huddle of cars
belting out music in the high school parking lot.
Kids, kegs, buckets of chips.
I walk and watch.

A guy in a Houston Texans jersey
      guzzles a bottle of beer
then raises his head and roars at the sky
as though downing booze is a superpower.
He stumbles, trips,
           totally wasted.

I pass through the gates
and drift around until I spot two girls
by the trunk of a car
pouring vodka into a bowl.
"Hey," I say.

The redhead looks up, eyes bloodshot.
"Hey," she replies.

Her friend, a curly blonde,
whoops and wraps her arms around my neck.
She smells like licorice.

"You came!" the blonde shouts, as though
expecting me.
"You're Lucy's cousin, right?
From Jacksonville?"
She dips a red cup into the bowl
and offers it to me.
It's sweet and toxic.

"I'm Peter," I say,
so I don't have to answer her question.

They both do some sort of wormy dance,
hands twirling,
asses wriggling.
Behind them in the trunk is a phone,
a wallet.

"Lucy told us you were cool," the redhead says.
"Where is Lucy anyway?"
She stands on tiptoe.

I take her hand,
twist her around so my back is to the trunk
and she's looking at me, not for Lucy.

The blonde pours more sauce into my cup.
I knock it back in two seconds flat.

"Oh, you're a bad boy," she whispers,
        lips brushing my ears.
But I'm not interested in being
a bad-boy-bit-of-rough,
a new guy who's
ripe for the picking
'cause she thinks sex
is the most terrible thing she could ever do to her
lousy parents.

I wrap an arm around her waist,
put my other hand behind me,
find the wallet and
        slip it into the band of my shorts.
I thought it would be easy,
but I didn't think it would be this easy.

I'm about to give the girls some story about
locating Lucy
when someone taps my shoulder.

I turn.

It's Nell.

"Wanna take off?" she asks.

"Yes, please," I say,
and follow her out of the parking lot
along the dusty, dark road
like a lost dog.

JUST NO

Nell leads me along the side entrance
to her yard.
She drops down into the deep end
of a dry-bottomed
swimming pool
and waves for me to follow.

"This is my dad's place.
Mom lives in Dover, next town over."
She pulls a crushed joint from her pocket,
lights one end,
inhales like her life depends on it.

Night insects whine to one another.
A car revs its engine, sounds its horn.
A dog is barking in the neighbor's yard.
"So, your *thing* is stealing stuff, huh?" she asks,
unimpressed.

I yank the wallet out of my shorts.
"I'll give the stuff back," I say.
"I was looking for cash."

Apart from some store loyalty cards
and a couple of photographs,
there's only ten bucks in it.
"I should have stolen her iPhone," I say.

Nell snorts. "In Wakeling?
You'd never sell it.
You'd get as far as *talking* about a stolen phone
and be down at the station."
She grabs the wallet.
"I'll pop it through Tanya's mailbox tomorrow.
Say I found it."

"So you approve of theft?"

"I don't care what you do, Joe."

"Are those girls your friends?"

"Friends? No. They'll be driving
rug rats around in minivans
before they're twenty years old."

"You don't like minivans?"

She passes me the joint.
I inhale, hold it in my lungs,

let it run through my blood
until the tiles of the swimming pool
        soften against my back.

"No to minivans, Little League, and baking.
No to all that shit.
I'm not going to be a statistic.
I'm getting out of this hellhole alive
and I'll fight anyone who tries to stop me.
I want more.
But you can't say that too loudly around here
'cause *who the hell do you think you are*, right?"

I exhale. "I understand."

She climbs the metal ladder
at the side of the swimming pool,
stands above me,
        a silhouette.
"I gotta go in.
And you better leave before my dad gets home."

"Can I see you again?" I say aloud,
but under my breath mumble Nell's words:
        who the hell do you think you are?

SUPERHERO

Ed told me that when I got older
I could be anything I wanted.
"Can I be Spider-Man?" I asked.
"Why not?" he said.
"And can I leave Arlington?"

He hesitated,
      just a second,
long enough for me to know something was up.

BEFORE THE SUN RISES

I wake at four thirty
and spend too long
calculating the number of days
left until Ed's execution.

It's July 9,
which gives us over a month
until August 18—
not that Ed will see
any of his execution day;
he's scheduled to die a minute past midnight.

Ed will be cold
before the sun rises.

I peel myself out of bed and go for another run.

I want to improve my splits.

COUNTDOWN TO CHRISTMAS

As soon as Thanksgiving was done,
I wanted it to be Christmas,
daydreamed about all the toys
Santa Claus would place beneath the tree.
"He won't come if you're naughty," Mom said,
scraping soggy cornflakes into the trash can.

Ed elbowed me,
    bit into a slice of burnt toast.
"Course he'll come, Joe.
You better write a letter
so you don't get a potato peeler."

We wrote the letter together
and mailed it early,
asking for stuff I knew Mom couldn't afford,
that Santa's elves would make in the workshop—
a *Star Wars* Lego set,
a superhero costume,
a set of paints, glitter and bright white paper.
Could they sew together new sneakers?

While heavy snow fell
and the bay almost froze,

I counted off the days until Christmas.
And I never realized that the reason
Ed and Angela were so busy
shoveling sidewalks
was to make sure
I didn't cry with disappointment
on Christmas morning
and believe that Santa thought
I had been bad.

BREAKFAST BAGEL

Nell tosses me a plastic-wrapped bagel.
"Sue made it. Cream cheese and tomato.
And it's soup for lunch again, if you'll be here."

"Thanks."
        A drop of sweat runs down my back.
"Hey, do you wanna hang out later?
We could get beers, sit in the back of the junker."

Nell rubs the end of her nose.
"I don't think so," she says.
Without an explanation,
        she returns to the diner.

I watch her go.

Has she searched Ed's name online?
Google would tell her everything she wanted to know
about him,
about me,
our whole family.

I bite into the bagel,
ticked off
Sue didn't send out a drink
to go with my breakfast.

FATHER MATTHEW

At the Section A entryway,
an old guy with
soft eyes
approaches
        nervously.

Despite the heat
he's wearing a wool sweater.
His beard has dandruff.

"I'm Father Matthew,
Ed's spiritual adviser."
He holds out a hand and I shake it.
"And you're his brother, Joseph?"

"Uh-huh," I mutter.

"I'm sorry you're going through this."
He waves at the prison walls.

A gray-haired guard looks up from
her gossip magazine.

"I'm available for you too.
And anyone else in the family," the priest continues.

"Look, Father—"

"Sometimes it's helpful to talk," he says quickly.

I sniff.
Does he think I haven't talked about this already?
It's all Angela wants to discuss:
Ed's crime, case,
        how long he has left,
playing on a loop in her head.

"I'm here if you change your mind," he says.
"Try to trust in God, son."

Rage rushes through me,
and I point
        my finger right between his eyes.
"You know what, Father?
God didn't put Ed in here.
Men did that.
And it's men keeping him here.
So go blow your God crap
at someone else, 'cause I'm not buying it."

The priest doesn't flinch.

"Joseph—" he begins.

"My name's Joe," I say.

"And you know nothing about me at all."

PUBLIC RELATIONS

When the news broke in New York
that Ed was a suspected murderer,
kids in my class were warned by their petrified parents
to keep away from me,
the bad boy, sad boy,
God-only-knows-what-goes-on-behind-that-door boy.
Ed came from our house—
a place they suddenly assumed
was cooking up evil like
chicken soup.
It's not like they were the Gospel-spreading types;
half the neighborhood was up to no good,
ducking taxes and stealing cable.

But Ed's crime put us in another league,
and that's where Aunt Karen stepped in—
she spat on us and shined us up to look
like a decent family,
stood in for Mom and Dad,
fed us and petted us,
            tried to turn things around.

And for this, I guess, I should be grateful.

But Karen never asked how happy we were or
what we wanted—
it was all about how things looked from
        the outside;
what other people thought
was all that was important,
and how we felt about ourselves was irrelevant.
Our desires didn't matter.

Karen stole Ed from us
and
we'll never get those years back.

THE WALL

Ed's knuckles are bruised a plummy purple.
He rubs them and laughs.
"You think *this* is something?
In here? Joe, this is nothing."

"Why'd you fight?"
I want to hear how he defended himself
against the toughest guys,
lunatics locked up for burying people alive,
monsters who are nothing like him.

"They wouldn't let me shower," he says.
"I missed my slot, so now I stink."

"Who'd you hit?"

He looks ashamed.
        Was it Father Matthew?
        A guard?
"I punched a wall," he says.
"And I know this looks painful,
but you should see the wall."

He winks
and the rest of the visit goes great.

A JOKE

Al Mitchell meets me by the prison gates
and shakes my hand like I'm a man.
"Good to meet you, Joe.
Let's take a walk," he says,
but we don't go far
before he stops
and kicks a stone
with the toe of his leather loafer.
"I was in Houston today.
The state denied our appeal. I'm sorry.
The cop's wife wants the sentence commuted to life
but she's not the one prosecuting Ed—
the state's doing that.
Anyway, the judge wasn't interested in her letter.
Listened with one ear, you know?
The Supreme Court will be more impartial.
If we can get the federal court to hear us,
we have a real chance of winning.
This isn't over."

"What can I do?"

He rests a hot hand on my arm.
"Keep your fingers crossed."

Is that it?
Is this all down to luck?
The judge Ed gets, the jury?
"Justice is a joke," I say.

Al nods.
"Look, Joe, this process will change you.
I've seen it plenty of times.
I've felt it myself in my heart.
What's happening is hell,
and as long as you survive,
you've done well."
He squeezes my arm, and I don't pull away,
don't play the gangster to fend him off.

Instead I ask,
"What are his chances?"

Al's cell phone rings.
Without glancing at it, he clicks it off—
shuts out whoever needs him.
It's a little thing, ignoring that call,
but it means a lot.

"We still have options," he says vaguely,
and turning us around,

heads back to death row
so he can break the bad news
to my brother.

MY LIFE NOW

I run to Nell's place quickly—
my splits around ten seconds quicker than usual.
I want to hang out with her,
chill in her backyard and guzzle beer.
Or we could sip water.
Whatever.
Anything.

But there's a blue truck in the driveway.
        The same truck that picked her up
        from the gas station.

So I return to the apartment,
put a frozen pizza in the oven
and set an alarm to beep after twelve minutes.

Angela calls and we talk about
the weather—compare New York summers
to Texan ones.

This is my life now.

THE PROSECUTOR

The morning news features Ed's story again—
his mean mug shot,
his handsome victim,
the state attorney
outside the courthouse
yesterday
looking so pleased with himself
you'd think he'd won
first prize in a meat raffle.

The state attorney puffs up his chest,
presses his mouth to the microphones.
"We are delighted that
Judge Byron did not reverse the decision
made by the original trial judge and jury,
nor saw any valid reason for a retrial."

Cameras flash,
        questions are asked
and the prosecutor beams,
dying to elaborate
and spout hate against Ed.

I turn the TV off;
I hate his face.

THE COST

It costs around four million dollars
to go through with an execution.
That's eight times more money
than to imprison someone for life.
Not that anyone gives a damn:
killing is worth every cent.

WHERE IT ENDS

Ed talks like a high-speed train.
"I seen over a hundred guys in this place
        go to the chamber,
and every one thought he'd get off in the end."
He scratches his head.
"And you know what's really screwed-up?
When those guys said good-bye,
they didn't do it properly, 'cause
they thought that a minute before midnight
the governor would *ring-a-ding-ding*
and say they've made a huge mistake.
But this isn't the movies.
No one's walking out the front door in a suit.
When folks here say you're headed to the chamber,
they aren't messing around.
The only way out is in a box."
He laughs bitterly.

I don't know this Ed.
So far I've only seen
the one who believes it'll be okay.

"This is where it ends, Joe," he whispers.
"I'm telling you the truth."

MY VERSION

He leans on a row of railings,
chews on gum
and pretty confidently squints away the sun.
He's older than me,
    but not by much.

"Joe?" he wants to know.
He's too friendly.

"Have we met?"

He picks up a canvas satchel,
throws it across his body,
runs, and stumbles to get to me
before I'm through the prison gates.
His shirtsleeves are rolled up,
shoes scuffed.

"How did Ed cope with losing his appeal?" he asks.
He lets his head fall to one side in sympathy
and I know then who he is and what he wants—
even Karen's takeover at home all those years ago
couldn't keep the newshounds from the door.

"I'm not talking to the press," I hiss.

He holds up his hands.
"Dude, I just wanna know how Ed's holding up.
Maybe you guys want *your* story told.
Your version of things."

"My *story*? This isn't a story,
        you asshole.
This is my life."
I make my expression mean.
"You interested in knowing more about me?
You wanna see the kind of guy I can be?"

He comes closer
        so we're nose to nose.
"You know what, dude,
that would also make an excellent story."
He laughs, taunting me,
steps back and snaps a photo with his phone.

"What's going on?"
a guard calls out,
inspecting us from Section A,
a hand on his holster.

My anger bubbles.

But it won't do Ed any good getting into a fight.

"My brother's innocent," I snarl.

"Write *that* in your stupid paper."

INNOCENT

Is Ed innocent?
I mean,
I've never actually asked him outright.

THE TIP JAR

Sue's lips are pinched around the
    butt of her cigarette.
"Any luck with the car today, hon?" she asks.

"Nah. But I'll try again tomorrow."
I take a seat at the counter
where Sue ladles lentils
from a copper pot into a brown bowl,
plops it in front of me.
"I got plenty, so shout if you're still hungry."

I slurp at the soup,
glance up at the wall clock.
Fifty minutes until visiting time.
"Hey, Sue,
I don't suppose you could spare a few bucks
so I can catch a bus?
I'll give it back."
I hate myself for asking
but I'm tired of trekking through the humidity.

Sue slides her tip jar,
filled with
crumpled dollar bills

and multicolored coins,
across the counter.
"Ain't much, but take what you need."

"I'll pay it back. I promise."

Sue pats my hand.
"Relax and eat your lunch, hon."

BAD NEWS

The diner door pings and Nell appears.
She doesn't see me at first,
hums her way to the counter
swinging a set of car keys.
"Thanks for taking such a late lunch order,"
she tells Sue.
"Daddy's at home
and all we have in the house is string cheese."

"Gimme a sec."
Sue disappears into the kitchen.

Nell sits on a stool next to me.

"You're avoiding me," I say.
"Like, just a fraction?"

She reaches for a menu to fan her face.
"Shit. I thought I was being subtle about it."

"Not really.
I mean,
one night we're hanging out, then I never see you.
I feel used."

I keep my voice light
so she thinks I'm teasing.

But Nell is serious.
"Look, Joe, I'm bad news to you."

I force a laugh.
"I love bad news."

Then Sue is beside us with a bag.
She shifts from one foot
        to the other.
"Here's your order, hon."

Nell sighs.
"Thanks, Sue."
She turns to me.
"Look, I have no interest in making fast friends."

"Me neither," I tell her.
And I mean it.
"I'm in Texas for Ed."

"See you around," she says.
        And she's gone.

A SODA

"I got a soda
with the money you put into the account," Ed says.

"I didn't send it," I admit,
wondering if Angela managed to find funds
after I told her Karen had been sending Ed money
every month
but had stopped.

"Well, whatever, man.
God, it was sweet. Best soda ever."
His eyes well up
and I want to reach through the Plexiglas,
grab him, shake him,
tell him to get a grip;
            it's just a soda.

Jesus, Ed, it's just a fucking soda.

But it isn't.
It isn't just a soda at all.

PEOPLE HERE

I'm on Main Street minding my own business
when a woman
      with a poodle under one arm
      murmurs something.

"Excuse me?"

"Your brother killed a police officer," she says
and shakes a newspaper at me,
noses the air.

So the journalist published a piece and pointed to me.
And here we go again—guilt by association,
strangers scared of my dangerous DNA.

"He isn't guilty," I tell her.
I seem to be saying this a lot
when I have no idea how true it is.

"People around here hope he fries," she spits,
just like that,
      straight into my face.

I take a deep breath.
"They don't use the chair anymore.
So no one's getting fried. Sorry."
 I pat the poodle
 and continue along the street.

WITHOUT THE CONS

Sue brews me tea and
pushes a large jelly doughnut
      across the counter.
"That old witch don't talk for the rest of us, Joe.
Wakeling wouldn't last a day without the cons.
Whole damn town is financed by the farm."

I bite into the doughnut. It's still warm.
"Can I have a tenderloin
with peppercorn sauce for lunch?" I ask.

Sue laughs.
"You can have a substandard burger and cold fries."

"Is that all you think I'm worth?"
I'm trying to make Sue smile
but she scrutinizes me.

"Real question is what you think
you're worth, hon."

DAD

It's not like they *all* ran away.
Dad was different.
I've seen pictures of him rocking me
with cheaply tattooed arms,
face furrowed from years of unemployment lines
and dealing crystal meth to junkies
who'd have cut him
rather than let him leave
without their hit.

But he died before I was a year old—
got himself killed:

       billiard ball hidden in a sock
       to the back of the head,
       like a real hero.

And the guy who did it?
Claimed it was an accident,
served four and a half years on Rikers Island,
    which seems,
    I don't know,
like a fucking disgrace
after everything that's happened to Ed.

NELL SENDS A MESSAGE

Come over to my house later.

I don't know how she got my number,
probably from Sue,
but it doesn't matter.
      She wants to see me.

ASK HIM

We are in Nell's swimming pool again.
She scatters shreds of weed on top of the tobacco.
"You look like a hillbilly hen farmer.
Wear some sunscreen."

My arms are peeling red.
My face must be worse.
"Back in New York this isn't who I am," I say.
"I've got kind of a life."

She lights the tip of the roll-up and inhales,
        passes the joint.
"Sue said your brother killed a cop.
I looked him up.
He was young when it happened.
Like, our age."

I breathe in the bud, cough,
and she smacks my back.
She takes the joint from me,
pinches the butt between her fingers,
doesn't put the paper to her mouth.
"Did he do it?"

"No!"
My voice is sharper, louder than I intend.

She hesitates.
"But he's still got appeals and stuff, right?
I mean . . ."

"He's got the Supreme Court,
if they agree to hear the case.
And the governor as a very last resort."

"So what happened?
Why'd they lock him up?"

"He confessed to it," I tell her.

"But if he didn't do it,
        why'd he say he *did*?"

"I dunno."
And I've never
        asked Ed outright,
not even since I started visiting.
Why is that?
        What is it about Ed's story
        that makes me doubt him?

Nell reads my mind.
"I'd wanna know exactly what happened
so I could get it straight in my head."

She's right.
I need the truth,
whatever shape it comes in.
I need to know Ed trusts me,
that we have no secrets between us,
no bullshit
now we're so close to the end.
We were always good friends.
I want him to tell me everything.

"Ask him," Nell says.

ED CONFESSED TO THE CRIME

Back when it happened,
Ed signed a sworn statement confessing
to shooting Frank Pheelan.

He told Mom on the phone
the cops forced him to sign
and he was too tired and confused to argue.

Little else links him to the crime.

This is all I know.

POINTLESS

The walls are sweating.
It must be a hundred and ten degrees
in the visiting room.
"I'm learning Spanish," Ed says, in greeting.

"Huh?"

"Spanish.
I figure I'm from New York
and I've been in Texas
for ten years so
there's no excuse.
Half the guys here speak it,
but to get good you gotta study.
Anyway, now I got Al
I can give up the law stuff.
Gotta fill my time somehow, right?"

I'm not sure what to say,
but I'm careful not to blurt out,
What's the point?

Ed counts to ten in Spanish,
tells me his name and where he lives.

I listen and eventually Ed simmers down.
"Do you speak another language?"
He wipes his forehead with the back of his hand.

My throat is chalk-dry.
I shake my head. "I hardly speak English."

He laughs and there is a lull,
            a conspicuous
            gap in the conversation,
a space for a question.

"Ed, I have something to ask."

He pulls his chair closer,
like that makes a difference.
"I'm right here, man."
His eyes are wide, waiting to give me advice,
        be a big brother.

It's always so damn hot here.
And they never set out water
or put a fan in the room.

"Joe?" Ed looks concerned.

I mean, the irony of it—
he looks concerned for *me*.

"I gotta ask . . ." I try.
But I can't.
I stare at him.
And he stares right back.

For a long time.

Time:
    the very thing we don't have to waste.

DID YOU DO IT?

"Did you kill that cop?"

WRONG

Ed removes the receiver from his ear and
squints at it like something might be
wrong with the prison equipment.

AGAIN

"What happened back then?"
            My voice is tinny.
I should shut up and let Ed answer,
but quickly new questions come and
            I spit them at him.
"Why did you confess?
Why didn't the old lawyer do the talking?
Wasn't there DNA to prove you never did it?"

Ed taps the table with his fingertips.
"You really gonna ask me that?"

I grit my teeth.
"I have to know one hundred percent, Ed."

"You're *really* asking me this stuff?"
He drops the phone.
The sound splinters my eardrum.

Then he stands and
            before I can do anything about it
is shackled and shuffling away.

"Ed. Talk to me!" I shout.
"Why can't we just talk about it?"

But it's too late.

He's gone.

Again.

IN ME

Before Ed got arrested,
Angela never stopped believing
he would come back
of his own accord,
once he quit being mad at Mom.

I knew better.
Ed was stubborn.

I knew better.
I had more Ed in me than
I've ever admitted.

THE WARDEN

What I definitely do not need
as I leave
is Philip Miller waiting for me.

"You got two seconds, son?"
I don't know where he gets off
      flashing that big, bogus smile
when he's the one who'll
put Ed down in the end.

In his office
we face each other,
a bulky desk between us
piled high with books
and paper cups.

"We haven't spoken.
My name's Philip Miller,
though I figure you already know that."
He pauses,
like maybe I'm supposed to
acknowledge his power.

I clench my jaw,
turn my hands into fists.

On his desk is a photograph of a girl in roller skates,
yellow jeans,
her hair held up in lopsided bunches.

"It can't be easy," he says.

"No," I admit,
"but at least I'm not organizing the injection."

He straightens his tie,
dabs his clammy forehead with a Kleenex.
"I'm doing my job, Joseph," he says,
like that's an excuse,
like that isn't what the prosecutor says,
the judge, the jury, the guards.

"I guess the Nazis claimed the same thing," I say.
I don't know a lot about history,
but I do understand that all it takes
is a whole bunch of bystanders
and people just doing their jobs
for ugly things to happen.

His smile fades.
"I wanted to introduce myself and reassure
you that my staff will be respectful
throughout this process.

I understand *you* committed no crime, after all.
Is there anything the prison can help with?"
He's trying to be considerate,
smooth over his guilt with bullshit benefits.

"You got a crucifix on the wall," I say.

He nods;
　　　　　he knows what's coming
　　　　　and doesn't try to stop me.

"I wonder what Jesus would do
if he were here for a day."

Philip Miller stands.
The meeting is over.
"Come see me if you need anything," he says.

BRAVE NEW WORLD

Nell is perched on the curb
near the gas station,
a book balanced on her knees.
Her sneakers rest on a beat-up skateboard
covered in oversize stickers.
"You been waiting long?" I ask.

She holds up her book: *Brave New World*.
"I've read fifty-four pages of this crap,
so yeah, pretty much been here a lifetime."
She stands and dusts herself off.
"Wanna go for a lemonade?"

"A what?"
The last thing I want is a soft drink.
I need to get numb.

"Lemonade, Joe.
It's a drink for quenching a thing called thirst."
She punches me full force in the thigh,
folds over the book and stuffs it into the
back pocket of her shorts.
"Come on."

A DECENT MAN

A fancy street,
lawns decorated with rock gardens
and a small stand where giddy girls
sell homemade lemonade
for fifty cents a pop.

Nell pays with a balled-up dollar bill
and we sit on the wall outside the girls' house.

"Did you see him?" she asks.

I sip, slurp, gulp.
"I screwed everything up."

> She puts a hand on my arm.
> I fix my eyes on her fingers,
> the broken, unpolished nails.

"But it got me thinking," I go on.
"Why wouldn't he answer?"

She sighs
like she might understand,

but she can't know how much I need Ed
to tell me he didn't do it—could *never* do it—
that evil isn't threaded through our genes
like everyone thinks.

      What I need is for Ed to say
      that I have a fighting chance
      of becoming a decent man
            someday.

ED WON'T SEE ME

So I trudge back to town
in the pot-roast heat
and work on the junker.

AND THE NEXT DAY

It is the same.

NOT DRIVING

Nell and I share a booth and drink Oreo milk shakes.
She's almost finished *Brave New World*,
turns the pages so violently
she's in danger of ripping them.
"Quit reading it," I tell her.

"I want to have an opinion," she says.

"What? I got opinions on a ton of stuff
I know nothing about.
Like . . . oysters."

"Oysters?"

"Yeah—I've never eaten one but they're gross.
And surfing. It's stupid. Arrogant.
Also, New Jersey.
Armpit of the universe.
I mean, who'd live in Hoboken?"

She thumps my leg.
"You're a genuine jackass."

"I know," I say,
and look out the window.

Her fingers tap my arm.
"I'm sure he'll see you tomorrow," she says.

THE THIRD DAY

"He has to see me," I say.

The marine-guard is back.
He shrugs and
makes a not-much-I-can-do face.

"Fine. Pass on a message.
Tell Ed from me that he's a prick."

HALLOWEEN

I was a werewolf
howling into the October sky,
fake fur fastened to my face.
Angela took me trick-or-treating,
and we filled two buckets with candy.
At home, Ed laughed at my costume:
"Are you supposed to be a scary beaver?"
I got so irate I stormed down to our room
and refused to come out.
Ed said it was a joke,
wouldn't apologize.
And even though we both
sulked for a few days,
by the end of it we were
friends
and couldn't
remember why it had gotten us all
steamed up in the first place.

CHARITY

A thin tap on my apartment door.
"From Ed," Father Matthew says,
holding out an envelope.
He peers into the gloom behind me.

"I'd invite you in
but I don't own a coffeepot
and the water runs yellow," I explain.

He waves away the suggestion.
"Maybe I can get you a drink in town?"

Some company would be nice,
but there's a limit to how much charity I can take.
I've reached it.
"I don't think so."

"Another time maybe," he says. "Good night, Joe."

"Good night, Father."

ANOTHER LETTER

Dear Joe,

So here it is:
        I was driving real late on Route 35
        just north of New Braunfels.
        It's true what they said,
            I was there that night
            and I got pulled over.
        The cop was mad as hell before I even spoke.
        He checked my license, but I didn't have
        registration documents for the wheels
        'cause they was Aunt Karen's—
        I never lied about that.
        He said he had to call it in.
        I panicked, man.
        I thought he'd see the car was Karen's
        and take me to the station.
        I didn't wanna go back to Staten Island.
        I didn't wanna live with Mom.
        So when he got on his radio, I split.
        I know it was stupid, but I wasn't
        thinking straight.
Anyway,
        I caught the cop by surprise
        and he had to run his ass back to the cruiser.

But I had my foot to the floor and was gone.
Didn't even see him in the rearview 'cause
I got off the highway quick as I could,
> *took some back roads.*
Thing is,
> *I was low on gas so I pulled into a*
> *Taco Bell. I remember that 'cause I was starving.*
> *I ditched the car there and took off,*
> *walked to a bus station.*
> *I seen tons of people along the road*
> *and no one took any notice of me.*
> *I was real glad they didn't that day,*
> *but after I wished I'd looked hard in*
> *someone's eye*
> *so they could tell the jury they'd seen me,*
> *you know, seen me and I wasn't*
> *covered in blood.*
Anyway,
> *I took a bus south, the hell out of Comal County.*
> *And I was sitting on that bus busting my ass laughing*
> *'cause I thought I got away with it.*
> *I imagined Karen would get her car back*
> *but I'd still be missing, which is what I wanted.*
> *Easy, right?*

So,

        the next week I'm pumping gas for tips in
        San Antonio,
        not thinking about that cop stopping me.
        I mean, he got my license but it's the
        Staten Island address.
        Then I get picked up.
        Just like that.
        These rookie cops pull into the station for a refill
        and take me in.
        I told them again and again
        how it happened,
        that I got stopped and got scared and bolted.
        But they started talking about a gun
        and that's when I got real confused,
        told them I didn't even own a gun.

Anyway,

        I go into the station at midnight and they leave me
        in an interrogation room for hours,
        though there's no record of that.
        Then they say they got a lawyer coming
        and was I okay answering some questions
        before the lawyer got there 'cause it was late?

Well,

        they tricked me good, 'cause no public defender's
        coming to a station at three in the morning,

but I said—sure I can answer your questions—
'cause I didn't do anything, so I wasn't too worried;
figured Karen would be pissed about her wheels
but wouldn't press charges.
I know they have zilch on me.
But they get mean, telling me I'm white trash.
And they give me a lie detector test and start
asking crazy questions about a cop
and a shooting and a murder
and I got no idea at all what's happening.
Anyway,
     later I heard I passed that damn test,
     but they tell me I failed.
Now,
     it's eight o'clock in the morning, and I got no lawyer.
     They say I'm lying, the test doesn't make mistakes.
     They show me some papers,
     like I can understand them.
     They say maybe I shot a cop by accident 'cause
     I was scared
     and I say no—that's not what happened—
     the cop was alive when I drove away.
     They say judges go easy on cons who confess,
     that if I lie they'll give me the death penalty
     and do I know how it feels to get
     put to sleep like a bitch?

I ask for my lawyer and they say he's coming.
I ask could I get some water and they say sure
   but they never bring it.
I ask can I sleep, 'cause by then it was the afternoon
and I thought I was gonna fall over.
So one officer says yeah, I can sleep.
But he doesn't take me back to the cell.
He takes me to a cruiser with some other cop
and they drive me to a street with no lights,
make me get out of the car.

So,

I can't see any people or houses or anything.
Just sort of a swamp. And the cops
put a gun to my head
and say they know I'm a killer
and I'm gonna confess, 'cause if I don't
they'll make sure I get what's coming.
And you know, I was thinking
that if I had skills and could get that gun,
I'd shoot him for trying to spook me.

So,

what would you have done, Joe?
I figured I didn't have a choice,
so I go back to the station and tell them everything
I think I heard them tell me about
what happened to the cop.

I said it, then signed a paper just before
my lawyer shows up and shakes his head
and asks why I did it
'cause
    he knows
    that it doesn't matter whether you're innocent or not—
    if they have a confession, a jury is gonna believe it.
But
    I was only eighteen, and I was thinking
    I could sign and later tell people what happened
        by that road
    and they'd believe me, 'cause why would someone confess
    then change his mind?

    But that signature did me in.

    Judge let them use it in court even though
    I didn't have a lawyer when I signed
    and the confession had no details about the murder,
    nothing that proves I knew what happened.
You know,
    when I was giving that confession,
    I asked for Mom.
    That's sort of stupid I know,
    but I was crying and I wanted Mom to get me out.

But we both know
she couldn't get herself out of a paper bag
if it was on fire.
Thing was,
    I didn't understand that
    the cop who stopped me the week before was dead.
    Shot.
    Routine stop a couple hours after mine.
    Camera in the cop car wasn't working,
    but the last call he made was when he busted me
    and they had my picture, so every crooked cop
    in the state was looking for me—
    I was a celeb in Texas and didn't even know it.
    Face was even on the news.
So,
    they got me and they had to get someone
    'cause a cop was dead and what they gonna do.
    Let a cop case go unsolved?
    People care big-time about white police officers
    and I'm just surprised they never tried to
    frame some black guy. Tons of black guys
    on the row say they got framed,
    and you gotta believe them
    if you see the news and all these cops
    shooting guys 'cause they're
    walking down a dark street or whatever.

So,

> *it took the jury an hour to find me guilty.*
> *An hour, man.*
> *I waited for trains longer than that.*
> *Never good when a jury comes back quick—*
> *that's what they say.*

There it is, Joe.

> *Black and white.*
> *Is this the stuff you wanted to know*
> *straight from my mouth?*

Joe,

> *I'd believe a confession if I didn't know*
> *how the damn things come about.*
> *I'd think,*
> *why would you admit to something you didn't do?*

But still,

> *I'm mad as hell.*
> *'Cause you gonna ask me now?*
> *This late in the game?*
> *I got guys who never asked me.*
> *Like Tyler in the cell next to mine—he knows the truth.*

Thing is,

> *he admitted what he did—killed his girl.*
> *Took a week for the cops to find her,*
> *and you know what?*

I could tell him if I was guilty and
he wouldn't bat an eyelash
'cause what he did was so dirty.
But he knows I'm not made like him.

Thing is,
if you lie about murder on the row
it makes you the worst kind of scum.
That's why guys end up telling more than their share.

Like last year,
Colin McConnors admitted
doing in those hitchhikers in Alaska,
though no one even knew he was in Fairbanks
when it happened.
We wasn't surprised 'cause McConnors is a sicko.
The crime they got him for was terrible.

Weird thing is,
McConnors is okay when you talk one-on-one.
He likes chess and politics.
He's got smarts too.
Reads all sorts of books by Russians
and spouts Shakespeare like a boss.

So,
you asked me to tell the truth,
kind of saying I didn't already,
so maybe I was a real scumbag,

worse than McConnors, someone who's
gonna lie
to save my own ass.
Well, that isn't me.
Anyway,
  I'm not writing to say screw you.
  I missed you and thought about you every day
  for ten years,
  I swear.
  Come visit me again.
  I don't have long, and I don't wanna waste any
  more time
  being pissed.
  And you gotta stop
  wasting time wondering
  whether or not
  I'm lying.
  And maybe you gotta stop being pissed too,
  'cause I seen some rage in you,
  quietly bubbling, man.
  See you tomorrow, okay?
  Ed x

NO LIES

There are no lies in Ed's eyes.
Just hurt.
"I don't know where to start," I say.

"The letter made sense?" he asks.

"Yes," I say.
The letter told me he was framed,
so that's what I'm going to believe.

"You need me to tell it to your face?" he asks.
His voice is barbed.

"Of course not," I say,
then realize I *do* need that,
no matter the outcome.
"Maybe," I admit.

Ed shakes his head.
"I'm trying not to be hurt, man.
But it's hard when your own blood won't believe you.
No one will listen.
I wanted one person on my side, and that was you."

He cracks his knuckles against the desk,
gestures for me to get closer to the glass.
"I didn't kill Frank Pheelan.
I never touched a hair on his head.
I was a petty thief when I came down to Texas,
but I've never been a murderer."
He clenches his jaw.

"I had to ask. I *had* to," I say.

He shrugs. "Okay."

"I also have to tell you something."

He narrows his eyes impatiently.
"What is it?"

"I'd still be sitting here if you did it.
I'd know you didn't deserve *this*."

      He blinks.
      I clench my fists.

"No one does, man," he says.
"And I can say that 'cause I live it.
Anyone who disagrees oughta try it out for a day."

He pauses.
"What does it matter?
No one cares.
You know they got petitions
to stop us from getting medical care 'cause of the cost?"

"Who does?"

"Crazy people," he says, and laughs.
"*Way* crazier than any of us.
And the worst thing is,
they're on the outside walking free."

RESPONSIBLE

They charged Ed as an adult,
locked him up and
sentenced him to die
three years before
anyone thought
he was old enough
to buy a beer in a bar.

WITH NELL

Nell drops down
into the swimming pool then
     moves away
so we aren't touching.

"He didn't do it," I tell her.
"He was a dropout, but not a killer.
I don't know why I had to ask.
I knew him back then."

I study her face under the dim moon,
wishing she'd move closer,
wishing I could be less of a creep
and just enjoy what we have—
stop wanting more.

Then she takes my hand.
Hers is sweaty, but so is mine.
"Wanna watch *Armageddon*?
Bruce is, like, an awesomely hot dad in it."

"That would be cool," I say,
     and we go inside.

WE DON'T KISS

We don't even keep holding hands.
We watch *Armageddon* and
eat marshmallows.
That's all.

It's a pretty great night.

THE CEILING FAN

The ceiling fan doesn't spin,
won't turn and churn
any sort of air around the room.
I glare at it from the bed
and then,
without really wanting to,
think of Nell.
Is she showering?
Sleeping?
Between sheets smelling soapy?

I want these thoughts to stir me, but they don't.
All I feel is loss,
an ache nowhere near my pants
but up in my chest
        and in my arms too.
I want to hold on to her,
have her lie on me—feel her full weight
pinning me down.

And I want to text her,
say good night,
but don't want to chase her away.
I plug in my phone on the other side of the room
so I can't check it every seven seconds.

I turn over,
    imagine Nell is next to me.
It makes me smile. It makes me sad.

I squeeze my eyes shut.
I wish the damn ceiling fan would work.

ROUTINE

Every morning
I work on the junker in the sun
and it never turns over.
Every afternoon
I visit Ed and we pretend that talking
through glass is normal.
Every afternoon
Angela calls to tell me she's working hard for tips,
that she'll
be in Wakeling soon.
Every night
Nell and I hang out—
    and it helps the other stuff
    seem a little less
    crappy.

ANGELA CALLS

"Hey . . . Ange . . ." I pant,
putting my mouth under the kitchen faucet,
gulping in lukewarm water
after my run.
"You find a flight?"

She clicks her tongue.
"I'm gonna call Aunt Karen and ask for a loan.
How you doing for cash?" she asks.

"Don't worry about me.
And don't ask Karen.
If she doesn't care, she doesn't care."

Angela is mute. Guilty.
But none of this is her fault.
We're doing our best,
and if *I* was the one with the job
then she'd be down here with Ed
instead of me.

Maybe I should blame Aunt Karen.
Or I could get pissed at Mom, Dad,
the State of Texas.

I could make a list, rank the culprits:
>*And making a new entry this week*
>*at number five is Ed's arresting officer . . .*

"Joe?" Angela whispers.

"I'm here," I tell her.

"I know," she says.
"And I'm coming soon."

USA

Another press conference was held in Houston
last night,
            aired on morning news.
It was following a Republican Party fund-raiser.
Governor McDowell had eaten a five-course meal
followed by scotch and cigars.
He'd met Miss USA
in her winning pink sash
and they'd posed for photos.

And McDowell, nicely juiced, stood at a podium
and said it was "premature"
to offer Ed executive clemency
and he'd be "waiting for the court's decision"
before reviewing the case again.

Then he climbed into a chauffeur-driven Cadillac.
I'm guessing he slept pretty soundly
in a Hilton penthouse suite.
I'm guessing he didn't dream of needles, but
maybe he did think about
Miss USA and her pretty pink sash.

Ed's life is in this guy's hands.

IF

Al Mitchell calls.
"Try not to worry.
These things often go down to the wire."

"But if the Supreme Court refuses to hear Ed's case
or denies his appeal,
that asshole will be the only person
with any power to postpone the execution.
It isn't right."
I am ranting.
I can hear myself.

Al sighs.
I can't tell whether he's frustrated with me
or annoyed with McDowell.
      Maybe it's neither of those things.
      He has his own life after all.
"It's bullshit. I agree.
And your brother's case is based on a false confession.
If I'd been the defense lawyer back then . . ."
He sighs again.

"You're his lawyer now," I say,
trying to bolster the guy
who's supposed to be bolstering me.

"Yeah," he says,
"And I promise.
I'm doing everything I can."

THIRTY MINUTES

Ed's eyes are bloodshot,
cheeks a little sunken.
"I haven't been sleeping," he says.
He rubs his face with both hands.
"I heard from Mom."
He smirks
       and I wonder if it's a joke.

"You what?"

"Our beloved mother called.
Warden let me talk to her for thirty minutes."

"Thirty minutes?"
It's been years since I've spoken to Mom.
I don't even know what her voice sounds like.

"She wanted to know how I was.
Wanted to know about this place,
how the guards treat us.
She asked how long she's got to come visit.
I swear, man,
       she said it like I was just moving."

He turns to the pale guard
    standing behind him,
        grins like we're all sharing a joke.

"Mom's gonna visit?" I ask.
My heart beats hard.

He sneers. "What do *you* think?
I told her we'd get it figured out.
She cried," he says.
"Real blubber show.
But those tears weren't for me, man—
she just wanted to be forgiven."
He pauses.
"She asked about you and Angela."

I am silent.

"And you know what?"
    He leans forward.
"I could hear a TV.
She never even turned off the TV to call me."
He laughs.
"What do you think of that?"

AUNT KAREN CALLS

"Joe? It's me."
Her voice is as hard
as the pit in an apricot.
"Hi, Aunt Karen."
"Are you still in Wakeling?"
"Yeah."
"And you're alive?"
"I am."
"And Ed's coping?"
"I guess," I say.
"Well, that's fine then," she replies,
and without
            any good-bye
            hangs up the phone.

My first thought:
            I didn't hear the sound of any TV
            in the background.

STRICT

For my eleventh birthday I wanted to go to a
football game.
"I don't have money for that," Aunt Karen complained.
So instead she made a chocolate cake,
used M&Ms to write my name,
KitKat sticks on the sides.
She stuck eleven red candles in it, lit them, and
we sang "Happy Birthday"
before eating our spaghetti bolognese,
the cake for dessert only.
Dad was gone ten years.
Ed was gone four.
Mom had left the previous summer.

Aunt Karen was under no obligation to stay.
"It's like being in the military," Angela and I said,
wishing she'd disappear and leave us to
have parties and eat junk food.
        But at least there was milk in the fridge
        and clean clothes in the closets.
Usually we were glad Aunt Karen was
        tougher than
        anyone else.
Usually we were glad she hadn't bailed.

THE WORST THING

"What's the worst thing you've ever done?" I ask Nell.

She bites into the steak sandwich
Sue sent out for me,
        then hands it over.
"Needs more onion," she says.

"So? The worst thing?" I repeat.

"Yeah, chill out, I'm thinking."
She examines the engine with her fingertips.
"I yelled at my dad," she says.

She fiddles with the oil cap,
and I can't tell if she's being sarcastic.
"I told him he was going to hell."

"Why?"

"'Cause of what he's responsible for."
She isn't looking at me.
Her fingertips are greasy now.

"Does he hurt you?"

She sniffs.
"No," she says. "He loves me.
That's the thing.
He's this big, gentle guy.
But he . . .
We're always arguing.
It's my fault.
He's nice to me.
I just can't be kind back."

"Why not?"

She looks away.
"Doesn't matter.
    Anyway, what about you?"

I've made out with my friends' girlfriends,
stolen stuff,
beaten guys up for no good reason.
I hated Mom for leaving and hoped she'd die,
hated Karen for caring and hoped she'd leave.

"I rarely admit I have a brother," I tell her.
"When I meet new people,
I pretend Ed doesn't exist
so I won't have to explain.

And now it's looking like he might not exist.
So yeah.
That's the worst thing."

Nell wipes her hands on her shirt.
"You didn't make this happen," she says.
"And you know what else?"
        She steps toward me,
            touches my elbow.
"We aren't the worst things we did
or the worst things that happened to us.
We're other stuff too.
Like . . .
We're the times we made cereal
or watched *Buffy the Vampire Slayer*
or helped an old lady off a bus.
We're the good, the bad, and the stupid, right?"
She smiles and
grabs the steak sandwich like it
spoke out of turn.
"I'll eat this and get you something else.
What do you want?"

Should I say, *I want you, Nell*?

"You stay there and mull it over.
I'll get you a cheeseburger."

"Actually the steak sandwich looked good."

"Well, it's too late. Last of the meat."
She bites into it again.
"But it definitely needs more onion.
Like, *tons* more."

POSSIBLE

Before I take off,
Sue comes out.
She peers under the hood.
"Maybe you should find another job."

"You fed up with feeding me?" I ask.

She pokes me in the arm.
"It's breaking my heart
      watching you melting out here," she says.
"Lenny told me it's hopeless."

"Not hopeless," I say. "Just difficult."

"*Really* difficult," she says.

"But possible," I remind her.
"I mean, anything's possible."

TOM HANKS

Ed isn't wearing the usual shackles
around his wrists and ankles.
And the warden is with him,
        behind him.
He pats Ed's back as
my brother sits.
Philip Miller mutters something before
wandering away.

Ed picks up the phone.
"Jesus, Joe, you been fried like bacon!"
He laughs.
His guard can't help grinning either.

I touch my forehead,
beet red and peeling.
It kind of hurts too.
"What did the warden want?" I ask.

"Ah, he's just saying thanks for getting
Tom Hanks to take a shower."

Is Ed going nuts?
It happens to guys on death row,

which wouldn't be such a bad thing.
I mean,
        you can't execute a lunatic.
"Tom Hanks?" I ask.

"That's what we started calling Kierney.
You seen *Cast Away*?
Tom Hanks is on an island,
beard like a hobo,
eventually goes crazy and
starts screaming at a volleyball.
        'Wilson! Wilson!'
        You remember?
That film was depressing though, man.
His fiancée married another guy.
Never waited for him.
I couldn't figure that out."
I want to say, *It's 'cause she thinks he's dead.*
Instead I say,
        "You convinced an inmate to take a shower?"

"Why didn't his fiancée ditch her husband?
Wouldn't you, if you loved someone?
I would.
I'd put love first, you know?"

"You convinced someone to shower."

"Oh, Joe, you woulda done the same.
Hanks was starting to hum,
then they went and moved him next to me
'cause they knew I'd talk that wacko down."

The warden reappears with
a can of Sprite in his hands.
He puts it on the desk,
then looks at me for far too long.
I pretend I don't notice.

     He leaves.

Ed continues to talk and
I listen but can't help staring at the soda
     —a gift from the warden—
a thank-you because Ed was helpful.
"Give back the soda," I say, stopping Ed midsentence.

"Huh?"

"I got work," I lie.
"I'll send money for more sodas.
Don't drink that one."

Ed holds the cold can to his forehead.
"It's just a drink, Joe.
Don't get silly."

I pound the desk with my fist.
"It *isn't* just a drink."

The guard in my room sucks her teeth.
"Cool down or you're done here."

Ed taps on the glass. "What's wrong, man?"

I take a deep breath.
"You did them a favor.
They know you're a decent guy,
yet they got you locked up like a serial killer.
Why's Tom Hanks here?
He probably butchered his own mother."

Ed shrugs.
"They're doing a job, I guess."
He opens the soda and gulps it down greedily.

"Yeah, well," I say loudly,
for the benefit of the guard behind me,
"I wouldn't work here for a million bucks."

Ed finishes the soda.
"You know, Joe,
you're made of stronger stuff
than most people."

He looks at me
like he can really see me.
But he doesn't know me at all.
If he did, he'd see how much I hate this,
how little more I can take,
how much I need Angela here
or even Aunt Karen.
The only thing I've got is Nell.
And I haven't got her like I want her.
"The soda was a payoff," I say.

Ed won't argue.
"Mr. Miller knows a soda isn't saving his soul."

"He knows you're a good guy."

"Am I?" Ed scratches his head.
"I didn't gun down a cop,
but I'm not a thoroughbred good guy.
I'm just plowing through.

It's all any of us can do, right?
Even the warden."

"Some people have power," I say.

"We all have power, Joe.
Just gotta know how to use it, man."

I don't know what he means,
but I can't ask 'cause the guard calls time.

Power?
I can't even pay for a soda.

BROKEN

Death row is a place for broken people
       just like Tom Hanks.
They can't be fixed,
warped all out of shape
by the cracks and splinters inside them.

And what else can you do with stuff that's broken
except throw it into the trash?

    Right?

THE APARTMENT

The apartment was gross when I rented it:
    bugs everywhere,
    sticky floors,
    stained carpets.

But now that Nell is visiting for breakfast
    I do what I can:
    clean the countertops,
    stick some frozen bagels into the oven
    to mask the smell;
        wipe down the sink with a dirty sock.
I do my best and still the place stinks,
not somewhere I want to be with Nell.

She knocks and I open the door,
planning to take her elsewhere.
        She pushes straight past me.
"I need the bathroom," she says.

I point down the hall and she disappears,
runs the water
so I can't hear her pee.

And she comes back smiling.
"I was bursting.
Shouldn't have had a gallon of juice.
So this is your place."
She stands in front of me,
puts a hand on my chest. "You okay?"

I nod. My heart pounds under her hand.

"Can I tell you something?" she asks.

I nod again. My heart pounds harder.

"I only came over for one thing," she says.

LIKE HELLFIRE

The longer I stand there, the fewer words I have.
But speechlessness never happens when I'm with a girl.
Like *ever*.
I don't have a lot going for me,
but I know how to talk to girls,
get them to like me.

Nell smiles.
It makes me want to
press her
against the wall,
kiss her until neither of us can breathe.

But I don't do this.
I just stand staring,
happy to know she trusts me.

"Holy crap. Are you *shy* all of a sudden?" she asks.

I don't wait anymore.
I put my hands behind her head,
pull her to me
and kiss her,
mouth open,
heart hammering like hellfire.

KISSING

Who knew kissing could feel so good?
Nell's lips, tongue, taste.
Gentle sips of her,
then great big gulps.
Her breath on my neck and
one word
in her mouth repeated over and over:
"Joe. Joe. Joe. Joe."

It was everything.

And when she left, I didn't go for a run.

I didn't need to run anywhere.

TURN OVER

Sue disappears from the window without waving.
She doesn't come out with food either.
I'm about to go into the diner,
check everything's okay,
      when,
for no good reason,
I slip the key into the ignition.

And the car turns over.

First time.
No sputtering.

Nothing but the colicky purr of an engine
      sucking on dregs of gas.

"What the hell?" I say aloud.
Yesterday the crap heap wouldn't hiss,
now it's purring?
Was it the oil change? The battery?
It doesn't seem likely.
But what does it matter?
It's fixed!

Joy shoots through me
'cause now I've got a job
and if Bob doesn't mind,
a car to see Ed in the afternoons
instead of walking and
baking my ass to a crisp.

Nell comes running. "You got it working?"
She pounds her fist on the hood, screams.
"Sue, get out here! Sue!"

Sue plods down the steps,
stands next to Nell, hands on her hips.
"I hope Bob still needs a delivery guy," she says,
     and winks,
     kidding,
     but it worries me
     because it's been forever since
     Bob talked about the job
     and it's not like I'll be in town
     for much longer.
Sue taps the license plate with her toe,
then heads back toward the diner.
     I watch her go, a slow, fragile step,
     but Sue's not fragile.
     She's tough,
     cunning.

And I know she did this,
fixed the car while I slept or
got her boyfriend to do it.

But I won't ask anyone how it happened.
I'll accept it and pretend this miracle
had something to do with me.

GO HOME

Sue is wiping tables with a gray dishrag.
I scan the restaurant. "Where's Nell?"
I've poured a can of gas into the car,
hosed it down and cleaned it out.
Despite the lumpy tires and rattling exhaust,
I'm taking the car for a ride. Nell too.

"In the bathroom," Sue says.

Her eyes are red. But they weren't this morning.
        I take a step backward.
"Everything okay?"

"Oh, you know," Sue says.
She picks a chocolate chip from a muffin,
pops it into her mouth, and
        slides the plate across the counter
            to me.
"It's my kid's anniversary.
He was a lifer at the farm.
Got knifed in a fight.
No one went down for it.
All lifers in his block,
so I guess it didn't matter much."

She pulls out a pack of cigarettes,
unpeels the cellophane.
"Listen, Joe,
you stay for as long as Ed needs you
but then go home.
I came here for Jason
and I ain't never left.
Not even after he died,
and now I'm going nowhere.
They might as well have locked me up.
It's different for someone like Nell.
Her family's got a good reason to be here."

Just then Nell appears, wiping wet hands on her shorts.
"Stupid hand dryer.
When's Bob gonna get a new one?"

"I'll leave you guys to it," Sue says,
and scuttles into the kitchen.

Nell leans toward me.
"So, you taking me for a ride?"

A JOB

The car lurches and grinds its way out of Wakeling.
"You're gonna spend half your time
        pushing this crap heap around," Nell says.

But I don't care.
        It's a car.
        Wheels.
I have a job.
For a few weeks anyway.

Until Ed no longer needs me
        in Texas.

MARRY ME

Ed uses his fingertips to flatten out his eyebrows.
"I got another marriage proposal in the mail.
Obviously on account of my looks."

"What are you talking about?"

"Women think I'm the atom bomb, Joe.
Didn't you know?
I've been propositioned twenty-eight times
since I got locked up."

"You're kidding."

He holds up his palms:
I can see a mark in the middle of one,
like the remnants of a cigarette burn.
"Women are out of their sycamore trees.
They *love* the idea of hooking up with a guy behind bars.
No way I'm nailing her best friend if I'm
in here, right?
You know,
Johnny Vinzano got a proposal and that guy
did something so skanky it'd give
Charles Manson nightmares."

"I don't get it," I say.

"No one gets it.
But plenty of guys say yes.
Pete Browne married a girl from Utah last year.
She visits him every month.
Thing is, everyone knows Pete's gonna fry,
'cause he's full-blown guilty of
murdering his mother-in-law."

"Do they get to . . . do the business?" I ask.

Ed bangs the table and laughs.
"No sex in here, man.
You're not even allowed to do yourself,
and that's the truth!
Guards catch you with your hands in your pants,
you're getting solitary."
He pauses.
"You got a girl back home?"

I shake my head, think of Nell,
her face, clumpy walk,
bossy voice and the way she kisses—
slowly then quick,
like she's hungry.

And I consider telling Ed about her,
but pity stops me—or guilt.

"I think that's what I regret," he says.
"That I never fell in love.
Maybe I'll marry that girl who wrote me after all."

We spend the rest of the time determining
how we'd pick a wife,
getting no further than talking about
Catwoman.

And at the end
Ed, still laughing, says,
"How many days left?
I haven't looked at the calendar."

It's twenty days
—twenty—
but I pretend I don't know either.
"Time's measured in moments, man," I say instead.

MONMOUTH BEACH

It was fall.
The ocean was gray, not blue,
waves cannonballing onto the beach.
Mom, Angela, and I were sitting on a blanket
eating peanut-butter-and-jelly bagels.
Ed was skipping stones into the sea,
his back to us.
Mom said,
      "Why the hell doesn't he just sit down?"

It wasn't a question.
She was irritated.
Always irritated by Ed,
like he was her annoying boyfriend
and not a son she should love.

I went to him,
      over the lumpy sand.

"That's Europe," Ed said, pointing to the horizon.
"Wouldn't it be great to live over there?"

"Where?" I asked.

"Across the ocean," Ed said.

I looked down at the sand for stones
to skip
but couldn't see any,
just washed-up water bottles,
cigarette butts,
candy wrappers.
My sneakers had a hole in the toe.

"Would you come with me?" he asked.
"If I got a job in London or Paris?
It would be super exciting.
We could see Buckingham Palace
or the Eiffel Tower.
Europe has history, man.
It's got buildings older than this country!"

I spotted a small coral-colored shell and
        picked it up.
"I'd go anywhere with you," I told him.
And I meant it.

But when the time came,
he took off without me.
And he never made it anywhere near Europe,
never got across the Atlantic.

Yet here I am,
with him
like I promised.

DELIVERY BOY

It isn't hard to navigate Wakeling's grid system,
and after a couple days delivering
grilled-cheese sandwiches,
I know my way around the whole town.
And I drive by Nell's house whenever I can:
I slow
      and search the windows for light.

I search for her.

BOTCHED

They botched an execution
in Louisiana last night.
The guy on the gurney
didn't
get the correct anesthetic,
wasn't even out cold
when they poisoned him
with potassium chloride
and he died of a massive heart attack.

It took Anthony Cruz, forty-six years old,
fifty-two minutes to die,
a vein in his neck bulging like a golf ball
where the nurse stuck in
the IV.
He was jerking, foaming at the mouth,
looked so horrific
they had to close the viewing gallery curtain
to stop anyone from witnessing it.

That's the second botched execution
this month.

Shouldn't they let Ed live
until they figure it out?
The governor of Texas says
he doesn't think so.

DAY TRIP

"You wanna see some nature?" Nell asks.
She's figured out the best route to the
Davy Crockett National Forest.
"I promise you'll be at the prison by two."

"Only if you got a playlist put together
for the ride," I say, my face serious.

She waves her phone at me. "Oh, *please*.
Think of this less as a drive,
more as an education,
or a musical cleansing, if you will."
She pinches my chin between her fingers,
pecks my lips.

"Screw you," I say, pushing her away
and putting the car into gear.

MONKEY BABIES

Nell strokes the nape of my neck.
"You want me so bad," I say.

"Oh, really?"
She withdraws her hand.

"No. Keep it there," I beg.
I take her wrist, make her limp hand paw my face.

She snatches her hand back,
hides it beneath her knee,
and suddenly
I imagine Plexiglas between us.

I push on the gas. The car jolts forward.
The world outside smudges by.
"You know, I can't even shake Ed's hand," I tell her.
"It's stupid.
It's not like I could smuggle in a rifle."

"A guy called Harlow did some study and
figured out that when faced with
a choice,
monkey babies
always chose comfort over food.

We can survive without anything except . . ."
She stares out at a passing truck,
        a mattress tied to its roof.

"Love?" I ask.

She nods. "Apparently.
We can survive without anything except love."

NIGHTMARES

I'd wake up screaming or in a wet bed,
and Ed never said "Grow up, Joe"
or got mad about being woken.

He'd pull back his blanket
and let me sleep next to him.
And when I did,
the nightmares and bed-wetting went away.

THE LAKE

We spread our sweaters on a rock
overlooking a lake.
It's early. No one's on the water yet.
The sky is pink. The air smells of pine.
Nell offers me some cranberry trail mix
but I'm not hungry.
"Isn't it weird how two worlds
can sit so close together?" I say.

Nell puts her head on my shoulder.
"It's people who build gray fortresses," she says,
understanding me completely.

"I wish there were a way—" I say.

A wet dog darts out of the forest,
barks up at us on our rock.
His tail wags.
"Come on, Max!" a voice calls,
and the dog bounds back into the forest.

A LITTLE WHILE

We get back to Wakeling early and
go to my apartment.
Nell takes my face in her hands,
kisses my cheeks.
      One.
      Then the other.

"I'm gonna stay a little while," she says.

MEANING IT

Being with Nell knocks my head back,
makes my bones thrum,
my blood ring and boil up
until we are
      reaching, grabbing, smothering
      each other.
And skin to skin our aching bodies press
      to find a way in—
and I mean pressing, pressing, pressing.

And there's teeth clashing, hands clutching,
as we pour our way into each other
until everything stops,
gives way to soft kisses,
quiet breaths of friendship,
and I say,
"Are you okay?"
      and actually fucking mean it.

AFTERWARD

We share a tall glass of milk.
And we doze.

AN E-MAIL FROM AL

Dear Angela and Joe,

Got good news:
Supreme Court says "Let's hear it!"
so we're going to DC August 15.
Here's hoping the federal judges
will be smarter than the ones in Texas.
We're getting there.
I'll be in touch . . .
Best,
Al Mitchell

THEY'LL HEAR IT

So the date is set—
three days before the
scheduled execution,
which is cutting it a bit close,
in my opinion.

BE HAPPY

I do my best to focus
on Ed's eyes,
brain batting away images of Nell in her underwear.
"The highest court in the country will hear us out.
That's gotta be good," he says.

I give him two thumbs-up.

Ed squints. "You okay, little brother?"

Be here, I tell myself.
For God's sake, be here while you still can.

He raps on the Plexiglas with his knuckles,
wiggles his eyebrows at me.
"Oh, I know that look."

"Huh?"

"You in love, little brother?"

I examine my hands.

"I'm happy for you, Joe.
Don't give up that stuff for me.
Don't give it up for anyone.
If you need to go back to Arlington
to see a girl,
          that's what you should do."

"I don't need to go anywhere," I say.
I want to hold him,
find out how he smells.
I want to say *thank you* and *sorry* and
Please don't leave me again.

"Be happy," Ed says.
"It's your duty to me, man."

THE WALKING DEAD

We are on Nell's sofa watching
The Walking Dead,
Nell insisting that Rick Grimes is the
      perfect man,
clutching her heart whenever he comes on-screen.

"You know the actor's English, right?
And the English are horrible kissers," I say.

She flutters her eyelashes.
"Not in my experience."

A zombie rips out a girl's throat and
Nell screams,
      hides behind a cushion.
"I can't watch," she says,
but then does,
as a woman with a baseball bat
bashes in the brains
      of a zombie.
The woman's face is spattered in blood.
She drops the baseball bat,
but looks totally unshaken by the massacre.

And that's when I start to cry.
Nell takes my hand,
strokes my fingers.

I say,
"I don't know why I'm crying. I'm not sad."

But I can't stop.

GRILLED CHEESE

We've paused the TV,
are making grilled-cheese sandwiches,
when a voice calls out from the front hall:
"Smells like dinner!"
There's a laugh—the sound of love in it.

Nell startles
like a cat facing an oncoming car,
a cat who knows her nine lives are up.
She tries to grab the sandwiches from the pan
with her bare hand,
burns her fingers.
She yelps.

I run the faucet,
drag her over by the wrist,
hold her hand under cold water.

"I'll go," I whisper,
wondering how quickly I could unlock
the patio doors and be in the backyard,
gone so she doesn't get into trouble.
But why would she?
Isn't she allowed to have a boyfriend?
It's not like we're rolling around naked on the rug.

Nell bites her trembling bottom lip.
"I should have said something.
I was going to, but I couldn't."

And then he walks in,
      one arm swinging,
      face fixed into a smile.
      A smile that fades
      when he sees me with his daughter.
      "Joseph Moon," he says evenly.

"Warden," I reply.

"Oh God. Oh God, I'm so sorry," Nell stammers.

DUEL

The warden eyeballs me
like we're about to duel.
He waits for me to make the first move.
I don't.
And neither does he.

Nell is shaking.
And why wouldn't she?
"You lied," I say,
       turning to her,
       turning *on* her,
       my tone toxic.
Roughly I let go of her wrist,
move closer to the patio doors.

The warden pulls up his pants by the waistband,
       takes two
       long strides toward Nell,
           stands in front of her making
           himself into a wall between us.
"What are you doing here, Joseph?" he asks.

"Me? Oh, I was deciding whether to steal
your blender, desk lamp,
or daughter."

Nell flinches.
"Joe's a friend. I can explain."
And maybe she tries,
but I don't wait around to hear it.

"Don't go, Joe!" Nell shouts. "Joe!"

I step into the darkness,
her voice calling behind me.

ANOTHER PICTURE MESSAGE

From Reed.
A photo of a girl in a bikini this time,
thin with tan skin
and a grin that says,
My worries are elsewhere.
She is holding an ice-cream cone;
her flip-flops are red.
Usually I'd confirm she's hot,
say Reed's one lucky bastard,
and ask for more pictures.

But I don't feel like it tonight.

A REMINDER

"Aunt Karen's been at the house
ranting about how psychologically damaging
seeing Ed will be," Angela says.
"She's, like, genuinely concerned
for both of us."

I don't have the patience for Angela's excuses,
her I'm-coming-soon promises.
"Are you flying down or not?
'Cause in case you didn't know,
time's running out.
The execution is in fourteen days."

"Yeah, Joe, I know that,
but thanks for reminding me what an
asshole I am."

FIREWORKS

My first Fourth of July without Ed,
and the whole island was at Fort Wadsworth
watching the fireworks.
Angela chewed on a licorice lace,
one arm around me.
Aunt Karen pointed into the sky
at every burst of color,
every whizz and bang.
Mom wasn't with us.
"She's not well," Aunt Karen told me.
I knew it wasn't true.
I'd seen Mom getting ready to go out
through the keyhole of her bedroom.
Aunt Karen
did that:

      protected us from Mom's lies,
      from knowing about her dates with losers
      or when she got drunk.
But I knew the truth.
Looking back now I know
I only ever pretended to be persuaded.

A MISTAKE

I push past Nell to get into the diner,
but more roughly than I mean to
and she stumbles,
grabs the handrail.

"Shout at me then," she says,
        following me inside.

Sue is stirring a hot pot of oatmeal.
        Seeing us, she slides into the kitchen.

Nell puts her hand over the bags ready for delivery.
"Tell me what I was supposed to do once I knew."

"You could have talked to me,"
I say through clenched teeth.

"I talk to you more than to anyone, Joe.
My whole life I've just been Miller's kid.
        A spoiled, surly bitch,
            the kid whose dad kills for a living.
With you, I wasn't,
and when that happened
I didn't want to be his daughter anymore,

especially not around you,
because of everything it meant.
You'd have hated me."
She is screeching.

"We can't be friends now.
I have too much to think about," I tell her.

"You don't mean that."

"I do. Please leave me alone, Nell."

"Whatever," she says,
and rushes out of the diner through the back door.

I'm breathing heavily. My heart is thumping.

Sue reappears looking flustered.
She must have heard everything.
"You're making a mistake letting her leave," she says.

I DON'T KNOW WHY

I don't know why I didn't
put my arms around her,
tell her it's okay,
that I know she never meant to hurt me,
that sometimes we like people we shouldn't
and by the time we feel
what we feel
it's already too late.

NO REHEARSAL

I arrive at the prison early, sit sweating in the car,
    waiting.
Father Matthew taps on the windshield.
"Time for a beverage today?" he asks.

He sits opposite me in the visitors' room,
sips at a peppermint tea.
He's wearing a lemon-colored shirt
    buttoned up to the neck,
      baggy brown pants with more pockets
      than any ordinary person needs.
And he's younger than I remember—
gray hair adding years to his life that aren't there.
He's definitely no older than forty.
"Ed tells me you got a job," he says.
"Wakeling ain't heaving with opportunity.
I reckon you done good."
The priest studies me like you might
a painting in a museum,
checking my face for revealing cracks and bumps.
"I do believe you got something on your mind."

"I'm fine."
I'm not sure why I agreed to sit
with the priest in the first place.

Was I planning a confession?
Did I want to tell him how I treated Nell?
Maybe I should explain I can't do what Ed's asked:
        I can't be happy.
        I don't know how,
                especially not now.

He rolls a paper napkin into a ball.
"I been watching you coming and going, Joe.
All that's in mind, when I see you, is respect."
He grins.
Is he mocking me?
"I mean to say, I admire you.
You coulda stayed in New York,
come down just before August eighteenth.
Or you coulda come down and skipped visits.
You haven't.
You've walked miles in mugginess,
and though I reckon you been
quietly
grumbling and grousing,
your brother don't know how tough it is.
Ed talks to me, see."
He scratches the bridge of his nose.
"You, Joe, leave the complaining at home."

We sit in silence for a minute.
Then I ask, "Will he die, Father?"

"We're all dying.
And in some ways they killed part of him already."

"I'm living in a parallel universe."

Father Matthew reaches across the table and
tries to take my hand.
Instinctively
        I pull it away.
        He doesn't react.
"You stay in today, Joe,
'cause tomorrow's a story that ain't been written yet.
No use in rehearsing it.
No use at all."

A couple at another table laughs,
forgetting where they are, I guess.

"It's two o'clock," I tell him.
"I gotta go."

POKER

"Don't you ever miss Mom?" I ask Ed.
He concentrates on my face.
"No," he says. "Do you?"

"Not usually. But I wonder why not.
Does that make me cold?"

Ed holds up a hand to stop me speaking.
"Hey. Think about it this way.
If you're playing poker
and you never get any good cards,
you might think,

>Damn, I put so much money into this game,
>I gotta keep going, 'cause
>eventually I'll get dealt an ace of hearts,

you know?
But I don't think about poker like that.
Makes no sense to keep betting on a losing game.
Cut your losses.
Run out of that casino and
spend your cash on a martini."

I must look confused.

"It's the same with people," he explains.
"You keep placing bets on someone
who never comes through,
you're just a total sucker.
Put your money on a sure bet.
Or a better bet, at least."

"Mom might visit.
She might be the ace of hearts that comes through."

Ed throws his hands in the air.
"Then let her come. But I sure as hell
won't be putting any money on it."

SID SIPS

"Sid sips from it," I read aloud really slowly,
sounding out each letter,
      each word,
            before I could understand the
            sentence.

Angela patted my hand, jiggled me
up and down on her lap.
"Nice job," she said.

Ed wasn't a book person.
He watched from the couch
making faces,
      making us laugh,
            making my homework take
            forever.

Angela said, "Keep going, Joe.
Don't you wanna know what Sid did next?"

Ed smirked. "Did he stick his finger up his ass?"

Angela threw an eraser across the room,
hit Ed on the side of the head with it.

"You are *not* helping!" she shouted.

Mom burst in from the kitchen.
"Keep the noise down,
I'm trying to take a call for God's sake."

"Joe can read," Angela said.
She held up the book,
waved it so Mom wouldn't miss it.

"That's great, Angela.
Once you're done teaching Joe,
give it a shot with Ed, huh?
Maybe if he learns to read he'll get a job
and stop sponging off his mother."

Ed opened his mouth to say something
but for the first time
didn't answer back.
It was like
he was trying to understand something new.

"She didn't mean it," Angela said.

Ed blinked. "Oh, I think she did."

SPECIAL PROVISIONS

The farm sends a letter:
they've made special provisions for prison visits
in the run-up to August 18.
The week before,
a meeting room will be available
to allow
full-contact
visits with Ed,
and on the day
prior to execution,
visiting hours will be
> extended
> for family members,
> a spiritual adviser,
> and one legal representative.

The letter suggests that if
I have questions I should contact
Philip Miller directly.

I have questions,
but none he could answer.

LIGHTENING

I drop off a hundred dollars' worth of pies,
      and my phone rings.
It isn't Nell.
It's Angela.
I don't have the energy to talk.
I answer anyway.
      "I'm flying to Houston tomorrow," she chirps.
      "Bus into Wakeling three hours later!"

"Really? That's awesome."
She isn't coming so we can see the rodeo but still . . .
She can visit the prison too.
I won't be alone in the apartment.
Someone can share this load,
      which is already lifting
          a bit
          with the news.

"Thank God you're coming," I tell her.

"Tomorrow."

DRAFT

I draft a text to Nell on my phone.
But I don't send it;
I change my mind and
      delete the whole thing.

I miss her, but I can't send a message.

Why not?

I mean,
      why the hell not?

LUGGAGE

Angela is thin,
hair flat and dirty,
a weakened smile.

She waves lightly,
letting go of the handrail and
slipping down the bus steps.

      I catch her at the bottom.

She's shaking like she'll
collapse if I let go.

The bus driver cracks open the undercarriage,
wrestles with suitcases,
grunting and shoving
      bags onto the sidewalk like garbage.

"Did you bring luggage?" I ask Angela.
She laughs so hard the sound
fills the station.
People look.

"I did. I brought luggage," she tells me
and presses her face into my neck.

CLOSER TO HOME

Angela puts her purse on the floor,
then quickly picks it up again.

Our house in Staten Island is small,
the neighborhood gritty,
but our place was always clean.
Aunt Karen saw to that.

"I'm sorry it isn't nicer," I say.

"I expected worse," she says.

We lean against the countertop.
"Thanks for the money," she says.
        "What money?" I ask.
        "The money you sent."
        "I didn't send you money, Ange."
        She frowns. "You didn't?"
        "No."

She gazes at a brown stain on the linoleum,
looks like she's working through every problem
that ever existed in her mind
all at the same time.

"Mom called Ed," I say.

"What for?" she asks.

I shrug.

> Angela shakes her head and
> goes to the bathroom,
> slamming the door closed.

The fan whirs and crackles,
water splashes from the faucet.
    This is noise
      in my apartment that isn't me.
And it makes me feel a little closer to home.

NOW

Now that I've got Angela,
I shouldn't miss Nell so much.
I shouldn't think about her.
But I do.
In the mornings I still
check my phone for messages
before my eyes have fully opened.
At night I go to sleep early
to stop myself from waiting for her call.

I should focus on my job,
my brother,
on why I'm here in the first place.

I shouldn't be fixated on Nell.
She isn't who I thought she was.

And anyway, she was a time filler,
a way to keep my mind off Ed.

I used her to tread water.

Isn't that all it was?

EVA

Angela plays Eva Cassidy through a Bluetooth speaker,
again and again,
"Autumn Leaves" and "Over the Rainbow,"
songs so sad I can barely listen.
"Cassidy died when she was thirty-three,"
Angela informs me.
"Tried to fight her cancer but couldn't.
Her last performance was 'What a Wonderful World'
for family and friends."

"Why are you telling me this?" I ask.

"I don't know," she says.
"Just makes you think."

"About death."

"About life. How little we're promised," she says,
and turns up the music.

A WAITING ROOM

The night before her first prison visit Angela asks,
"What's it like?"

"Like limbo,
a place where nothing lives,
a waiting room," I say.

She twirls her hair around her fingers
                                    tirelessly.

ANGELA'S FIRST VISIT

Instead of running a metal detector
down my body and
      waving me through
         as they usually do,
a guard gestures for me to follow, and a
female guard accompanies Angela.

I'm taken to an office. The guard closes the door.
"I need you to strip."

"Sorry?" I don't know the guard.
Maybe he's new and
doesn't understand Section A regulations.
"I need to search you before the contact visit."

I flatten my back against the door.
I know what a strip search means,
how much of myself I'll have to expose.
"Did the warden approve this?" I ask.

He snaps a latex glove against his wrist
like he's in a goddamn movie.
Another guard comes in yawning—
a chaperone.

I glance at the wall clock.
It's already two minutes after two.
Ed will be waiting.

I can't make him wait.

REAL

It's a different room,
an ordinary room, like a place you might meet
a school counselor,
and no Plexiglas—
nothing to divide us.

Angela is already there with Ed,
arms around him,
hanging on as though he might
     float away
       like a helium balloon.

When they hear the door,
they look up,
see me standing next to the guard.

"My little brother," Ed says,
     and I rush to him.

I hold on to him too.

He's real.

THE LAVENDER ROOM

Angela is definitely not a contender for
America's Got Talent.
She sings for Ed anyway,
getting the words to the songs wrong,
laughing when the melody is
        too high
                for her to reach.

She sings stuff by Adele,
songs Ed doesn't know all that well.
Yet he grins the whole time.

And so do I.

Because being in this lavender room
with bars on its windows,
guards on both sides of the door,
        we are on the verge
        of being a family again.

"I missed you guys," Ed says.

"You aren't ticked off that we didn't come
to Texas before all this?" I ask.

Ed claps me on the back.

"Life's too short for that crap, man.

Nah.

    We're together now."

MAJOR-GENERAL

Ed was Major–General Stanley in his school
production of *The Pirates of Penzance*.
We had a video recording of it at home
we watched sometimes,
laughing so hard
at Ed singing
and at the haircut he had when he was thirteen.
Mom would come in
to investigate the noise.
"Oh, you're watching that again.
Haven't you seen it enough?"

"It's the Ed show," I told her.

"Yeah. And I'm sort of wondering
when it'll be over."

OUTSIDE THE PRISON

Nell's leaning against the car,
earphones in, head down.
She kicks at the dirt.
"What do you want?" I snap,
when all *I* want is to kiss her,
tell her I forgive her,
beg her to see me later—
      somewhere we can be alone.

But a stupid part of me wants to make her suffer,
      see if she'll fight for me.
      Am I worth an argument?

"I came to see my dad and saw your car," she says.
"I decided to say sorry. Again.
Like it'll help."

Angela wanders off without a word,
pokes at her phone.

"Your sister looks like you," Nell says.
"She's pretty. But she needs some of Sue's
high-calorie apple pie. You do too."
She tries for a laugh.

"Come on . . .

    At least tell me to go to hell."

"I don't want you to go to hell, Nell."

She leans toward me. "Tell me what I should do.
If you say you need me to leave you alone,
I'll understand.
I won't like it,
but I'll understand."

"In a week, your dad will
kick my brother off the face of the earth."

"It's all he talks about, Joe.
He doesn't believe Ed's phony confession.
And he said there are a dozen scumbags who should've
got their dates before your brother.
But if Dad refuses to execute him, he'll lose his job."

"And save Ed's life."

She looks down at her grubby sneakers.
"For how long? An hour? A day?

You think they wouldn't replace my father in a
      heartbeat?
He isn't the one keeping him here."

"He's part of the crooked system.
He's as much a murderer as any of
the guys on the row."

"So what does that make me?
Guilty by association?"
She reaches for a stone,
wipes it clean on her shirt,
polishes it between her thumb and forefinger.
"Out of everyone, I thought you'd
understand how shitty that is."

"You wanna meet later?" I ask.

She squints. "Yes. I really do."

HEALING

Nell is beside me in a booth
drinking hot chocolate and chatting with Angela
like they've known each other

                                    forever.

It's no big deal.

Just sitting.

Talking and drinking.

But this helps me feel better.
Nell heals me.

And I have no idea how she does it.

PREPARATION

"They weighed me and took my measurements,"
Ed says.
"I mean, they fucking *weighed* me."

Angela squeezes my knee
so I know this must signify something.
I try to figure out what he means.
I don't want him saying the bad stuff aloud.

Ed puffs out his cheeks.
"They gotta know how much drug to use.
And every dead guy needs a coffin, right?"

"They measured you for a coffin?" I ask slowly.

He ignores me. "I don't really get it.
Why not just use a truckload of poison
for everyone?
If we overdose, who cares?
Dead is dead."

Angela pulls her chair next to Ed's.
"It's *not* gonna happen," she tells him.

"They moved me to the end cell," he murmurs.
"That's so I'm closer to the chamber.
And also so fewer people have to
walk by my cell every day.
You know the worst part of it?"

I can't even imagine.
And part of me doesn't want to know.

"They made me carry my own mattress and
blanket and stuff.
They watched me do it and didn't help.
They watched me carry my bedding
to the last cell."

My mind is mud:
nothing moves in it.
What can I say to this?
What possible comfort could any words have?

"It isn't fair," Angela says.
She holds his chin,
forces him to look at her.
"It isn't fair," she repeats.

NOT FAIR

It was a snow day.
Every school in the city closed
except mine.

"It's not fair!" I screamed,
still in my pajamas.

"Oh, get over it! Life isn't fair!" Mom screamed back.
"Now get dressed."

Ed walked me to school.
      We stomped fresh paths
      of bootprints through snow
and watched kids playing,
adults shoveling sidewalks,
snowplows pushing away their snow mounds
      to God-knows-where.

Ed tied a knot in my scarf,
patted my head,
nudged me through the school gates.
"I'll collect you at two thirty," he said.
"It's not fair," I repeated.

"I know it isn't, little man," he said.

"And I'm sorry.

But I promise I'll be here to pick you up."

THE GALLERY

It's seven days until the scheduled execution
and Angela has Al Mitchell on speakerphone:
"Ed can have a family member or friend
sit in the gallery as a witness.
But Angela's the only one approved.
You have to be eighteen.
I get a seat and also Father Matthew."

"She's invited to watch him die?" I ask.

He doesn't answer.
"A member of the victim's family has
requested a spot in the gallery.
The press would have places and
some of the prison staff.
My advice is don't take the seat."

"Why would anyone watch?" I ask.

"I want to be there," Angela says.
"I won't let him do it on his own
and there's nothing you can do
to change my mind."

THE RETURN

Nell and I are lying on the sofa.
Angela's in the bedroom on the phone
but keeps calling out.
"You guys better be behaving."
She hoots like it's the funniest joke ever,
goes back to whispering.

And the doorbell rings.
A jangle that makes Nell jump.
"Is it your dad?" I ask.

She shrugs. "I hope not."

I peer through the peephole.
It's not Philip Miller.
It's someone I never expected to see in Texas:
it's Aunt Karen.

A MISTAKE

I don't tell Aunt Karen to leave or
slam the door in her face.
I don't shout at her for making me live
in hell for so long
when she had money to help.
I don't blame her for leaving
Ed here
for all these years
when he needed someone,
when he hadn't done anything wrong.
I say, "You came,"
            and she nods.

WHAT CAN WE FORGIVE?

Anything.
      If that's what we choose.

TOO LATE

Aunt Karen takes her coffee light
with a lot of sugar.
I make it to her liking, but she doesn't
even taste it.
She balances on the sofa,
absorbing her surroundings
and asking a hundred legal questions
that Angela and I don't have a clue how to answer.
We needed her to take an interest a month ago,
or when Ed first got locked up.

It feels too late to fight now.

LAND OF THE FREE

Al Mitchell orders a cheesesteak sandwich from Sue,
opens his briefcase,
      making a shield of one half,
      ducking behind it,
      shuffling through papers.

"So,
we have the Supreme Court
in three days," he says loudly,
      reappearing,
      slamming it closed.

Angela sips at iced tea.
Aunt Karen frowns.
I listen.

"We have a solid case.
Anyone with two brain cells can see Ed's
a victim of circumstance."

"How's that?" Aunt Karen asks steadily.
She didn't even order a water.

Al throws his shoulders back.

"Ed was convicted on a false confession
he made when he was eighteen,
tired, hungry, and threatened.
Nothing else links him to the crime apart from a
run-in with Frank Pheelan hours earlier.
They don't have any witnesses,
no DNA.
It's laughable."
Al grins
but not like he's encouraging anyone
to join him.

Angela exhales.
"Someone else did it," she says.

Al narrows his eyes.
"Prosecutors told the jury his DNA was found
        in the cruiser.
        Which it was.
But they weren't told it was only found
        on his driver's license,
which the cop had taken from him."

Sue arrives with a steaming cheesesteak sandwich
and shuffles away again.

Al looks at it, grimaces,
taps his temples with his fingertips.
"It's reasonable doubt."

"Have you *ever* convinced the Supreme Court?"
I ask.
I want him to admit what we all know,
forget all the lawyer-speak
and tell us the truth.

He looks me straight in the eye.
"The court ensures justice is done, Joe."
And he wants me to believe it,
wants to believe it himself.
But how can he when he's been
representing guys like Ed forever?
                              He knows the deal.

I slide out of the booth, the diner,
            into the heat of the afternoon
            hating with every inch of my bones
            the so-called free country I live in,
            the home of the brave.

HOW DO YOU SAY GOOD-BYE?

I count down our time together
as soon as I sit,
one eye on Ed,
the other on the clock,
sometimes wishing Angela wouldn't sing
'cause the songs take so long,
wishing Aunt Karen hadn't turned up to share
this time and space
which I want to
      myself
      now.

And in those final five minutes
while I'm waiting for the guard to tap his watch,
I never know how to sew up our time together,
                make it count,
                dilute the sadness.
Anger rises in my throat
and I leave with a rock of molten rage
      burning up my guts.

Angela, Karen, and I don't talk on the way out;
we walk side by side,

but I always feel totally alone
trying to figure out
how the hell I'll ever say good-bye for good.

REMOVAL

Philip Miller sends a letter
reminding us to make arrangements
for the removal of Ed's body
after his execution.

        He vouches for Vander & Sons
        on Wakeling's Main Street.

I hand the letter to Aunt Karen.
"You wanna help?
Deal with this," I tell her.

Because I can't do it.

PLANNING

A neighbor in Arlington had diabetes
that did her in last December.
I'd never seen so many flowers,
lilies that stank up the church.

Angela's friend Susie-May died
in a car accident on her way home from Montauk.
She was tanned,
newly engaged.
Everyone said she would've made a great hairdresser.

But it happens, doesn't it?
    Death.
Either suddenly or steadily.

But you never put it on your calendar,
    X marks the spot—
       let's get the headstone in a Black Friday sale
       and have the name chiseled into it.

You can never usually plan on death like that.

A CHANCE

In a pocket of silence
between greedy
bites
of jelly doughnuts
in Wakeling's strip mall parking lot,
Nell says,

> "Dad thinks Ed has a chance in
> DC tomorrow
> at the Supreme Court."

"Really?" I ask.

It's raining heavily for the first time since
I arrived,
washing all the humidity out of the air.
The car's wipers swish

> back and forth.

"Yeah," she says,

> so what do I do?
> I start to
> get my hopes up.

HOPE

It's the hope that'll kill you.

UNITED STATES SUPREME COURT ORDER

(ORDER LIST: 576 US)

AUGUST 15, 2016

CERTIORARI DENIED

15-6898
(15A6644)

MOON, EDWARD R. V. COMMISSIONER, TX DOC. ET AL.

The application for stay of execution of sentence of death presented to Justice Williams and by him referred to the Court is denied. The petition for a writ of certiorari is denied.

THE WRIT

So.
I guess that's it.
The Supreme Court has denied Ed's appeal.

GET OUT

Angela is in her nightgown,
hair piled on top of her head,
eyes ringed with black makeup.
"The lawyers *always* have final appeals.
I've seen documentaries. I'll call Al,"
Angela says.
She rummages in her purse
then turns it upside down,
the entire contents chaotically spilling onto the
                                        unmade bed.
She grabs her phone
        scrolls through it.

Ed's only hope now is Heath McDowell, and
there's little chance of the Texas governor
showing leniency toward a convicted cop killer—
        not when he's up for reelection.
And yet I say, "It's gonna be okay," 'cause
it's what Angela needs to hear.

Suddenly
she swings at me
        like a feral cat.
"Get out!" she shouts. "I don't need your horseshit."

"Angela."

"Get *out!*" she screams.

I leave,
    closing the door gently behind me,
        while Angela trashes the bedroom.

MORNING RUN

I keep my eyes firmly fixed ahead,
    don't look
    left or right,
        hammer the cement with my feet,
        pummel my way through town
running faster, faster, faster.
If this were a race
it would be my personal best.
I can feel it without checking my watch for the time.

And at Nell's, I stop,
    morning sweat
    dripping from the end of my nose.
I call. She picks up after two rings.
"The Supreme Court said no," I tell her.
"I'm outside. I need to see your dad."

Her bedroom blinds open
    from the bottom
        up.
She is at the window in a purple tank top,
    one strap down at the shoulder.
"I'll wake him," she says.

HUDDLE

Philip Miller isn't wearing any shoes
and it makes him seem vulnerable,
with those very old white feet.
He sits opposite me, at the table,
        hands clasped.

Nell puts a plate of cookies between us,
                two mugs and a coffeepot.
"I'll go get ready," she says, and rushes away.

The warden
        pours himself a large, steaming mug of coffee.

I hold my head in my hands.
"I have no idea why I'm here," I say,
staying where I am 'cause Ed needs help
and I don't know who else to ask;
Nell's dad is the only person I know with power.
"Washington denied our appeal," I tell him.

He nods. "I got a message. I'm very sorry."
His eyes are bloodshot;

I'm sure he'd go back to bed, if given the option.
But I guess he's going to be kept pretty busy now.

"Can you predict which guys will get a call
from the governor?" I ask.

He frowns. "No. A stay of execution
happens for so many reasons."

"Like what?"

He brushes his hands through his hair.
He doesn't want to do this,
explain the process or give me any insight into the
unpredictability of it—
        the randomness.
"A few years ago a guy called Neil Huddle
set fire to his house and killed his
wife and kids for insurance money.
You know how much?
        Sixty thousand bucks.
That's what his family was worth.
There was so much evidence against Huddle,
his own mother said he was guilty.
But two hours beforehand the governor
called me up,

told me to put on the brakes because Huddle's lawyers
proved he was crazy."
He pauses.
"I mean, you kill your family for peanuts,
I'd say you're a few eggs
short of an omelet."

"So he got off?"
            Should Al put forward this case for Ed?
            Could we say it's unnatural to be so calm
                        about your own death?
            Or maybe I could convince Ed to
            attack a guard or eat his own crap.
            It would be a long shot,
                        but that's the stage we're at.

"I had to send him to a maximum-security
            mental hospital
so he could get better," Philip Miller says.
"And he did. They said they
made him *not crazy* anymore,
then sent him back to us for execution."
He is talking quickly, angrily.

I wait a moment
            to summon up some courage.
            "And can *you* stop it?

If you called the governor and explained
that Ed's a good guy
and doesn't deserve death?"

"What do *you* think, Joseph?"
He holds my gaze,
and I want to hate him
but I can see he isn't proud of his power,
the position he holds in the system.

"No one ate the cookies," Nell says.
She looks at us anxiously.

"I gotta go be with my family," I say, and stand,
then sprint away
as I did the last time I was here.

I don't stop running
until I'm back at the apartment.

NOSY PEPPERS

Ed knows about the Supreme Court decision,
smiles anyway and says,
"Let's make the best of our last couple days."
And we try.
We rag on each other,
tell stories from when we were kids.

Then
Ed turns to one of the guards and asks,
    "What does a nosy pepper do?"

She searches for a serious answer.
    "I don't know, Edward."

    "It gets jalapeño business," he says,
        and laughs from the pit of his tummy,
which makes me laugh
and Angela
and even Aunt Karen.

After a couple of minutes the guard snorts.
    "Jalapeño business. Oh, okay, I get it."

JOKES

"Knock-knock," Ed said.
"Who's there?" I asked.
"Moo."
"Moo who?"
"Cows don't say who, they say moo."
Ed tittered
       while I fell
       onto the rug laughing.
I was four.
I couldn't tell my own jokes,
only laugh at Ed's.
But I tried.
"Knock-knock," I said.
"Who's there?" Ed asked.
"Moo."
"Moo who?"
"Moo-boo-too-loo!" I told him.
I laughed. Clapped my hands.
       Ed rolled his eyes.
"Not quite," he said. "You gotta have a punch line.
Like, a bit that makes people laugh 'cause
you were clever with your words."

"I got smarts," I announced.
"You're a smart*ass*, you mean," he said and
patted my head.

I chewed my sweater cuff,
tried to figure out what made Ed's joke funny,
my joke lame.

And then I said, "Knock-knock."
"Who's there?"
"Ghost."
"Ghost who?"
"Ghosts don't say who, they say BOO!"

Ed winced as I screamed the punch line at him,
then put up a hand for me to high-five.
"Now we're cooking, little man," he said.
"Hell, that joke was better than mine!"

THE VIGIL

Candles and poster boards held high,
hymns and prayers mumbled
into the night air.
"That's for Ed," Al says,
meeting us as we leave the prison
and stating the obvious.
These are Ed's supporters,
people who don't want my brother to die,
gathering around the prison like the survivors
of an apocalypse.
"They come every time.
And they'll be here until the end."

The End:
the words burn,
and I have to
        rest my hands on my knees to keep myself from
        falling over.

Angela rubs my back.
"Let's go," she says. "Tomorrow will be a long day."
But it won't.

August 17 will
    come and
    be gone again
before we've had time to do
    anything
    that will ever matter.

WHEN YOU KNOW BETTER

Aunt Karen doesn't get into my space much,
sleeps next to Angela and only speaks
when she's asked for her opinion.
But tonight she's in the kitchen baking
cinnamon buns,
the smell
      filling up the apartment with a feeling
of family,
which I'm sure it's never known before.

Angela sits on the floor in the living room,
piles of papers around her,
trying to
find a loophole somewhere,
a way to
postpone
what is speeding
toward us
like an unstoppable freight train.

"Anyone hungry?" Aunt Karen asks.
Her skin is gray,
her hair so thin and white
she's turned into an old lady.

I go to her.
"Don't feel guilty anymore.
You're here. It's more than Mom's managed."

"Guilt would be easy," she says.
"Guilt would be about what I've done.
But it's shame I feel, Joe.
Shame that what I've done is
a reflection of who I am.
Who *am* I?"

Angela joins us.
"You were an aunt doing her best."

"It wasn't good enough," Karen says.

Angela elbows her tenderly.
"Hey, when you know better, you do better."

The oven begins to beep.
It beeps and beeps.
The cinnamon buns are done.

I DREAM

Kids in camouflage sprint and stumble through smoke,
their faces smeared with blood and dirt.
It's a burned-out city with kids tearing into enemy lines,
no weapons,
scrabbling around in torn tank tops looking for
scraps of paper
                    to use as shields.

The guerrillas aren't interested in words,
don't care how young the soldiers are,
that most couldn't grow beards.
They pull out machetes, slice right into them,
        these boys,
leaving them
bleeding to death on the ground.

And in the background,
a diner's broken neon sign
flashes ceaselessly.

LAST DAY

I   wake before five.
I   can't get back to sleep.
I   clock-watch,
flipping through photos of Nell on my phone.
She is scowling in each one.
I don't have any of Ed—
they won't let me bring my phone in.

Angela wanders into the living room in the dark,
and then we're sitting
side by side on the
air mattress,
watching out the window,
Ed's last sunrise,
a poppy-red sky he can't see from his cell.
        "We can do this," Angela says.
        "Can we?" I ask.
        "We have to," she reminds me.

NEED

Nell arrives at ten o'clock with a lasagna.
"Sue said you have to eat."
I put the dish in the refrigerator.
"I can stay or leave. Whatever you need," Nell says.

"I need to buy milk and toilet paper," I tell her.

It's close to a hundred degrees,
the air hazy with humidity.
At the convenience store I put
milk, Pepsi, and toilet paper into the basket.
Then I slip some hard candy
into the pocket of my shorts.
I have an urge to steal,
take something that doesn't belong to me.

At the counter, Nell wraps her arm around my waist.
"Do you want company later?
I can wait for you outside the farm."

"Definitely," I say. "I need you."
As I say it, I realize it's true.

"I need you too," she says.

READY

Angela, Karen, and I scrape around the apartment,
              heat up
              squares of lasagna
              we never eat,
and check our phones for updates,
the TV for news that never comes.

Nothing changes.
And all day long,
while we tread water,
the farm is getting ready—
filling needles,
checking straps,
rehearsing their parts like actors in a play
so everyone knows what to do,
won't miss a cue
and mess up the whole operation.

I guess that by now
they're pretty much ready.

AMAZING GRACE

The protesters sing outside the prison,
giving Ed a voice.
They mean well,
but they're too late.
He needed support during his trial
and the early appeals.

They're just here for the night,
the countdown,
'cause this is what they do;
it doesn't matter to them who's on the gurney
or whether they're guilty or not.

They notice us drive in, wave cautiously.
I wave back my weak-willed appreciation.
Maybe, afterward, I should join them—
sing a couple of verses of "Amazing Grace."
What harm could it do?

But not now.
Now it's time to see Ed.

The last time.

It is too soon.

THE LAST SUPPER

Ed rushes at us and
    a guard reaches with his arms to stop him
    but thinks better of it,
    allows
    the four of us to stand in a
    tight huddle.
Ed smells sour, like he hasn't showered in days,
but I don't let go.
I breathe him in until he unpeels himself
from us,
waves toward a table.
"KFC!" he announces.
"I told them I didn't want anything special,
but the warden ordered this anyway.
Chicken, fries, coleslaw, potato salad.
Looks good, right?"
He drums the air with his hands.
"And what made me happiest of all . . ."
He points to a bucket filled to the brim
with cans of Dr Pepper.
"Soda!" he shouts.

"You'll spend all day in the bathroom," Aunt Karen says,
crossing her legs,

pawing the gold crucifix
hanging around her neck.
"Thank goodness," she says,
touching an electric fan next to her which
is slowly whisking hot air around the room.

At the table,
Ed fills a plate with food and
brings it to Angela. "Wanna drink?"

"You eat it.
We'll get something later," she says.

Ed shakes his head.
"I want us to eat together.
A last supper.
You can pretend I'm Jesus."

The guard laughs, but not unkindly.

Ed turns to him.
"You want something to gnaw on, John?" he asks.
"You haven't had lunch yet."

"No, Ed. I'm good. You dig in."

Ed fills a second plate
hands it to Aunt Karen,
then another for me.

I stare at the food on my lap.
How will I force it into my mouth?

Ed fills his own plate and sits next to me,
hands me a can of Dr Pepper.
"This is nice," he says. "Right?"

I try for a smile
because Ed's right—it is nice
not spending our last hours
        fenced off from each other
        by Plexiglas.
But I can think of better days
                we've had
                together.

LIBERTY STATE PARK

It was spring.
Ed was fifteen.
I was five.
Angela had made
a lopsided sponge cake
with Reese's Pieces stuck into the cream frosting.
Aunt Karen brought a bag of cold burgers.
Mom was wearing sunglasses.

We sat on a blanket and ate.
Ed cut the cake and we all sang him "Happy Birthday."
He said,
"That's a kick-ass cake, Ange,"
biting into the first slice.

I couldn't keep my eyes off the jungle gym,
wondering when we'd be done
so I could play.
Ed noticed. "Let's go have fun, Joe!"
He reached for two more slices of cake,
handed one to me,
stuffed the other piece into his mouth.

Then
he grabbed my arm,
        pulled me up.
"God, Angela, you're some baker," he said.
        And we were off.

    That was a better day.

SIX O'CLOCK

Father Matthew shows up at six.
As Ed is introducing him to Angela and Karen,
a yellow phone attached to the wall rings.
The guard answers it,
mumbles into the mouthpiece.
He holds the handset over his head,
calls over. "It's Alan Mitchell."

Angela puts her hand over her mouth.

       Ed shuffles to the phone.

Everyone in the room is silent.

"Yeah. Okay.
I understand.
Yeah. Okay.
Yup.
Okay, thanks, Al."

Angela goes to Ed, puts a hand on his arm.
"Gotta wait," Ed says.
"Al's driving up here now. Said he'll explain."

I exhale;
I've been holding my breath since the phone rang.

Ed looks at the clock over the door.
Six hours left.

Six hours and one minute.

IRREGULAR

Al storms in at seven thirty,
shakes everyone's hands,
takes a seat.

His blue suit is wrinkled.
His tie is undone.

He's out of breath.
He glances at the guard,
     the door.
"I was in the governor's office in Austin earlier
to file the petition for clemency.
As I was doing it,
I looked over at his secretary's desk,
and the denial was coming out of the printer."

Father Matthew sits up. Aunt Karen frowns.

"What does that even mean?" Angela asks.
She twirls her hair
     around and around her
     pointer finger.

Despite the fan it is sweltering in here.
                    I need air
                    but I can't leave.
                    Not now.

"I don't know," Al says.
"But it's highly irregular and probably illegal.
I asked to speak to the governor personally.
He told me it was a clerical error and that
he'd be getting to our petition
before eleven o'clock."

"We leave at ten," Angela says.

Father Matthew mutters beneath his breath,
a prayer,
and Aunt Karen joins him,
a final call
        to God
        to intervene
where man has
                    stood aside
                    and watched.

TEN O'CLOCK

Before I have time to decide on the last words to say
        to Ed
it's ten o'clock.
A different guard comes in.
She doesn't speak,
stands there seeming sorry for herself,
like she's the one being tortured.

Al stands. "Time to go," he says. "I'll wait outside."
He grabs an envelope, shoots through the door.
Father Matthew follows along with the guard.

Aunt Karen takes Ed's hand.
"I'm praying for you all the time," she says.
"And I'm so very, very sorry."
Ed kisses her forehead and she scurries out,
so
it's just the kids now,
the three of us
alone
for the first time in ten years.

Angela holds the back of a chair.
I steady myself on her arm.

I want to whimper,
feel like collapsing.

But I have to hold it together
        for Ed.

No use in him seeing his siblings crumble.

He has to know we're okay.

Ed faces us. "This isn't the end.
In an hour Heath McDowell
will make a call and you'll be back
tomorrow afternoon
wondering when the hell you get to go home."
        His voice is wispy;
        he hardly believes it himself.

Ed feels out of reach,
like I'm seeing him from
        across a football field.
Will he hear me if I speak?
Can he understand
        when he's so far away?
"Ed," I whisper.

"Come here, Joe." He reaches for me,
takes me in his arms, squeezes.
Then he pulls Angela into us too
and we are silent,
'cause nothing can be said now
        that matters
        all that much.

The clock ticks loudly.

I don't know how many minutes pass
but Al returns. "I'm sorry," he says.
"They're calling time."

Ed releases the embrace
        and Angela stumbles,
            saves herself by reaching for my hand.
I hold her up, help her step away from Ed.
She isn't crying.
She sounds like she might be sick.

I reach forward one last time and hold him.
"I'm glad we got this time together," I say.

Ed pulls away, his eyes swollen with tears.
"Take care of yourselves, okay?"
And then he turns,
puts his back to us completely.

I hold Angela's hand,
      pull her
            out of the room as quickly as I can.

The guard shuts the door.

I fall to the floor.

And from the closed room we can hear Ed.

He is howling
      our names.

WITNESS

Angela collects her bag,
about to follow Father Matthew to the visitors'
cafeteria
in the main prison,
where they'll wait a couple of hours
until the witness gallery is ready.
Angela will watch the state murder Ed,
something she can never unsee,
a movie that will play
for the rest of her life.
"There's no reason to do this," I tell her.

She is crying,
        snot running into her mouth.
"He can't be alone," she snivels.

"But *you'll* be alone," I tell her.

Aunt Karen offers Angela a Kleenex.
"*I'll* be the witness," she tells us. "It's the least I can do."

But Angela is adamant.
She will not relinquish this role.
"He'll be expecting me," she says.

"Then I'll wait with you," Aunt Karen insists,
and all three of them
leave through a
heavy metal door.

BELIEF

Nell opens her arms and takes me in.
"Let's go for a drive," she says.

Behind her,
      protesters' candles blink.
I could join them, as I planned,
but my voice will make no difference.

I'm not in any mood to pray anyway.
I don't believe in God today.

      I don't even believe in people.

IN THE DARKNESS

A hill overlooks the farm.
I drive, Nell grasping my knee.
She pats it now and then, and asks, "Are you okay?"
I nod, though I'm not.
I'm afraid I might pass out,
                veer off the road into a ditch,
        vomit all over myself.
I fix my eyes on the road,
focus on the car moving.
If I cause an accident I'll hurt Nell;
        I don't want that.

We stop at the lookout point.
From up here you can see the whole farm—
every rotten thing happening below;
cars and vans come and go,
lights in cells go out,
        and Section A
        to the right,
        the only part of the prison lit up—
        bright lights against the black.

I reach for the radio. Nell stops me.
"If anything changes, they'll call," she says,

and she's right; what else will I hear
over the airwaves
but people gunning for Ed?

Nell hands me a beer and a bottle opener,
strokes the back of my neck with her fingertips.
"What can I do?" she asks.

"Nothing," I say.
        "Just sit in the darkness with me."

A MINUTE BEFORE MIDNIGHT

Nell and I have had three beers each,
shared a titanic pack of Twizzlers.

My phone pings.
A text from Al:
    Governor denied our appeal
    for a stay. I'm sorry, Joe.
    I'll call you afterward.
    Al

MIDNIGHT

I stumble out of the car,
breathe in the moist air.

Nell is out the
       passenger side,
       comes to me. "What was it?"

I hold out my phone; she reads the text.
       "You're going to survive this," she says.
She tries to wrap her arms around me,
but I step away,
lay my hands flat on the hood,
face the farm, their lights,
and imagine
the strap-down team
       taking Ed from his holding cell
           to the death chamber,
the murmurings of the priest's final prayer,
Angela's face as the curtains open
       and she sees Ed, IVs in his arms,
          head shaved,
              body fastened down
              too tight
              for him to move.

And there's Philip Miller nodding,
giving the go-ahead for poisons to be pumped
        into Ed's body. .

I stare at the moon,
        round and the color of oatmeal.
"The moonrise was beautiful all month," I tell Ed.
"It's beautiful underneath this sky."

IT IS DONE

Ed is gone.

TIME TRAVEL ME

Time travel me back.
Let me say good-bye again.
A minute more,
      a moment,
a chance to see Ed's face
      alive,
hold his hand like we did when I was a kid—
feel his skin and smell him.

Time travel me back.
Let me relive *any* moment with Ed;
I'll take him at his worst,
      his moodiest.
Anything at all so long as he can hear me.

Time travel me back
so I can say good-bye and mean it.
Give me the final moment again
to use the words no one in our house
ever dared say to one another—
scared of being sappy or overemotional.
Give me the three seconds with Ed,
and I will tell him the words and I will mean them.
I will say,
      I love you.

DRIVING HOME

Nell drives and we don't speak.

Every limb is numb
or aching.
My mind is racing
        and then slow.

Never
        again.

                        Never.

Never
        again.

That's when I'll next see my brother.

BODY CURLED UP

I bolt upright on the air mattress
on the living room floor.
"Angela?"
She is standing over me,
body shuddering.
I pull her down
and she lies on her side,
face to the window,
body curled up like a baby.
She starts to shake.
I lie on the sheet next to her,
wrap her in my arms,
do nothing useful at all
except listen to the hurt.

ANOTHER NEXT MONTH

I get up early and
step around the air mattress, where
Angela is still curled up into a small ball,
asleep,
dressed in her clothes from last night.

The door to the bedroom is closed.
Maybe Aunt Karen is awake,
but if she wanted to talk, she would have come out.

I dress for my run and take off,
down the apartment stairs,
through the parking lot,
        and along Main Street to the edge of town.

Usually this is where I head home,
where the sidewalk ends.
But this morning I keep going
down unlit streets,
past empty fields
and buzzing factories.

I run and run in the predawn light,
not noticing too much the aching in my legs.

And I find the prison,
where I expect to see cameras,
a few remaining protesters holding banners aloft.

But it's finished.
Over.
Like nothing ever happened here.

A janitor collects something from the ground
and throws it into a trash can.
The place is strewn with candy bar wrappers,
cigarette butts,
candle wax.
"The party's over, I guess," I say to him.

The janitor shrugs.
"They got another party planned for
September sixteenth."

"Another execution?"

"Sure. Dick Reese got a date last week."

"I missed that news," I say.

"Yeah, well,
Dick ain't got a chance in hell.
You know what he did?"

"Does it matter?" I ask.
"Does it really matter what he did?"
and without waiting for an answer,
I turn around and start running.

THE NEWS REPORTS

Philip Miller refuses to make a statement to the media,
but speaking straight into the camera Al says,
"I now have to go and speak with Mr. Moon's family.
I wish someone at Governor McDowell's office
would tell me how I explain this to them.
I doubt anyone could.
In any case, McDowell's team
is probably all sound asleep."

A journalist explains
that Ed's body will remain at the farm
until an autopsy has been carried out.

Only then will he be released to us.

But the autopsy
won't tell the truth—
                which is that my brother was
                murdered.

BELONGINGS

I collect Ed's belongings,
everything tossed untidily into a plastic bag.
The guard makes me sign something, then says,
"Plenty of others deserved to go ahead of him,
you know?"
I nod politely
as the warden saunters in.
He gestures for the guard to leave us alone.

"I wanted to say good-bye," Philip Miller says.
"To give you this"— he hands me a letter—
"and also tell you I'm sorry.
Not officially.
But as a person.
I'm sorry for what's happened here," he says.

He reaches forward,
but he's out of his mind if he thinks
I'm going to let him touch me.
     I step away
     and we watch each other.

When he senses I'm not about to absolve him,
he opens the door for me to leave, and I do,
without another word.

WHAT IS LEFT BEHIND

There's nothing unusual in the bag:
a pair of Adidas high-tops;
tattered jeans, the knees faded;
a fake TAG watch;
a wallet with a Walmart card in it;
one dollar and seventy-eight cents in change;
a calendar with happy penguins on it,
check marks counting down his last days,
    and, circled in red,
    August 18.

I stuff everything back into the bag
and reach into my pocket for the
letter Philip Miller handed me.
It's Ed's handwriting.
His last letter.

THE LAST LETTER

Dear Joe and Ange,

So,

> *you left half an hour ago,*
> *and I'm writing 'cause I*
> *don't have much else to do.*
> *Al is here.*
> *We are waiting to hear from the governor.*
> *Could get the call real soon.*
> *It's five after eleven now.*
> *I got Father Matthew here too.*
> *And he's a good guy even though*
> *he smells like*
> *a bacon and frankincense sandwich.*
> *He keeps reading the Bible*
> *but I can't concentrate on that stuff.*

Thing is,

> *it's real quiet here.*
> *I'm in a new cell next to the chamber.*
> *Just a bench.*
> *No bed or anything.*
> *And they don't allow radios now.*

Thing is,
> *I want you to know I'm okay.*

I mean,
> *I'm scared.*
> *My hand's shaking a bit writing this*
> *but I'm okay.*

So,
> *don't worry about me,*
> *about how it was*
> *if it happens*
> *or what I've been through.*
> *Think about yourself. Take care of each other.*
> *I'm no poet so I don't know how to say the hard stuff*
> *but I can still feel the hug you guys gave me*
> *before you left.*
> *I know I was sticking to you pretty tight,*
> *but I wanted to remember it,*
> *and I want you to feel that cling.*

You know,
> *I reckon people sit here with a mountain of*
> *regrets*
> *but I haven't got many.*
> *I'm here 'cause I was tired of being trapped,*
> *and it didn't work out great, but I can't say*
> *I'd change much,*
> *even after everything that's happened.*

So,

> do all the stuff you want even
> if someone tries to deadlock your front door.
> Be brave about it.
> Open the back door at night
> and let in the noises, or hell,
> I don't know, run, escape if you have to.
> If that's the only way to live.
> And if someone tries to stop you,
> you tell them you can't save anyone's life
> but your own.

Okay,

> it's almost time.
> Guards want to get me ready.

So,

> I'm leaving for now.

Thing is,

> if I write any more I might quote Oprah and
> NO ONE wants that!
> Al's back actually.
> Hopefully it's good news.
> Hope. Ha!

And the thing is,
  if it's not good news,
  at least I'm free.
  We all are.
Love always. Always.
  Your brother—Ed xx

THE PAIN

I knew this day was around the corner,
that I should have been prepared
for the coughing,
the heaving in my body,
the tears
that won't stop,
        the scream
        I let out,
the scream that fills up the apartment
and makes Karen come running.
"Joe?"

    I should be ready for this pain,
    but I'm not
    because I never believed
    that Ed would die.

REMEMBERING

Sue arrives with homemade moussaka,
Nell with bottles of wine and water.
No one eats, but we drink a lot and talk,
and I tell them about the time Ed dressed up
as a snow queen for Halloween.
He nearly gave Mom a seizure
when she arrived home from work to see a
six-foot-tall guy in drag
      standing in the middle of our kitchen
      frying liver in a pan.

Angela laughs and says, "Ed loved to dress up.
When you were real small he was Santa.
You remember?
He almost frightened you to death.
And he forgot to bring a present!"

"Of course I remember," I say,
and for the rest of the night that's what we do:
      we remember the Ed we knew.

RELEASED

They release Ed now they're happy with how he died.
Apparently it was cardiac arrest.
That's what the report says.

TO HOUSTON

Angela and Karen are already on the bus,
pretending not to watch.

"I like the idea of Columbia for college," Nell says,
lightly punching my arm,
"so I guess I'll see you around New York sometime.
Maybe I'll cheerlead your track-and-field events . . .
except I won't."

"I'll visit when I've got some money," I say.
I open my backpack, pull out a large bottle of water.
"Want this? I won't be able to take it on the plane."

She hits me again, and it hurts.
"You romantic, Joe Moon.
But you better keep it.
It's a few hours to Houston.
I don't want you dying of thirst."

The bus wheezes and spits.

Angela raps on the window and waves.
Nell smiles up at her.

"You better go," she says.

"Sue told me to leave
as soon as this was over.
I have to take her advice."

Nell waves me away. "I know you can't stay.
It's just . . ."
She bites her lip.

"I know," I say.
And I do. Of course I do.
"But what about you? You and your dad?"

She shrugs. "We'll be fine," she says.

I don't reply.

"We *will*," she insists.
"Now get out of this shithole before it buries you!"

BACK IN ARLINGTON

The sky is bright blue,
the sidewalk peppered with old wads of gum and
cracked from years of carrying people.

I go into our house,
my bedroom,
the place I used to share with Ed.

My bed is made
but the blinds are shut,
making it seem like nighttime.

Something glitters
on the bookcase.
I follow the glint.

It's a plastic, glow-in-the-dark
crescent moon
no wider than a dime.

I hold it in the palm of my hand.

The arc smiles up at me.

I didn't know I had this in here.
It must have been Ed's from years ago.

I fold my fingers around the plastic piece
and scan the room for other signs of moons or stars,
Ed
hidden in the everyday,
burrowed away in my life forever.

Because,
      hell,
      you never know
      what you might find in the dark.

AUTHOR'S NOTE

I was fifteen yeas old when I first saw a 1987 BBC documentary called *Fourteen Days in May* about a man called Edward Earl Johnson, whose courage and dignity while on death row in Mississippi had a profound and lasting impact on me. *Moonrise* is, in so many ways, inspired by that brave film. It is also inspired by the lawyer representing Johnson at that time, Clive Stafford Smith, now the director of Reprieve and author of *Injustice: Life and Death in the Courtrooms of America*. I urge the reader to see *Fourteen Days in May*, if possible.

I also encourage the reader to seek out *Just Mercy: A Story of Justice and Redemption* by Bryan Stevenson, a book about the American justice system, which hugely influenced this novel. Finally, please do check out the wonderful work done by the Equal Justice Initiative (EJI.org) for death-row prisoners, as well as the many other men and women unfairly treated by the system.

ACKNOWLEDGMENTS

First and foremost, thank you to Maureen Price, my Religious Studies teacher at school, who forced her classes to watch *Fourteen Days in May* despite its devastating effect. She was right about how important it is. She also believed in me way back when, and that faith led to so much.

This novel wasn't easy to complete and would never have seen the light of day had it not been for Brian Conaghan, who read and gave feedback on every version of the project—I owe you so much. Nikki Sheehan, thank you for the inappropriately hilarious encouragement and professional advice.

Thank you to my editors, Zöe Griffiths, Hannah Sandford, and Helen Vick, for their patience and hard work, and to my publicist, Emma Bradshaw, as well as the entire children's team at Bloomsbury—this has been a massive team effort and I love being on your team! Thank you to Julia Churchill, my agent, for it all.

Thanks also to Repforce Ireland, Combined Media, The Big Green Bookshop, CLPE, Children's Books Ireland, CILIP, David O'Callaghan, Hélène Ferey, and all my friends and family for being bloody fabulous.

31901064327135

REPAIR

Redeeming the Promise of Abolition

Katherine Franke

Haymarket Books
Chicago, Illinois

© 2019 Katherine Franke

Published in 2019 by
Haymarket Books
P.O. Box 180165
Chicago, IL 60618
773-583-7884
www.haymarketbooks.org
info@haymarketbooks.org

ISBN: 978-1-60846-624-5

Distributed to the trade in the US through Consortium Book Sales
and Distribution (www.cbsd.com) and internationally through
Ingram Publisher Services International (www.ingramcontent.com).

This book was published with the generous support
of Lannan Foundation and Wallace Action Fund.

Printed in Canada by union labor.

Cover design by John Yates.

Library of Congress Cataloging-in-Publication data is available.

10 9 8 7 6 5 4 3 2 1

For Janlori and Maya

Contents

Introduction

> *"The past is all that makes the present coherent, and further . . . the past will remain horrible for exactly as long as we refuse to assess it honestly."*
>
> **—James Baldwin**, *Notes of a Native Son* (1955)

THE SEA ISLANDS of Georgia and South Carolina are stunningly beautiful. *Travel + Leisure* magazine describes the area in this way: "On South Carolina's once-isolated Sea Islands, Gullah is still spoken, African traditions are carried on, and salty marshes perfume the air." The high-end travel magazine delights in the telling of a magnificent tour with a local preacher of the tidal and barrier islands on the Southeastern Atlantic coast. "'Welcome to the best place on God's earth,' says the man behind the wheel of the gray 1985 Oldsmobile. . . . Born Joseph P. Bryant, he grew up speaking English, but gained fluency in Geechee and Gullah—the languages of his slave great-grandparents who toiled on the islands' rice plantations—as a child."[1]

The *Travel + Leisure* article goes on to praise the unique richness of the local culture on the Sea Islands, a place that has kept its African history and culture alive unlike anywhere else in the United States:

After the Civil War, the Gullahs were abandoned in the

islands flung off the Carolina coast because the land was considered worthless. That abandonment and the century of isolation that followed have preserved the Gullah language, culture, and daily way of life. Families live for generations on the same farm, grow much of their own food, pick sweet grass to make baskets, and attend the one-room praise houses of their slave ancestors, where hymns are harmonized in Gullah and Geechee.

Vogue magazine describes Beaufort, one of the most beautiful ocean-side towns in the area: "Today Beaufort is respected for its preservation of antebellum architecture—classic plantation style mansions with deep porches made for sipping Bittermilk mixed cocktails. Locals liken the town to a modest millionaire who never puts on airs."[2]

The violence, torture, dehumanization, and brutality of slavery slide off the page in these tales, and in their place the travel writer delights the potential visitor with ancient and exotic African tongues, food, and civilization. If that's not enough of an enticement, articles describing the area also mention that the Sea Islands served as the settings for the blockbuster movies *Forrest Gump* and *The Prince of Tides*, movies in which white people are the protagonists, heroes, and only characters whose lives we are meant to care about.

Given this rich history, the Sea Islands are the site of a curious form of remembrance of the past coupled with strategic forgetting. The travel-magazine portrayal of the Islands' history renders slavery a kind of quaint, benign historical note. In this telling, it was the "migration" of hundreds of thousands of Black people to the region that makes the Sea Islands such an alluring spot for tourists today. Mentioning that their "migration" was forced, in chains, and deadly would interrupt a plot animated by the "dusky" (one author actually uses the adjective "dusky" to describe the landscape) combination of Southern charm and exotic African traditions. The fact that the kidnapping and violent enslavement of Black people were the means by which African culture "ended up" in the Sea Islands lurks as a kind of bothersome and thus ignored fact, haunting the otherwise fabulous experiences to be had on the coast of South Carolina and Georgia today.

Narratives of local culture, like that provided by glossy travel magazines, reflect, perpetuate, and sometimes invent a palliative history that makes little in the way of moral demands on the present. These narratives of exoneration normalize a contemporary status quo by emplotting history in a way that severs the present from the past and renders the present ordering of life somehow inevitable. But as William Faulkner observed, especially about the South, "The past is never dead. It's not even past."[3]

That past has an enduring afterlife in the present, indeed its residue binds present injustice to unaddressed wrongs of the past. *Repair* makes the argument that the failure to provide any kind of meaningful reparation to formerly enslaved people in the 1860s has ongoing structural effects today. While the sources of contemporary Black poverty, disenfranchisement, and systematic disadvantage are complex, the original sin from which the evil of structural racism has grown is clear. It is chattel slavery: the unrelentingly vicious, sadistic, torturous enslavement and exploitation of Black people for profit. Emancipation put an end to the formal system of slavery, but as a prospective legal reform, emancipation did nothing to repair the rape, torture, death, and destruction of millions of human souls through the institution of chattel slavery. At the same time, slaveholders were never required to disgorge the profits they made from enslaved labor, or retroactively compensate enslaved people for the theft of their labor, safety, dignity, and lives. Quite the opposite, former slaveowners were compensated generously for their lost land and property with US tax dollars.

Property ownership is one of the key reasons why there is comparatively much more wealth held by white than Black people in the United States. The median wealth of white households in 2013 was thirteen times greater than for Black households (the largest gap in a quarter century),[4] and the average Black household would need 228 years to accumulate as much wealth as its white counterpart holds today.[5] While 73 percent of white households owned their own homes in 2011, only 45 percent of African Americans were homeowners.[6]

Formerly enslaved people entered civil society in the aftermath of the Civil War at a distinct economic disadvantage as compared with their former owners who retained all of the profits they had reaped from the purchase, sale, and use of formerly enslaved human beings. These income and accumulated family wealth disparities didn't just happen, rather they are the result of systematic, structural race discrimination in this country, much of it attributable to government policy. This book urges us to face our collective responsibility for ongoing racial inequality in the United States, and traces that responsibility back to the failure to provide meaningful repair, or reparations, to formerly enslaved people. By "us" I mean American society generally. Not just the descendants of enslaved people, not just the descendants of slave-owners, but all of us today who have inherited a legacy of opportunity that is ineluctably structured by our racial history.

The distribution of people and wealth in the Sea Islands today should provoke us to honestly assess the horrible history that lies beneath such an alluring tourist destination, and to repudiate a familiar story of emancipation that absolves the present from being morally implicated in that hideous past. Recently renewed calls for reparations for slavery from the likes of journalist Ta-Nehisi Coates, the Movement for Black Lives, and the United Nations serve as an invitation to revisit that past in a way that discloses contemporary culpability for the failure to meaningfully remediate the crime of enslavement. Replotting this history, as I set out to do in this book, not only reveals the kind of justice that formerly enslaved people were owed and did not receive, but also lays bare how white people have been the discrete beneficiaries of that failure to repair.

❧

How could the story of freedom for formerly enslaved people have been told differently than the familiar middle school history book chapter: we fought a civil war over slavery; the South lost; the slaves were freed, and America became a society newly committed to racial equality and freedom? How might we view this version of the story as one that suits the interests of the descendants of slave-owners more than the descendants of enslaved people? At what junctures were other, more robust, forms of Black freedom imaginable, and indeed possible? Have the possibilities that lay in that more robust form of freedom been lost to history, or can we recuperate a more ambitious idea of freedom today? *Repair* returns us to critical moments when the lives of Black people were set on a course of being freed, yet not truly free, and urges us to remedy the way in which being set free did not accomplish justice for enslaved people.

Repair returns to the moment of emancipation and imagines what freedom would have looked like if formerly enslaved people had been given a stronger voice in shaping what it meant not just to be freed, but to be free. Over and over, as I have read and lived with the voices of formerly enslaved people preserved in archives across the South I have been humbled by what it must have been like to be freed. Imagine yourself, your parents, your grandparents, being a person that was owned, like a horse, a piece of land, a farm implement. Frederick Law Olmsted described the experience after a visit to Mississippi in 1853:

> A cast mass of the slaves pass their lives, from the moment they are able to go afield in the picking season till they drop worn out in the grave, in incessant labor, in all sorts of weather, at all seasons of the year, without any other change or relaxation than is furnished by sickness, without the smallest hope

of any improvement either in their condition, in their food, or in their clothing, which are of the plainest and coarsest kind, and indebted solely to the forbearance or good temper of the overseer for exception from terrible physical suffering.[7]

And then, the next day they were freed. What would this experience be like? What would freedom mean to freed people? The new experience of being freed had to have been replete with relief, exhilaration, and triumph, but also disorientation, bewilderment, and fear.

With few exceptions the course and contours of Black emancipation were charted by white people who refused to respect the humanity of enslaved people and thus locked Black people into a truly inferior second-class status once they were freed. White supremacy saturated the meaning of Black freedom every bit as much as it justified the enslavement of Black people. What kind of incredible resilience did enslaved Black people possess that they could endure not only the crushing violence of enslavement, but also the chimeric parallel universe of freedom? In her novels, including *Song of Solomon* and *Mercy*, Toni Morrison portrays this troubling transition through her characters. Because I am not a writer with a fraction of Morrison's talent, in *Repair* I present a narrative gathered from actual voices and experiences of some freed people from the Sea Islands of South Carolina and at Davis Bend, Mississippi. In these two places where government policies left them largely on their own, freed people were able to take greater control of what it meant to be free than in any other community in the South at the end of the Civil War. Their vision of freedom provides a model of what could have been, and places a demand on us today to repair the enduring afterlife of slavery and white supremacy in the present.

◦

Emancipation in Mississippi provides a critical example of a more robust form of freedom: as Northern troops moved through the South in the spring of 1864, enslaved people fled the plantations where they had been held captive and sought out the safety of the Union army. The following first-hand description of the living conditions of escaped people seeking refuge behind Northern lines just outside Vicksburg, Mississippi, bears witness to the bare life that characterized the condition of being freed by military occupation:

> In a cattle shed without any siding, there huddled together were thirty-five helpless people, one man who had lost one eye entirely, and the sight of the other fast going, he could do nothing. Five women, all mothers, and the residue of twenty-nine children, all small and under twelve years of age. One of the women had the small pox, her face a perfect mass of scabs, her children were left uncared for except what they incidentally received. Another woman was nursing a little boy about seven whose earthly life was fast ebbing away, she could pay but little attention to the rest of her family . . . I inquired how they slept, they collect together to keep one another warm . . . There is no wood for them nearer than half a mile which these poor children have to toat . . . and the same with water, this has to be carried the same distance and the only vessel they had to carry it was a heavy two-gallon stone jug, a load for a child when empty.[8]

Federal troops set up "contraband" camps throughout the South to receive the formerly enslaved people as they fled their owners' violence, dominion, and control. Military leaders had not anticipated that a collateral project to their defeat of the Confederate army was the care and feeding of destitute escaped slaves. From the start of the Northern conquest of the Confederacy, the federal government waged parallel military and humanitarian campaigns. The humanitarian was enabled by the military and threatened to bring it down if the swelling Black population that attached itself to US troops wasn't disposed of in some way that would free up the troops to fight without being encumbered by the basic human needs of Black people who sought safety in their care.

The vivid portrayal above of the horrible conditions into which Black people were freed in Vicksburg, Mississippi, in the spring of 1864, provides a framework for the distinction I draw in this book between being freed and being free. No longer enslaved, what was the status of the Black people once under the protection of the US government? While enslaved they were legally considered property,[9] but their civil, legal, and moral status were transformed instantly when they were brought within the wide arms of the US military. But transformed how? It was easier to say what they *were not*—enslaved—than what they *were*: free men and women, captured chattel, spoils of war? Some officials regarded them unhesitatingly as savages, others took the view that they were men and women—humans—for whose welfare they were now responsible. Today we would consider them refugees. But in the terms available in the nineteenth century, they weren't citizens and they weren't freemen, instead they came to be called freed men and women. (I would prefer to use the less gendered free people and freed people rather than freemen/man or freedmen/man. However de-gendering identity, and freedom itself, would be anachronistic and would sound clunky when used in the context of historical references. So in *Repair*, I try to use the terms as they were used in the nineteenth century, where "men/man" was used to refer to all people, but did so in a way that usually used men's experiences as a norm, and thus erased the differences men and women experienced in their lives as enslaved people, as free or freed people, or as citizens. I won't hesitate, however, to note the gendered implications of life in the contexts I explore.)

In the nineteenth century, a freeman was understood as the opposite of a slave, as a man[10] with robust civil and political rights and status.[11] A freedman by contrast was not a slave, but was also not the opposite of a slave.[12] The experience of the newly freed people during the Civil War and in its immediate aftermath make clear that slavery and freedom were not a binary, but were instead graded categories with ample middle ground between them—an uncomfortable middle occupied by freed men, women, and children. The "d" bore witness to their immanent ability to be enslaved, enjoined for the moment by questionable operation of law, but ever present in a way that distinguished them from free men. The "d" also marked a person as a former slave, a label that carried forward the stain of the past as an enduring badge of inferiority. The freedman was a refugee from slavery occupying a precarious place, the significance of which was entirely unclear to any of the players—Black and white—during and in the immediate aftermath of the Civil War.

The badge of being freed has produced intergenerational forms of disadvantage for which reparation remains past due. As Dr. Martin Luther King Jr. put it during a tour through Mississippi in 1968 as part his Poor People's Campaign: "At the very same time that America refused to give the Negro any land, through an act of Congress our government was giving away millions of acres of land in the West and the Midwest, which meant it was willing to undergird its white peasants from Europe with an economic floor. . . . We are coming to get our check."[13] Michelle Alexander's notion of the New Jim Crow challenges us to understand the mass incarceration, felony disenfranchisement, and enduring poverty of Black people in this country as vestiges of enslavement as well.[14]

Early on in the Civil War, federal officials settled on the legal category "contraband" to describe formerly enslaved people.[15] Contraband goods, under their reading of the term, were items of personal property that could not be imported into enemy territory and could be seized lawfully when found in the enemy's possession. Strong Northern abolitionists forswore this term as it retained the notion that Black people were property, but at such an early stage in the war Northern military officials did not want to unsettle the power brokers in Washington and Boston who did not yet regard the Civil War as a mission to end slavery. Edward Pierce, a young, white lawyer from Boston who had been assigned the task of overseeing the first "contraband camp" at Fort Monroe, Virginia in 1861, was met by his charges with disbelief that they were still being treated like chattel. When they learned that they were being held in "contraband camps" they asked Pierce "Why d' ye call us that for?"[16] Pierce quickly came to agree with the formerly enslaved people in his charge that "contraband" was an offensive term. On his next assignment at the Sea Islands of South Carolina he refused to call them contrabands adopting instead the more dignified term freedmen.

In 1861 it was not clear, nor indeed knowable, what would lie on the other side of slavery for Black people. Repatriation back to Africa, the Caribbean, or some territory in the West? Settlement of the freed men and women on land confiscated from white planters? Full citizenship on a par with white people? Or some variation on any of these or other possibilities? Of course, the Confederacy had to be defeated first before full attention could be paid to these post-victory questions.

During the period from 1861 to 1865, military and civilian, public and private, religious and secular men and women from the North came south to offer aid and comfort to the newly freed Black people. At the same time, formerly enslaved people took care of themselves and each other and began to dream about a life that had seemed impossible a few months earlier. While all the rights and privileges enjoyed by freemen remained out of reach, freed-dom was exhilarating for the men, women, and children liberated by Northern troops. For the first time families did not face the prospect of separation by sale to parts unknown, never to see one another again. Freed people did not wake to a fear of the lash for the most minor infraction or for no infraction at all. And the freed people had to adjust to a new reality where their time was their own. The contraband camps may have been slapdash, short on provisions, and full of disease, but freed people were safe there from the daily violence, degradation, and exploitation that characterized enslavement.

No sooner had the contraband camps been set up than vision-
ary military officers and abolitionists from the North set out to experiment with Black freed-dom. Starting in late 1861 and continuing
throughout the war, utopian experiments in Black emancipation
were begun in the Sea Islands of South Carolina and Vicksburg,
Mississippi, among other places. These experiments in freed-dom
had multiple objectives: proving that freed labor was more efficient
than slave labor; seizing the lucrative cotton crop for the benefit of
the Union treasury with freed rather than enslaved labor; exploring
methods of reparation for the indignity and theft of Black peoples'
labor while enslaved; teaching the freed men, women, and children
to read and write; "civilizing" the formerly enslaved people to respect
the marriage sacrament, honesty, loyalty to nation, and keeping one's
word; preparing newly freed Black people for a life in the not too dis-
tant future as citizens; and exploring whether freedmen might make
suitable soldiers in the Union army should President Lincoln be
persuaded to muster them. Not all these goals were compatible with
one another, and not every benevolent actor was committed to all of
them, indeed, today we would not consider every goal benevolent.
But each of them was a stage in the humanitarian project that sought
to render visible the humanity of enslaved people in the wake of their
wrecked lives. Law figured centrally in this recovery project, framing
the very terms of freed-dom, the human,[17] and the tactics of uplift
and social "improvement" that were brought to bear on freed people.

⁓

Repair returns us to the imperfect conditions of emancipation.
Relying as much as possible on primary sources that give voice
to people for whom being freed was a new and often frustrating
experience, this book traces the complex ways in which formerly
enslaved people negotiated a radical transformation in their lives
and horizons of well-being.

We begin in 1861 with a utopian experiment in Black freedom and landownership at Port Royal, South Carolina. These islands were captured by Northern forces early in the Civil War and were inhabited by between eight and ten thousand Black refugees. Federal officials, working closely with private Northern aid societies, sought to set up a radical free labor project at Port Royal in the hope of demonstrating that freed labor was as, if not more, efficient than enslaved labor. The version of freedom implemented at Port Royal was tightly administered by Northern white do-gooders who regarded themselves on a mission to lift up their Black charges. Importantly, newly freed Black people at Port Royal were able to work, and in some instances purchase, their own land; this provided a model for what a free Black agrarian society might look like after the end of the war. The Port Royal experiment provides an example of what Reconstruction could have looked like had President Lincoln not been assassinated, and his political course not been radically transformed by his successor Andrew Johnson.

Repair then moves to the tale of a different radical experiment in Black self-governance that took place just outside of Vicksburg, Mississippi, at Davis Bend, the plantation owned by Jefferson Davis's eldest brother, Joseph. Like Port Royal, Davis Bend served as the testing ground for an experiment in Black independence that some federal officials hoped would serve as a model for Reconstruction. While in Port Royal the discipline of law was imposed on Black people largely by white missionaries and government agents as part of a wider project designed to civilize newly freed people, at Davis Bend formerly enslaved people were left alone to govern themselves free from white oversight. Though the Davis Bend project offered a more radical and autonomous approach to Black self-governance than that tried at Port Royal, in the end, it too could not withstand the overwhelming pressure to situate the emancipation of Black people within and under the control of white people, rather than in autonomous zones, free from white oversight, judgment, and discipline.

A return to the historical archive can be transformative. In important ways, the archive provides a stockpile of possible futures, "from a moment . . . when the future appears guaranteed by the present to one in which it seems undermined by it."[18] Literary theorist Paul Saint-Amour observes that reverse engineering contemporary trauma can illuminate how the present can be haunted by past expectations. Thwarted expectations can become encysted in our histories thereby impairing self-understanding and commitment in the present. Revisiting key historical moments at which things could have gone differently—and after emancipation there was some expectation that they would—can provide the opportunity not only for regret and reflection, but to revive those lost and more just futures in the present.[19]

This is precisely why it is imperative that we return to the history of incomplete emancipation at the end of the Civil War: to recover possible futures, and to reactivate those futures now, via reparations. *Repair* takes up this prospect, returning to the archive not to relive and relent to a horrendous moment of moral failure and disappointment, but instead to reimagine a version of freedom/freed-dom, to recognize that the emancipation of enslaved people is not "over," and that there are things we can do now to heal a national wound left festering for 150 years.

The Sea Islands of South Carolina have become an affluent, white enclave. The market value of real estate property in Beaufort County in 2017 was $35,756,421,947.[20] Census data from 1860, just before the start of the Civil War, lists 6,714 white people, 809 "free colored" people, and 32,530 enslaved people in Beaufort County. Roughly half of the enslaved population was held by ninety-eight white slaveholders who ran large plantations on the Islands.[21] The kind of future that would have been made possible had formerly enslaved people been emancipated with both rights *and* resources, rather than merely with limited rights, would likely have produced a quite different, more just, and less unequal present. Specifically, the riches to be found in the Sea Islands today would likely have a different racial character entirely.

The initial intent after emancipation was to redistribute land to formerly enslaved people. In fact, the distribution of land to newly freed people was undertaken in the Sea Islands and at Davis Bend as an explicit form of reparation, but the land was redistributed back to former slave-owners when the Johnson administration assumed control of post–Civil War operations after the murder of Abraham Lincoln. Both of these early and unrealized experiments in land-based reparation exemplify what it would have meant to take repair seriously. Yet in the end Johnsonian politicians structured Black freedom around contract labor and other legally mediated relationships with white people. Government and white enterprise were not only complicit in but directly responsible for the failure of an approach to Black freedom that would have set four million newly freed people on an entirely different course of self-sufficiency, wealth accumulation, and full citizenship. This book shows the extent of that complicity and a means by which reparations might still be made today. It is both the promise and the failure of reparation in the 1860s that should animate a return to reparations now, not in the form of individual cash grants but through collective resource redistribution. The last chapter of the book offers some potential steps toward how this kind of repair might be possible today. The book does not aim to chart a precise blueprint for how that redistribution would work, but rather offers an overview of what it would look like.

⟡

Whatever notion of justice one might embrace, emancipation was a necessary, but insufficient, component of its fulfillment at the end of the US Civil War. The disestablishment of the institution of slavery released four million people from bondage, but it did little to redress the horror of slavery itself. That horror stretched backward to cover

the loss of dignity, forced labor, family separation, sexual exploitation, human commodification, and sheer sadism that enslavement
entailed, and forward into an afterlife that marked Black people as
inferior and relegated them to a second-rate form of freedom than
that enjoyed by white people. This was what enslaved people got
when they were emancipated: freedom on the cheap. The dangling
"d" at the end of "free" stood as a kind of residue of enslavement that
bound freed people to a past, and marked their future as freed, not
free, people. It served as a racial mark that structured the kind of
freedom formerly enslaved people received as something less than
that with which white people were endowed as a matter of natural,
or God's, law. Structural, comprehensive, and ongoing reparation
continues to be required to address the wounds of the past and ameliorate an enduring social, political, economic, and legal identity of
freed people as something less than white people.

Because innovative experiments in Black freedom and reparation were sabotaged and subsequently failed, they impress us with
the strength of the moral demand made for reparations today by
the likes of Ta-Nehisi Coates, the Movement for Black Lives, and
others.[22] So often the claim for reparations is lost in the cul-de-
sac of debates about intergenerational responsibility, intervening
causation, exculpatory pleading of white innocence, and complex
actuarial calculations. Yet, the stories of the Black families on the
Sea Islands and Davis Bend and the manner in which enslaved
peoples' abjection was denied adequate repair sidesteps these dead-
end diversions and invigorates the moral potency of the demand for
reparations. The call for reparations is premised on the notion that
the past has enduring moral relevance today, and that we should
face and know that past. This book offers us the opportunity to face
the past and recognize the moral claims it makes on us today.

Repair seeks to link the fragile history of land ownership by formerly enslaved people at the end of the Civil War with calls today
for racial repair to be mobilized by redistributing land ownership

to Black people. The turn to land trusts and creative financing of collective Black property ownership in the contemporary context echoes experiments in land redistribution to Black people in the Sea Islands and Davis Bend in the 1860s, experiments that were undermined by white supremacists seeking to lock formerly enslaved people into a permanently inferior status of being freed, not free. This history renders today's call for repair through the use of third-sector housing mechanisms—private non-market alternatives to publicly owned housing projects—more powerful, and more morally compelling.

The last chapter of the book takes up what reparations might look like today. Not direct payments to individuals who can prove a lineal blood relation to an enslaved person, but rather a collective reckoning with the badge of inferiority associated with Blackness and the unearned endowment enjoyed by white people, or persons "who think they are white," to borrow from James Baldwin.[23] Reinvestment in Black communities through community land trusts, limited-equity housing cooperatives, zero-equity co-operatives, mutual housing associations, and deed restricted housing—sometimes referred to as "third-sector housing"—has emerged as a transformative form of repair of Black communities that transfers resources and property into those communities and empowers them.[24] How, then, to pay for investment in this kind of collective repair? I propose a tax on the intergenerational transfer of wealth, from the "greatest generation" to the "baby boomers." Real estate investment has been the great wealth-generating machine of my parents' generation, yet African Americans have been systematically locked out of this unique opportunity to buy in, sit tight, and get rich. The lucky few of my generation who stand, in the next twenty years, to benefit from a lottery-like windfall, are burdened—and should *feel* burdened—by an obligation to disgorge what is truly an unjust enrichment made possible by the failure of the nineteenth-century upper-class actors to deliver meaningful justice to millions of people when slavery was disestablished in this country.

For a group of people who suffered the atrocity of being property, remedy of that outrage makes most sense with property. As I argue at the end of the book, in important ways property is like no other kind of right, it is the central right on which all others rest.[25] Socially, politically, and legally property should be understood as a keystone right. Property can be a source of both wealth creation and identity creation. Owning property and having those rights of ownership respected by others is a necessary predicate to freedom and citizenship. As this book reveals through the stories of failed emancipation in the Sea Islands and Davis Bend, the federal government had in place a plan, which was ultimately unsuccessful, to provide land and tools to freed people explicitly as a form of reparation for slavery. That plan reflected the freed people's idea of what it meant to be free: living autonomous lives independent of white people. The land and other resources that freed people owned were stolen from them and given to former slaveowners or sold to white land sharks from the North. Freed people were almost categorically denied the right to own property and were granted contract rights as an inferior substitute. The disappointment of partial emancipation suffered by Black people in this country rests, to a significant degree, upon the failure of the Johnson administration to figure property ownership at the core of what freed people were owed as repair for their enslavement and to recognize their identity as persons not property. Given this history, *Repair* shows how the story of reparations for slavery is not over. The outstanding promissory note still held by Black people in this country can be paid off today and the last chapter of the book offers steps to begin the process.

CHAPTER 1

Land and the Question of Reparative Justice in the Sea Islands

"They had been the only cultivators, their labor had given it all its value, the elements of its fertility were the sweat & blood of the negro so long poured out upon it, that it might be taken as composed of his own substance. The whole of it was under a foreclosed mortgage for generations of unpaid wages."

—**Rufus Saxton**, March 15, 1865[1]

The Port Royal Experiment

THE LARGEST ATTACK fleet ever to sail under the US flag was amassed to undertake the capture of Port Royal, South Carolina in November 1861. The choice was obvious given its strategic location midway between Savannah and Charleston, with easy inland passage to both cities, and its deep and well protected harbor.

It would make a key coal depot for US naval ships fighting in the Atlantic. The Sea Islands were comprised of six large islands—Edisto, St. Helena, Lady's, Port Royal, Hilton Head, and Paris—and a number of smaller islands. St. Helena Island was the largest and most populated island, measuring fifteen miles long and seven miles wide and containing fifty plantations and approximately three thousand Black people when the US fleet arrived in 1861. Beaufort, located on Port Royal Island, was the largest town, having been settled by Europeans from Scotland in 1682, then the Spanish, and then later the British. Beaufort was most likely named after Henry, Duke of Beaufort, one of the lord proprietors while Carolina was a province of Great Britain.[2] Its first Episcopal Church was built in 1720. The library was founded in 1802, and by the time the Northern troops arrived, it had about 3,500 volumes. Besides the strategic military value of Port Royal, the rich cotton and rice fields on and adjacent to the Islands could be harvested to finance the Northern war efforts. Cotton prices in 1861 were better than many planters had ever dreamed, thus floating very opulent lives for the planters and their families of the Sea Islands.[3]

Late in the afternoon on Sunday, November 4, 1861, Admiral Samuel F. DuPont's fleet arrived at Port Royal with General Thomas W. Sherman's troops aboard the Navy's vessels ready for a ground invasion. They were met with an enthusiastic defense from the white locals, the St. Helena Riflemen, aided by over a thousand reinforcements from the German Artillery from Charleston, the Charleston Artillery Battalion, the South Carolina Infantry, and the South Carolina Volunteers. Almost immediately it was obvious that the Islanders were outgunned and outmanned, and by Wednesday nearly all of the local white men had packed their wives, children, and favorite "servants" into boats and rowed to the mainland.[4] Many of these families had lived at Port Royal for as long as 140 years, and most of them left reluctantly. More than a few tried unsuccessfully to get the people they owned to leave with them, telling them that the Yankees would either kill them or sell them to Cuba.[5] When cajoling failed, friends and relatives had to physically remove a prominent planter, Captain William O. Fripp.[6] He "exhorted his Negroes to watch out for themselves and to obey the white strangers who would soon be telling them what to do . . . Thomas B. Chaplin told Robert, Isaac, and Jack to take care of the plantation in his absence, until normal life could resume."[7] One Black man later explained to Charlotte Forten, a Black missionary from Philadelphia, why he chose to stay on the island: His master told him that the Yankees would shoot him. "Berry well sur," he replied, "if I go wid you I be good as dead, so if I got to dead, I might's well dead here as anywhere. So, I'll stay and wait for the Yankees."[8] Many Black people who remained reported that as white planters fled the islands they turned to shoot "negroes who refused to accompany them into the woods." The flag officer of the invading Union Naval fleet reported that "the negroes are wild with joy and revenge. They have been shot down, they say, like dogs, because they would not go off with their masters."[9] Another commander of a Union vessel encountered three Black men in the St. Helena Sound who told him "the rebels, three hundred strong were at Mrs. March's plantation killing all the negroes."[10] No sooner had the white planters left, than the "loyal" Black people set about to "take care of things until normal life resumed," but not exactly in ways their owners had expected. They moved into their former masters' grand homes, smoked their cigars, and tried out the billiard tables. They wrapped their bodies and rebuilt their homes in what remained of the slave-owners' lives: "Clothes were the first items taken, and when the clothes gave out, women made dresses out of lace curtains and men cut suits from 'gaudy carpeting just torn up from the floor.' The very floors were ripped up, recut, and laid down in the Negro cabins."[11] Barnard K. Lee, Jr., one of the first white civilians to arrive at Port Royal who came down from Boston in November of 1861 to work as a plantation superintendent described the same scene: "they had taken up their master's old carpets from the floor and were clothed in it, presenting a grotesque appearance."[12]

When General Sherman landed on Hilton Head Island on

November 8, he immediately issued a proclamation, addressed not to the freed people he found there, but to the absent population of white planters who had fled. To this phantom audience he announced: "Citizens of South Carolina, the civilized world stands appalled at the course you are pursuing; appalled at the crime you are committing against your mother—the best, most enlightened, and heretofore most prosperous of nations."[13] While there were no "Citizens of South Carolina" to receive this proclamation, there were approximately 10,000 Black people living on the islands on 189 plantations. They were neither free nor enslaved, and they presented both a burden and an opportunity to the Northern military officials who occupied the Sea Islands.[14] As the Northern whites would later describe it, the Black people they found were destitute, degraded, illiterate, child-like, uncivilized, and clothed in carpets. The Black population of Port Royal was liberated by Northern troops into what Giorgio Agamben would call "a bare life."[15] They occupied a middle ground between slave and citizen—that of contraband—property liable to being confiscated from the enemy during time of war.[16] Of course, this dubious status was concocted to placate the sensitivities of abolitionists and more conservative supporters of the Northern war effort. As one federal official put it: "The venerable gentleman who wears gold spectacles and reads a conservative daily, prefers confiscation to emancipation. He is reluctant to have slaves declared 'freemen,' but has no objection to their being declared 'contrabands.'"[17] This political/legal status prohibited their re-enslavement, but it was unclear what it enabled and to what their new status and identity entitled them. What sorts of demands could they make on the authorities who now asserted control over them? To whom could they appeal if they felt their treatment was unjust? Were they entitled to be treated justly? Against what norm would these claims to justice be measured? Surely not the Constitution, as they were neither citizens nor persons, and the Constitution did not recognize "things" or "contraband" as rights-holders. Neither the federal authorities nor the Northern missionaries who followed on their heels had any ready answers to these difficult questions.

Here as elsewhere, what it meant to be freed yet not free, was being made up on the fly by people with complex and demanding interests that did not necessarily coincide with the interests of the Black people of the Sea Islands. The military was interested in the profits that could be generated from the agricultural work the freed people could undertake—otherwise they wanted them out of the way. Northern missionaries were determined to save the souls and educate the minds of these people who had been subjected to a life of barbarism, and Northern land speculators were soon to arrive eager to turn a profit through the use of a cheap source of labor. What assurance did the freed people have that their treatment by a new set of white men would be any better than what they had suffered in slavery? None. Thus, began the experiment in freed-dom at Port Royal.

Contraband, Fortress Monroe, Library of Congress, 1861

Management and control of abandoned property, including the cotton plantations and the refugees who had worked them, was the responsibility of the Department of the Treasury, headed by Secretary Salmon P. Chase. He held among the strongest antislavery views of anyone in Lincoln's cabinet.[18] Chase saw the seizure of the Sea Islands as a tremendous opportunity to demonstrate the value and productivity of freed Black labor. Yet as winter set in, and the former slaves faced near starvation and the cold without adequate clothing, Chase had to deal with a desperate situation. These problems were compounded by the fact that some freed people believed (not unreasonably) that freedom meant that they no longer had to work. Thus, the cotton fields, a potential source of significant income to the federal government, laid untended. In Chase's view these fields could not remain ignored past mid-February, as the federal government was counting on the income from the cotton produced there to finance the costs of feeding and providing for the more than 10,000 Black men, women, and children who either remained on the islands or fled there once the word of Union occupation spread to the plantations on the mainland.

As a first step, in December, Chase dispatched chief resident cotton agent William H. Reynolds to Port Royal to take custody of the harvested cotton, to oversee the employment of Black people to harvest what remained in the fields, and to pay them for their work in rations and clothing. Reynolds seemed to Chase to be the right man for the job, because he had ample experience in the cotton business in Rhode Island. Shortly thereafter, Chase wired Edward L. Pierce to enlist him to oversee the entire Port Royal refugee project and to make recommendations about the ongoing management of cotton production. Pierce, a young attorney in Boston who had worked in Chase's Cincinnati law office, and later as his secretary in Washington, held strong antislavery views and, unlike most Northerners, he had some experience with freed people, having overseen their care at Fort Monroe, Virginia, when he was a private in the Third Massachusetts Regiment. He agreed to visit Port Royal and to provisionally oversee the freed population there. Like Chase, he viewed the experiment at Port Royal as vital to the antislavery cause, for neither of them believed that this population would be returned to slavery.[19] Instead, they could concentrate all their efforts on showing the benefits and utility of freed labor and "the success of a productive colony that would serve as a womb for the emancipation at large."[20] "Port Royal, in Chase's eyes, would become the scene of a social experiment of importance to the entire South."[21]

One signal of Pierce's commitment to the humanity of the Black people at Port Royal was that here, unlike at Fort Monroe, he declined to refer to the formerly enslaved people as "contrabands," instead insisting on using the term "freedmen."[22] Notwithstanding the respect conferred on the freed people by Pierce, it never occurred to him or to Chase that the freed Black population of Port Royal should be emancipated into a condition of self-governance in which they would build lives free from white oversight. Rather, Pierce shared the view held by even the most enlightened white actors of the day: the freed people needed the moral and practical guidance that white people could give them, and this entailed strict discipline and control from whites. General Sherman put it thus in February 1862:

> The helpless condition of the blacks inhabiting the vast area in the occupation of the forces of this command, calls for immediate action on the part of a highly favored and philanthropic people . . . Hordes of totally uneducated, ignorant, and improvident blacks have been abandoned by their constitutional guardians . . . a suitable system of culture and instruction must be combined with one providing for their physical wants. In the meanwhile, . . . the service of competent instructors will be received whose duties will consist in teaching them, both young and old, the rudiments of civilization and Christianity.[23]

Word got out quickly to Northern entrepreneurs that Port Royal's abandoned plantations might offer a fantastic investment opportunity. As early as mid-December, Chase began to get inquiries from investors in New Jersey and Vermont suggesting that they be allowed to lease Sea Island plantations and oversee the continuation of cotton production using paid Black labor.[24] Reynolds, the cotton man from Rhode Island, liked the idea, suggesting "whether it would not be well to consider the plan of leasing Plantations in our possession to loyal citazens [sic] at a fair rate, under proper restrictions, the Negroes to be paid a fair compensation for their services."[25] Pierce, having gotten wind of these proposals, strongly counseled Chase against them. He felt it unwise to turn the project over to "doubtful men" who would exploit the beleaguered Black people of Port Royal in order to gain "a speedy fortune." Pierce cautioned:

> No man, not even the best of the guardians of these people, should be put in a position where there would be such a conflict between his humanity and his self-interest—his desire, on the one hand, to benefit the laborer, and on the other, the too often stronger desire to reap a large revenue, perhaps to restore broken fortunes in a year or two. Such a system is beset with many of the worst vices of the slave system with one advantage in favor of the latter, that it is in the interest of the planter to look to permanent results. Let the History of British East India, and of all communities where a superior race has attempted to build up speedy fortunes on the labor of an inferior race occupying another region be remembered, and no just man will listen to the proposition of leasing, fraught as it is with such dangerous consequences.[26]

In these early observations Pierce was astutely prescient, anticipating the wrong turn that this project would later take. At this early juncture, however, Pierce was able to convince Chase that the Port Royal experiment required the enlistment of philanthropic, rather than capitalistic, white enterprise. The challenge, for him, was recognizing the difference.

Realizing that an enormous project lay well beyond the capacities of a federal government with its hands full fighting the war, Sherman wrote the War Department in January 1862 asking "that suitable instructors be sent to the Negroes, to teach them all the necessary rudiments of civilization, and . . . that agents properly qualified, be employed and sent here to take charge of the plantations and superintend the work of the Blacks until they be sufficiently enlightened to think and provide for themselves."[27] Key to Sherman's, Chase's, and Pierce's plans for Port Royal was an ad hoc collaboration with Northern missionaries who would be engaged as teachers and moral guides for the freed people on their path from enslavement to citizenship. Once he accepted Chase's invitation to join the Port Royal experiment, Pierce turned not to capitalists in Vermont and New Jersey who had already expressed an interest in running the Port Royal cotton plantations, but to antislavery religious leaders in Boston, New York, and Philadelphia. He promptly arranged meetings in the private homes of the members of the Boston Educational Commission and the National Freedmen's Relief Association in New York, seeking volunteers to head south with him as teachers and superintendents of cotton production.[28] Pierce wrote Chase in early March of 1862:

> To both the Boston and New York Committees,
> I have said that persons accepted must have in the first place profound humanity—a belief that the negro is a human being and capable of elevation and freedom . . . These qualities being found, a knowledge of cotton culture was not expected and a knowledge of farming not required, though the last would be of value; what was most needed was the moral power of the presence of a white man on the plantations to guide and direct, and the laborers themselves understanding their work better than the master or overseer generally did.[29]

He sought their aid in order to teach the "fundamental lessons of civilization, voluntary industry, self-reliance, frugality, forethought, honesty and truthfulness, cleanliness, and order. With these will be combined intellectual, moral and religious instruction."[30] Pierce selected forty-eight men and twelve women for the journey. "You go to freedmen to elevate, to purify, to fit them for the duties of American citizens," Pierce told the new recruits.[31]

The Port Royal Experiment was truly underway when Pierce and his group of missionary recruits from Boston, New York, and Philadelphia set sail for the Sea Islands at 11:00 a.m. on Monday, March 3, 1862. Known in the less-friendly Northern press as the "Gideonites," the group arrived four days later, on Friday, March 7, in the early afternoon—having weathered very windy and rough seas as they approached their destination.[32] Seventeen more recruits from New York sailed for Port Royal on March 19.[33] Given that President Lincoln was unwilling to commit any financial resources to the Port Royal project, the missionary societies provided not only personnel but also financial aid to pay the meager living expenses of recruits who headed south. At the start of the mission, the superintendents from Boston received a stipend of between thirty and fifty dollars per month, while members of the New York contingent were paid between five and twenty-five dollars per month. When Pierce learned of this discrepancy, he wrote to his agent in New York that they weren't paying their people enough and that they should send fewer, or better-paid, men.[34] The men and women who undertook this work arrived to perform two principal tasks: the men largely acted as overseers of the agricultural work to be done by the freedmen, and the women served as teachers primarily of the freed children. The practical demands of the war effort mandated that the 189 plantations at Port Royal continue to produce both cotton and other edible crops to finance the war,[35] while more symbolic interests motivated a desire to use the Black people of the Sea Island as an example for the antislavery cause. The Northern actors in this experiment shared one goal in this enterprise: to demonstrate to the world that Black people would work without the lash, and indeed, "to prove that free labor could grow more cotton more cheaply than slave labor."[36] Careful stewardship of the Black people on the islands was key to accomplishing this task. Indeed, Pierce reported that the superintendents chosen to oversee the freedmen should be given authority "to enforce a paternal discipline."[37] Of course, no one in this project seemed concerned that the Northern missionaries enlisted to act as superintendents of cotton production knew almost nothing about how to raise cotton, while their Black charges were experts in doing so,[38] nor were they well suited for the hot, mosquito-ridden climate they would encounter. In fact, four of the missionaries died in the first summer.[39]

Notwithstanding the flaws that lay at the heart of the enterprise, the most pressing problem to the Northern overseers was keeping the land in cotton production. The climate and soil of the Sea Islands made it one of the few places in the United States where long-staple

Plantation view at Port Royal, South Carolina, 1862.

cotton could be grown. Regular, or short-staple, cotton possessed fibers of five-eighths to one inch in length when combed, whereas the Sea Islands long-staple cotton measured one and a half to two inches long and was of strength far superior to short-staple cotton. Due to its length and strength, long-staple cotton was used for the warp or longitudinal threads in many high-end woven fabrics coveted by wealthy Europeans, thus gaining prices at least double that of short-staple cotton on the markets in New York. None of the Sea Islands cotton made its way to New England mills, as all of it was shipped overseas, largely to England.[40]

Pierce and other treasury agents were given the responsibility to make sure that the cotton crop was not interrupted. Pierce had suggested to his boss, Secretary Chase, that the plantation hands be paid $0.40 cents per day or $12.00 per month,[41] but Chase thought this price too high. In January, General Sherman had issued an order that mechanics be paid between $8 and $12 per month, and that other laborers receive between $4 and $8 per month; three months later government wages were set at $9 to $12 per month for Mechanics and Drivers of Gangs, $6 per month for First-class laborers (healthy adult males doing field work), and $4 per month for Second-class laborers (healthy adult females doing field work). All wages included one food ration daily.[42]

Displaying what would be routine unfamiliarity with the sentiments of their charges, neither Pierce nor his missionary friends had expected Black resistance to working the cotton crop at a wage. The superintendents were instructed not to resort to the lash or other violent means of punishment that had been frequently used by white planters. Nevertheless, other coercive means were used by the Northern overseers to discipline noncompliant workers: "the delinquent, if a male, is sometimes made to stand on a barrel, or, if a woman, is put in a dark room . . . such discipline proved successful."[43]

Oblivious to the culture of work among enslaved people prior to emancipation that ranked "house slaves" well above "field slaves," Northern managers of freed Black labor were taken aback when the

former house slaves were particularly set against doing what had previously been the work of field slaves.[44] What is more, before the Northern superintendents took over the supervision of freedmen's labor, the
freed people had begun to plant corn for their own consumption on
land they had claimed for themselves, and were resistant to returning
to the cotton fields under white supervision, "regarding it as a badge
of servitude."[45] They were generally ill-disposed to planting cash crops
like cotton, preferring instead to put the land to use to feed themselves
as part of a longer-term plan toward independence from white people.
In his second report to Secretary Chase in June of 1862, Pierce wrote:

> The negroes had commenced putting corn and potatoes into
> their own patches, and in some cases had begun to prepare a
> field of corn for the plantation. No land had been prepared for
> cotton, and the negroes were strongly indisposed to its cul-
> ture. They were willing to raise corn, because it was necessary
> for food, but they saw no such necessity for cotton, and dis-
> trusted promises of payment for cultivating it. It had enriched
> the masters, but had not fed them.[46]

So great was the ex-slaves' hatred of cotton that among the first
things they did when their former masters fled was destroy many
cotton gins, with the aim of never "planting cotton for white folks
again."[47] "No more driver, no more cotton, nor lickin," freed people
were known to declare.[48] Getting them to plant cotton was made no
easier by the fact that the federal government lacked the funds to make
good on the meager wages Pierce had promised. As early as March
1862, superintendents complained to Pierce that they were having
trouble getting their hands to work without paying them.[49] During
this period, Pierce repeatedly wrote to the cotton agent in New York
pleading for funds to pay the Port Royal laborers for bringing in the
previous year's crop. In his reports to Chase he frequently voiced frus-
tration at the prospect of gaining the trust of the freedmen or their
commitment to the notion of wage labor since the government was so

delinquent in paying promised wages. When you work for a wage but never get paid, it's hard to distinguish free from enslaved labor. Freedmen often complained that their rations and clothing allotments had been much better before their white masters had fled.[50] Meanwhile, their clueless overseers from the North were earning up to ten times as much as they were, and they were having no trouble getting paid by their Northern sponsors. From the freed people's perspective, freedom wasn't getting off to a very good start.

⚬

In April 1862, when responsibility for overseeing Confederate abandoned lands passed from the Treasury to the War Department,

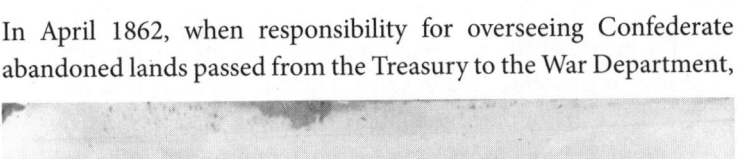

Large group of enslaved people, standing in front of buildings on Smith's plantation, Beaufort, South Carolina, 1862.

Brigadier-General Rufus Saxton assumed the governorship of the Sea Islands.[51] Saxton, Sherman, Chase, and Pierce shared the view that an essential part of their mission was the reallocation of confiscated land to the freed people so that they could till for themselves. A people who have land "will never be nomads or vagabonds,"[52] wrote Pierce in the *Atlantic Monthly*. In February 1862, well before he became Governor of the Islands, Saxton observed, "it would be well to parcel out the fertile lands of these islands among the different families in lots large enough for their subsistence."[53] Chase echoed this view in his own correspondence.[54]

Port Royal Island, S.C. enslaved people preparing cotton for the gin on Smith's plantation. Port Royal, South Carolina, 1862.

Upon assuming control of Port Royal, Saxton continued a land allocation plan originally recommended by Pierce: two acres of land were assigned to each working hand, plus an additional five-sixteenths of an acre for each child. In exchange for working the government's cotton fields Black workers were permitted to raise corn and potatoes sufficient for their own use. In addition, they were required to cultivate enough food supplies for the superintendents, disabled, and elderly members of the community. The government supplied the implements and seeds and paid twenty-five cents for a day's work under a task system.[55] Under the task system workers were given a task to complete within one day, and once they were finished they could have the time to themselves. The other way labor was organized on plantations was the gang system in which groups of workers labored until their superiors told them that they were done. Not surprisingly, formerly enslaved workers preferred the "task system."

Pierce reported that notwithstanding their previous antipathy towards cotton, after some time they willingly took it up. "[T]he culture of the cotton is voluntary," he wrote in the *Atlantic Monthly*.[56] But Pierce failed to mention that this "voluntary" compliance was bought at the price of a punitive tax of two dollars per month if they refused to plant cotton.[57] Thus, the new land settlement policy kept Black workers tied to wage labor, working on the island's cotton plantations—exactly what the Northern administrators wanted.[58]

Renting the confiscated lands to freed people under these conditions was merely a temporary solution to get through the 1862–1863 planting season. For Saxton and Pierce, the permanent transfer of land to freed people was the longer-term goal. A range of plans were being developed, at Port Royal and in Washington, for the allocation of the land confiscated from Confederate loyalists. The Confiscation Act of 1862 imposed a property tax in "insurrectionary districts" to raise revenue for the war and authorized the confiscation of land when taxes were not paid. Of course, Congress knew that none of these taxes would be paid and that this measure stood on shaky constitutional ground as a way of confiscating Confederate land.[59]

Despite the murky legal grounds on which Confederate property was seized by the federal government, under the new law almost 77,000 acres of land confiscated for unpaid taxes were to be sold in lots not exceeding thirty-two acres to "loyal citizens".[60] The first auction of land seized at Port Royal was scheduled for February 11, 1863, but given the prices that thirty-two acre lots were likely to gain in an open auction, Saxton and others worried that the freedmen would be practically prohibited from purchasing any land of their own, and that Northern white speculators would buy up all the land. Under this scenario, the thirty-two-acre plots would concretize, in perpetuity, an economy made up of large, white-owned plantations that would continue to exploit Black labor. Saxton urgently wrote Secretary of War Edwin Stanton in December of 1862, "I regard this law as eminently wise and just; but still it makes no provision for the negroes, who have been for so many years regarded as a portion of the livestock for the plantation, that it is not easy to separate them entirely from its future." He continued: "The prospect now is that all the lands on these sea islands will be bought up by speculators; and in that event, these helpless people may be placed more or less at the mercy of men devoid of principle, and their future well being jeopardized, thus defeating in a great measure the benevolent intentions of the Government towards them."[61]

The view that the land auctions would be a good way to allocate land to the freed people as a kind of reparation for enslavement was widely held, even by some Northern missionaries: "The announcement of the intended sale of 24,000 acres in large lots was received with great dissatisfaction by the friends of the freedmen, an informal group of people who conceived of themselves as helping the freedmen. Many thought that the Blacks had an exclusive claim to these lands which had so long been drenched with their sweat and blood, and nearly all saw with alarm the threatened revival of the old system of large proprietorships."[62] This view was echoed by Mr. R.

Tomlinson, Esq., who had been sent from Philadelphia to Port Royal as a teacher in the summer of 1862. When he returned to Philadelphia, he told his peers: "if there is any class of people in the country who have priority of claim to the confiscated lands of the South, it certainly is that class who have by years of suffering and unrequited toil given to those lands any value they may now possess."[63]

Out of concern that the freed people would be outbid by white speculators, Saxton, Stanton, Chase, and others desperately tried to hold off the auctions through Congressional action or otherwise.[64] They fought hard to be sure that the freed people would be granted the right to bid first, and at below market prices, on the confiscated lands of the Sea Islands when they were auctioned or allotted. "Their attachment to place is a marked trait in the negro character, and in my humble opinion the enforcement of a law of this kind would be the means of establishing them in permanent homes, would secure the careful cultivation of the lands allotted to them, and consequently their own independence; and in addition would furnish a large supply of willing laborers, who could be hired to cultivate the purchased lands," wrote Saxton in 1864.[65] In his view, the freed people had a right to land as reparation for enslavement and allocating land to them was necessary to adequately address their current state of impoverishment. Indeed, he viewed the freed people as holding an equitable mortgage on the land, secured by their past unpaid wages, sweat, blood, and lost lives. According to Saxton, "They had been the only cultivators, their labor had given it all its value, the elements of its fertility were the sweat & blood of the negro so long poured out upon it, that it might be taken as composed of his own substance. The whole of it was under a foreclosed mortgage for generations of unpaid wages."[66]

Saxton was joined in his sentiments by Abram Smith, one of the three tax commissioners who had been sent by Washington to inventory the land in arrears and administer the land auctions. Smith had been a tax attorney in Wisconsin and had had a hand in drafting the 1862 Direct Tax Act. Smith's view was that Black people on the

Sea Islands "did not want to go away; they were attached to their homes and wanted to stay [t]here provided they could be free and protected. But in order to get that encouragement and hope, they must have the family organized, and a homestead must be given them—they <u>must</u> <u>have</u> <u>land</u>, <u>land</u>. A mere military title furnish [sic] no security, no permanence."[67] Saxton and Smith were concerned that under the president's plan the size of the lots left in the general auction would place them well beyond the means of even the most enterprising freedmen.[68] The result of such a land allocation scheme would be "to fix the people for a long time in the condition of a peasantry only a little higher than chattelism, and that, too, when so many of them had proved their fitness to be owners of the soil, and some their competence to manage large estates."[69]

In January, Abram Smith traveled to Washington and met with Secretary Chase, and several members of Congress, all of whom, he reported, agreed with his concern about the dangers of the lands falling into the hands of white speculators. They had Smith draft an amendment to the Direct Tax Act that would assure that the government could reserve enough lands for all of the Sea Islands' freedmen. The amendment became law on February 6, 1863.[70] As a matter of policy and fairness, a better course of action may have been for the federal government to satisfy the debt they owed to most of the freed people of the Sea Islands in the form of back wages. The cruel twist of this situation lay in the fact that the federal government seized this land based on a dubious tax debt owned by the Confederate plantation owners, yet the government itself was a debtor to the newly freed people who lived and worked on that land and had not been paid the wages to which they were entitled. An easier transaction, and a more just one, would have been for the government to satisfy the debt owed to the freed people by paying them in land, rather than staging a series of complicated auctions at which the Black people of the Sea Islands had to bid against white Northern speculators.

But that wasn't to happen. Instead, when the land auction was held in March, the tax commissioners held back 40,000 acres on St. Helena Parish for ongoing government use and the government bought another 20,000 acres in open bidding, leaving approximately 20,000 acres (forty-five plantations) for private purchase at the auction. Saxton acknowledged that the theory behind the selection of which lands would be sold, which would be reserved, and the size of lots that were auctioned "was to alternate the plantations sold to private individuals with those reserved by Government for the negroes; thus by a judicious location of houses a supply of labor will always be at hand which can be hired at reasonable wages to cultivate the land."[71]

The land bought by private parties ended up selling for an average price of one dollar per acre.[72] Of the 20,000 acres that were sold in open bidding and ended up in private hands at the March 1863 auction, 2,595 acres were bought by freed men and women. The freed people would have been able to buy significantly more land had they had their full wages in their pockets when the bidding started. Nevertheless, they engaged in smart bidding strategies that optimized their ability to purchase land notwithstanding their comparative disadvantage relative to white men from Boston and other points North who showed up with bags of cash. Some freed people pooled their resources and bought land collectively, others bought land individually. By and large they had built up savings from the proceeds from selling pigs, chickens, and eggs, and by saving the small amount of wages they had been paid by the government.[73] Edward Pierce wrote of Harry, his former guide, who "bought at the recent tax-sales a small farm of three hundred and thirteen acres for three hundred and five dollars."[74] In fact, what had happened was much more complicated. Harry McMillan was about forty years old, had been born in Georgia, but had been sold to Abraham Eustis, a Port Royal planter, when he was a small boy and had been enslaved by the Eustis family until federal occupation and his emancipation. He had served as Pierce's "faithful guide attendant, who had done for me more service than any white man could render."[75] He had saved some money and was preparing to bid on a plantation called The Inlet on Lady's Island, a plot that he wanted very much. Edward Philbrick, one of the men brought down by Pierce from Boston to run cotton production on the Coffin Point plantation, the largest plantation in the Sea Islands, heard of Harry's intentions and counseled him against it. Warning him of the risk involved in owning and running a plantation, Philbrick suggested that he, Philbrick, buy the plantation and then Harry work it for wages, while the profits from the crop would be Philbrick's. Harry, unsure of the wisdom of this advice, consulted Laura Towne, one of the missionary teachers on the Island, and Captain E. W. Hooper, an aid to General Saxton for whom Harry worked as servant. Both Towne and Hooper were furious about Philbrick's advice. Hooper was so angry that he bid on and bought the plot in Harry's name for about $300. Harry did not have the full purchase price, but Hooper lent it to him along with some extra cash to buy tools and equipment. Harry worked the land with his wife Celia, two daughters aged sixteen and seventeen, and three hired hands. Pierce went to see Harry in April of 1862 and reported that he was plowing the fields with a twenty-five-year-old blind horse, led by a rope, was living in the home of the former overseer and "delights, though not boastingly, in his position as a landed proprietor."[76] Saxton noted his success two years later: "Harry took the acres into his own hands, working diligently and hiring the necessary assistance & managed his affairs with so much shrewdness, judgement & success, that with the avails of his cotton crop alone he paid the price of his land, $305, the current expenses of the farm & of his family, increased his farm stock, & found himself in possession of a clear cash capital of nearly $500, & a large store of corn, potatoes, etc. for future operations."[77]

In a manner similar to Captain Hooper assisting Harry McMillan's land purchase, Reverend Solomon Peck, a sixty-year-old Baptist minister from Massachusetts, bought the eight-hundred-acre Edgerly plantation for $710 for the "people of Edgerly and the adjoining Red House plantation."

They had raised $500 of their own money and he advanced the

United States of America,

TAX SALE CERTIFICATE, NO. *43.*

This is to certify, That at a sale of lands for unpaid taxes, under and by virtue of an act entitled "An act for the collection of direct taxes in insurrectionary districts within the United States, and for other purposes," held pursuant to notice at *Beaufort*, in the District of *Beaufort*, in the State of South Carolina, on the *tenth* day of *March*, A. D. 186*3*, the tract or parcel of land hereinafter described, situate in the *District* of *Beaufort*, and State aforesaid, and described as follows, to wit: *The tract of land on Port Royal Island known as "Edgerly". Bounded Northerly by Red House, Southerly by The John G. Chaplin Place, Easterly by Beaufort River, Westerly by The John G. Chaplin Place and by The Rice land tract. Containing Eight hundred acres more or less.*

was sold and struck off to *Solomon Peck*, for the sum of *Seven hundred and ten* dollars and —— cents, he being the highest bidder, and that being the highest sum bidden for the same; the receipt of which said sum in full is hereby acknowledged and confessed.

Given under our hands, at *Beaufort S.C.*, this *eleventh* day of *March*, A. D. 186*3*.

A. D. Smith
W. C. Wording   } Commissioners.
Wm Henry Brisbane

rest, which they repaid as soon as they received their back wages from the government. They surveyed the land, divided it up into plots for each of the thirteen or fourteen families who formed the buying cooperative, and began to build homes and till the land. The first year they planted melons, corn, and rice and produced more than 1,200 pounds of high-quality ginned cotton. To the astonishment of Northern observers, they did all this without a white superintendent or overseer, instead relying only on one of their own men, Francis, to work as foreman to oversee the common land.[78]

This arrangement in collective land purchase and living was typical of the freed people who purchased land. Relatives or households related as kin would buy land collectively, divide it up so that each household would have its own plot on which they would build a home and plant provision crops, and then keep the pastures and woodlands as commons for grazing, firewood and other collective needs. Records reflecting government-run sales of abandoned property during this period show that freed men and women were regular purchasers of cows, mules, carts, wheels, buggies, and other implements necessary for successful farming. On the Fripp plantation, for instance, Plenty bought a pair of wheels for $2, and Cupid bought a mule for $16. On the Sam's Point plantation, both Mingo and Carolina bought cows for $12. As with the purchase of the land, it was not uncommon for freed people to buy farm implements collectively. The register of sales of the chattel from the James Fripp plantation indicates that the "people on the place" bought one whipper and one corn sheller for $5.75. Yet, with these sales, just as with the land sales, Edward Philbrick ended up buying almost everything he could get his hands on. On Coffin's Island he bought almost 90 percent of the goods up for sale.[79]

Five generations on Smith's plantation, Beaufort, South Carolina, 1862.

Recall that the Confiscation Act permitted the sale of land at auction to "loyal citizens." Thus, for the purposes of these sales, freed people were considered citizens which is a remarkable, and historically underappreciated, fact. Indeed, their successful participation in the first Port Royal land auction should be understood as the first "acts of citizenship" by freed people.

Philbrick, who professed to have the former slaves' interests in mind, bought over 7,000 acres comprising eleven plantations at the auction and leased two more plantations from the government. He purchased these properties "on behalf of a joint-stock-company in Boston formed for the purpose."[80]

NO.	NAME.	PLACE SITUATE.	ACRES.	DATE OF SALE.	PAGE.
5	Pritchard E.	Beaufort		Feby 28	5.
6	Philbrick E. S.	"	500	March 9	6
7	Philbrick E. S.	"	100	" 9	7
8	Philbrick E. S.	"	147	" 9	8
11	Philbrick E. S.	"	900	" 9	11
12	Philbrick E. S.	"	750	" 9	12
13	Philbrick E. S.	"	750	" 9	13
14	Philbrick E. S.	"	500	" 9	14
19	Philbrick E. S.	"	300	" 9	19
20	Philbrick E. S.	"	1425	" 10	20
21	Philbrick E. S.	"	300	" 10	21
28	Philbrick E. S.	"	255	" 10	28
43	Peck Solomon	"	800	" 11	43

In so doing, he became the largest landowner at Port Royal and controlled the labor of nearly a thousand freed people. While this promise was later denied by Philbrick, the freed people of Coffin Island swore that before Philbrick bought these large tracts he pledged to sell the land back to them at one dollar an acre.[81] His true, more white-supremacist, motives were revealed in his correspondence back to his investors in Boston:

Whether this course of granting special privileges to negroes, to the exclusion of whites, is best for the future of the community, remains to be proved. If the freed negro is ever to become civilized in any degree, or elevated above his present ignorant and degraded condition, it must be through his own industry, led on by the example and encouraged by the capital and superior energy and enterprise of the whites. It can hardly be doubted that the industry of our own race is the most efficient agent in its advance in civilization during the past thousand years; and even the Anglo-Saxon race was never made an industrious race except through the stern hand of necessity.[82]

At this point, it was widely understood that a significant portion of the 60,000 acres of land reserved by the government was designated to be farmed by freed people. There was some discussion about whether it was in the best interests of the freed people to have them farm as tenants on government-owned land, as laborers on land run by private white superintendents, or as outright owners of the land themselves. Saxton believed strongly in the third strategy and did much to raise those expectations in the Black residents at Port Royal.[83] "Most of the places reserved were selected for the purpose of selling land to the negroes next year, after the crop is in."[84] Meanwhile the current year's crop had to be planted and tilled under the labor regulations promulgated by General Saxton.

In the fall of 1863, plans began for the auctioning of the remaining land in the possession of the government at Port Royal. Much debate and strategizing surrounded the terms under which the land would be made available. In September 1863, President Lincoln issued orders to the tax commissioners in South Carolina that the auction take place in early 1864 in lots no greater than 320 acres, and he included a special provision reserving a large block of land to be sold in lots up to twenty acres in size for sale to "heads of families of the African race" at a rate of one dollar and twenty-five cents per acre.[85] Saxton, Smith, and others sympathetic to the freed people's interest in owning land were alarmed at these instructions, as the amount of land set aside—16,629 acres, enough for 831 families in twenty-acre lots—would not come close to meeting the needs of the remaining freed men and women who sought to own homesteads— certainly not in twenty-acre parcels. Those who would be forced to bid on the land not reserved at below-market prices were sure to be outbid by Northern speculators.

While Saxton again tried to persuade officials in Washington to reconsider the instructions, he acted aggressively on the local scene, exceeding Lincoln's order and issuing additional instructions on November 3 to the freed people encouraging them to build cabins and squat on parcels of the unreserved government land that they should expect to have "a pre-emptive right in equity to the soil."[86] Saxton's aggressive tactics infuriated two of the three tax commissioners, as they did not feel their instructions presupposed the sale of land to every freedman on the Sea Islands, but only to a deserving few.[87] The tax commissioners assigned to implement the president's order did not take kindly to Saxton's aggressive strategy with respect to securing land for the freed people. To them, he was undertaking "an attempt to get up among the Negroes a sort of 'squatter sovereignty' to have them stake out their lands which they want, and then make a public opinion which will frown down a bidder over a certain sum."[88] At stake here, as all were aware, was a land redistribution program breaking up the old plantations that would serve as a model for the rest of the South.[89]

Mansfield French, a fifty-two-year-old Methodist minister from New York who had been sent to Port Royal by the American Missionary Association shortly after the federal occupation of the Sea Islands, strongly believed that formerly enslaved people should receive land as a form of reparation and had been attending Sunday church services all over the Port Royal area for months encouraging the freed people's expectations to land and urging them to stake out preemptive claims on the land they considered home and theirs by right. When word of instructions for the second auction got out,

Reverend French was sent by Saxton to Washington to plead the case to Secretary Chase, one of French's close friends, that more land be reserved for subsidized sales to the freed men and women of the Sea Islands. French's arguments were persuasive, and on December 31, 1863, President Lincoln instructed the tax commissioners in South Carolina to put up for auction the 60,000-odd acres that they had reserved the previous March with the instructions that those who had resided on the land for the last six months or were currently cultivating the land had a preferred right to purchase up to forty acres of land at a price of one dollar and twenty-five cents per acre.[90] Saxton, anxious that the Port Royal freed people secure as much land as they could at this sale, distributed President Lincoln's order with an encouraging statement:

> I also recommend the people to lose no time in pre-empting their claims and in preparing their grounds for the coming harvest . . . Freedmen, you should plow deep, plant carefully and in season, cultivate diligently, and you will reap abundant harvests. First provide for an ample supply of corn and vegetables, then remember that cotton is the great staple here. I advise you to plant all you can of it. So profitable was its culture in the old days of slavery that your former masters said: "Cotton is King." It is expected that you will show in a free South that cotton is more of a king than ever.[91]

Almost immediately, the tax commissioners' office was inundated with freed people's preemption claims. Given that almost none of the Black people of the Sea Islands could read or write, these documents were handwritten by white people who were sympathetic to the idea of allocating property to formerly enslaved people, yet they were signed by the claimants with an often shaky "X". Most of the preemption documents identically recited the language of President Lincoln's instructions authorizing the set aside of certain land for Black preemption, noting that the claimants were heads

of households and were loyal citizens. It must have been incredibly
powerful for the Black people of the Sea Islands, recently emancipated from enslavement, to be able to sign a document that would
have legal force and that they believed would secure them a permanent home on the land they had worked for generations.

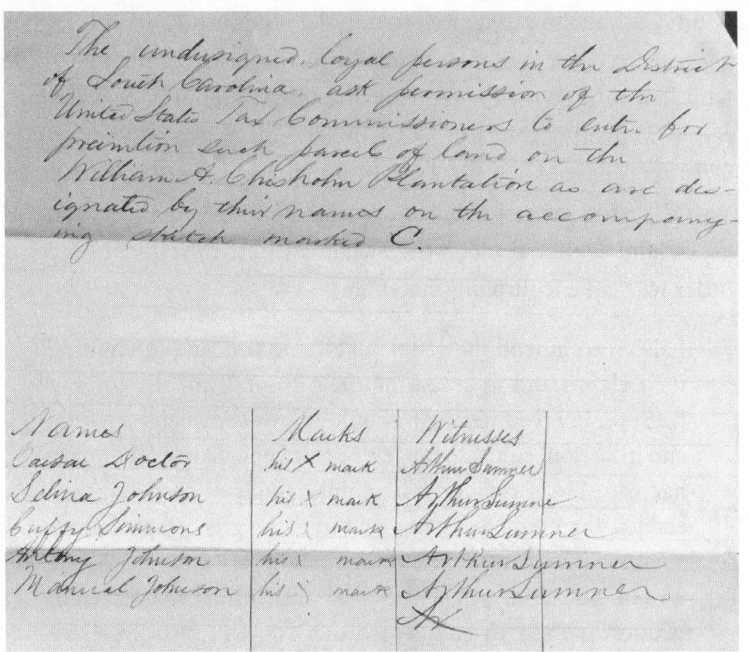

Within two weeks, over a thousand Black families had filed applications for up to four thousand acres and deposits of $8,000 with
the tax commissioners. In 1964, historian Willie Lee Rose examined these preemption documents and noted "packet after packet
of these musty little papers may be found as the broken hopes to
which they are the mute witness." As I examined the preemption
claims, fifty-four years later, and gingerly touched documents that
may have been opened only by Rose and myself since 1863, I was
moved to see the Xs where freed people signed applications for land
on which they and their people had been enslaved. Next to the "X"

for many freed person's signatures are ink smudges bearing witness to hands undertaking this remarkable act of freedom.

Often their preemption claims were made collectively. For instance, on January 29, 1864, ten formerly enslaved men and women filed a preemption claim collectively for what had been the Gabriel Capers plantation.

Nine days later, five freed people filed a claim for the Pleasant Point plantation, accompanied by a hand-drawn map that indicated how they would share the parcels as a community.

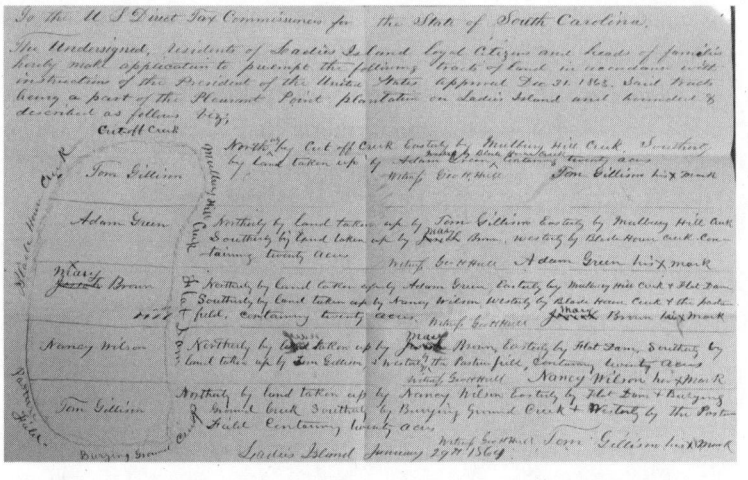

They began to build small cabins on the land they claimed and started planting provision crops. Others who had no plans to farm the land staked out claims with the intention to resell the land at a substantial profit—they had learned the game of land speculation from the example set by their Northern white tutors.[92] Some freed people had accumulated money from working as plantation hands for the government, and many had earned extra money as truck farmers, selling fish and chicken to the superintendents and soldiers. William Gannett, a young Unitarian teacher from Boston who ran two plantations owned by fellow Bostonian Edward Philbrick, wrote in 1862 that a freedman named Limus had earned four or five hundred dollars since Union occupation: "He is ready to buy land, and I expect to see him in ten years a tolerably rich man. Limus has, it is true, but few equals on the islands, and yet there are many who follow not far behind him."[93] Another agent reporting on the financial state of the Sea Island freed people wrote:

> I know one man on St. Helena island—a slave formerly on an adjoining plantation—who now owns a farm of 315 acres, works twenty laborers, has twelve cows, a yoke of oxen, four

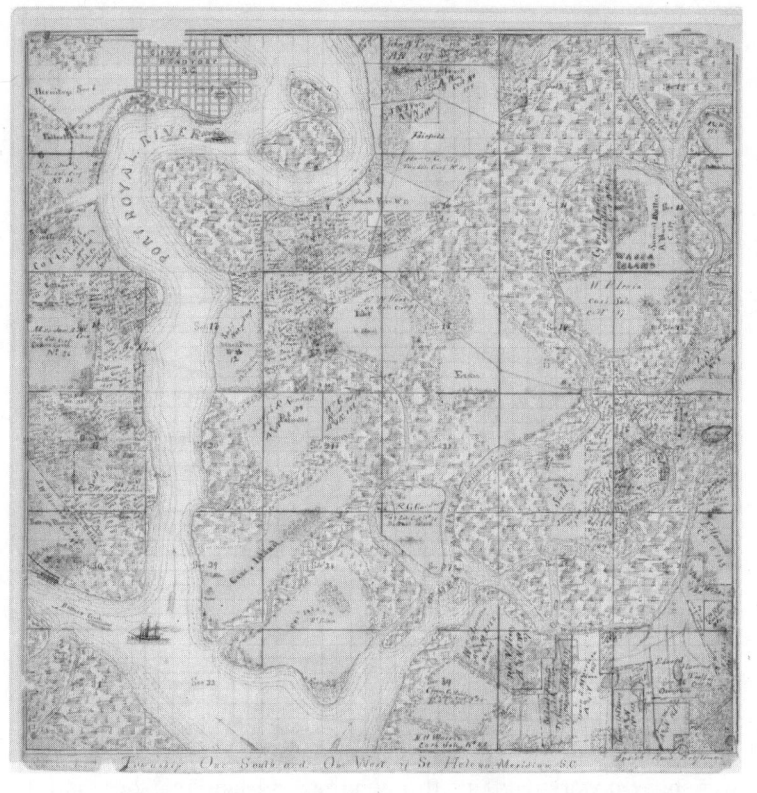

horses, twenty swine; and he showed me, with very pardon-
able pride, his fifty-eight acres of the best sea-island cotton
I saw anywhere . . . There are a number of men on Edisto
and the other sea islands who are only waiting the action of
government in permitting them to have lands to engage in
similar operations.[94]

The entrepreneurial spirit of many of the freed people was un-
ambiguous and needed no cultivation from the Northern tutors
who had come to teach them to be good capitalists. When a representative of the New York National Freedmen's Relief Association
sought to understand "Why, Sambo, [do] you work much harder

"Gwine to de field," Hopkinson's plantation, Edisto Island, S.C. Edisto Island, South Carolina, 1862.

now than you did for Master?" a freedman responded: "We used to work for the lash, now we works for the cash."[95]

In anticipation of the second auction, scores of federal surveyors were busy at work trudging through the Sea Island marshes marking out perfect rectangular plots. The tax commissioners described St.

St. Helena Village, St. Helena Island, South Carolina.

Helena Parish as "comprising islands of irregular form, and of various size, serrated by firths and coves, occupied with plantations of every conceivable shape, with landmarks obliterated and boundaries obscured, if not entirely demolished."[96] This absurd project of imposing modernist order on the chaotic topography ignored existing plantation boundaries that had been in place, in some cases, for well over a hundred years and respected the unruly salt marsh terrain. Speaking of the land in pejorative terms that echoed the judgment in which the missionaries held the Black residents of the Sea Islands, the commissioners sought to civilize the land through surveyance, "to bring order, distinctness, definiteness, valuation, assessment and adequate certainty of description."[97]

No one found the surveyors' project more absurd than the Black people of St. Helena. They refused their help in identifying property lines and landmarks, and instead resisted this ludicrous project by following behind the surveyors pulling up survey markers. Much was at stake for these people who were busy laying their own claim to this land they considered home. They expected to bid on plots of land they were familiar with, not absurdly concocted rectangles fashioned in the style of French arrondissements. This was land that they had worked on for their whole lives; indeed, property lines ran the same course as blood lines for the Sea Island Black people. The old plantation boundaries told you who your kin were in this system. "The new land lines were laid down as if the land were virgin, unpopulated, free for the taking. When the freedmen saw this, they felt uprooted, alienated from their rights."[98] The Black people of the Sea Islands were confounded by the way the white Northerners related to land. An elder from a local church told one of her Northern teachers: "We born here; we parents' graves here; we donne oder country; dis yere our home, antee? What a pity dat dey don't love der home like we love we home, for den dey would neber come here for buy all way from we."[99]

Others who had not earned as much as Limus pooled their resources and, as in the last auction, planned to bid on land as clubs.[100] Meanwhile Saxton was inundated with inquiries from Northern speculators interested in buying land at the next auction. To Saxton's horror, someone had placed an advertisement in the *American Agriculturalist* magazine announcing the land auction and listing Saxton as the person to contact for more information. Saxton wrote them all back, discouraging their participation in the land sale with well-meaning exaggeration. He tried to ward off these investors looking for a fast buck by telling them that there were so many Black people who had preempted plots that "the amount and quality of the lands remaining after the preemption claims are satisfied will not be thought worth very sharp competition."[101]

Unfortunately, two of the three tax commissioners did not share Saxton's view that the Port Royal properties were best allocated to the freed people, and they refused to accept the freedmen's money or recognize their land claims. After much wrangling both locally and in Washington, in February, Secretary Chase reversed the December auction instructions, including the preemption provision and instructed that the sale go forward as previously set out.[102] When the auction finally took place, Saxton's worst fears were realized. "The auction sales held under the first instructions, were the very carnival of speculators and sharpies. They were here in swarms, Jew and Gentile, with claws sharpened for a clutch at the fat carcass," wrote Saxton.[103] "The farms, reserved for educational purposes, & some plantations, were offered for lease by the Commissioners. Eleven of these were leased to one individual,—Irving, I believe of NY, who was among the most eager of auction bidders—although negroes had applied for them, with the money in their hands for the payment of the rent."[104] The land was sold at an average of $11 an acre and a high price of $20 per acre, well beyond the means of the freed people.[105] White buyers, mostly outsiders to the Port Royal experiment, bought close to one hundred thousand acres, while 110 Black families bought 2,750 acres of land, both individually and collectively, largely from the tracts that had been reserved for subsidized sale. Few freed people were able to meet the prices that had been established in the open auction, given the competitive bidding and the land being sold in very large lots. A notable exception was the sale of the 614-acre Thomas James Fripp plantation to a group of Black families; the sale was registered with a shared heads of family certificate.[106] So too, freed people bought a 280-acre farm on Wassa Island for $2,100 and Bolus Point, a 190-acre tract, for $1,250.[107] But such large purchases were unusual; by and large freed people who were able to buy land ended up with twenty-, ten-, and five- acre plots, if they got any land at all.

The open auction resulted in overwhelming heartbreak for the freed people of the Sea Islands. Pooling their resources for the open auction, they bid two thousand dollars for the Ashdale tract but were outbid by a white man who got it for $2,550. The people who resided on a three-hundred-acre farm on Dathaw Island bid $3,100 for their home but lost it when the property went for $3,500. The freed people of Bluff farm lost out to a white Northerner when he bid $3,025, besting their $2,000 bid.[108] "A plantation on which the people have always resided, and who by industry and frugality had saved up two thousand dollars, their little all, to buy it back lost to them at the sale because some speculator bid $2,500. They are now homeless, except at his mercy, and God help them when they are in the power of a man who could do them such a wrong," wrote Saxton to Senator Sumner.[109] Over and over the freed people lost control of their homesteads, their crops and the land they had hoped would be home to a new kind of freedom.[110]

In the end, just over 1,000 Black families were able to buy land at the two auctions—a fraction of the freed people who had selected plots, planted crops, and made down payments. Their devastation cannot be overstated, "the disappointment to them is almost unbearable. They see neither justice nor wisdom in such treatment," wrote Reverend Mansfield French to the head of the Commissioner of Internal Revenue in Washington.[111] As Saxton described it, "The action of the commissioners proved a sad blow to their hopes, and

the disappointment and grief of all were in proportion to their previous exaltation in the hope of soon becoming independent proprietors, free men upon their own free soil; for the attachment and
love of the soil is one of the marked traits of the negro character."[112]

Not surprisingly, the freed people were outraged by their land
being sold out from under them. What is worse, shortly after the land
auction, the government, desperate for cash, set out to appraise and
then auction all of the other farm equipment and other chattel that
had been found on the plantations. Some of the freed people who
had lost out in the land auction organized themselves and bought
at auction all the work animals and farm implements on the plantations on which they lived and worked—outbidding the white owners
who had spent all of their money buying land. This clever strategy
infuriated the likes of William Gannett, who wrote of this period:
"At the sale of abandoned chattels in the spring of 1864, the negroes
carried off nearly the whole stock of some estates, bidding against
white men. On a single plantation three men paid each upwards of
two hundred dollars for the horse that was to 'call him massa.'"[113]

Edward Philbrick along with Henry Brisbane, who served as
chair of the Tax Commission, had had a plan for the distribution of
the Sea Islands land, and in the end they more or less prevailed. As
Saxton described it to a friend,

> Their idea of complete justice to the negroes, in present cir-
> cumstances, is to get the bulk of the land into the hands of
> white men—Christian philanthropists & special lovers of negro
> humanity as all white Yankees are—& to allot to the negroes
> enough—their estimate is two acres apiece—to raise their own
> hominy, thus save the planter all expense for their subsistence.
> This is an experiment, in its lowest terms, of the ability of the
> negro to take care of himself. Then, as the negroes, in their new
> conditions of freedom, will be likely to want something more
> than hominy, it is calculated that he will go for it where only he
> can find it, to the planters' cotton fields.[114]

The newly freed Black people who had lost out at the land auctions were not only devastated; they were angry and, in many cases, were not going to give up the expectation of gaining real homesteads willingly. Resistance to the new white owners was not uncommon. E. P. Hutchinson had bought land at the auction. He reported that when he came to Port Royal from Massachusetts and tried to enter his land, the people he had outbid shot at him and warned him not to come near the place.[115] When Mansfield French urged the freed people to defend their claims with hoe handles, troops were deployed to protect the white purchasers who sought to take possession of their newly purchased land.[116]

The freed people used every means they could to remain on the land they regarded as their own. Once it became clear that the tax commissioners were committed to frustrating their expectations to own the land they had staked out, nineteen freedmen signed a petition to be delivered to President Lincoln demanding that he intervene to set matters right, particularly with respect to Philbrick's refusal to make good on his promise to sell his land back to them for a dollar an acre.

> Wee hav gon to Mr Philbrick & Ask'd him to sell us our Land, and get for an answere he will not sell us one foot, & if he does sell to any one he will charge $10. Ten Dollars per Acre. Wee have work'd for Mr Philbrick the whole year faithfully, and hav received nothing comparatively, not enough to sustaine life if wee depended entirely uppon our wages . . . Why did Government sell all our Masters Land's to Mr Philbrick for so trifling a sume; we are all redy & willing of truth anxious to buey all our Masters Land, & every thing upon them; and pay far more than he did for them.[117]

Upon receipt of the freedmen's petition Secretary Chase dispatched special agent Austin Smith to investigate the complaints the freedmen had lodged against Philbrick. Besides his refusal to sell them the land he had bought at the first auction, they also claimed that he was grossly underpaying them for their work, overcharging them for goods sold at stores he ran, and in one case flogged a young girl in contravention of Saxton's orders that no whipping or physical punishment be used on lands owned by either government or private parties in the areas under his command. At this point Philbrick owned eleven plantations on which about nine hundred people were living, of which 371 were adult working hands. Smith wrote a report of his investigation, confirming that Philbrick had represented that he had bought the land "for the benefit of the freedmen," and that "Mr. Philbrick promised to let the negroes have lands for homes, *when the war should close.*"

Smith did not doubt the veracity of this promise, but he urged the Treasury Secretary to arrange to have the land transferred to the freed people sooner rather than later stating, "I think it would be better if their hopes were no longer deferred." He also affirmed the notion that the land be sold at the promised price of one dollar per acre. He argued:

> In view of the large profits realized upon the investment, these gentlemen can well afford to grant homesteads to these people at a nominal price. Justice & equity demand that the freedmen should be provided with homes, [and that they should be regarded] as having an equitable lien upon the lands of their masters for compensation for what they had done. If the law does not hold these men to the fulfilment of their promises, public opinion will.[118]

Would that Austin Smith had had greater power, for neither the law nor public opinion forced the satisfaction of Philbrick's promise.

In the aftermath of the tax sales, freed people who had not been able to buy land were faced with either entering into labor contracts with the new white owners or being ejected from the land altogether. Given their attachment to the land and their poverty, most of them entered into written labor contracts to work their land for wages.

Saxton was very concerned that the freed people would be taken advantage of and thus ordered that all labor contracts be in writing and were subject to his approval.[119] The freed people's bitterness and disappointment manifested itself in resistance to enter into labor contracts with the white men who had bought "their land," and complaints about how much they were being paid. Freed people on four islands refused to enter into contracts of any form. Some of them were so adamant that they preferred to walk away from their homes rather than contract with their former masters. On St. Catherine's Island, eighty men, women, and children left the cotton in the fields and their household goods in their houses and rowed to Savannah rather than be tied by contract to white land owners. In Colleton District the freed people gathered their cotton, slaughtered the livestock, cut all the timber and headed off to Charleston. Other freed people tore up bridges to impede the return of the white planters, armed themselves, prepared to fight, and took returning planters prisoner in defense of their claim to the land they felt was rightfully theirs.[120]

None of them were interested in working for wages and many made pleas to Saxton that, at a minimum, they be allowed to rent land and work it autonomously. Given that the government still possessed enormous tracts of land, the freed people continued to assert demands for their forty acres argued for by Lincoln in 1863. A new development at Port Royal brought this issue back into greater focus.

᳇

Beginning Christmas night of 1864, thousands of cold, tired, hungry, and sick freed people sought refuge on the South Carolina Sea Islands.[121] These refugees came to be known as "Sherman refugees,"[122] as tens of thousands of them accompanied General Sherman's troops on his great march to the sea. After some time, he found them a hindrance to his military operations,[123] and sought some means by which to address both their destitution and his need to continue the military mission. On January 12, 1865, Sherman and War Secretary Stanton gathered twenty Black leaders at Sherman's headquarters and asked their views on how he should address their problems.[124] Among the issues they discussed was the settlement of Sherman's refugees on land abandoned by Confederates. Like the freed people of the Sea Islands, Sherman's refugees from the mainland expressed a strong desire for land: "[t]he way we can best take care of ourselves is to have land and turn it and till it by our own labor. . . . We want to be placed on land until we are able to buy it and make it our own," declared Garrison Frazier, a sixty-seven-year-old man who had been born and enslaved in Granville County, NC, and who had bought his and his wife's freedom before joining the safety of Sherman's military operation. Stanton asked Frazier whether the freed people would prefer to be settled in communities of mixed white and Black people or in areas restricted to Negroes entirely. To Sherman's surprise, Frazier had a ready answer: they preferred to live alone, apart from white people, "for there is a prejudice against us in the South that it will take years to get over."[125]

Clearly Sherman was moved by his meeting with the freed people in Savannah. Five days later, General Sherman issued his famous Special Field Order No. 15, reserving exclusively for Black settlement the entire Sea Islands area, as well as a strip of land thirty miles wide from the coast inward and bounded from the north at Charleston and the St. John's River on the south.[126] On this land, Sherman ordered, "no white person whatever, unless military officers and soldiers detailed for duty, will be permitted to reside," and the freedmen would be left to their own control.[127] "The negro is free, and must be dealt with as such."[128] This is what most of the freed people imagined freedom would look like: land, tools, and complete independence from white people. Each respectable family was to be allotted forty acres of tillable land.[129] Sherman's order is the source of the demand still made today that freed people receive "forty acres and a mule."

In the following months, four hundred and eighty-five hundred thousand acres were divided up among forty thousand freed people. At this point titles had already been issued for almost all of the land on St. Helena Island at the two auctions, and Sherman's Field Order exempted Port Royal Island from his land resettlement program. This left Sherman's Field Order No. 15 covering Edisto and Hilton Head Island, plus a few smaller islands, and most of the plots were much smaller than forty acres.[130] Given that the large number of freed people in Port Royal who had not gained land at the auctions far outweighed the amount of Port Royal land available for Sherman's settlement plans, many of Port Royal's Black population who sought land through Sherman's Field Order were faced with choosing between Sea Island contract-wage labor or establishing homesteads on the mainland on land seized by Sherman. No doubt this was a wrenching decision for them, particularly since most of them had never set foot on the mainland. Saxton and others told them: "In selecting your lands, be sure to get such as were owned by men who have taken up arms against the government or aided in the rebellion or have abandoned the plantations—then you can be sure to keep your land."[131] Saxton, who had been charged with settling Sherman's refugees, was skeptical about the integrity of these land grants, as Sherman's order promised only possessory titles to the freed people.[132] (A possessory title is the most vulnerable legal form of land ownership, as it is "good title" so long as no one else makes a claim to the land by presenting a valid deed—something the former Confederate landowners would do after the war.) He undertook this task reluctantly, as he feared he would be responsible for disappointing the freed people once again in their claims for land.[133]

Notwithstanding the questionable legality of the Sherman land titles, Saxton's men began to issue titles to freed people even before proper forms were printed. Thousands of possessory titles were haphazardly provided "to every Freed person except single women claiming that they had staked out and then held a tract of land within that portion of the Country defined in Major General Sherman's. S.F.O. No. 15."[134]

Little more than two months later Congress passed a law establishing the Bureau of Refugees, Freedmen, and Abandoned Lands, commonly known as the Freedmen's Bureau, a federal agency charged with supervising all relief and educational activities relating to the freed people, including issuing rations, clothing, and medicine. The Bureau also assumed custody of confiscated lands or property in the former Confederate States, border states, the District of Columbia, and Indian Territory. In effect, the new law authorized Sherman's field order by permitting the Bureau to divide up the confiscated land into forty-acre lots. The law did not, however, reserve these lots exclusively for freed people, but instead authorized their lease or sale to freedmen, refugees, and other male citizens.[135] These lots were to be leased for three years, at which point they could be sold by the government with "such title as it could convey." Thus the Freedmen's Bureau Act acknowledged the fact that the confiscated or abandoned land that had been seized by the Direct Tax laws, the Confiscation Act, or Sherman's field order was vulnerable to legal challenge.[136] Significantly, the final version of the bill provided governmental responsibility for the education and general welfare of the freed people, but it did not establish government-operated plantations. This resolution of the issue of the oversight of the freed people's labor put to rest, at least temporarily, a question that had received much debate both inside the government and among private parties: Would the freed people's transition from enslavement to free labor be best facilitated by the establishment of government-owned plantations, independent Black yeoman farmers working land they owned themselves free from white involvement, or private white-owned plantations on which freed people would work as contract laborers? This third plan, clearly the worst, tragically became the blueprint for Black freed-dom in the post–Civil War period.

❧

Lee surrendered to Grant at Appomattox in April 1865, while the freed people began their spring planting on the land they had been allotted under Sherman's Order and the Freedmen's Bureau Act. Nevertheless, they proceeded with caution, not sure what the end of the war would mean for them, their freedom, or their land. They had placed so much trust in Lincoln, that his assassination in May shook their confidence in the stability of their newfound freedom. Edwin Ruggles, one of the Gideonites who had come down to Port Royal from New York in March of 1862 to teach the freed people, observed, "The death of Lincoln was an awful blow to the negroes here. One would say, 'Uncle Sam is dead, isn't he?' Another, 'The Government is dead, isn't it? You have got to go North and Secesh come back, haven't you? We going to be slaves again?' They could not completely comprehend the matter—how Lincoln could die, and the Government still live. It made them very quiet for a few days."[137] This insecurity was reinforced by the return of some of the former white planters who had fled when Sherman's troops took Port Royal in 1861.[138] The former Confederate owners of the Sea Islands property wanted their land back, and the freed people were determined not to abandon the lots that they, and Saxton, felt were rightfully theirs.[139]

The freed people's fears about the federal government's commitment to their land claims without Lincoln in the White House were realized when the new president, Andrew Johnson, issued an Amnesty Proclamation on May 29, 1865. Not only did he grant amnesty to all former Confederates (except Confederate military and political leadership) upon the signing of the Iron Clad Oath of allegiance to the United States, but he included "the restoration of all rights in property, except as to slaves." Thus, Johnson set up an even more complicated set of problems related to land ownership. Did the March 3, 1865, Freedmen's Bureau Act or the Amnesty Proclamation control the disposition of land subject to Sherman's field order? After consulting with Stanton, Saxton and the Attorney General, the Commissioner of the newly created Freedmen's Bureau, General O. O. Howard, issued an order that the lands set apart for the freed people in the March 3, 1865, Act were not subject to the Amnesty Proclamation, and that the Bureau should continue to convey the land to freed people in forty-acre lots.[140] This work proceeded even though it was not clear whether the titles they were conveying could withstand legal challenge from the pardoned rebel planters who sought the return of their confiscated land.

In mid-August, President Johnson stepped in and put an end to the Bureau's attempts to undermine the restoration of planters' land envisioned by his Amnesty Proclamation. He unequivocally instructed the Bureau to restore land to pardoned Confederates. General Howard sought to comply creatively with the President's order, issuing a new circular to his agents ordering them to restore all abandoned property, but to retain within the Bureau's control all property for which confiscation proceedings had been commenced.[141] This infuriated Johnson, and he personally issued an order in September to all Bureau agents demanding that they restore all land except that which had already been sold under a court decree. Prior to Johnson issuing this order, Howard had worked hard to gain a modification that would condition the restoration of lands on the grant of plots to the freed people in possession of those lands. Johnson found this suggestion amusing and rejected it out of hand.[142]

Almost immediately, Saxton's office at Port Royal was overrun with former Confederate planters seeking to get their land back. General Howard arrived shortly thereafter to deliver the terrible news to the freed people. His task was made more difficult by the fact that his aim was to make them leave their farms, but not the islands, as it was the Johnson administration's goal that they would work as contract laborers for the planters once they were back in possession of their land. None of this sat well with the freed people. "One of the strongest motives preventing the making of contracts, is the hope of possessing land of their own," a subordinate reported to General Howard.[143] He continued:

> The impression is universal among the freedmen that they are to have the abandoned and confiscated lands, in homesteads of forty acres, in January next. Our own acts of Congress, and particularly the act creating this bureau . . . still strengthened them in the belief that they were to possess homesteads, and has created a great unwillingness upon the part of the freedmen to make any contracts whatever . . . so deep-seated a conviction has been found difficult to eradicate, and, although many contracts have been made, I doubt that much greater success in this direction will attend our efforts in the future."[144]

Even worse, from the perspective of the Johnson administration's plan, the freed people were "reluctan[t] to work under overseers especially the same overseers they had had in slavery."[145] Bureau officials reported that "planters coming to claim lands in some cases find the people unwilling to give them up."[146] The freed people holding a "Sherman title" to Sea Cloud, a plantation on Edisto Island, greeted the returning white owner thus: "the people received us much to my surprise with feelings of angry excitement."[147]

In response to the influx of returning planters, the freed people held meetings and signed written pledges not to contract with any white owners.[148] At these meetings, General Howard found the freed people well organized and very clear in their resistance to a contract labor system. "The freedmen of Edisto, having organized resistance to being deprived of their farms, claimed that no one could force them to work for their old masters. The freedmen held regular weekly meetings, and when they heard of Howard's approach, they gathered in a large church on the island to tell the Commissioner that they would not be put off their lands."[149] The angry and desolate group refused to come to order until a Black woman began to sing, "Nobody knows the trouble I feel—Nobody knows but Jesus."[150]

After all joined in singing, the group came to order. They were adamant in their demand to own the land they worked. They regarded
the proposed contract labor system as a return to slavery.

In a report Saxton filed with General Howard in December of
1865, he urged Howard to appeal to Congress to force the government to recognize the freed people's right to the abandoned or confiscated land:

> Inasmuch as the faith of the government has been pledged to
> these freedmen to maintain them in the possession of their
> homes, and as to break its promise in the hour of its triumph
> is not becoming of a just government, which can only live in
> the hearts of its whole people, I would respectfully suggest
> that a practical solution of the whole question of lands . . .
> may be had by the appropriation of money by Congress to
> purchase the whole tract set apart by [Sherman's Field Order],
> and have a fair and liberal assessment of its value made, and
> offer to pay to the former owner that sum, or give him pos-
> session of the land, as he may elect. In case he should prefer
> the land to the money, then pay the money to the freedman
> who occupies it."[151] Howard felt strongly that it was "an act of
> gross injustice to deprive the freedmen of these lands now."[152]
> General Howard seemed convinced by this position, and in
> his first public break with the Johnson administration, agreed
> that Congress had to act to assure that the freed people were
> provided land that had been abandoned or confiscated.[153]

Howard saw to it that the local Bureau officers dragged their feet
in restoring land to the returning rebels. In particular, they would not
award any land to a former white owner who had not yet entered into
a contract with the freed people who would work the land. A rather
clever ploy since the freed people were refusing to sign labor contracts, leaving the whole process at a standstill. Further complicating
matters, if they were to get their land back, planters had to agree to
leave the existing crops to those who had planted them.[154]

Shortly after the Thirteenth Amendment abolishing slavery became effective in December 1865, the abolitionist members of Congress turned their attention to another Freedmen's bill. Among their priorities was extending the life of the Freedmen's Bureau, securing funding for its activities, and statutorily recognizing the Sherman land grants. Both houses passed bills by large majorities that confirmed Sherman's field order and protected the possessory titles to that land for three years and authorized the Bureau to "procure other lands for them by rent or purchase, not exceeding forty acres for each occupant," if the freed people's land was restored to its former Confederate owners. It authorized the president to reserve three million acres of public land in Florida, Mississippi, Alabama, Louisiana, and Arkansas to make good on this promise, and gave the Freedmen's Bureau the power to protect the civil rights of freed people, including the power and duty to try and punish anyone who violated those rights, authorizing criminal penalties "by fine not exceeding one thousand dollars, or imprisonment not exceeding one year, or both."[155]

Johnson was indisposed to sign the bill, and even before it had been voted on by Congress, he consulted General Sherman about the Field Order No. 15 land grants and whether he had intended that they be binding. Sherman responded: "I knew of course we could not convey title to land and merely provided 'possessory titles' to be good so long as war and our Military Power lasted. I merely aimed to make provision for the negroes . . . leaving the value of their possessions to be determined by after events or legislation."[156] On February 19, 1866, Johnson vetoed the bill, arguing in his veto message that it was unnecessary to the larger national policy of conscripting freed people into the contract labor system:

> To the Senate of the United States:
>   I have examined with care the bill which originated in the Senate and has been passed by the two Houses of Congress, to amend an act entitled "An act to establish a bureau

for the relief of freedmen and refugees, and for other purposes." Having, with much regret, come to the conclusion
that it would not be consistent with the public welfare to
give my approval to the measure, I return the bill to the
Senate with my objections to it becoming a law.

I might call to mind, in advance of these objections,
that there is no immediate necessity for the proposed
measure. . . . I have, with Congress, the strongest desire
to secure to the freedmen the full enjoyment of their freedom and their property and their entire independence and
equality in making contracts for their labor. But the bill
before me contains provisions which, in my opinion, are
not warranted by the Constitution and are not well suited
to accomplish the end in view. . . .

It is no more than justice to them to believe that, as they
have received their freedom with moderation and forbearance, so they will distinguish themselves by their industry
and thrift, and soon show the world that in a condition of
freedom they are self-sustaining and capable of selecting
their own employment and their own places of abode.[157]

With respect to the bill's provisions relating to the enforcement
of the Civil Rights of freed people, Johnson justified his veto with
concern that Bureau agents charged with adjudicating complaints
may not be familiar with local custom. "The agent who is thus to exercise the office of a military judge may be a stranger, entirely ignorant of the laws of the place, and exposed to the errors of judgment
to which all men are liable." And he elevated concerns about injustice suffered by white people unfairly charged with discrimination
over the legitimacy of claims of bias lodged by freed people: "The
safeguards which the experience and wisdom of ages taught our fathers to establish as securities for the protection of the innocent, the
punishment of the guilty, and the equal administration of justice, are

to be set aside, and, for the sake of a more vigorous interposition in behalf of justice, we are to take the risks of the many acts of injustice that would necessarily follow."[158] (It is difficult not to hear the echo of Johnson's veto message in the remarks of a different US president 150 years later, when he responded to calls to prosecute white supremacists with a concern that some of them were "very fine people" and were unfairly judged.[159]) Johnson's veto message emits the noxious odor of white innocence combined with the notion that enough had already been done for the freed people, let's move on.

In the end, there were not enough votes in Congress to override Johnson's veto. With his veto pen President Johnson put an end to the notion that justice for formerly enslaved people required, at a minimum, reparation for their stolen labor, systematic torture, and treatment as property not human beings. Almost immediately thereafter, Johnson arranged for the Bureau to come under the control of the occupying military command in the South. As a result, the military seized control of the land restoration process. At Port Royal, they administered to the repossession of the land by the former owners, and those freed people who refused to enter into labor contracts were forced to leave the islands.[160] When a federal agent returned to the Sea Cloud plantation on Edisto Island just after Johnson vetoed the Freedmen's bill, he was hoping to pave the return of its former white owner. Instead he "was beset by the [Black] women on this place, in a very serious manner, and was obliged to use decisive measures for the preservation of the property as well as for my own head . . . They said they would not make any arrangement whatever, for me or anybody else: that they cared for no United States officer: the Govt brought them to the island & 'they would burn down the house before they would move a rag' or 'from it themselves until put out.'"[161]

The Congressional radicals regrouped and were able to pass another version of the Freedmen's bill in July that they hoped would overcome Johnson's veto. Yet this bill contained a more timid approach to the Sherman land grants. Those freed people who had been ousted from the Sherman lands would have no claims to redeem those land grants, but instead were permitted to lease twenty-acre lots on other government-owned lands, with a six-year option to buy.[162] One month before the Second Freedmen's Act became law, Congress passed the Southern Homestead Act that addressed some of the land allocation issues that had appeared in earlier unsuccessful legislation.[163] The new Homestead Act opened up public land in Alabama, Mississippi, Louisiana, Arkansas, and Florida for homesteading in eighty-acre plots. It prohibited ex-Confederates from applying for land until January 1, 1877, and included a provision prohibiting discrimination on the basis of race or color.

This land grant program fell well short of what the freed people would have seen had their Sherman titles been honored. Land without tools, farm animals, or seeds was of little productive value.[164] Land was not a fungible good to the freed men and women of Port Royal who had lived their entire lives on the isolated Sea Islands plantations. This was home, their families were buried here, their kin were here, and they spoke a dialect quite incomprehensible to outsiders—a combination of English and West African languages. "What is the use of giving us freedom if we can't stay where we were raised and own our own house where we were born and our own piece of ground?" they objected.[165] For most people who had never set foot on the mainland, abandoning the Sea Islands on the basis of a promise by the government for a plot in Arkansas or Florida was unimaginable, not to mention the fact that they had little reason to trust the government. That mistrust in this case, as before, was not mislaid, as most of the land made available by the Homestead Act was of very low quality, often mostly sand and rock. In the end, out of 23,609 homesteads awarded under the Act, General Howard reported that by 1870 only four thousand were for freed people's families, out of the nearly four million people who had been freed at the end of the war.[166]

This aid from Congress was too little too late. By then, virtually all of the land temporarily owned by freed people under Sherman land grants had been repossessed by their former owners who were happy to implement a system of contract labor. For example, on January 16, 1865, Daniel Middleton along with eighteen other freedmen had received possessory titles for forty-acre lots from Saxton on what had previously been the Whaley plantation on Edisto Island. They planted an ample cotton crop in for the 1885–1886 season, however in the midsummer of 1866 Whaley rented the land to Heinrich Herman van Houten, a white man. Two months later van Houten seized all the cotton that the freed people had harvested and locked it away to prevent them from accessing it. Middleton and his colleagues filed an action in the Charleston District Court to recover the cotton van Houten had stolen. The extant court records are unclear as to whether the Middleton plaintiffs won their lawsuit. Tragically, the complaint asked only for compensation for the seized cotton, not for the enforcement of their Sherman titles to the land. It is likely that they had been advised by Freedmen's Bureau officials that the best they could hope for was the proceeds from the cotton.[167]

Middleton's experience was not unusual. In many cases freed people forced to enter into contracts with white planters, found the planters unwilling to live up to their contractual obligations. In March of 1865, the mayor of Port Royal reported to a military official that "there are other deceptions and impositions practiced upon the freedmen, such as letting land to them pretendingly [sic] on shares, then for some pretend offense committed after the crop 'is made', driving them from the plantation, seizing and taking the whole of the crop from them."[168] Provost Court records from November of 1866 indicate that Samuel Morris and twenty-seven other freed people who had contracted to work for Mr. van Houten sued him for breach of contract for his failure to pay them at the end of the growing season. The court ordered him to pay them and to pay the court costs. Another entry shows that Richard Finnick and five other freed people successfully sued van Houten for the same offense. Similarly, John Clark and nine of his coworkers sued George Lee in December of 1866 for firing them in November without paying them a cent. They too won their wages.[169] After suffering a series of broken promises about their right to the land, the freed people were left with a cause of action to collect owed wages, and no meaningful claim to land.

It is undeniable that the freed people of the Sea Islands would have been able to purchase much more land at auction had the US government paid them for their back wages. But as the land redistribution project was structured, the government seized land from Confederate landowners who owed back taxes, then required the freed people to compete with white speculators from the North in the sale of that land. Given that the federal treasury was facing a liquidity shortfall at the time, they could have paid the freed people for their labor in land rather than cash. But that was never proposed.

Notwithstanding the tireless efforts of devoted Bureau officials, the Port Royal experiment in freedom and reparations had come to an end. In a matter of months, the Johnson administration transformed a radical experiment in reparations through the redistribution of land ownership to Black people into the testing ground for contract labor and converted the land *reallocation* project into one of land *restoration*. From this point forward, freedom in general, and freed labor in particular, took the form of legally binding labor contracts between a class of Black peasant agricultural workers and white landowners.

This is not to say that Black people did not own land on the Sea Islands. The 1870 census, for instance, showed 6,200 residents in St. Helena Township, the area of highest population density in the Sea Islands. Ninety-eight percent of the township's residents were Black, and at least 70 percent of the Black families owned property. These numbers are less impressive when viewed in contrast to white ownership. Of a total of 21,608 acres in St. Helena Township, 8,459 were owned by Blacks, while 13,149 acres were owned by whites, who comprised just over 1 percent of the population. Most of the plots owned by Blacks were small, ranging between five and twenty acres. Almost half of them were about ten acres in size. Large enough, in many cases, to feed their families, but not large enough to assure economic independence from whites.[170] More freed people ended up owning their own homesteads on the Sea Islands than in most of the postbellum South, but the small size of plots, particularly compared to the large farms owned by white planters like the despised Edward Philbrick, meant that at best the allocation of land to freed people at the tax sales produced a landed agricultural peasantry who would live hand-to-mouth on small tracts of land, economically dependent on white planters for their families' support. In this sense, the aspirations of the majority of tax commissioners in making small lots available to the Sea Islands freed people were realized: by owning land, they wouldn't leave, but having small plots they would need to work and would thus be a permanent ready labor force for the larger farms owned by white planters. This arrangement locked formerly enslaved people into economic dependence on white people, denied them any form of compensation or reparation for the obscene crime of slavery, and secured a postbellum socioeconomic structure within which white people would accumulate wealth through property

Group of freed people on their way to the cotton field, St. Helena Island, South Carolina, 1863.

ownership, while Black people's relation to property resulted in their generations-long impoverishment. In the end, white people were the primary beneficiaries of the federal government's land policy.

Many freed people from the Sea Islands found themselves land-less and bound to white planters—often their prior owners—through yearlong labor contracts that they could not escape. This was a curi-ous freedom indeed. The dreams of the freed people of the Sea Islands were of a very different kind of freedom, one that was cut short by President Johnson, the Sea Islands tax commissioners, and pardoned Confederate white planters. In the postbellum society they envi-sioned, freedom presupposed a form of justice that recognized that slavery was something not merely to abolish, but was an injury and a theft that justified, if not required, reparation. What they got instead was a strange brand of emancipation that locked most freed people in a bare life, neither free nor enslaved, but bound to whites through legally mediated relationships of labor, production, and discipline.

⚬

The successes and ultimate failures of this utopian experiment teach us something important about the difference between being free and being freed, and how that difference structured a path for Black people later marked by a second-class US citizenship. Freed-dom for so many former slaves meant the acquisition of a kind of "burdened individuality," of "being freed from slavery and free of resources, emancipated and subordinated, self-possessed and in-debted, equal and inferior, liberated and encumbered, sovereign and dominated, citizen and subject."[171] As Dr. King's Poor People's Campaign made clear a hundred years later, fighting only for a right to be equal under the law is a mere reform movement. Radical change must include a demand for the redistribution of resourc-es.[172] Most rights are meaningless if you are too poor to exercise them, so in important respects in the space between being freed

and being free lies economic justice. Though better than being enslaved, to be sure, being freed was by no means the same as being
free, a status reserved exclusively for white people.

⚭

Today there are 183,149 people living in Beaufort County, of which
77.4 percent are white (141,757), and 18.7 percent are African American (3,425). The median household income for white residents of
Beaufort County is three times that of African Americans[173]—a dis-
parity significantly wider than can be found in the national median
income statistics.[174] Much of the wealth held by residents of Beaufort County today is reflected in the value of property. And nearly
all of the most valuable property is owned by white people. This contemporary reality has a racial history. Land speculators like Edward
Philbrick and his Northern investors profited handsomely from the
Port Royal land auctions. For instance, Philbrick bought Coffin Point,
a property making up 1,438 acres, for $1,150 at the tax auction on
March 10, 1863.

United States of America,

TAX SALE CERTIFICATE, NO. *20.*

This is to certify, That at a sale of lands for unpaid taxes, under and by virtue of an act entitled "An act for the collection of direct taxes in insurrectionary districts within the United States, and for other purposes," held pursuant to notice at *Beaufort* , in the District of *Beaufort* , in the State of South Carolina, on the *tenth* day of *March* , A. D. 186*3*, the tract or parcel of land hereinafter described, situate in the *District* of *Beaufort* , and State aforesaid, and described as follows, to wit: *The tract of land on St Helena Island, known as "Coffin Point Place". — Bounded Northerly by Morgan River, Southerly by Harbor River, Easterly by St Helena Sound, Westerly by the Fripps Point Place and by Pine Grove. Containing Fourteen hundred and thirty eight acres more or less. —*

was sold and struck off to *Edward S Philbrick*, for the sum of *Eleven hundred & fifty* dollars and ——— cents, he being the highest bidder, and that being the highest sum bidden for the same; the receipt of which said sum in full is hereby acknowledged and confessed.

Given under our hands, at *Beaufort S.C.*, this *tenth* day of *March* , A. D. 186*3*.

A. D. Smith

W. C. Wording

Wm Henry Brisbane

Commissioners.

The government had appraised the property as worth $5,752 when they listed it for auction, so he got an extremely good deal. He then sold Coffin Point, the largest property in the Port Royal area, in 1891 to Pennsylvania senator J. Donald Cameron who was looking for a hunting and fishing retreat where "he and his wife would winter at Coffin Point . . . arriving in their yacht."[175] It remained in the Cameron family, though rarely occupied, until 1952 when trustees for the estate sold all 932 acres to J. E. McTeer, who had been sheriff of Beaufort County since 1926. A few years later McTeer laid out residential lots as part of a plan to break up the plantation, and a hurricane in 1959 caused extensive damage. McTeer retired from the police force in 1963 and went into real estate. The Old Coffin house was sold in 1969 to writers George and Priscilla Johnson McMillan. George McMillan, a *Life* magazine reporter, gained notoriety for writing "The Making of an Assassin," about the life of James Earl Ray, the murderer of the Rev. Dr. Martin Luther King, Jr.[176] Priscilla Johnson McMillan, a reputed Central Intelligence Agency (CIA) agent who had lived in the early 1960s with Marina Oswald (wife of Lee Harvey Oswald, the alleged killer of President John F. Kennedy), had served as an aide to John F. Kennedy when he was a US Senator, spoke several languages including Russian, and was translating the memoirs of Josef Stalin's daughter when she resided at the Old Coffin house. The house was listed by the McMillans with the National Register of Historic Places in 1975. At the head of the chain of title to this property held by a string of prominent white people from Philbrick to the McMillans, perhaps best termed "Johnson titles" in contrast to the Sherman possessory titles held by Black people, lurks a damaged link traceable to Philbrick's deceit and predatory real estate purchases.

Many of Beaufort County's largest plantations were ultimately sold by their former Confederate owners to white Northerners, who used these sprawling estates once or twice a year for hunting and other recreation, otherwise they sat empty. By the mid-twentieth century they had been subdivided into much smaller lots and sold to full-time white inhabitants. The Fripp and Coffin Point plantations are good examples of this history. The Tombee plantation, owned in the 1860s by Thomas Chaplin, who fled the Island when the Northern troops invaded in 1861, remains largely intact.[177] It was

listed for sale in 2011 at $3,250,000.[178] The Sam's Point plantation
was listed for sale in 2018 at $2,695,000.[179] The Coosaw plantation
had been owned by Alexander Robert Chisolm, who in 1852 inherited the land and 250 enslaved people from his father.[180] In 1861,
Chisolm brought some of his enslaved men to Charleston upon the
request of the South Carolina governor to help build batteries to
protect against a Union invasion. Coosaw was seized by the Northern government as part of the Port Royal experiment and the freed
people living there filed preemption claims to the land on January
29, 1864. The land was returned to Chisolm after he was pardoned by
the federal government in December 1865. He sold the plantation in
1877 to the Pacific Mining Company. In the early 1900s most of the
property was sold to William and Michael Keyerling, who then sold
it to Edward Hutton, founder of the stock brokerage firm E. F. Hutton, in 1917. Hutton gave Coosaw plantation to a stockbroker friend
Juan Ceballas in return for introducing him to his second wife, General Foods heiress Marjorie Merriweather Post. (Edward and Marjorie Hutton's collective wealth allowed them to build Mar-a-Lago in
Palm Beach, Florida, several years later.) Hutton also gave his long-
time dog handler, Marshall Smith, six hundred acres of other land.
In 1965, Dr. Marshall Clement Sanford, Sr., father of former South
Carolina governor and former US senator Mark Sanford, bought the
Coosaw plantation and bought back the six hundred acres that had
been given to the dog handler. Mark Sanford wrote in his Furman
University senior thesis: "Thus Coosaw Plantation has come full cir-
cle, returning to its original use as a family farm." The Sanford family placed the property, 1,584 acres, under a conservation easement
worth $2,500,000 in 2011.[181]

Mark Sanford's use of the term "family farm" has such a quaint
ring to it, erasing entirely the history of enslavement and failure to
make good on the promise of land-based reparations for the people
who had been enslaved by the Chisolm family. The claims of freed
people to the land as a means of achieving justice were deemed less

compelling than the efforts of a bourgeois stockbroker to procure a second wife, or the service given by a dog handler, as the chain of white title to this land reveals.

Seaside plantation, comprising 1,284 acres on St. Helena Island, was owned by Edgar Fripp. Like Coosaw, Seaside was confiscated by Union troops in 1861. The freed people living at Seaside were among the first to file claims to the land in advance of the tax auction in early 1864. With this, like so many other properties, Edward

Philbrick outbid the freed people at the tax auction. In 1872, 732 acres of the plantation were returned to the Fripp family. In 1920, Fripp sold the plantation to Dr. Arthur W. Elting, a surgeon from Albany, New York. Dr. Elting went on to acquire 150 Beaufort County properties, covering thousands of acres, many of which he used for hunting when he visited the area. In 1959, Dr. Elting sold Seaside to Margaret Sanford, the future governor and senator's mother.

Solomon Guggenheim, born into a wealthy copper mining family in Pittsburgh in 1861, gained his own wealth by founding the Yukon Gold Company in Alaska. He also purchased considerable property in Beaufort County. Guggenheim bought five hundred acres of land on which to found the Lady's Island Hunting Club and the twelve-thousand-acre Elgerbar plantation.[182]

Contemporary narratives of Beaufort's "grand past" resting on the systematic erasure of the history of slavery and the tragedy of land-based reparations in the Sea Islands is illustrated clearly in the story of the Edgar Fripp house, also known as Tidalholm. Several blogs that document quaint stories about the history of Beaufort include the following anecdote about Tidalholm in which white innocence figures prominently:

> The house . . . is a large absolutely beautiful home built in Beaufort in 1853. Mr. Fripp built this home as a summer retreat, as did many of the plantation owners during the antebellum period. Heat and mosquitoes made life very intolerable on St Helena. The home was enjoyed by the Fripp family up until the Civil War. When Union troops occupied Beaufort on November 7, 1861, Tidalholm was among the mansions seized by the Union and served as Union Hospital #7 during the occupation of Beaufort.
>
> After the Civil War ended, these mansions were put up for tax auction, and Tidalholm was included in this massive auction. According to Fripp family legend, when James

Fripp returned after the war he arrived just as the house was being auctioned for taxes by the US Tax Commission. He was unable to bid on his home, so he stood with tears coursing down his cheeks. It is said that a Frenchman, who had been living in the area and who was sympathetic to the South, purchased the house. He walked over to Mr. Fripp, presented him with the deed, kissed him on both cheeks, and left, returning to France *before Mr. Fripp had a chance to repay him.*[183]

While this Fripp "family legend" about the history of Tidalholm is moving, the historical record illuminates a much more complicated story of the mansion's history, and that of the Fripp family. Edgar Fripp, the man who built the house, was one of the largest antebellum landowners in the Sea Islands. He was described by those who knew him as "a wealthy and arrogant man, [who] sometimes made his slaves work all night by the light of the full moon during the heaviest part of the season." Even worse, he had a reputation for whipping "any black man he met who did not immediately remove his hat as a sign of respect."[184]

Mr. Fripp was known locally as "Proud Edgar," a very difficult man known to be a "colossal egoist" who would "flaunt his money among those of lesser means. He had the traits of a petty tyrant." When he died, in 1860, he was buried in the "Egyptian style" vault he had built for himself in the Episcopal churchyard on St. Helena. Edgar chose not to leave his property to his wife Eliza, and not having had children, he left his estate to his nephew Edgar W. Fripp, who was a minor at the time of his uncle's death. Edgar W.'s father, James Fripp, acted as the guardian of the younger Edgar's property holdings until the property was seized by the Union army when it occupied the Sea Islands in 1861.

The history of wealthy white Northern speculators buying land in Beaufort and neighboring counties is extensive. It started with

Edward Philbrick and his compatriots and continued after the former Confederates, whose land had been returned after confiscation, decided that they too could profit handsomely from a Confederate-friendly executive in the White House who was willing to restore their property rights out of fidelity to the language of the Constitution that declared that "no persons shall be deprived of life, liberty, or property without due process of law."[185] Thus, the property rights of former slave-owners were elevated over the rights of repair owed to enslaved people whose "life and liberty" had been systematically deprived not only by the Confederates who sought return of their land, but by a constitution that protected the institution of slavery itself until the Thirteenth Amendment was ratified in 1865.

For this reason, we should be clear that the failure to deliver on a promise of full repair to formerly enslaved people in the Sea Islands is not just a local problem that imposes a moral demand on the white people of South Carolina. Rather, doctors in Albany, mining barons in New York, investors in Boston, future governors and US senators, and a wide variety of more regular white people living all over the country were able to acquire property in the Sea Islands precisely because formerly enslaved people were stripped of any claim to that land. As such, this history, retold with a focus on the frustrated attempts to provide reparations to people who had been enslaved, raises a problem of national, not merely local, proportion that demands a collective national remedy.

CHAPTER 2

Black Self-Governance at Davis Bend

T HE DAVIS BROTHERS, Jefferson and Joseph, owned two substantial plantations on the banks of the Mississippi River thirty miles south of Vicksburg, Mississippi. Jefferson, the younger brother, was well known as the father of the Confederacy and a staunch defender of chattel slavery. Given this fact, it is particularly ironic that a form of Black self-governance that rivaled the best utopian aims of the Port Royal experiment was set in place on the Davis brothers' plantations during and after the Civil War. The experiment in Black self-governance at Davis Bend provides a searing example of the necessary relationship between economic opportunity and the self-determination of a community, both as slavery was ended in the nineteenth century and today.

Above: Jefferson Davis, 1857, William S. Pendleton, photographer; below: Joseph Davis, Mississipi Department of Archives and History

Joseph was the eldest of ten children, and his youngest brother, Jefferson, was twenty-four years his junior. Joseph distinguished himself as a lawyer in Natchez, a founder of the Mississippi Bar Association, a delegate to the Mississippi constitutional convention in 1817,[1] and finally as an innovative plantation owner. In 1818, Joseph

Davis gave up his career as a lawyer and bought eleven thousand acres of land abutting the Mississippi River south of Vicksburg in an area that came to be known as Davis Bend.

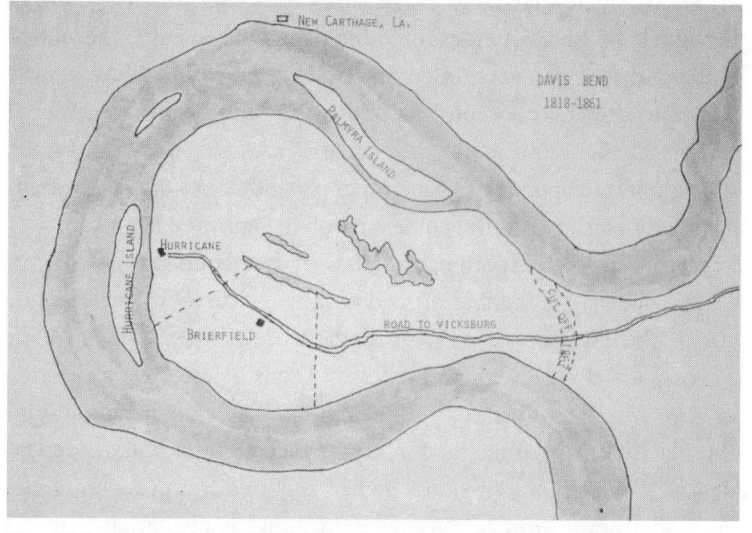

Map of Davis Bend. Courtesy of Old Court House Museum, Vicksburg, MS

Over time, he sold portions of the land to people whom he welcomed as neighbors. In 1835, he offered a substantial tract adjacent to his own Hurricane plantation to his brother Jefferson, as payment for the interest Joseph owed him for the enslaved people that their father had left them, and that Joseph had been using on his plantation.[2] Jefferson, known to family and friends as Jeff, named his plantation Brierfield, due to the abundance of briers on the property.[3] At the start of the Civil War, the Hurricane plantation covered 1,700 acres and included 345 enslaved people.[4] (Unlike other parts of the antebellum South, Mississippi planters did not, by and large, own enormous plantations and control vast numbers of enslaved people. Joseph Davis, for instance, was one of only nine Mississippians who owned more than three hundred enslaved people.)[5] Joseph Davis was very attracted to

the theories of reform and progressive thinkers of the time who advocated collective principles of organizational management and industrial structure. He was particularly interested in the work of Robert Owen, often referred to as the father of British socialism.[6] Owen
brought his cooperative ideas of industrial management to the United
States and set up an experiment in collective labor and living in New
Harmony, Indiana.[7] Joseph Davis, interested in learning more about
Owen's ideas put into action, accompanied Owen on a US tour in 1825
with a mind to applying Owen's progressive theories of factory management to an agricultural context involving enslaved labor.[8]

From his own experience as a lawyer, and from Owen's writing,
Davis believed that people worked best by the carrot rather than the
stick. "The less people are governed, the more submissive they will be
to control."[9] Both Joseph and Jefferson Davis detested centralization
of governance, and believed it the best course for the nation and for
the plantation to pursue a system of "widest community independence."[10] Joseph took the ideas he had acquired from Owen and developed a novel form of self-governance on his plantation that was
surely unique for its time. He was known for providing the people
he enslaved with comparatively generous housing, food, and medical
care—indeed he was one of the only planters to provide dental care to
the enslaved people at Hurricane.[11] He also provided incentives and
rewards to the people he enslaved for exceptional cotton picking, paid
them for extra work, and allowed them to sell their own chickens and
eggs.[12] Benjamin Montgomery, one of his most trusted slaves, was allowed to open up a store on Hurricane, and Davis extended him credit
as an advance on merchandise to be sold in the store. Montgomery's
store was quite successful, selling goods to the people of Hurricane
and Brierfield, as well as to steamboats that docked at Hurricane on
their way up and down the Mississippi River.[13] Montgomery's store
was so profitable that he was able to pay Davis for the cost of his wife's
labor so that she could stay home with their five children, a kind of
gendered freedom nested within the slavery system itself.[14]

At the core of this structure of self-governance, however, lay a legal system, run entirely by the enslaved people on Hurricane. Davis devoted a building on the plantation to a slave court and called it the Hall of Justice.[15] Court was in session every Saturday, and a jury made up of enslaved people would hear cases and complaints of misconduct among their peers. They would take testimony, and issue sentences where appropriate. Davis served as judge but intervened only to grant a pardon if he regarded the sentence too severe.[16] Davis also insisted that the white overseers he employed on Hurricane bring their complaints before the Saturday court, and they were not allowed to punish enslaved people without the court's permission. For this reason most overseers in the region preferred not to work at Hurricane.[17]

Brierfield plantation, 1864, courtesy of Old Warren County Court House Museum

This form of local justice was unheard of in the Southern plantation system, and set Joseph Davis apart from his contemporaries.[18] When Jefferson had Brierfield up and running, he borrowed many of his brother's progressive approaches to slave management, including the court system.[19] But in the end, Jefferson took a very different view towards Black people than did his elder brother. While Joseph treated his slaves with a modicum of dignity, calling them by the names they preferred and referring to them as servants, not slaves, Jefferson shared the view of most of his contemporaries that Black people were inferior to white people and that slavery was ordered by divine law. Fortunately for the enslaved people at Brierfield, Jefferson was away from the plantation on political business most of the time after 1845, and the rules and norms adopted by his brother at Hurricane were enforced at Brierfield in his absence.[20]

Joseph Davis regarded himself a benevolent patriarch who had a responsibility to serve as a moral example and steward for his slaves. Despite his progressive views about how to manage his plantation and the enslaved people who worked on it, he remained, albeit ambivalently, committed to the institution of slavery. The people he enslaved no doubt appreciated the privileges they enjoyed as compared with other plantations, but surely, they preferred not to be enslaved at all. In the end, not one Davis slave was ever manumitted.[21]

Joseph Davis discovered that the loyalty of the people he enslaved was not unbounded. In May of 1862 he fled Hurricane on account of the war and a particularly high flood season. He sent a boat to rescue his personal effects and papers, and as many enslaved people as could fit on the boat. He was then shocked to learn that most of them had fled into the woods after he had repaired to higher ground. When the boat left with as many items of personal property as could be retrieved, the enslaved people of Hurricane who remained broke into Joseph's mansion and confiscated what they could for their own use or sale, thus proving the limit of their respect for Joseph Davis. A month later, a raiding party of Union troops further ransacked the house and burned it to the ground.[22]

Slave Quarters at Brierfield Plantation, home of Jefferson Davis, Davis Bend, Mississippi, Library of Congress

After the arrival of Union troops, many of the people Joseph Davis had enslaved remained at Hurricane to fend for themselves, including Benjamin Montgomery, who took over agricultural production and the care of the population at Hurricane for a short time. Yet by June of 1863, Montgomery had retreated with his family to Cincinnati.[23]

As General Ulysses S. Grant moved through the South he, like General Sherman in Georgia and the Carolinas, found his troops' progress burdened by increasingly large groups of formerly enslaved people seeking protection and food. W. E. B. DuBois described it so:

> The moment the Union army moved into slave territory, the Negro joined it. Despite all argument and calculation and in the face of refusals and commands, wherever the Union armies marched, appeared the fugitive slaves. It made no difference what the obstacles were, or the attitudes of too low wages to the commanders. It was "like thrusting a walking stick into an ant hill," says one writer. And yet the army chiefs tried to regard it as an exceptional and temporary matter, a thing which they could control, when as a matter of fact, it was the meat and kernel of the war.[24]

One Northern paper estimated that as early as August 1863, 155,140 formerly enslaved people had been liberated by Union forces in Mississippi.[25] Military officials set up refugee camps, but they had limited resources to tend to the refugees' needs and they were quickly overwhelmed by the large numbers of Black people fleeing their conditions of enslavement.

Like Sherman, Grant sought to find a way to free his troops from the refugees' needs, and in November 1862, appointed chaplain John Eaton as superintendent of freed people to take charge of the problem. Eaton witnessed the inundation of Black people running to the safety of Northern troops: "an army of slaves and fugitives, pushing its way irresistibly toward an army of fighting men . . . The arrival among us of these hordes was like the oncoming of cities.

There was no plan in this exodus, no Moses to lead it."[26] Eaton immediately organized the freed people into companies, and "set them
to work picking, ginning, and baling all cotton now out and ungath-
ered in the field."[27] Eaton, following Grant's orders, set up a system
of wage labor in Mississippi, employing the freed people not only for
agricultural work, but also in labor battalions for the army, largely
constructing military fortifications.[28]

Eaton kept the freed people housed in camps through the winter, and in the spring sent them out to plant the abandoned cotton
fields that were closest to the camps. It was becoming clear that this
system of government-run camps was not a plausible long-term
solution to the problem, as there was no support in the North for
such a monumental public works project. The American Freedmen's Inquiry Commission recommended to the Secretary of War
and the Senate, in June of 1863, that the contraband camps be used
not as a permanent, structural solution to the problem of the refugees in the South, but as a temporary place of "reception and distribution" of the fleeing refugees who should be expeditiously settled
on abandoned plantations to work for "loyal and respectable owners or lessees who will hire the freedmen at fair wages."[29]

Given the overwhelming needs of the freed people, the imperative that the cotton crop keep in production, and the absence of government wherewithal to continue oversight of the camps, military
officials overseeing Davis Bend decided to bring in private entrepreneurs to rent the land at very low rates, use the equipment they
found on the plantations,[30] and feed, shelter, and pay wages to the
freed people to do the field work.[31] Unfortunately, this plan turned
out to be a disaster, as the so-called entrepreneurs who leased the
land were "generally men of low character who came largely from
the group of 'sharks' who followed the army."[32] James Yeatman
observed, "The desire of gain alone prompts them, and they care
little whether they make it out of the blood of those they employ
or from the soil."[33] Yeatman was president of the Western Sanitary

Commission, a private philanthropic organization, and was actively engaged at this time in visiting Mississippi and making recommendations for the treatment of the freed people.[34] In Mississippi, as in South Carolina and throughout the South, the Treasury and War Departments fought bitterly over control of the freed people, until Congress stepped in and established an independent Bureau in 1865.

Vicksburg became the largest gathering point for formerly enslaved people in the state, and Eaton had an enormous humanitarian crisis on his hands. He desperately needed a reliable assistant, and looked to Captain Samuel Thomas, who in August 1863 was placed in charge of the freed people in the Vicksburg area.[35] Even before General Grant took Vicksburg on July 4, 1863, he had decided that the plantations of the President of the Confederacy would make a wonderful "negro paradise."[36] This plan was provisionally put into place by Admiral David Porter, commander of the Union fleet on the Mississippi, who ordered that Davis Bend be used as an independent Black colony for the refugees who were left there.[37] In December of that year, General Thomas stationed two companies of Black troops at Davis Bend, and a reporter for the *New York Herald* noted that the Davis plantations had become a colony for freed slaves.[38] At that time, over six hundred freed people were living at the Bend and the crops were being prepared for the following year.[39]

A wedding at Hurricane plantation, credit, J. Mack Moore Collection, Old Court, House Museum, Vicksburg, MS

For most of 1863, starting with Grant's capture of Vicksburg in July and well into 1864, chaos reigned in the Davis Bend area. Northern troops, Northern civilian speculators, and other miscellaneous white people from the South engaged in all manner of fraud, theft, and exploitation, not limited to stealing bales of cotton and whatever else they could get their hands on.[40] The Treasury Department was given authority to oversee and protect the successful production of cotton in the abandoned and confiscated lands in the area, but their presence set up foreseeable conflicts between Treasury agents, the military officers in the area, civilians seeking to assist the destitute freed people,[41] and Colonel Thomas's oversight of freed people's affairs.[42] Finally, in the fall of 1864, Eaton was able to obtain President Lincoln's authority to restore control over the plantations and people at Davis Bend.[43]

At this point, the people who had been enslaved by the Davis brothers who remained at Hurricane and Brierfield were joined by hundreds of Black refugees from other parts of the region. In September of 1864, General Lorenzo Thomas visited Davis Bend and reported back to Secretary of War Edwin Stanton, "there is a large home farm where the negroes are cultivating on their own account, and I understand, are doing very well . . . This colony, containing many indigents, will, I understand, be self-supporting."[44]

Just as at Port Royal, the civilian and military officials responsible for the freed people at Davis Bend had two principal objectives: caring for the needs of the indigent and destitute freed people and keeping cotton production going in order to provide a source of financing for the ongoing war.

On November 5, 1864, General Thomas issued Special Order No. 15, confiscating virtually all of Davis Bend "for military purposes, on which will be established a home farm, and to furnish land for freedmen for their own cultivation."[45] The order was to be implemented by one of General Thomas's subordinates, Major General Napoleon Jackson Tecumseh Dana. Dana instructed that the Bend be set aside for "colonization, residence, and support of freedmen . . . The home of Jefferson Davis is a suitable place to furnish the means of support and security for the unfortunate race he is being so instrumental in oppressing."[46] And, just as Sherman had done in the Sea Islands under his Special Order No. 15 setting aside land along the coast for freed people, Dana ordered that "all white persons not connected with the military service will be required to leave the above limits before the 1st day of January, 1865, and after that date no white person will be allowed to land on any part of the same without written permission."[47] Dana appointed Colonel Samuel Thomas to oversee the Davis Bend colony. Davis Bend was one of several Mississippi Valley plantations that had been converted to Black-run "home farms" that were not only self-sustaining,[48] but could send profits up North to fund the war effort.[49]

Major Dana's plan for the Davis Bend colony prevailed over an earlier plan developed by Quakers working in the area. Samuel Shipley, a representative of the Friends' Association of Philadelphia sent to assist in setting up a model freed people's colony at the Bend, had developed a plan to divide up one thousand acres of land for cultivation by one hundred freed people.[50] Shipley felt strongly that the contract labor system resulted in the exploitation of the freed people:

> Under these circumstances, it is evident that this system does not furnish the best mode of elevating the colored man into the position of an intelligent and self-directing laborer. The true friends of the negro in the Southwest recognize these facts and deplore their effects but see no present remedy. Between the cupidity of the lessees and the indifference of the officials, the true interests of the Freedman are little thought of."[51]

He preferred that the freed people be allotted plots at the colony under the supervision of the Quakers.[52] "Without it, the great mass cannot easily rise from their present position,"[53] wrote Shipley to his executive committee in Philadelphia. The Quakers' plan was never adopted, and it was quickly overshadowed by Colonel Thomas's experiment, ultimately embodied in General Thomas's placing the Bend under the Colonel's control.

Another idea for how to use the confiscated property at Davis Bend came from Colonel S. W. Preston in October 1865. Preston commanded a unit of the "colored" infantry and suggested to General Thomas that the Bend be settled by colored soldiers, who, in his opinion, were reckless in spending their military pay:

> The Colored soldiers here, have been in the habit of spending all their money within a few weeks after receiving it and many of them in a way that brings no substantial benefits to themselves or to their families . . . Their reckless expenditures of their earnings if indulged and as is too often the case, encouraged, will create habits of prodigality that cannot be eradicated, and they must remain a demoralized and dependent race.

Preston recommended that their pay should be directly invested in homesteads at Davis Bend, which, under Preston's tutelage, was a plan sure to succeed. "I believe I have an unbounded influence over my men and shall have no difficulty in controlling them in this enterprise for their welfare," he humbly offered. General Thomas never seriously considered this plan.[54]

Thomas set aside roughly five hundred acres at Davis Bend for a Home Farm that housed almost a thousand orphaned children, and older and disabled freed people, overwhelmingly women.[55] He then parceled up five thousand acres for 1,300 adults and 450 children who formed 181 cooperatives. The freed people were left alone to manage their own affairs, free from paternalistic white supervision recommended by the Quakers and Colonel Preston.

This experiment in independent land management, not contract labor under white governance, was enormously successful. Despite heavy rains in June that hurt the crop, the freed people of the Davis Bend Colony turned a $25,929.80 profit, most of which was paid directly into the Bureau's coffers.[56] John Trowbridge reported that fifty Black planters earned $5,000 each year in 1863 and 1864, and one hundred others accumulated between $1,000 and $4,000 annually during this period—absolute fortunes by contemporary standards. Trowbridge remarked that "the signal success of the colony perhaps indicates the future of free labor in the South, and the eventual division of the large plantations into homesteads to be sold or rented to small farmers. This system suits the freedmen better than any other; and under it he is industrious, prosperous, and happy."[57]

Freedpeople's self-governance included an autonomous legal system that the freed people ran themselves. Presumably, some of the people previously enslaved by Davis remained at the Bend and continued to implement a system of justice that they had learned when Joseph Davis had been present.[58]

The freed people's court system at the Davis Bend Colony was as unique and remarkable as its antebellum predecessor. Formally established in January 1865, the Freedmen's Court was set up as follows:

> three judges who shall constitute a court, with authority to try all cases that may be brought before it. This court shall be elected to hold office 3 months . . . The court shall meet at 9 a.m. Saturday, at the Jeff Davis place. There shall be one Sheriff on each plantation to whom all complaints will be made by parties aggrieved, and he on Saturday will bring the case before the court. He will arrest parties when necessary . . . The court will proceed to the trial of cases, swear witnesses, examine them and decide the case according to their ideas of justice and the evidence produced. The judges and sheriffs shall be elected by the people. The court will inflict as punishments fines not to exceed one thousand dollars, forfeitures of crop, expulsion from the Bend, confinement in the guard house, hard labor on the home farm. All decisions of the court must be approved by the post Supt Freedmen. If the judges fail to

do their duty or the sheriff to perform their part, they shall be fined and punished by the Post Supt. Freedmen.[59]

Captain Gaylord Nelson, Provost Marshall of Freedmen at Davis Bend, formally established the Court as a matter of Freedmen's Bureau policy and kept spotty records of the cases brought before it. The judges, all formerly enslaved people, were Simon Cable, Daniel Davenport, and J. A. Gla.[60] Colonel Eaton was much impressed with their "shrewdness" and found the court system itself quite remarkable.[61] The extant records document only ten sessions of the court, between June 10 and December 2, 1865, during which time the judges heard a total of twenty-one cases. Ten resulted in criminal convictions, three civil cases resulted in judgment for the plaintiff, two people were fined for failure to appear, one defendant was acquitted, and five civil cases were dismissed for lack of evidence. All of the court's orders were approved by Captain Nelson.[62] The cases ranged from minor infractions such as stealing fruit, wood, or clothing, to adultery, shooting a neighbor's dog, and charges by a woman against her husband for assault and battery with intention to kill. On Saturday, December 2, 1865, Ms. Phila Davenport charged Abe Davenport with "striking and otherwise abusing her." The court fined the defendant $5. In the next case on the docket, William Hall charged Cesare Johnson with shooting his dog, for which Johnson was fined $10.[63] Under the justice system established at the Bend, the penalty for shooting a dog was twice as severe as that for beating your wife.

While the minute book that recorded the cases heard before the Davis Bend Court of Freedmen did not include any testimony or details about the cases, John T. Trowbridge described one Saturday court session in a published narrative of his tour of "the battlefields and ruined cities of the South."[64] On a visit to the Bend in late 1865, he reported that the judges in the Freedmen's Court did more than listen to community complaints and hand down judgments.

When a freedman and his mother were brought before the court for stealing a bag of corn, one of the judges chastised the defendant:

> Now you listen, you. You and your mother are a couple of low-down darkies, trying to get a living without work. You are the cause that respectable colored people are slandered and called thieving and lazy niggers. Now this is what I'll do with you. If you and your mother will hire out today, and go work like honest people, I'll let you off on good behavior.[65]

This example is remarkable not only for the detail it reveals about the sophistication of the legal proceedings before the Freedmen's Courts, but even more important, as an illustration of how the legal actors involved expressed, performed, and enforced the civilizing power of law. As the judge, himself a Black man, put it to the defendants: the choice is yours, either act like a civilized, law-abiding and industrious citizen, or pay the price as a "low-down darkie."

Freedmen's Bureau and military officers alike regarded the Davis Bend Home Farm as enabling all manner of uplift, as one Bureau agent noted in a report: "The community distinctly demonstrated the capacity of the Negro to take care of himself and exercise under honest and competent direction the functions of self-government."[66] As at Port Royal, this experiment provided an alternative blueprint for emancipation, a path ultimately abandoned, but one that would have laid the way for a very different story of Black freedom, citizenship and reparation structured around separation and independence from white people rather than integration with and subordination to them.

Notwithstanding its financial, moral, and agricultural success, the Freedmen's Colony at the Bend was disbanded after only one year. As soon as President Johnson started issuing pardons to former Southern planters, four of the plantations at the Bend were returned to their antebellum owners.[67] The army closed its post at the Bend in October 1865, and Gaylord Nelson was relieved of duty shortly thereafter. Colonel Thomas was relieved of command in May of 1866. "Colonel Thomas' transfer removed the last federal official with an interest in creating an ideal colony on the Bend. Henceforth, the Bureau would be more concerned with defending past actions than with initiating new projects."[68]

The Davis brothers were not among the former planters whose land was immediately restored, thus the Hurricane and Brierfield plantations remained in the control of Benjamin Montgomery, who had been running them almost continuously since he had returned from Ohio in the beginning of 1865.[69] During this time, Montgomery had been corresponding with his former owner Joseph Davis, and kept him apprised of developments at the Bend, including difficulties Montgomery was having with Colonel Thomas and other Bureau officials. More than once, Davis intervened on Montgomery's behalf to resolve conflicts relating to matters such as the control over the Bend's cotton gin.[70]

In October 1865, Joseph Davis met with Benjamin Montgomery in Vicksburg where they signed a contract permitting Montgomery to lease Brierfield and Hurricane for the next year.[71] Thus, while the Bureau regarded itself in full control and ownership of the land "abandoned" at the Bend, Joseph Davis and his loyal former slave Benjamin Montgomery were contracting in the shadows as if Davis had never lost title to the property. Joseph Davis was fully pardoned by President Johnson on March 20, 1866; however, he did not receive notice of the pardon until five months later. Davis was to be restored the full title, use, and enjoyment of his property as of January 1, 1867, with rent paid to him from the effective date of the pardon.[72] By this point, the elder Davis was over eighty years old and had no intention of returning to Davis Bend to farm. In November of 1866, he and Montgomery agreed to a method by which Davis would finance the sale of four thousand acres of land at the Bend to Montgomery for $300,000. Yet, the Black Codes recently enacted by the Mississippi legislature made this contract of sale unenforceable because the new law prohibited freed people from owning land. Nevertheless, both

Davis and Montgomery intended to abide by its terms.

Montgomery was elated to be in full possession of the Bend and almost immediately took out an ad in the *Vicksburg Daily Times* announcing that on January 1, 1867, he intended to "organize a community composed exclusively of colored people, to occupy and cultivate said plantations, and invites the cooperation of such as are recommended by honesty, industry, sobriety, and intelligence, in the enterprise."[73] Montgomery went on to outline a form of self-government and taxation that would be instituted at this new colony. This new regime would surely include the system of freedmen's courts that had been maintained at the Bend after the Freedmen's Bureau had retreated.

Over the years, Montgomery and his family struggled to make the payments to Davis, never, in the end, paying off any of the principal on the loan, and only making partial payments on the 5 percent annual interest upon which they had agreed. Davis was content to receive a steady income of interest payments from Montgomery in his old age.

Jefferson Davis, 1888. Courtesy of the National Portrait Gallery, Smithsonian Institution, Washington D.C.

But his heirs were not so tolerant, neither of the lost income, nor of the noble project in Black self-sufficiency to which Benjamin and Joseph had been committed. After years of successful farming,[74] indeed innovation,[75] Benjamin Montgomery died a poor man in 1878. His son, Isaiah, abandoned the Bend in 1883 due to recurring floods,[76] and went on to establish another utopian all-Black community at Mound Bayou, Mississippi in 1887.[77] In the spring of that year, an enormous flood raged down the Mississippi River, cutting out a new channel just upriver from the Bend. Almost overnight, Davis Bend became Davis Island, significantly complicating the logistics of running the former Davis plantations. Much of the best land remained under water until well into the planting season.[78]

The experiment at Davis Bend, in ways similar to the Port Royal project, was both enormously successful and tragically short-lived. While a fraction of the freed people of Port Royal ended up with land on the Sea Islands or along the southeastern coast as envisioned by General Sherman, Benjamin Montgomery and his family were the only freed people to gain longer term title to land at Davis Bend. But even Montgomery's title was highly leveraged and contingent upon the ongoing beneficence of his former owner. Surely no one underappreciated the irony of the fact that the Montgomery family enjoyed this privilege on account of the kindness of the elder brother of the President of the Confederacy. To his death, Isaiah Montgomery praised Jefferson Davis as "a wonderful man . . . My thoughts frequently go back, now that I am approaching the end of my days, to the time I was his personal servant as a barefoot boy. I truly believe, when he got his last sickness, had I been here to serve and care for him, that he would have lived many more years . . . It was the influence of Jefferson Davis and his sweet life that has guided all my efforts in bettering the life of my colored brothers and if I have succeeded it was because of them."[79]

The story of Black freedom at Davis Bend is replete with paradox. Time and again, Joseph Davis came to the aid of his former slaves in defense of their interests that were being disregarded by Northern officials. One wonders what Benjamin Montgomery could have accomplished had he not been saddled with the debt to his former owner or made to suffer the ravages of the weather and a river that despite its apathy seemed to be against his interests. Davis could have forgiven the debt in his will, or even better could have deeded the property outright to Montgomery as compensation for the many years in which Montgomery's labor was stolen while he was enslaved, but instead Davis passed it on as an asset to his children, thus assuring that neither the Montgomery family nor any of the formerly enslaved people had a future at Davis Bend. Today, the land that was the Bend is abandoned and overgrown.[80]

Law played a significant role in the civilizing mission that was undertaken at the Bend, but in ways that differed somewhat from law's utility at Port Royal. Both before and after emancipation, legal self-governance subsidized the production of cotton—first with enslaved Black labor and later with freed Black labor. Unlike at Port Royal, Black people at Davis Bend were not merely governed by law, but they served in positions of legal authority as well. So too, law's governance at the Bend was largely intra-, not inter-racial. Black men, both free and enslaved were enlisted to undertake fairly well-scripted performances of legal authority—as police, as judges, and as jurors. Thus, the call of law and the kinds of legal subjects that it summoned, were more complex at Davis Bend than at Port Royal insofar as the legal roles made available to Black men allowed them to distinguish themselves as more or less civilized. Here we see the seeds of the notion of the good Black, the civilized negro, the successful product of moral uplift, who never completely achieves the full civility and subjectivity of white men, but rather is asked to mimic what those men are by nature, always and already.

CHAPTER 3

The Ongoing Case for Reparations

"Revolution is based on land. Land is the basis of all independence. Land is the basis of freedom, justice and equality."

—**Malcolm X**, "Message to the Grassroots," November 10, 1963

O N THE EVENING of December 31, 1862, Black people across the South gathered together for what they called "Freedom's Eve" celebrations and counted down the minutes, then seconds until the Emancipation Proclamation took effect. "At Beaufort, South Carolina, over five thousand Black people gathered and sang what one white observer called 'the Marseillaise of the slaves . . . The effect was electrical.'"[1] They sang: "In that New Jerusalem, I am not afraid to die; We must fight for liberty, in that New Jerusalem."[2] In that electric moment at the stroke of midnight, Black people were transformed from objects of enslavement to subjects of freed-dom. But, as they would shortly learn, the freed-dom they were about to enjoy was every bit as peculiar as the soul-killing institution that Lincoln's pen sought to destroy.

While the Emancipation Proclamation officially ended the nightmare of slavery for masses of Black people throughout the South,[3] those freed by Lincoln on January 1, 1863, joined thousands of formerly enslaved people who had been freed through military occupation in the Sea Islands and Mississippi. Meanwhile, the enslaved people in four slave states that had remained loyal to the Union (Kentucky, Missouri, Maryland, and Delaware) and so were not covered by Lincoln's freedom proclamation would have to wait until the end of the war to be freed.[4] Consequently, more enslaved people were emancipated by the US military than by Lincoln's proclamation, though his declaration of freedom served as an important catalyst in shifting the focus and momentum in the Civil War.

Union troops had overseen the creation of "a negro paradise" just south of Vicksburg, Mississippi, and a radical experiment in free Black labor, land ownership, and self-sovereignty at Port Royal, South Carolina. These two utopian experiments provided a model for what freedom, reparation, transitional justice, and citizenship could have looked like for African Americans had President Johnson not put an end to them shortly after he entered the White House. Their initial successes and ultimate failures help illuminate the peculiar form of freed-dom that Black people experienced in the newly united States.

Freed men and women had a very different notion of what it meant to be free than did the white military officers, missionaries, and politicians who controlled the terms of their emancipation. The freed people made ardent demands for land redistribution and separation from white people, while the white people who ran Reconstruction governance preferred an approach that nested both freedom and transitional justice for Black people in a web of legally mediated relationships with white people—contract laborer/planter and sharecropper/landowner. In lamentably similar ways, both before and after the end of slavery, Black people were workers and white people were owners. Hence, labor and capital remained essentially raced resources regardless of the formal abolition of slavery. While formerly enslaved people expected that their freedom would take place in homestead farms on forty-acre lots, Northern officials, paternalistically, thought it better that the freed people learn the lessons, responsibilities, and discipline of freedom through legally structured institutions such as the contract labor system. Keeping to the obligations of labor contracts that the head of the Black household would sign for a year was the best method by which to teach freed people a necessary form of self-mastery, so their thinking went.

The experiment in a productive freedom at Port Royal undertaken by Philbrick and colleagues illustrated what has been manifest in many other colonial contexts: economic interests underwrite "common sense notions of who (or what) is responsible for social inequalities."[5] For Edward Philbrick and William Gannett, by 1865, the articulation of benevolent, unself-interested concern for the welfare of the freed people became a fig leaf for promoting economic interests in Southern cotton production that they shared with their Boston investors, who, it should be pointed out, made a handsome profit on Philbrick's "experiment" in free labor. Philbrick's success at Port Royal served as a model for Northern industrialists, such as Horace Greeley, who "insisted that what the South needed most was not talk of confiscation, which would paralyze investment and economic development, but an influx of Northern capital, settlers, and industrial skills."[6] Nowhere in their plans did Black people figure as agents of a postwar economy or social order. The temptation for those on colonial missions to do not only good but also do well monetarily is not unique to the Port Royal project.[7]

The global implications of this venture in virtue for profit were anything but extenuating. The United States sought to improve its advantage in the international cotton market, then dominated primarily by India, Egypt, and Brazil.[8] Cotton industrialists like Edward

Atkinson, the author of *Cheap Cotton by Free Labor*, sought to sell the antislavery campaign as one that would improve the standing of the United States in an increasingly globalizing cotton market.[9] Industriousness and a commitment to a single-crop economy by the freed people were key to the success of these plans. While these Northerners were committed to the destruction of the system of chattel slavery, they favored the retention of the plantation system, but with Northern capital and management. These plans could not tolerate independent Black yeoman farmers engaged in subsistence or just above subsistence farming of crops other than cotton. "Their vision of the freed people as agricultural peasants devoted to a single-crop economy and educated to a taste for consumer goods supplied by Northern factories fulfills the classic pattern of tributary economies the world over."[10]

In the end, the policies of both the Freedmen's Bureau and Northern settlers favored a role for the freed people in the post-war economy as "an essentially propertyless plantation force, whose basic legal rights would be recognized," and would "hardly be in a position to challenge propertied whites for political and economic dominance."[11] This policy received strong endorsement from Northern industrialists and members of the Johnson administration, who, in the end, viewed land confiscation and redistribution as an outrage. Property rights were a bedrock American value that could not be sacrificed for a cause of less importance, such as the freedom of Black people. This reasoning explained President Johnson's veto of the second Freedmen's Bureau Act, a law that would have legally recognized Sherman's land grants to the freed people along the Eastern coast, if only for three years.[12] Once public sentiment in favor of aiding the freed people dimmed with the end of the war, prominent Northern journals issued editorials urging that the allocation of land to formerly enslaved people not violate well-hewn American ideals of hard work and deservedness. *The Nation* commented that giving homesteads to the freed people would teach the wrong lesson, that "there are other ways of securing comfort and riches than honest work . . . No man in America has any right to anything which he had not honestly earned, or which the lawful owner has not thought proper to give him."[13] Somehow all the unpaid labor done by four million people while enslaved did not count as "honest work" to the editors of *The Nation* and their supporters. A consensus was emerging among white people that freeing enslaved people was all that justice required; doing anything more—such as providing reparation for the crime of enslavement—was more than recently freed people deserved and would be unfair to white people from whom any kind of redistribution of resources might be required.

Once the war was over, outrage toward the atrocity of chattel slavery was expeditiously replaced by indignation at the specter of an erosion of the natural right to property. Once emancipated, Black people were successfully bound into a peasant status through an interlocking web of legal relationships, responsibilities, and rights. By 1867, all but a few of the nation's leaders were looking forward to the economic future of the unified nation, no longer mindful of what moral imperative the atrocities of slavery might demand, nor interested in the economic needs of African Americans. US Representative Thaddeus Stevens was a notable exception. He continued to fight, until his death in 1868, for confiscation and homesteads for the freed people. But he became a minority in the increasingly less progressive Republican delegation in Congress.[14] Confiscation triggered self-serving concerns about the integrity of private property interests—regardless of the fact that the property was that of disloyal Confederates who had waged war against the republic. The fundamental integrity of capitalism was at stake, not to be undermined by backward looking claims made by poor Black people in the South. The *New York Times* gave voice to this view in July of 1867 when it editorialized: "If Congress is to take cognizance of the claims of labor against capital . . . there can be no decent pretense for confining the task of the slave-holder of the South . . . An attempt to justify the confiscation of Southern land under the pretense of doing justice to the freedmen, strikes at the root of all property rights in both sections. It concerns Massachusetts quite as much as Mississippi."[15] The interests of capital forged solidarity between white men who only a couple of years earlier had been shooting at each other.

The defenders of white people's property rights were unmoved by arguments that justice demanded that some form of reparation was owed to formerly enslaved people, and they doubled down on their position in ways that amplified this injustice. Not only did President Johnson grant amnesty to the former slave-owners and restore confiscated land to white planters who returned to the Sea Islands with the aim of reestablishing an earlier status quo, but once that land was restored to white planters, the freed people of the Sea Islands who had bought confiscated land at the tax auctions were not reimbursed for what they had paid for those properties. Even worse, Congress passed a law in 1891 that would compensate the white planters who had not returned to reclaim land that had been seized pursuant to the Direct Tax Act and then sold at auction to white speculators and some freed people for the value of the land seized, albeit at a substantially discounted rate.[16] The US Court of Claims was then charged with tracking down the heirs to that land who had dispersed throughout the country as far as New York, Florida, Washington, DC, and Texas.[17] Court of Claims records indicate that the US Treasury settled these interests in land in Beaufort County for a total of $207,166.58 ($5,518,373.73 in 2018 dollars). Thus, white slave-owners were ultimately "made whole" for any costs they may have incurred from seceding from the Union and siding with the losing, proslavery cause. Meanwhile, formerly enslaved people have never received anything as compensation for their confiscated labor, dignity, and life. "The poverty which afflicted them for a generation after Emancipation held them down to the lowest order of society, nominally free but economically en-slaved,"[18] wrote Carter G. Woodson in *The Mis-Education of the Negro* published in 1933.

Without question, the freed people of the Sea Islands and Davis Bend expected—and were promised—land and independence from white people as a kind of enabling condition for real freedom. What that more robust form of freedom might have looked like is hinted at in all-Black communities created in Davis Bend by the Montgomery family and in other communities peppered across South Carolina, Tennessee, and Georgia, where freed people were able to buy land collectively and create model "Black Utopias" of their own design. The Nashoba Commune was the first of its kind, founded outside Memphis in 1825 by Francis "Fanny" Wright, a Scottish-born white abolitionist, feminist, and suffragette. Curiously enough, Wright, like Joseph Davis, was a devotee of British socialist Robert Owen and, like the brother of the President of the Confederacy, set out to create a communal experiment in Black freedom in the South. In 1825 Wright published a pamphlet, *A Plan for the Gradual Abolition of Slavery in the United States Without Danger of Loss to the Citizens of the South*, that she hoped would persuade Congress to set aside land for the purpose of promoting emancipation.[19] Her proposal was to purchase the freedom of enslaved people and set them up in collectively run all-Black communities with land, seed, animals, and implements. She had a detailed budget for the project that would start off with the purchased manumission of a hundred people. The Nashoba Commune was a prototype, founded with thirty formerly enslaved people. The experiment was not successful and provided a mediocre model for Black freedom since Black people were not allowed to assume leadership positions, and in some cases freed people were admitted only if they were accompanied by their former owners. What is more, the Commune was built on a mosquito-infested swamp and many of its residents, including Wright, contracted malaria. It ended after three years when Wright chartered a ship and moved the Commune residents to Haiti, where they could live their lives under conditions of greater political freedom.[20] Nevertheless, Fanny Wright's unorthodox and forward-thinking approach to abolition envisioned much more than "mere emancipation," and included substantive repair that, at least in theory, would make free and independent lives possible.

The Combahee River Colony was another, and better, example of Black independent living. The project was founded by freed Black women whose husbands had left home to fight with the Union army. Neighboring Beaufort County to the northeast, along the Combahee River, several hundred freed women settled on land abandoned by Confederate planters and grew cotton, potatoes and other crops, and made crafts for sale. They refused to allow white people into the collective and gained a reputation for independence and pride in building their own autonomous community.[21]

These self-supporting Black communities, formed as positive alternatives to failed white-led abolition efforts, provide a model of what freedom might have looked like had formerly enslaved people been given the resources and opportunity necessary to start new, free lives. "They were political and economic havens for escaped enslaved people and impoverished freedmen, operating under ideals of Jeffersonian agrarianism and, later, urban-industrial entrepreneurship."[22] Rather than serving as the blueprint for Black freedom, they serve as the exception that proved the incomplete justice of the rule.

The wisdom that lay at the heart of these Black utopias, as well as the efforts of officials who insisted that formerly enslaved people were owed an enormous debt of repair, still calls us today to consider in what ways we continue to live with a legacy of both advantage and disadvantage traceable back to unjust enrichment at the time we collectively ended slavery. General Rufus Saxton framed the question so eloquently in 1862: "It seemed to be the dictate of simple justice that [the freedmen] have the highest right to a soil that they have cultivated so long under the cruelest compulsion,

robbed of every personal right, and without any domestic or social relations which they could protect."[23] By 1865, the debt owed
to formerly enslaved people had matured in Saxton's mind, and he
argued to his superiors that the freed people's demand for land was
secured by an "equitable mortgage on the land" for "generations
of unpaid wages."[24] This summons from the past need not be seen
only as a model for a counter-history that never came to be, but
rather as inspiration to act in the present.

⌐&

This history makes a compelling case for the renewed call for reparations today, especially in the form of property redistribution. To
be sure, modern principles of human rights and dignity—familiar
to today's ear but not yet articulated in the mid- to late nineteenth
century—fully embrace the notion that a kind of restorative justice
must be awarded to the victims of human enslavement for the loss
of liberty, torture, hatred, and degradation that they suffered and
that characterized the institution of chattel slavery.[25]

Clearly, enslaved people gained a set of important rights when
they were freed. They could have their marriages honored legally,
enter into contracts, and sign documents in their own names. But
for the most part, the right to own property was not acknowledged
as something to which they were fully entitled. In fact, complying
with the legal rules of marrying and making contracts were seen as
practices that could impose the kind of disciplinary training that
would prepare them for other, more fundamental, rights—such as
owning property.[26]

Yet rights, are not rights, are not rights. That is to say, all is
not equal among fundamental rights. In important ways, property
rights serve a keystone function—they are the rights upon which all
other rights rest, some have argued.[27] Arthur Lee, an early colonial
diplomat, born in Virginia and educated in Britain, and a strong

opponent of slavery, addressed the British Parliament in 1775 on the question of colonial independence, arguing that "[t]he right of property is the guardian of every other right, and to deprive a people of this, is in fact to deprive them of their liberty."[28] In making this argument, Lee relied heavily on John Locke's approach to property: "For the preservation of property being the end of government, and that which men enter into society . . . for I truly have no property in that which another can of right take from me, when he pleases, without my consent."[29] Twelve years earlier, Adam Smith observed that a core aspect of the importance of property rights was its centrality to successful governance.[30] Giving Smith's thoughts a more modern gloss, property rights could be understood to be essential to both self-governance and governance by the state. In this sense, property rights are necessary not only to the creation of personal wealth and well-being, but to the creation of civic personhood. According to the dominant thinking at the time slavery was abolished in the US, to deny to a group of people the status of property rights–holder is to deny their humanity and membership in civil society. From this perspective, property rights can be a particularly "dense transfer point for relations of power" in the process of identity formation.[31] Or, to borrow from Franz Fanon, property becomes a kind of "glowing focal point where citizen and individual develop and grow."[32]

It was precisely this kind of recognition—of full personhood through property rights—that was denied Black people when they were freed. While the missionaries from the North who regarded themselves as caretakers of Black freedom—almost all well educated, elite white men—likely had read Smith and Locke and had a keen sense of the role that property rights played as the predicate for the exercise of all other rights, the freed people likely intuited that they were being emancipated on the cheap and without full justice. The freed people of Port Royal and Davis Bend fully expected that the abolition of slavery would entail the exchange of their condition of *being* property owned by white people for the status of being property-*owners* who could tell white people to get off their land. Remarkably, not all of the freed people of Port Royal expected to be *given* land—as later promised by Generals Sherman and Grant—rather they aimed to *buy* it, often in clubs, kinship groups, or in co-operatives. They worked hard to save enough money to buy land at public auctions, and the federal officials that set the terms of these sales understood that if title to land was to play a meaningful role in the reparation of slavery, the land could not be priced at what the market would bear, but rather at what the community could afford.

The strategy for doing justice to formerly enslaved people, including individual and collective ownership of land, can be found in the histories of Port Royal and Davis Bend. The failures of these experiments in repair testify to the triumph of the notion of white innocence, or at least redemption (thus justifying amnesty, pardons, and restoration of confiscated Confederates' land) as a justification or excuse for the refusal to face the atrocity and horror of enslaving human beings in this country. The idea that merely setting people free was enough to satisfy the demands of justice in this context is, and remains, well, obscene. The failure to deliver adequate justice to formerly enslaved people at the end of the Civil War locked Black people into an enduring and subordinate second-class status of people who were free*d* but not free.

There is little disagreement that most freed people wanted and expected that the Southern plantations would be distributed to them at the close of the war. So too, there can be no denying the fact that they were devastated and outraged when the promises of land, often made to them by public and private officials, were broken by President Johnson's amnesty program. Even after it became apparent that General Sherman's land grants were no more valuable than the paper on which they were written, and that the efforts of Senators Sumner and Stevens to allocate land to the freed people would fail, Sojourner Truth, among others, continued to make demands for reparations in the form of free public land for the former slaves: "America owes to my people some of the dividends. She can afford to pay and she must pay. I shall make them understand that there is a debt to the Negro people which they can never repay. At least, then, they must make amends."[33]

There is no doubt that the formerly enslaved people were entitled to something more than being freed. Yet what would have warranted the granting of land and some tools to the freed people as a substantive component of the larger project of abolishing slavery? Did justice require this? Would the granting of land have gone some distance toward eliminating or repudiating the underlying racist values that made Black people enslaveable in the first place?

I pose these questions after telling the stories of betrayal of the freed people of the Sea Islands and Davis Bend because we have never, as a nation, come to terms with the ongoing moral and material legacies of slavery. Today, when societies are struggling to make the difficult transition from tyranny and inhumane exploitation to greater legitimacy and respect of human rights we bring to bear a set of tools loosely organized around a notion of transitional justice. Take for instance Darfur, Sierra Leone, Chile, South Africa, Rwanda, Bosnia, or post–World War II Germany. In these settings a just future is not possible without naming and taking account of the injustices of the past. Yet in the United States, the transition from a nation that permitted, if not encouraged, slavery to one that abhorred it did not include an acknowledgment that the nation as a whole needed to undergo some sort of reckoning, that the freed people were owed something more than declaring slavery constitutionally impermissible, and that that something would be understood as a necessary element of the nation's reconstitution as a more just society than the one that had been vanquished by the Civil War.

Was land redistribution what justice required or was it simply the resource that the Northern troops and the Freedmen's Bureau had available? Recall that at the time it was widely viewed that exempting the slaves from the restoration of property rights as part of the amnesty granted by President Johnson to the former rebels amounted to a kind of theft. Even President Lincoln clung to the idea that the best way to abolish slavery was through compensated emancipation, such that the slave-owners would be paid something in the neighborhood of $400 million (in 1864 dollars) for the value of their freed slaves.[34] It never entered his mind that funds should be allocated to the enslaved people to compensate them for the theft of their labor and the violence, indignity, separation of families, sexual abuse, and social death caused by enslavement. Frederick Douglass was also dubious about the practicability of a demand for reparations for formerly enslaved people, but he came to the view that the nation "had robbed [African Americans] of the rewards of his labor during more than two hundred years."[35] In 1875, reflecting on the failure of both reconstruction and justice toward freed people, Douglass declared that the nation had not done enough for freed people: "The world has never seen any people turned loose to such destitution as were the four million slaves of the South . . . They were free without roofs to cover them, or bread to eat, or land to cultivate, and as a consequence died in such numbers as to awaken the hope of their enemies that they would soon disappear."[36]

There are a number of ways to justify an entitlement, or better yet, a right to some kind of reparations for free people. It is not clear, however, which of these theories of justice best heals the wound of enslavement, as if such an injury could be adequately addressed through its liquidation in the form of ex post damages.

One approach would be to calculate the value of the theft of the enslaved peoples' labor. In law we call this a "make-whole" remedy: the injured party is made whole by the payment of monetary damages equivalent to what they lost due to the injuring party's conduct. These make-whole remedies are premised on the fiction that important aspects of human life—such as a limb, a life, or freedom— are possessed of a kind of fungibility that render them amenable to valuation in terms of dollars. Most laypeople find this kind of commodification of humanity and the human body impossible and offensive. Yet this second-best approach to justice is often all we have when we are dealing with the problem after the fact. Contemporary law and economics scholars have tried to infuse these calculations with the illusion of rationality when they ask, in advance: what would you pay to give something up—a leg, the company of your wife, your professional status? The number you pick tells us what it's worth to you, and that's how we know how much the tort system should value the loss of these "personal assets." How much would any of us be willing to pay for our freedom? Indeed, the thirteenth amendment to the Constitution, in essence, stands as an injunction against the very asking of this question. Thus, any attempt to commodify the harm of enslavement in terms of money-based reparations is from the start a morally compromised enterprise. Never mind the compounding intergenerational dilemmas, a century and a half after emancipation, of determining who should pay and who should receive these funds.

Mindful of these ethical conundrums, many efforts have been made to rationally calculate monetary reparations for enslavement, on the notion that some payment is a less bad option than no payment at all. In 1972, economist Jim Marketti offered one of the first rigorous calculations of the debt owed for enslaved labor performed between 1790 and 1860: between $448 billion and $995 billion—in 1972 dollars. (The difference between the lower and the higher numbers here turned on the rate of compound interest that should be applied.) Marketti arrived at these numbers not by calculating the amount of money the slaves should have been paid in wages, but by assuming that the purchase price paid for each slave was a reliable proxy for the net income or profit stream derived from that slave. Of course, these figures represent the lost value owed to enslaved people *only* up to the point of emancipation. Others have urged that the reparations owed Black people should include not only lost wages, but also the amount of underpayment after emancipation due to the persistent and brutal discrimination against Black work-ers.[37] Marketti's calculations also neglect a calculus for compensat-ing for physical torture, including rape, death through hard labor, forced reproduction, separation of families, and the systematic deg-radation of enslaved people's dignity as humans.

Marketti's approach would lead us to conclude that at the end of the Civil War the freed people were owed reimbursement for their value in the slave markets of the time. In a sense, the society would sell the slaves back to themselves. If this had been done, would jus-tice have been accomplished? While the approach is attractive to an economist, those, such as myself, who come at the problem as one of human rights are troubled by the idea of framing what is owed to former slaves in terms that ratify the idea of human beings having a market value.

If Marketti's approach is less than satisfying from the perspective of human rights and human value, then might we feel better if the financial compensation were calculated differently? In other words, does the discomfort derive from the fact that the injury of slavery is translated into a cash value, or how the cash value is calculated? To answer these questions adequately one must imagine what it would have meant in 1865 to have abolished slavery and then have made cash payments to the freed men, women, and children. The federal government, through the auspices of the Freedmen's Bureau, could have confiscated the land of the former Confederate planters and sold the land at auction and then used the proceeds of those land auctions to pay reparations to the freed people. Would justice have been done in the minds of the freed people under this scenario? Maybe some would have thought so, indeed I suspect that the peo-ple at Davis Bend would have found this approach more attractive than those living on the Sea Islands. The people in South Carolina were so attached to the land that they would have been devastated to have it sold out from under them—as indeed they were when this is what happened. Of course, getting a cash payment would have been better than what actually happened, but I don't think the Port Royal freed people would have walked away feeling that a form of justice had been done if they'd been paid the proceeds from the sale of confiscated Sea Islands land.

At the close of the nineteenth century a movement mobilized in support of federal legislation that would create a pension system for the formerly enslaved people, specifically understood as a form of reparation for enslavement. The reasoning behind this effort was motivated by the creation of a federal pension system for military veterans: if men who had served in the Union army were entitled to a pension to recognize their service, so too were the former slaves entitled to compensation for the years of involuntary labor. While the movement itself drew much support among formerly enslaved people and white allies, none of the several bills introduced into the Congress to create such a pension system were successful.[38]

An equally creative effort to gain reparations for the former slaves took the form of a lawsuit filed by a class of formerly enslaved people against the Secretary of the Treasury seeking an equitable lien in the amount of $68,072,388.99, a sum collected between 1862 and 1868 as a tax on cotton that they argued was due them because the cotton had been produced by them and their ancestors as a result of their "involuntary servitude." They maintained that "their ancestors 'were subject to a system of involuntary servitude' in states of the South, and that as a result of such servitude many million bales of cotton were produced; that between the years 1862 to 1868 the then Secretary of the Treasury secured possession of the above-named sum of money, 'being a portion of the proceeds of the identical cotton heretofore mentioned, and that said money is designated on the books of the defendant, named on said books, and known as 'Internal Revenue Tax on Raw Cotton.'"[39] Unfortunately, the suit was unsuccessful.

In the end, given the levels of Black illiteracy, inexperience with managing savings, the paucity of opportunities to invest, and the depth of disdain that white people still felt for the freed people, would freed people have been well-served by cash payments in the immediate aftermath of the war? Surely some of them might have followed in Isaiah Montgomery's footsteps and set up autonomous Black communities with the money they had received. To be sure, the best investment the freed people could have made at the time was in land. But a large number might have been swindled out of their money, made bad investments, or had it stolen. Indeed, some Black leaders at the time voiced concern that cash payments to freed people would only serve the interests of white "southern business but not uplift[. . .] the African American community" as they were likely to spend these funds too quickly.[40]

Does this concern about the freed people's ability to responsibly and safely manage a large infusion of cash smack of ugly paternalism? Does being free necessarily include the freedom to make bad decisions and be taken advantage of? Doesn't this echo Donald Rumsfeld's response to the looting and chaos in Baghdad in the immediate aftermath of the US ouster of Saddam Hussein: "Freedom is untidy . . . free people are free to make mistakes and commit crimes"?

As an alternative, would the redistribution of land instead of cash payments have better accomplished the justice aims of a society seeking to make amends for the enslavement of millions of people? Land redistribution has been pursued in other contexts, such as part of decolonization programs in sub-Saharan Africa, in part to address past injustices but also as part of a comprehensive, forward-looking effort to reduce poverty within a framework of rural development that aims to create sustainable livelihoods for impoverished and oppressed peoples.

Zimbabwe offers an example of how not to undertake land redistribution in the name of reparation for past injustice. The government of Robert Mugabe violently seized land owned by whites with the stated goal of redistributing it to landless native

Zimbabweans. Yet the reality is that the land was redistributed as a reward to Black people who were loyal to the Mugabe government, and the Black farmworkers who were living and working on the seized lands have not been included in the resettlement efforts, instead they were treated violently and ejected from the land when government officials moved in to remove the white owners. Very few of the farms that were seized have become fully functioning again, resulting in a 90 percent drop in food production in Zimbabwe. After Mugabe left office the new administration sought to ameliorate the chaos created by the Mugabe government's land reform programs by compensating white farmers for the cost of land appropriated by the government.[41]

Namibia's land reform program has avoided some of the dangers of the Zimbabwean program but has proceeded far too slowly by most accounts. Preferring an approach of "willing seller, willing buyer" the government has sought to purchase land from the overwhelmingly white owners of the estimated four thousand farms in Namibia. It has avoided the violence that characterized the program in Zimbabwe, but the government is short on cash to purchase those farms that have willing sellers.

In South Africa, black people make up 80 percent of the population but own only 4 percent of all farms and agricultural land that is owned by individuals.[42] This inequality of land distribution in South Africa can be traced to the 1913 Natives Land Act that reserved almost 93 percent of the land for the white minority, legalizing what had been an ongoing historical dispossession of African-owned land since European colonial settlement. Land reform figured prominently in the African National Congress's (ANC) platform upon gaining power in 1994, and the post-apartheid constitution included a specific clause that called for the restitution of land or fair compensation to people and communities who had been dispossessed of their rights to land during the colonial and apartheid eras. The World Bank has concluded that land redistribution is essential to remediating economic inequality in South Africa.[43] Yet progress here, like in Namibia, has been slow, adopting a "willing buyer, willing seller" approach as well.

The South African land reform program has three components: restitution, which seeks to restore land ownership or compensate those forced off land during white rule; redistribution of mainly agricultural land to redress the discriminatory colonial and apartheid policies by providing the disadvantaged and poor with access to land; and land tenure reform, which seeks to secure tenure for all South Africans, especially the more vulnerable such as farm laborer tenants. The Zuma government planned to redistribute 30 percent of commercial farmland currently owned by white farmers to landless Black people by 2015, yet when Zuma was forced out of office, in early 2018, land redistribution fell way short of this target. When the new president, Cyril Ramaphosa, took office in February 2018, he proclaimed that he would speed up the transfer of land to Black people, and legislation to accomplish this goal moved quickly through the South African parliament. President Donald Trump intervened in President Ramaphosa's efforts to improve land equity with a tweet in the summer of 2018 that repeated white supremacist falsehoods about Ramaphosa's policy goals that he had heard on Fox News: "I have asked Secretary of State @SecPompeo to closely study the South Africa land and farm seizures and expropriations and the large scale killing of farmers. 'South African Government is now seizing land from white farmers.'" The South African president responded quickly and firmly, insisting on the importance of land reform in his larger goal of repairing the injustice of the apartheid era. Land reform activists in South Africa have grown impatient and have urged the government to implement more radical land redistribution now rather than face the long-term consequences of a drawn-out process that is likely to devolve quickly into deep resentment and violence, as it already has in KwaZulu-Natal.

These experiences in Southern Africa teach us that successful land reform as part of a program of transitional justice is always hard to achieve and can be painful. This doesn't mean, however, that it should not have been tried at the end of the Civil War in the United States. There are important differences in the experiences of the postcolonial African nations and the postbellum United States. First of all, at the moment of emancipation, many, if not most of the Southern landowners had abandoned their plantations in the face of federal military occupation. Thus, war had forced their removal, leaving, in many cases, the formerly enslaved people to run the plantations on their own. Indeed, in many contexts the freed people were just as, if not more, proficient in doing the agricultural work and running the plantations than were the land's legal owners. Thus, many of the pitfalls of the South African experience could have been avoided, as there would have been no need to use a "willing seller/willing buyer" approach. Whites need not have been ejected, as they forfeited any claim to the land when they declared insurrection against the United States; the transition in ownership would not, necessarily, have interrupted the productivity of the plantations; the freed people did not need to be trained in agricultural methods; and the government did not have to come up with the purchase price for the land (although reimbursing the evicted white landowners for the fair price of the land was one of the proposals floated by Senator Sumner). The government could have gone ahead with subsidized auctions in the Sea Islands and in other parts of the South, including the Sherman lands, thus making it the case that freed people fully owned the land with defensible titles.

The confiscation that would have been required for such a land redistribution program would have been justified as a way to disgorge the planters' ill-earned gains, or for the reimbursement of the purchase prices of all of their slaves. Whichever way one accounts for the transfer of assets from slave-owner to newly freed person, there would be a justice-based justification for doing so.

Whether the reparation was forty acres or forty dollars, land reallocation or cash payments to the freed people would have been better than the coercive adoption of the contract labor system they were forced into. Yet returning to the question of how to repeal or eradicate the racist ideology that situated Black people as grossly inferior to whites such that they were socially and legally enslaveable, one wonders whether money or land would have been more effective in undermining and dismantling that racism. While it is compelling to tell an alternative history where greater justice was afforded the freed slaves when they got the land they so desperately wanted and deserved, I want to resist the urge to construct a utopian counternarrative that, had it taken place, everything would have been great for the Black people of the South. Eradicating the deeply ingrained sense of racial superiority felt by most whites was, and continues to be, a hugely intractable problem. As Frederick Douglass sagely observed about human nature, no one ever gives up power willingly.

The experiences of Native Americans in the same period in which Black people were emancipated could tell us something about what might have happened had the freed people received land rather than contract labor. Just as officials in Washington were convinced that giving or selling land to the freed people would not teach them the right lessons about what it meant to be civilized and responsible people, the opposite approach was being pursued with respect to Native peoples. Secretary of the Interior Carl Schurz recommended providing land allotments to heads of Native families on all reservations because of "the enjoyment and pride of the individual ownership of property being one of the most effective civilizing agencies."[44] Indeed, it had been the federal government's view since the nation's founding that it was in both the government's and the Native peoples' best interest to tie them down to homesteads by allotting them plots of land that they would own outright. An 1805 treaty with the Choctaws allocated parcels for individual tribe members, and as more and more eastern Native tribes were moved westward, the treaties that did so contained provisions granting plots of land to heads of Native households. In 1862, the

Commissioner of Indians stated that "one by one, the tribes are abandoning the customs of holding their lands in common, and are becoming individual owners of soil—a step which I regard as the most important in their progress towards civilization."[45] Thus, the views of government officials dealing with the demands for land rights by freed Black people were exactly the opposite when it came to Native Americans. For the government, freed Black people weren't civilized enough to handle land ownership, yet land ownership was thought to be the right tool to civilize Native Americans.

Federal policymakers were realistic about what it might mean to place land titles in the hands of Native people who had never owned land before. Among their concerns was the danger that fast-talking white swindlers would trick them into selling their land. The Commissioner of Indian Affairs, Ezra Hayt, gave voice to this concern:

> The reservations in such cases are infested by a class of land-sharks who do not hesitate to resort to any measure, however iniquitous, to defraud the Indians of their lands. Whiskey is given to them, and while they are under its influence they are made to sign deeds of conveyance, without consideration [i.e. without any payment for the land].[46]

For this reason, the government took steps to protect Native Americans "from their own improvidence." Take, for instance, the land owned by Victoria Smith, to which she, a "half-breed" Kansas Indian, had received title in a treaty between the Kansas Indians and the US government in 1825. That treaty named fourteen "half-breed" families who were allotted one-mile square plots of land on the reservation onto which the Kansas Indians were being relocated. By the terms of the treaty, those families were not allowed to sell their plots without the permission of the federal government. In 1860, Congress made it even harder for these lands to be sold, giving the Secretary of the Interior the sole power to sell the land and to decide what should be done with the proceeds. Victoria Smith brought a lawsuit testing the legality of these Congressional restraints on her ownership of the land, and the Supreme Court found them valid to "safeguard against their own improvidence."[47]

Thus, the government's policy of favoring the allotment of land to Native Americans was fueled by the view that owning land on which they would farm would better civilize and assimilate the Native people to the "evolved ways" of settler-Americans, and by a concern that without paternalistic constraints on individual titles to land, the Native Americans would be swindled out of their property by fast-talking white tricksters. Perhaps most importantly, the wholesale carving up of the reservations into individual plots for Native families would have the added benefit of freeing up large swaths of land for white settlement. The size of the reservations was so vast that after each Native family got their plot there would remain enormous tracts available for white homesteaders. This fact was not lost on some of the Native people, such as members of the Cherokee Nation, who strongly opposed the allotment plans. Other tribes, like the Creeks in the Dakota Territory, the Senecas in New York, and the Santee in Nebraska, were reported to favor the subdivision of the land and allotment with clear title. One can imagine that given how poor most Native people were, the thought of owning land that could generate income was irresistible for many. Notwithstanding the government's stated benevolent reasons for giving the Native Americans land titles, their real aim was to destroy tribal culture and assimilate them into white society. Teddy Roosevelt was reported to have put it bluntly: the goal of allotment was that it be "a mighty pulverizing engine to break up the tribal masses."[48]

In 1887, Congress systematized the allotment of reservation land to Native Americans with the General Allotment Act, also known as the Dawes Act. This authorized the Bureau of Indian Affairs to survey reservation lands and allot 160 acres to each head of family, 80 acres to each single adult or orphan child, and 40 acres to all other children. For at least twenty-five years the allotted land would be held in trust by the federal government on the Native peoples' behalf, and it could not be sold or leased by its owners. In short order the government came under strong pressure to allow whites to lease the land that the Native Americans were not fully exploiting. At the same time, it became clear that the Native people were unable to purchase the equipment they needed to farm the land allotted to them. If they could lease part of the land they could use the proceeds to buy materials to farm the remainder. So, in 1891 Congress amended the Dawes Act to allow the land to be leased for farming or grazing for three years, or mining for ten years. Within a matter of a few years, significant amounts of Native-owned land were leased to white people, and by and large the proceeds from those leases were not used to productively develop the remaining land, but instead went to alcohol and other non-productive ends. One observer, a member of the Omaha Nation, observed in 1900:

> The leasing business is ruining the Omahas in every way. It is producing idleness among them, and idleness brings out the worst that is in man. It has proved to be injurious rather than a help. Nearly all of the land is leased, and most of the Indians have scarcely a thing to show for the rent they receive. Many of them loaf about the towns, and some of them come to my house in a shameful state of intoxication and expect hospitality of me.[49]

At the same time, there was strong pressure put on Congress and the Bureau of Indian Affairs to cut short the twenty-five-year-trust period, and in 1902 Congress amended the Dawes Act once again, so as to allow the heirs of the original recipients to sell their land, subject to governmental approval—and this approval was liberally given. The Dawes Act was amended again in 1906 and once more in 1907, further liberalizing Native Americans' ability to sell their land. In all, by the time allotment ended in 1934, the government had allotted more than forty million acres of land. Yet by that same year, nearly twenty-seven million of those acres had been sold, largely to white people. Some of the Native owners sold wisely, making good profits on their property, using the proceeds to pursue business ventures other than farming, and were otherwise not taken advantage of in the sales of their land. Yet many of the sales were the product of trickery, coercion, fraud, or the exploitation of the Indians' illiteracy or ignorance.

And of course, there was the reservation land that was not allotted to Native Americans under the Dawes Act that was sold by the government in 160-acre tracts to interested white settlers. Between the passage of the Dawes Act in 1887 and the end of allotment in 1934, the amount of land held by Native people had been reduced from 138 million to 52 million acres. Under the terms of the Act, the proceeds of these sales were "benevolently" held in trust for the education and benefit of Native Americans. But the US Treasury's gross mismanagement of these funds is among the largest crimes committed by the US government against the Native Americans. The government was finally sued in 1996 by Elouise Pépion Cobell, a member of the Blackfeet Nation of Montana, because it had mismanaged the funds so badly that it had no idea how much money was in the trust, nor how many accounts it held. Cobell claimed that were the trust funds properly accounted for, the balances would be close to $137.5 billion.

The end result of the Native American allotment program was that less than fifty years after the Dawes Act was passed the vast majority of land held and controlled by the tribes had been sold to non-Native white people, or divided into parcels owned by Native people that were so small that they were not practically usable for grazing or mining. One of the aims of the allotment program was to turn Native Americans into peasant farmers, but this never happened. As Stuart Banner writes in his book, *How the Indians Lost Their Land: Law and Power on the Frontier*, "by 1930 there were fewer Indian farmers, farming less land, than there had been in

1910. By the end of allotment, Indian agriculture lagged even further behind white agriculture than it had at the beginning. The Indians seemed no more assimilated in 1930 than in 1880."[50]

Banner's book recounts the devastating story of how American Indian tribes were given land titles in an effort to civilize them, and how those policies worked against Native Americans' interests in every respect. The story of the Native peoples, their culture, and their land mirrors, in so many important respects, the heartbreak of the freed people that is the focus of this book. The government made promises, broke those promises and neglected the well-being of a people over whom it had asserted paternalistic control. Native Americans' experience with allotment suggests that even if the freed people had been awarded clear title to the Sherman land and other land confiscated from the Confederate planters as reparation for the injustice of their enslavement, it would be naive to assume that all would have been put right. Instead, they would have been set upon by a different array of exploitive and racist tricks and schemes developed by white land sharks from the North and the prior owners of the land alike. So too, we could not be assured that the federal government would have done the right thing to insure against the unfair and violent confiscation of the freed people's land. The US government has had a sad history of adopting policies that explicitly discriminated against the property interests of African Americans—whether it be in government loan programs after the Second World War or forcing residential segregation through federally subsidized housing projects. Racism and greed so often win in a battle with benevolence, best intentions, and neglect. But whatever one might say about the challenges that the freed people would have faced if they had received land titles as part of their emancipation, that scenario would likely have been better than what they faced once Johnson returned almost all of the land to their former owners.

CHAPTER 4

Reparations Today

"I'm not giving up . . . Slavery is a blemish on this nation's history, and until it is formally addressed, our country's story will remain marked by this blight."

—**Representative John Conyers**, in 2017 on re-introduction of a bill into Congress for the fourteenth time to create a commission to examine the institution of slavery in the United States and its early colonies, to recommend appropriate remedies.[1]

I N THE SUMMER of 2016 the Movement for Black Lives issued a platform containing a specific, ambitious, and comprehensive roadmap for racial justice in the United States.[2] Reparations figure centrally in the platform's programmatic demands. Reparations not only for the enslavement of Black people, but Jim Crow segregation, systematic housing discrimination, environmental racism, inferior educational opportunities, mass incarceration, and long-term disinvestment in the Black community all of which, the platform argues, comprise the legacy of slavery in this country.[3]

The Movement for Black Lives's call for racial reparations

appeared at a time of reinvigorated attention to this issue. Ta-Ne-hisi Coates wrote in the *Atlantic* in June 2014, "Two hundred fifty years of slavery. Ninety years of Jim Crow. Sixty years of separate but equal. Thirty-five years of racist housing policy. Until we reckon with our compounding moral debts, America will never be whole."[4] In January 2016, after completing an investigation of the situation of African Americans and people of African descent in the United States, the United Nations Working Group of Experts on People of African Descent issued a strong statement in which it noted "a lack of attention to the matter of reparatory justice for enslavement and its effects."[5] The UN Working Group concluded that "[p]ast injustices and crimes against African Americans need to be addressed with reparatory justice."[6] Professor Charles Ogletree, Jr. has noted, "The reparations movement has experienced ebbs and flows through periods of both forceful repression and abject depression."[7] The movement for reparations is now clearly experiencing a flow. Even the 2018 Emmy awards program featured "Reparations Emmys" given to overlooked African American actors. When a "Reparation Emmy" was awarded to actor John Witherspoon for his role in *I Spy*, Witherspoon said, "I can't have this at my house. Reparations is not for an Emmy, it's for forty acres and a mule." When the host, Michael Che, responded, "I don't have forty acres and a mule," Witherspoon shot back: "Well get me forty mules and an acre. I'll take that."

If we were to seriously undertake reparations today for the failed, or incomplete, abolition of slavery at the end of the US Civil War, what should we do? Unfortunately, what might have been the right thing to do in 1865 could be impossible or unwise to do now. Even though freed people were entitled to land in 1865, it is impossible to imagine a scenario today in which the land set aside by General Sherman's Special Field Order No. 15 would be confiscated from its current owners—Black, white, and others—and allotted to the descendants of US slaves. One of the objections to the paying of reparations now for the human rights violation of slavery is that slavery existed a long time ago and all the enslaved people are now long dead. Japanese Americans received reparations for their internment during World War II, but those payments were made in close enough proximity to the internment itself that the people who were interned could be identified. Who should receive reparations for slavery today? Are all Black people entitled? Only those who can demonstrate through DNA or some other method that they are descendants of slaves? On the other hand, don't all Black people today suffer from forms of racism that are the vestiges of slavery? Then who should pay? My family didn't own slaves, indeed all my ancestors arrived in the United States well after slavery was abolished. Yet, forms of white privilege that are also the vestiges of the racist ideology have helped white people like me benefit from the greatest engine of wealth generation of the last two hundred years: investment in real estate.[8]

The histories of repair and its failures told in chapters one and two make clear that racial reparations then, and racial reparations now, are a collective national problem. Former slave-owners were not the only people to benefit from the denial of land-based reparations to formerly enslaved people. White speculators from Boston, New York, Philadelphia, and Pittsburgh capitalized as much or more than former rebels returning to their old plantations. And the racist policies that tainted Black freed-dom and citizenship with a badge of inferiority did not attach only to people who had been enslaved—it attached to Blackness itself. In this sense, the enslavement of Black people was more a feature of American white supremacy than a bug we could isolate and excise from our national story. White supremacy is the founding value of American society that metastasized in laws and customs supporting the enslavement of Black people, in Black Codes that secured their subordinate status after slavery was formally abolished by the Thirteenth Amendment, and in old and new Jim Crow laws that secured a separate and unequal status for African Americans on the books and in practice until today. As Michelle Alexander has well documented in her book *The New Jim*

Crow, the mass incarceration of African American people today can be directly linked back to the sin of slavery in this country. Just as slavery was a society-wide atrocity over which we fought a civil war, so too is the justice that atrocity demands today.

There is no perfect, obvious form that justice should take today. As I have traveled the country talking about this issue I have received very little pushback about the claim that we failed to deliver justice to enslaved people at the end of the Civil War. But I do get pushback about what we ought to do today. Some of this resistance is motivated by the inoculating myth of white innocence: "My family didn't enslave people. Why should I have responsibility for an injustice I had nothing to do with? It was so long ago, and today's racial inequality bears no relation to any shortcomings with national policy when we abolished slavery." Other pushback is more related to the perfect being the enemy of the good: "Your proposals might not work (whatever 'work' might mean). Educational opportunity is more valuable in terms of building human resources today than is real estate." The first set of objections about who bears responsibility today strikes me as an easier concern to address than does the method by which we redistribute resources today as part of a commitment to racial reparations.

With respect to the query of why we ought to use land as the means of repair: recent studies have shown that increasing educational opportunities to African Americans will not meaningfully ameliorate the gaping wealth gap to be found between white and African American people.[9] "[B]lacks cannot close the racial wealth gap by changing their individual behavior—i.e., by assuming more 'personal responsibility' or acquiring the portfolio management insights associated with [sic] financially literacy—if the structural sources of racial inequality remain unchanged. There are no actions that black Americans can take unilaterally that will have much of an effect on reducing the racial wealth gap."[10] Perhaps more interestingly, recent studies have shown that educational advantages facilitate wealth accumulation most effectively *after* a wealth transfer, such as the transfer I suggest in this book.[11]

The aim of this book is to move us as a nation to act, to feel the moral imperative to do so, and to be willing to try innovative approaches to make payment on a long-overdue promissory note. Any one approach does not eliminate the possibility of others. Just as the horror of slavery took many forms, so should its repair. As scholars of racial justice at Duke University have recently argued:

> America must undergo a vast social transformation produced by the adoption of bold national policies, policies that will forge a way forward by addressing, finally, the long-standing consequences of slavery, the Jim Crow years that followed, and ongoing racism and discrimination that exist in our society today . . . This could take the form of a direct, race-specific initiative like a dramatic reparations program tied to compensation for the legacies of slavery and Jim Crow.[12]

One of the most compelling means by which racial reparations could be undertaken today is through creative new forms of collective land ownership in which property is placed in trust for a community, removing it from the speculative market and placing it in the hands of community-controlled nonprofits. Since speculative real estate markets were used to divest freed people of the land they had been promised as reparations for enslavement, it is fitting that we turn to remedial measures today that repudiate a market-based approach to land use.

Today's call for innovative alternatives to individual, for-profit, market-based land ownership are a compelling modern approach to reparations, especially when they are seen as honoring the demands of the formerly enslaved people in Port Royal and Davis Bend for land redistribution as a debt owed for enslavement. Indeed, the first community land trust was established in 1968 by civil rights activists seeking a way to assist African Americans in rural

Georgia, continuing the tradition first established by the women of the Combahee River Colony almost a century and a half earlier.

Limited Equity Cooperatives (LECs) are democratic, member-run cooperative organizations that limit the equity individual home-owners can accumulate, thus preserving long-term affordability; Resident Owned Communities (ROCs) are member-run coopera-tive organizations that own the land in manufactured housing com-munities, thus protecting against displacement, poor conditions, and exploitative management practices; Community Land Trusts (CLTs) are multi-stakeholder organizations that own land for the permanent benefit of the community and sell and rent homes with various resale restrictions in order to maintain long-term affordabil-ity; Community Benefits Agreements (CBAs) are legally enforceable contracts between developers and local community groups that of-ten include various land and housing related benefits and require-ments; and Land Banks are publicly owned or nonprofit entities that allow local governments to acquire abandoned or tax delinquent properties and prepare them for productive uses.[13]

These modern ownership structures echo the spirit of the exper-iments in freedom in the immediate aftermath of the Civil War, re-fusing to surrender a commitment to reparation to 1) the values of a "free market" that assign real property ownership to the "carnival of speculators and sharpies,"[14] 2) the individualization of injury and dis-advantage that undermines collective remedies, and 3) the work that white innocence does in justifying and normalizing the intergener-ational accumulation of property-based wealth by white people and the relative structural poverty of African Americans. The underlying philosophy of the early CLTs reflected a notion that "Land is treated as a common heritage, not as an individual possession,"[15] and priori-tizing housing as a right, not a commodity that is bought and sold in a market that is subject to speculation, gentrification, and price gouging.

So, remuneration today *could* take the form of collective property-based solutions, such as those described above. This would amount to a substantial reinvestment in communities that have essentially been abandoned by modern society—an abandonment resulting in those communities having inferior schools, no jobs, little health care, and no meaningful economy. Not coincidentally, African American people are over-represented in these blight-zones.

Jackson, Mississippi, proves an interesting case study for how racial justice advocates have turned to CLTs as a form of reparation for historic and systemic race discrimination. In the aftermath of the election of African American mayor Chokwe Lumumba in 2013, progressive activists in Jackson developed a political program to implement a revolutionary and reparative vision of the city. This vision was based in a commitment to cooperative, bottom-up democratic governance and included the creation of a community land trust and "freedom farms"—urban, worker-owned cooperative farms that would produce organic vegetables for the community. The movement has purchased almost forty lots in West Jackson, a working-class, predominantly Black, and underdeveloped neighborhood not far from the downtown Capital district. They named it the Fannie Lou Hamer Community Land Trust. Echoing the land redistribution project in the Sea Islands, most of the land they have purchased in West Jackson was acquired through state tax auctions—the state is able to confiscate and then auction off land for which taxes have not been paid for three years. The plan is to build and run housing for the community as a self-sustaining collective. Collectivized ownership and energy independence (stressing solar power) are designed to hold off gentrification, displacement, and housing vulnerability for the working-class and poor members of the community.[16] As one of the founding members of Cooperation Jackson, Sacajawea "Saki" Hall, told me when I interviewed her in the spring of 2017: "We're not about getting in on the American Dream, we want to get beyond individual ownership of property. We want control of our own dreams." The activists in Jackson, Cooperation Jackson and the Malcolm X Grassroots Movement, are working closely with national campaigns, such as the Right to the City Alliance, that have prioritized collectivized land ownership as a form of racial repair.

Similar efforts to create affordable housing, fight gentrification, rebuild economically devastated urban communities, and create community rather than developer control—all with a racial justice lens—have been undertaken in Baltimore, Oakland, Miami, New York City, and other cities.[17]

A program in New York City, however, provides an example of how not to preserve affordable housing and community control of development. In the 1980s there were many blighted and burned out buildings in New York City that were sitting empty and became an "attractive nuisance" creating conditions for undesirable or illegal activity. (Recall the opening montage in Tom Wolfe's *Bonfire of the Vanities* when the book's wealthy, white Wall Street executive protagonist Sherman McCoy takes a wrong turn in his Mercedes and ends up in the blighted and violent South Bronx.) To address this problem, the city was empowered to foreclose on buildings or units that were vacant or distressed—meaning having significant building code violations, or in arrears in property or water taxes. The Third Party Transfer (TPT) program, as it is called, allowed the city to seize these delinquent properties and sell them to new owners who would rehabilitate them and put them back on the market, ideally at an affordable rental price ("definitions of affordability based on area median income are notoriously out of sync with neighborhood income levels" and vacant units could be sold at market rates).[18]

While the TPT program successfully enabled the return of uninhabitable buildings to the rental market in poor and low-income communities in New York City, it has also created a great deal of controversy. The program, in effect if not design, conscripted the city in the project of neighborhood gentrification, and emphasized the interests of developers over the community itself. Fixing up the empty buildings increased the real estate values of other buildings nearby, cascading into a situation where the neighborhood did not remain affordable for long-term residents. Community Land Trusts have been proposed as a better alternative to TPT foreclosures, and groups such as the New Economy Project have been working to promote the use of CLTs in urban areas such as New York City.[19] Even worse, the city has been accused of foreclosing on properties in predominantly African American neighborhoods that are in the process of gentrifying, even seizing single family homes owned outright by African American families who have fallen behind in tax or water payments.[20]

~❖~

But how would we pay for this kind of repair? The Movement for Black Lives has adopted a divest/invest approach to justice—urging divestment from the structures that produce and perpetuate race-based inequality and investment in Black community institutions that enable human flourishing rather than waste. They demand "investments in the education, health and safety of Black people, instead of investments in the criminalizing, caging, and harming of Black people. We want investments in Black communities, determined by Black communities, and divestment from exploitative forces including prisons, fossil fuels, police, surveillance and exploitative corporations."[21]

The complexities of this issue led me to an intergenerational approach to reparation: treat the enormous accumulation of wealth that is about to be transferred to my generation as having been held in a constructive trust for the benefit of the descendants of slaves and other Black Americans who have borne the badge of inferiority imposed by American slavery. White Americans, like myself, who were fortunate enough to have been born at the right time and place have no greater claim to that financial windfall than do the Black Americans, Black families, and Black communities in which we have underinvested and intentionally disinvested for the 150 years since slavery was abolished. It's time we made good on Sherman's promise of land and tools as a form of reparations for the theft of the slave's labor, and it's time we acknowledge that being emancipated without any resources with which to make that freedom meaningful is like telling the person stranded on a deserted island without a boat that they are free to leave. Freedom is much more than the absence of bondage; it requires the tools, the capacities, and opportunities that make independent human action possible. African Americans need and are entitled to their boat. Without the means to be truly unshackled from an unjust past, freedom will never be truly free. That's what the reparations movement is about today, and that's why I want to argue as strongly as I can that we stand in a particularly fortuitous moment to repair the damage of under resourcing the former slaves' promise of freedom.

Experts report that an "estimated $59 trillion . . . will be transferred from 93.6 million American estates from 2007 to 2061, in the greatest wealth transfer in US history."[22] The heirs of white baby boomers are poised to inherit sums ranging from nice nest eggs to veritable fortunes from our parents. Currently not much data exists on whether those heirs have all benefitted equally. For this reason, some suggest that it may be more practical to institute a corporate tax or one targeting individuals and corporations that were directly involved in enslavement and its profits. But I think a more systematic approach is best, one that captures not only the role of particular business interests in profiting from slavery, but the payoff to individuals who have no direct link to the pre–Civil War plantation economy. In essence, my aim is to reframe the entire US economy as a plantation economy, insofar as there is no principled way to cordon off the profits and pain of this corrupt business model to one geographic area, period of time, or discrete set of investors. The wages of this evil have been woven into the entire warp and weft of the nation's modern economy, as a structure of inextricable links between the enslavement of people of African descent and contemporary global capitalism. Scholars such as Sven Beckert and Seth Rockman argue that American economic development rests on what they term "slavery's capitalism":

> Slave grown cotton was the most valuable export grown in America, that the capital stored in slaves exceeded the combined value of all the nation's railroads and factories, that foreign investment underwrote the expansion of plantation lands in Louisiana and Mississippi, that the highest concentration of steam power in the United States was to be found along the Mississippi rather than the Merrimack.[23]

While anti-aristocratic impulses may motivate some to renounce their inherited fortunes, any entitlement to such a lottery-like windfall must be understood in the historical context of race discrimination in the United States and contemporary notions of racial justice. All boomers who stand to profit from this impending intergenerational wealth transfer should feel compelled to question their entitlement to the proceeds from this lottery.

Real estate investment has been the great wealth-generating machine of my parents' generation, yet African Americans have been systematically locked out of this unique opportunity to buy in, sit tight, and get rich.[24] The GI Bill underwrote segregated housing through discriminatory lending policies. For decades real estate agents steered Black buyers to Black neighborhoods and white buyers to white neighborhoods, and local and federal governments invested in the infrastructure in white neighborhoods but not in Black neighborhoods.[25] Even today, we see the burden of the mortgage lending crisis falling disproportionately higher on Black homeowners. As a result, white people have been given opportunities to profit from a booming real estate market in which African Americans had no part. The racially unequal investment market started well before the end of the Second World War. Slavery was abolished in 1865, but promises made to the freed slaves that they would receive land—as reparation for enslavement and as the leg up they needed to start their lives anew—were not honored. The failure to see land rights as a key component of what the ex-slaves were owed meant that the formerly enslaved—and their descendants—were unable to get in on the land boom of the twentieth century. This goes a long way toward explaining why today the median net worth of African American households is only 8 percent of that of white households.[26]

Against this historical reality, I am compelled to ask: Do I have a greater moral claim to inherit the wealth of my parents' generation than do the great-great-grandchildren of slaves? Should we understand the real estate profits of the twentieth century as a form of unjust enrichment? The way wealth has accumulated along racial lines in this country leads me to think that the color of one's skin determined whether you had any bootstraps with which to pull yourself up. I can't help but see the wealth of the "Greatest Generation" and the baby boomers as the residue of the unfinished business of the abolition of slavery.[27] What if we understood the causes of the racial disparities in wealth accumulation in this country as vesting an ongoing right to some of the real estate profits of the last century? As I see it, my parents and their peers are de facto trustees of an IOU long owed to the descendants of people who were enslaved. Ironically, racially discriminatory policies ended up making these investments more profitable, and it's time that the beneficiaries in whose interest this constructive trust was created be recognized.

For these reasons, I have come to the view that my contemporaries and I who, by law, stand to inherit significant sums from our parents, should acknowledge that we are not morally entitled to do so. It is all the more compelling that we do this voluntarily because it is the right thing to do. Rather than contributing to and benefitting from the even greater concentration of wealth in a few white purses, we ought to renounce some of this racially tainted land and fortune and redirect this bounty to the cause of racial justice in our communities.

The lingering debt owed to the freed people should not be viewed as having been extinguished by the passage of time. Crimes against humanity should not have a statute of limitations. Reaching some national consensus that the enslavement of millions of Black people in the United States constituted the gravest form of injustice, which was not adequately addressed at the time slavery was abolished, would itself be a profound step forward. This would entail not only the payment of reparations, but also the difficult project of amending and correcting our memory of what happened in the period prior to and immediately following the Civil War. For Jews, the idea of "never forgetting" the Holocaust both constitutes them as a people and serves, albeit symbolically, as insurance against a similar form of genocide ever happening again.

Yet we have largely forgotten the history of slavery in the United States. We put it behind us and moved on. By "we" I mean the official story of the United States that is taught in elementary schools and that animates a collective national memory, a story that is inevitably told by white people. In contrast to the experience of white Americans, for many African Americans the legacies of slavery—in both symbolic and material forms—remain a visceral part of daily life. The legacy persists in the form of the death by a thousand cuts that daily racism inflicts on Black people, or structural inequality, impoverishment, police shootings, over-incarceration, and lack of opportunity that knocks down Black people individually and as a community. White people simply don't experience this day in and day out, and we certainly don't relate it back to the institution of slavery. James Baldwin reminds us of the impossibility of Black people forgetting and moving on: "The man does not remember the hand that struck him, the darkness that frightened him, as a child; nevertheless, the hand and the darkness remain with him, indivisible from himself forever, part of the passion that drives him wherever he thinks to take flight."[28]

While material reparations may be appropriate to redress the unaddressed crime against humanity that was slavery, other forms of remembrance should not be ignored in an effort to come to terms today with our failures in the past to address this injustice. The methods of accomplishing transitional justice today in places like Rwanda, Sierra Leone, and the former Yugoslavia for example, suggest cultural mechanisms through which the sins of our past may be acknowledged in the present. In contemporary contexts, healing and justice have been pursued through the use of prosecutions (domestic and international); truth and reconciliation commissions; lustration (the shaming and banning of perpetrators from public office); public access to police, military and other governmental records; public apology; public memorials; reburial of victims; compensation or reparation to victims and/or their families (in the form of money, land, or other resources); literary and historical writing; and blanket or individualized amnesty. Some of these approaches were actually used in the case of North American slavery: lustration (to a limited degree as part of the fourteenth amendment to the Constitution in 1868); access to public records; literary and historical writing (for example, the Works Progress Administration's publicly financed effort to document slave narratives); and, of course, President Johnson's ignominious grant of amnesty.

While we debate the practical hurdles to paying out reparations, we should simultaneously pursue an apology for slavery and erect memorials to its history and legacy. Virginia, Maryland, North Carolina, and Alabama have recently officially expressed "profound regret" for the state's role in slavery, and the city of Montgomery, Alabama, voted unanimously to apologize to Rosa Parks for her mistreatment in the 1955 bus boycott six months after she died in October of 2005. "This proves Alabama is open for everyone and we are ready to improve race relations," said state representative Mary Moore, an African American Democrat from Birmingham who sponsored the resolution. "The issue of slavery and its impact on the country had been kept in the closet until a few Southern states said, 'We want to take it out of the closet.'"[29]

Closet metaphors aside, at best, these public proclamations about intergenerational responsibility for slavery merely commence rather than complete a contemporary reckoning with the meaning and implications of the incomplete emancipation of enslaved people at the close of the Civil War. The Equal Justice Institute's National Memorial for Peace and Justice, informally known as the National Lynching Memorial, and the Smithsonian's National Museum of African American History and Culture bear witness to the history of racial violence in this country, including slavery. Numerous memorials to the Holocaust have been built in the United States, including on the mall in Washington, DC, but slavery—a domestic genocide and human rights atrocity—has scarcely been acknowledged and mourned in such a public way. Memorial-based remedies for historical injustice serve as cultural benchmarks, in a way. They provide testimony and witness to an atrocity or shameful past in such a way that says: *this is what happened, we abhor it, we denounce it, and in so doing declare that we, as a society, commit ourselves to never allowing that state of affairs to take place in our nation again.*

To memorialize the atrocity of slavery, just as we have done with the Holocaust, is to approach the question of justice for the people enslaved in the United States as, at least in part, a matter of *collective memory* rather than of history. Memory, understood as remembrance that is organized for present purposes, has a special character to it insofar as it operates as a live link to the past. Collective memory, argued French sociologist Maurice Halbwachs, functions as "essentially a reconstruction of the past [that] adapts the image of ancient facts to the beliefs and spiritual needs of the present."[30] By building continuity with the past, memory does the work of laying the foundation for identity, on an individual and a cultural level.[31]

Yet history, unlike memory, is a representation of events now completed. History is self-consciously a story we tell about and coherence we give to a period or era now over. History is behind us, memory lives on with us. The problem we have in this country when it comes to making amends for slavery is that we have relegated it to history, thereby vanquishing it from memory and its horror from any relevance to our present. One of the things we can do today to address our failure to adequately redress the injury suffered by enslaved persons in the eighteenth and nineteenth centuries is to make it a part of our collective memory, such that we understand the enslavement of millions of Black people in the United States as part of who we are, then as now, just as the Holocaust is part of who the Jews understand themselves to be. Americans love our founding stories, we love to relate the events of today to the founding fathers, the severing of ties with the British, and our commitment to life, liberty, and the pursuit of happiness. Yet the collective memory that plays an important role in our present sense of national identity inevitably skips over the enslavement of millions of Black people. Our national integrity grants us no license to cherry-pick the stories we like while denying—or closeting—the ones we don't. They are *all ours*.

To recast, or replot, the collective sense of the road we have traveled in such a way that includes slavery by memorializing it in meaningful ways is not merely a "symbolic project". Collectively forgetting about slavery cuts off certain political projects in the present. Forgiving and forgetting the enslavement of millions of Black people by white Americans only six generations ago renders some racial justice projects today less plausible, less necessary, and less just. Affirmative action, voting rights, welfare and prison reform, and race-conscious remedies to the unequal distribution of public and private resources—whether they be housing, jobs, wealth or health care—can appear to many as unjustified, undeserved or downright contrary to American values of merit and hard work when they are viewed outside of a national autobiography that remembers both the fact and the effects of slavery.

So too, white people have never really undertaken the exercise of identifying with what it meant to be enslaved, or to have had your ancestors enslaved. Instead, we have asked Black people to identify with us, often in the name of equality and justice: "you deserve the opportunities we have," "you should dream to live like we do," "you too can have a piece of the (white) American dream." Transitional justice mechanisms such as apologies and memorials—in addition to reparations—could have the effect of forcing a national reckoning about slavery that would force us—white people—to identify with the experience of American slavery, while owning its legacy as part of both our own past and present. At a minimum, we owe this kind of recognition and remembrance to the freed people who were promised so much, who dreamed so big, and were given so little. Black lives will continue to be treated as though they do not matter until we take meaningful steps to repair the intergenerational wreckage that slavery inflicted on Black people.

Acknowledgements

I N WRITING THIS book I have benefitted enormously from the generosity of a community of scholars who offered thoughtful comments and provocations on the book's premise and argument. This community included faculty and students at Columbia University, Harvard Law School, the University of Wisconsin Law School, the University of Minnesota Law School, the Wharton School, Florida State University College of Law, and the Law and Humanities Senior Scholars Workshop. Cathy Albisa, Richard Briffault, Robert Ferguson, Ariela Gross, Martha Jones, Carol Rose, Paul Saint-Amour, and Kendall Thomas provided early feedback for which I am especially thankful. Gabrielle DaCosta provided important assistance with cleaning up the manuscript.

The research for this book took me to archives throughout the South, in Washington, DC, and in New Haven, Connecticut. My research would not have been possible without the generous assistance of archivists working in those locations who were willing to point me toward a special collection that only they knew of, sneak me in the back to look through unindexed boxes, and helped me think through the meanings of gaps in the records. These archivists included Reginald Washington at the National Archives, and Gordon Cotton, Blanche Terry, and Jeff Giambrone at the Vicksburg Courthouse Museum. Reference librarians at Columbia Law School's Diamond Law

Library have been enormously generous with their time and ingenuity when asked to help track down an obscure citation. They include Dana Neacsu, Jody Armstrong, Jennifer Wertkin, Deborah Heller, and Patrick Flanagan. All of my research was enabled by generous support from Columbia Law School.

My thanks to the editors at Haymarket Books. First for agreeing to publish this book, second for their enthusiasm for its argument, and third for their careful editing of the text. Every writer needs a good editor, and Anthony Arnove, Maya Marshall, and Dao Tran each lent the manuscript a careful eye, and in so doing, made the book much stronger.

Finally, my enormous gratitude to my first and best readers, Janlori and Maya Goldman. They lived inside this project along with me, pushed me to be clear about my own motivations for writing the book, and offered critical edits on multiple readings of the manuscript. Thank you.

Notes

Introduction

1. Catherine O'Neal, "The Sea Islands of South Carolina," *Travel + Leisure*, May 8, 2009, http://www.travelandleisure.com/articles /nothing-could-be-finer.
2. Daniel Scheffler, "Beaufort: One of South Carolina's Most Charming Small Towns," *Vogue*, March 3, 2016.
3. William Faulkner, *Requiem for a Nun*, (New York: Random House, 1951).
4. Rakesh Kochhar and Richard Fry, "Wealth Inequality has Widened Along Racial, Ethnic Lines Since End of Great Recession," *Fact Tank* (blog), Pew Research Center, December 12, 2014, http://www.pewresearch.org/fact-tank/2014/12/12 /racial-wealth-gaps-great-recession/.
5. Institute for Policy Studies and the Corporation for Economic Development, *The Ever-Growing Gap: Failing to Address the Status Quo Will Drive the Racial Wealth Divide for Centuries to Come* (August 8, 2016), https://ips-dc.org/report-ever-growing-gap/.
6. Demos, *The Racial Wealth Gap: Why Policy Matters* (2016), https://www.demos.org/publication/racial-wealth-gap-why -policy-matters.
7. Frederick Law Olmsted, "An English Traveler in Mississippi Writing to the London Daily News, 1857," in Frederick Law Olmsted, *A Journey in the Backcountry in the Winter of 1853–4*, (New York: G. P. Putnam's Sons, 1907) 59–60.
8. Agency Civ. Cont. Relief Comm., Jeff Davis Mansion, 4 mos 13, 1864, Record Group (hereinafter RG) 393, National Archives

(hereinafter NA).

9.   As property they were not understood by white people to be fully human. Here, as is so often the case, Mark Twain put it best in *Huckleberry Finn* when Huck explains to Aunt Sally why he was delayed in visiting her. He tells her that the steamboat "blowed a cylinder-head." 'Good gracious! anybody hurt?' asked Aunt Sally. 'No'm. Killed a nigger,' Huck responded. 'Well, it's lucky; because sometimes people do get hurt," Aunt Sally replied with relief.' (Mark Twain, *Huck Finn and Tom Sawyer among the Indians and Other Unfinished Stories* (Berkeley: University of California Press, 1989), 279.

10. Of course, at this time freedom was not something enjoyed by white women to the same degree as white men.

11. In debates concerning the adoption of the Thirteenth Amendment, Senator Howard remarked, "Its intention was to make him the opposite of a slave, to make him a freeman. And what are the attributes of a freeman according to the universal understanding of the American people? Is a freeman to be deprived of the right of acquiring property, of the right of having a family, a wife, children, home? What definition will you attach to the word 'freeman' that does not include these ideas?" Congressional Globe, 38th Congress, First Session. 1364 (1864), 504.

12. "Freeman" connoted a particular meaning in the mid-nineteenth century, a meaning quite distinct from the status of being freed. Legal dictionaries at the time defined a freeman as "One who is in the enjoyment of the right to do whatever he pleases, not forbidden by law. One in the possession of the civil rights enjoyed by the people generally." "Freedman" was "the name formerly given by the Romans to those persons who had been released from a state of servitude." John Bouvier, *A Law Dictionary, Adapted to the Constitution and Laws of the United States of America* (Philadelphia: J. B. Lippincott & Co., 1889), 548–49.

13. Dr. Martin Luther King Jr. speech, "We're Coming to Get Our Check," YouTube video accessed July 2, 2018, https://www.youtube.com/watch?v=pLV5y4utPKI.

14. Michelle Alexander, *The New Jim Crow: Mass Incarceration in the Age of Colorblindness* (New York: The New Press, 2012).

15. Edward L. Pierce, "The Contrabands at Fortress Monroe,"
     Atlantic Monthly, November 1, 1861.

16. Pierce, "The Contrabands."

17. Enslaved people were incapable of entering into contracts, owning
     property, being legally married, or otherwise acting as legal
     subjects because of their status as chattel, not persons. "Slaves
     were treated legally as 'property' and under the law had no more
     capacity to enter into a contract than would a horse or a plow."
     Katherine Franke, *Wedlocked: The Perils of Marriage Equality* (New
     York: NYU Press, 2015), 43. Once emancipated, "not only were
     they subject to law, in the sense of being required to heed the law's
     demands for marital fidelity and adherence to the strict rules of
     contract labor, but they also now regarded themselves as subjects
     who could make use of the law by turning to legal authorities
     to sort out the complicated disputes that arose in their lives,
     especially their intimate, domestic lives." Franke, *Wedlocked,* 165

18. Paul K. Saint-Amour, *Tense Future: Modernism, Total War,
     Encyclopedic Form* (New York: Oxford University Press, 2015),
     31, quoting David Scott, *Conscripts of Modernity: The Tragedy of
     Colonial Enlightenment* (Durham, NC: Duke University Press,
     2004), 44.

19. Saint-Amour, *Tense Future,* 31–32. Here Saint-Amour draws
     from the work of David Scott, Frantz Fanon, Gary Wilder, and
     Reinhart Koselleck.

20   Beaufort County, South Carolina, *Comprehensive Annual
     Financial Report for the Fiscal Year Ended June 30, 2017,* p. 154. If
     the aggregate property value were divided equally among all the
     residents of the county, each person would possess $195,231.33
     worth of real property.

21. 1860 US Census Slave Schedules for Beaufort County, South
     Carolina (NARA microfilm series M653, Roll 1231).

22   Ta-Nehisi Coates, "The Case for Reparations," *The Atlantic,* June
     2014, https://www.theatlantic.com/magazine/archive/2014/06
     /the-case-for-reparations/361631/; "Platform," Movement
     for Black Lives (website), https://policy.m4bl.org/platform/;
     Statement to the media by the United Nations' Working Group
     of Experts on People of African Descent, on the conclusion of

its official visit to the US, January 19–29, 2016.

23.   James Baldwin, "On Being White . . . and Other Lies," *Essence*, April 1984.

24.   The Movement for Black Lives Platform makes specific calls for land trusts and alternative, collective land ownership in Reparations Demand #3, Divest-Invest Demand #7, and Economic Justice Demand #8. See also National Economic and Social Rights Initiative, *Community + Land + Trusts: Tools for Development Without Displacement* (January 28, 2016), https://www.nesri.org/resources/community-land-trust-tools-for-development-without-displacement; Michelle Chen, "Can Community Land Trusts Solve Baltimore's Homelessness Problem?" *The Nation,* October 2, 2015, https://www.thenation .com/article/can-community-land-trusts-solve-baltimores -homelessness-problem/. Mayor Chokwe Lumumba supported the development of community land trusts as a form of reparations for former sharecroppers in Jackson, Mississippi, and the social justice organization Cooperation Jackson, founded to mobilize Lumumba's vision, have charted out a comprehensive land and housing reform program in Jackson, Mississippi. See Nathan Schneider, "The Revolutionary Life and Strange Death of a Radical Black Mayor," *Vice Magazine*, April 2016, http://www.vice.com/read/free-the-land-v23n2; https:// cooperationjackson.org/sustainable-communities-initiative/.

25.   Carol Rose, "Property as the Keystone Right?" *Notre Dame Law Review,* 71, no. 3 (1996), 329, 333.

Chapter 1

1.   Letter of Rufus Saxton to Professor J. J. Child, March 15, 1865, Rufus nd Willard S. Saxton Papers, Yale University, Manuscripts and Archives.

2.   Edward L. Pierce and United States Treasury Department, *The Freedmen of Port Royal, South-Carolina: Official Reports of*

Edward L. Pierce (New York: Rebellion Record, 1863).

3.   Cotton prices increased sixty-three percent in 1861. See David
      G. Surdam, "King Cotton: Monarch or Pretender? The State of
      the Market for Raw Cotton on the Eve of the American Civil
      War," *The Economic History Review* 51, no. 1 (1998), 113–32.

4.   "Beaufort has been taken by the gunboats, the town having
      been abandoned by the whites," in Letter from Captain John
      Rogers, US Steamer Bienville, Port Royal Harbor, Off Port
      Walker, Saturday, November 9, 1861, in *Rebellion Record: A
      Diary of American Events,* Edward Everett Frank Moore, ed.,
      v. 3, Document 36, 112 (1871); "We are informed that the
      families on the mainland as well as this group on the sea islands
      have fled to the interior, in some cases taking their negroes."
      ("Another Account, By An Officer of the Frigate Pawnee,
      Steam-Frigate Pawnee, Port Royal Bay," November 11, 1861, in
      Rebellion Records v. 3, Document 137, 320).

5.   Laura Josephine Webster, *The Operation of the Freedmen's
      Bureau in South Carolina* (Northampton, Mass., 1916); Guion
      Griffis Johnson, *A Social History of the Sea Islands: With Special
      Reference to St. Helena Island, South Carolina* (University of
      North Carolina Press, 1930).

6.   Theodore Rosengarten, *Tombee: Portrait of a Cotton Planter* (New
      York: McGraw-Hill, 1987). Edward Pierce reported that upon his
      first contact with the former Fripp slaves on St. Helena Island, they
      spoke kindly of "the good William Fripp" as well as his brother
      Dr. Clarence Fripp, "but that they all denounced the cruelty of
      Alvira Fripp, recounting his inhuman treatment of both men and
      women." Clarence Fripp, while beloved by some of his slaves,
      acknowledged that before 1860 he had fathered two children by
      his slave and housekeeper Rachel (Theodore Rosengarten, *Tombee:
      Portrait of a Cotton Planter: With the Journal of Thomas B. Chaplin,*
      reprint edition [New York: Quill, 1992]).

7.   Rosengarten, *Tombee,* 218.

8.   Charlotte L. Forten, *The Journal of Charlotte L. Forten: A Free
      Negro in the Slave Era* (New York: Collier Books, 1967), 161.

9.   Letter from Flag-Officer Samuel F. DuPont to the Assistant
      Secretary of the Navy, Wabash, Port Royal, November 9, 1861, in

Rebellion Records v. 3, Document 36, 112; see also "Letter from Captain John Rogers, US Steamer Bienville, Port Royal Harbor, Off Port Walker, Saturday, November 9, 1861, in *Rebellion Record*, v. 3, Document 36, 113: "Negroes are pouring in; they believe their condition is to be bettered. The white men have all fled. . . . They said the whites were shooting them right and left, in order to drive them back into the interior"; "They had been worked up to a pitch of frenzy by their masters, who had shot several negroes who refused to accompany them into the woods, and away from the village," A Correspondent of the New York Herald, Fort Walker, Port Royal Harbor, SC, November 11, 1861, in *Rebellion Record*, v. 3, Document 137 ½, 319.

10. W. T. Truxtun, Commander of the USS *Dale* to Commander of the South Atlantic Squadron, June 13, 1862, in Ira Berlin, ed., *The Destruction of Slavery. Freedom, a Documentary History of Emancipation, 1861–1867*, ser. 1, v. 1 (Cambridge; New York: Cambridge University Press, 1985).

11. Rosengarten, *Tombee*, 254; Port Royal Correspondence: Edward L. Pierce to Samuel P. Chase, February 3, 1862, RG 366, Entry 574 NA, College Park, MD, hereinafter "Port Royal Correspondence".

12 Port Royal Correspondence: Edward L. Pierce to Samuel P. Chase, February 3, 1862, RG 366, Entry 574 NA, College Park, MD, hereinafter "Port Royal Correspondence".

13. General Sherman's Proclamation to the People of South Carolina, November 8, 1861 in *Rebellion Record*, v. 3, 111.

14. In June 1862, Edward Pierce reported to Salmon Chase that there were 9,050 people living on all the plantations (Letter from Edward L. Pierce to Salmon P. Chase, June 2, 1862, Port Royal Correspondence). The numbers of refugees at Port Royal varies depending upon the source. Willie Lee Rose marks it at 10,000, while Edwin Hoffman reports that 15,000 slaves were liberated in November 1861. See Willie Lee Rose, *Rehearsal for Reconstruction: The Port Royal Experiment* (Athens: University of Georgia Press, 1999); and Edwin D. Hoffman, "From Slavery to Self-Reliance: The Record of Achievement of the Freedmen of the

Sea Island Region," *The Journal of Negro History* 41, no. 1 (1956), 8–42. The population of the refugees at Port Royal bulged again in December 1864 when General William T. Sherman concluded his famous march to the sea, accompanied by more than 30,000 refugees from Georgia who regarded Sherman's troops as an army of liberation, and had accompanied Sherman's forces as they moved eastward. They needed to be relocated to some territory under Union control—Port Royal was that territory; "Report of Brev. General Rufus Saxton to Major General O. O. Howard," December 6, 1865, Sen Exec. docs. 27, 39th Congress. First Session. (1865-66),141. "Some forty thousand destitute freedmen, who followed in the wake of and came in with [Sherman's] army," Hoffman, "From Slavery to Self-Reliance," 20.

15. Giorgio Agamben, *Homo Sacer: Sovereign Power and Bare Life* (Stanford: Stanford University Press, 1998).

16   Notwithstanding the fact that the Fugitive Slave Act remained good law until mid-1864, (Act of June 28, 1864, ch.166, 13 Stat. 200, repealing "the Fugitive Slave Act of eighteen hundred and fifty, and all Acts and Parts of Acts for the Rendition of Fugitive Slaves") it was federal policy well before that time to treat escaped slaves as "contrabands" recognizing their status in between confiscated property and human refugees. In May 1861, General Benjamin Butler declared fugitive slaves "contrabands," on the ground that the Fugitive Slave Act did not apply in a foreign country—Virginia. See Edward L. Pierce, "The Contrabands at Fortress Monroe," *Atlantic Monthly* 8 (1861) 626, 627; see also Leon F. Litwack, *Been in the Storm So Long: The Aftermath of Slavery* (Chapel Hill, N.C.: University of North Carolina Press, 1979), 52–53; Vernon Lane Wharton, *The Negro in Mississippi 1865–1890* (Chapel Hill: University of North Carolina Press, 1947).

17. Pierce, "The Contraband."

18. See Albert Bushnell Hart, *Salmon Portland Chase* (Boston, Houghton, 1899). Edward Pierce later reported that the only well-placed officials that took any interest in the gravity of the situation at Port Royal were Chase and Frederick Law Olmsted, who served as the executive secretary of the United States

Sanitary Commission, a private agency formed to advise and
supply the US Army's Medical Bureau. Edward L. Pierce, "The
Freedmen at Port Royal," *Atlantic Monthly* (September 1863)
291, 296. Even President Lincoln, less than a year before issuing
the Emancipation Proclamation, was disinterested in the fate
of the freedmen who sought safety behind Union lines. Pierce
attributed Lincoln's distraction and indifference, in significant
part, to Lincoln's grief about his son Harry's fatal illness. Pierce,
"The Freedmen at Port Royal."

19. Pierce, "The Freedmen at Port Royal," 29; Rose, *Rehearsal*, 22–23.
20. Rose, *Rehearsal*, 31.
21. Forten, *Journal*, 29.
22. Pierce, "The Freedmen at Port Royal."
23. General Order No. 9, "New York National Freedmen's Relief
     Association," *Annual Report,1866*, 5–6.
24. See Letter from Sam'l H. Terry to Honorable S. P. Chase,
     December 18, 1861, Port Royal Correspondence; Letter from
     Ellis, Britton, & Eaton to Hon. Salmon P. Chase, February 3,
     1862, Port Royal Correspondence.
25. William H. Reynolds to Salmon P. Chase, January 1, 1862, Port
     Royal Correspondence.
26. Edward L. Pierce to Salmon P. Chase, February 3, 1862, Port
     Royal Correspondence.
27. Forten, *Journal*, 29.
28. The Boston Education Committee, later known as the New
     England Freedmen's Aid Society, was founded on February 7,
     1862, and the Port Royal Relief Committee, later named the
     Pennsylvania Freedmen's Relief Association, began work on
     March 5, 1862. See Pierce, "The Freedmen at Port Royal," 297.
     The National Freedmen's Relief Association of New York was
     formed on February 22, 1862. (American Freedman's Union
     Commission. New York Branch, *Brief History of the New York
     National Freedmen's Relief Association: To Which Are Added Some
     Interesting Details of the Work Together with a Brief View of the
     Whole Field, and the Objects to Be Accomplished, Concluding
     With the Fourth Annual Report of the Association for 1865, With
     Statement and Appeal* (New York: NYNFRA, 1866), 5.

29. Letter from Edward L. Pierce to Salmon P. Chase, March 2, 1862, Port Royal Correspondence.

30. Report of Edward L. Pierce to Salmon P. Chase, February 3, 1862, Port Royal Correspondence, 36.

31. Austa M. French, *Slavery in South Carolina and the Ex-Slaves; or, The Port Royal Mission* (New York, W. M. French, 1862), quoted in Hoffman, "From Slavery to Self-Reliance."

32. Letter of Edward L. Pierce to Salmon P. Chase, March 2, 1862, Port Royal Correspondence.

33. Letter from John W. Edmonds, President, National Freedmen's Relief Association, to Salmon P. Chase, March 19, 1862.

34. Letter from Edward L. Pierce to Hiram Barney, March 27, 1862, Port Royal Correspondence.

35. See Pierce, "The Freedmen at Port Royal," 299.

36. Rose, *Rehearsal*, 204. The same macroeconomic principles motivated the white missionaries who colonized Jamaica in the 1830s: "[T]heir case against slavery was centrally linked to their economic argument that slavery was a less productive system than that of the free market." Catherine Hall, *Civilising Subjects: Colony and Metropole in the English Imagination, 1830–1867* (Chicago, IL: University of Chicago Press, 2002), 120.

37. Report of Edward L. Pierce to Salmon Chase, February 3, 1862, in Rebellion Record supp. vol. 1, 3.

38. "A knowledge of the culture of cotton was found not necessary in a superintendent, though it would have facilitated his labors. On this point the laborers were often better informed than their former masters." ("Second Report of Edward L. Pierce to Hon. S. P. Chase, Secretary of the Treasury," June 2, 1862, in *Rebellion Record*, supp. vol. 1, 315, 317.

39. See Pierce, "The Freedmen at Port Royal," 299–300.

40. Whitemarsh Benjamin Seabrook, *A Memoir on the Origin, Cultivation and Uses of Cotton from the Earliest Ages to the Present Time* (Charleston: Miller & Browne, 1844); George Watt, *The Wild and Cultivated Cotton Plants of the World; a Revision of the Genus Gossypium, Framed Primarily with the Object of Aiding Planters and Investigators Who May Contemplate the Systematic Improvement of the Cotton Staple* (Calcutta:

Longmans, Green, and Co., 1907); Stuart Weems Bruchey, *Cotton and the Growth of the American Economy, 1790–1860* (New York: Harcourt, Brace & World, 1967).

41. "He should receive about forty cents a day in order to enable him to lay up thirty dollars a year." "Second Report of Edward L. Pierce to Hon. S. P. Chase, Secretary of the Treasury," June 2, 1862, in *Rebellion Record*, supp. vol. 1, 312.

42. Edward L. Pierce to Salmon P. Chase, February 3, 1862, Port Royal Correspondence; Capt. Hasard Stevens to the Superintendent of the Department of Contrabands, March 1862, reprinted in Ira Berlin, Thavolia Glymph, and Leslie S. Rowland, *The Wartime Genesis of Free Labour: The Lower South, Freedom, a Documentary History of Emancipation, 1861-1867*, ser. 1 vol. 3 (Cambridge: Cambridge University Press, 1982), 177–78

43. Edward L. Pierce to Salmon P. Chase, February 3, 1862, Port Royal Correspondence; "Capt. Hasard Stevens to the Superintendent of the Department of Contrabands," March 1862, reprinted in Berlin et al., *Freedom*, 148.

44. Pierce, "The Freedmen at Port Royal," 308.

45. Pierce, "The Freedmen at Port Royal," 298.

46. Letter from Edward L. Pierce to Salmon P. Chase, June 2, 1862, Port Royal Correspondence.

47. Letter from Edward Philbrick, March 20, 1863, in Pearson, *Letters from Port Royal*, 181; Pierce, "The Freedmen at Port Royal," 308; Johnson, *A Social History of the Sea Islands*, 161.

48. Letter from Edward Philbrick, March 20, 1863, in Pearson, *Letters from Port Royal*, 181.

49. Edward Philbrick to Edward L. Pierce, March 26, 1862, Port Royal Correspondence; Richard Soule, Jr. to Edward L. Pierce, March 29, 1862, Port Royal Correspondence.

50. For example, see Edward L. Pierce to Salmon P. Chase, June 2, 1862, Port Royal Correspondence. "Again, the laborers had but very little confidence in the promises of payment made by us on behalf of the Government."

51. On July 1, 1862, control of the Sea Islands passed from the Treasury Department to the War Department.

52. Pierce, "The Freedmen at Port Royal," 310.

53. Rose, *Rehearsal*, 211.

54. Rose, *Rehearsal*, 211.

55. Circular, Head Quarters, Beaufort, SC, July 3, 1862, enclosed in Brig. General R. Saxton to Hon. Edwin M. Stanton, July 10, 1862, Letters Received, RG 94, NA.

56. Pierce, "The Freedmen at Port Royal," 308.

57. Rose, *Rehearsal*, 211, 225; Pierce, "The Freedmen of Port Royal," 308. This recipe for land allotment mirrored that undertaken by missionaries who set up free Black villages in Jamaica in the 1830s in lots large enough to qualify Black Jamaicans to vote, but not adequate to produce a living. See also, Hall, *Civilizing Subjects*.

58. Hall, *Civilizing Subjects*, 127.

59. Vermont Senator Jacob Collamer made an impassioned speech on the floor of the Senate arguing that the Confiscation Act was unconstitutional. Congressional Globe, 37th Congress, Second Session, April 25, 1862. 1807. The Kentucky Supreme Court held the Confiscation Acts unconstitutional in Norris v. Doniphan, 61 Ky. (4 Met.) 385 (1863). Despite disagreement about the constitutionality of the Confiscation Acts in Congress and in various state courts, the US Supreme Court upheld them after the close of the war as a legitimate exercise of the war power in seizing enemy property (Tyler v. Defrees, 78 U.S. (11 Wall.) 331 (1871); Miller v. United States, 78 U.S. (11 Wall.) 268 (1871); McVeigh v. United States, 78 U.S. (11 Wall.) 259 (1871); G. Randall, *Constitutional Problems Under Lincoln*, rev. ed. (Champaign: University of Illinois Press, 1951); James R. Maxeiner, "Bane of American Forfeiture Law-Banished at Last?,"Law Review, 62 n. 2, Cornell (1977)).

60. An Act for the Collection of Direct Taxes in Insurrectionary Districts within the United States, and for other Purposes, 37th Congress, Sess. II, Chapter 98, 12 Stat. 589 (June 7, 1862).

61. Letter from Rufus Saxton to Hon. Edwin M. Stanton, Secretary of War, December 1862, Group 431, Series I, Box 1, Folder 1, Letterbook Headquarters—2nd, Beaufort SC 1862, Correspondence of General Saxton, June 30, 1862 to October 15, 1864, Rufus and Willard S. Saxton Papers, Yale University,

Manuscripts and Archives.

62. *Second Annual Report of the New England Freedmen's Aid Society (Educational Commission)* April 21, 1864, 15.

63. "Testimony of R. Tomlinson Port Royal Experiment," *Pennsylvania Freedmen's Bulletin*, vol. 1, no. 1, February 1865, 20.

64. LaWanda Cox, "The Promise of Land for the Freedmen, *Mississippi Valley Historical Review* 45 no. 2, (1958) 413, 428; "[T]he Abolitionists and negroes' friends up North are striving so hard to have the sale postponed . . ." Letter from William C. Gannett, January 26, 1863, in Pearson, *Letters from Port Royal*, 147.

65. Report of Rufus Saxton to Edwin Stanton, December 30, 1864, *War of the Rebellion*, Official Records (hereinafter OR), vol. 4, no. 3, 1025.

66. Letter of Rufus Saxton to Professor J. J. Child, March 15, 1865, Saxton Papers, Yale University.

67. Testimony of Judge A. D. Smith to American Freedmen's Inquiry Commission, June 1863, M619 Roll 200, NA, emphasis in original.

68. Report from Saxton to Stanton, December 30, 1864, 1025: "To put the lands at auction in large lots was virtually to place them beyond the reach of the freedmen. In a free competition of their weakness, ample means of persons eager to grasp the prizes offered here to speculation their chances could be stated only by very small fractions or minus quantities."

69. Report from Saxton to Stanton, December 30, 1864, 1025: "To put the lands at auction in large lots was virtually to place them beyond the reach of the freedmen. In a free competition of their weakness, ample means of persons eager to grasp the prizes offered here to speculation their chances could be state only by very small fractions or minus quantities."

70. Statutes at Large, vol. 12, 640-41.

71. Testimony of Judge A. D. Smith to the American Freedmen's Inquiry Commission, June 1863, M619, Roll 200, NA; Report of R. Saxton to Brigadier General M. C. Miegs, October 2, 1863, reprinted in Berlin et al., *Freedom: A Documentary History of Emancipation*, series I, vol 3, 271.

72. Letter from William C. Gannett, March 14, 1863, *Letters from*

Port Royal, 177.

73. Edward L. Pierce, "The Freedmen at Port Royal."

74. Edward L. Pierce, "The Freedmen at Port Royal."

75. Report of Edward L. Pierce to Salmon P. Chase, June 2, 1862, Port Royal Correspondence.

76. Pierce, "The Freedmen at Port Royal," September 1863.

77. Letter of Rufus Saxton to Prof. J. J. Child, March 15, 1865, Saxton Papers, Yale University.

78. This report derives from a letter written by a northern missionary who ran the school that the Edgerly and Red House children attended. Letter from Martha A. Wight to Mr. C. C. Leigh, March 22, 1864, printed in Appendix to the Second Annual Report of the New England Freedmen's Aid Society, April 21, 1864, 68–69.

79. Sales Book of Captured, Confiscated or Abandoned Moveable Property in Sea Islands Region of South Carolina, RG 366, Entry 588, NA.

80. Results of Practical Experiments. Letters from Mr. Edward S. Philbrick. Boston, February 24th, 1864. Second Annual Report New England Freedmen's *Aid Society.*

81. Edward L. Philbrick to Hon. W. E. Wording, January 14, 1864, reprinted in Berlin et al., *Freedom: A Documentary History of Emancipation,* series 1, vol. 3 pp. 279–81; Pierce, "The Freedmen of Port Royal," 309; Laura Matilda Towne, *Letters and Diary of Laura M. Towne: Written from the Sea Islands of South Carolina,* 1862–1884 (Cambridge: Riverside Press, 1912), 106–07; Testimony of Capt. E.W. Hooper to the American Freedmen's Inquiry Commission, June 1863, M 619, Roll 200, NA; Rose, *Rehearsal,* 214–15.

82. Results of Practical Experiments. Letters from Mr. Edward S. Philbrick. Boston, February 24th, 1864. 2nd Annual Report New England Freedmen's Relief.

83. Johnson, *A Social History,* 186.

84. Letter from Charles P. Ware, March 10, 1863, in *Letters from Port Royal,* 171. See also, Rose, *Rehearsal,* 214.

85. Report from Saxton to Stanton, December 30, 1864, 1025; Rose, *Rehearsal,* 272.

86. Kerry S. Normand, "'By Industry and Thrift': Landownership Among the Freedpeople of St. Helena Parish, South Carolina, 1863-1870," unpublished thesis, Hampshire College (1994), 20; Rose, *Rehearsal*, 274.

87. Normand, "By Industry and Thrift," 276.

88. Normand, "By Industry and Thrift," 275, n.6.

89. Normand, "By Industry and Thrift," 279.

90. Abraham Lincoln, "Additional Instructions to the Direct Tax Commissioners for the District of South Carolina in Relation to the Disposition of Lands," December 31, 1863, *War of the Rebellion, Official Records* (hereinafter "OR"), vol. 4, no. 3, 120.

91. Rufus Saxton Report, February 7, 1864, OR, 120.

92. Letter of Rufus Saxton to Charles Sumner, December 6, 1863, Saxton Papers, Yale University; Pearson, *Letters from Port Royal*, 230, 247; Mary Jennie McGuire, "Getting Their Hands on the Land: The Revolution in St. Helena Parish, 1861-1900," unpublished dissertation, University of South Carolina 1985, 75–76.

93. Letter of William C. Gannett, May 11, 1862, *Letters from Port Royal*, 37–38, n.1.

94. Report of J. W. Alford to Major General O. O. Howard, January 1, 1866, Sec. Exec. Docs. no. 27, 39th 1st Sess. (1865-66), 121.

95. *Brief History of the New York National Freedmen's Relief Association*, 8.

96. "Preliminary Report from the Tax Commissioners of South Carolina under the act of Congress June 7, 1862," January 1, 1863, cited in Rosengarten, *Tombee*, 265–66.

97. Preliminary Report from the tax commissioners of South Carolina under the act of Congress June 7, 18, 37th Congress, Session Three, Exec. Doc. no. 26 January 1, 1863, 2.

98. Rosengarten, *Tombee*, 267. Theodore Rosengarten and William Allen, a Wisconsin school teacher and song collector who left a remarkable diary of his time on the Sea Islands, offer very moving accounts of the freedmen's views toward the land; *The William F. Allen Diary*, State Historical Society of Wisconsin, Madison, Wisconsin.

99. James M. McPherson, "The Negro's Civil War (New York,

1965)," *Philadelphia Press*, May 31, 1864.

100. Johnson, *A Social History*, 190.

101. "Land for Sale and to Lease at the South—The Commissioners appointed by Government, are selling land of rebels for the taxes, at rates but little higher than Government wild land. Officers appointed for the purpose, in the cotton and sugar districts, lease plantations under certain conditions to men who come well recommended. Concerning lands in South Carolina and Florida, information may be had by writing to Brig. Gen. Rufus Saxton, Beaufort, SC Or a letter to Secretary Usher, of the Department of the Interior at Washington DC, would probably bring out the facts relative to all such matters." *American Agriculturalist for the Farm, Garden, and Household,* February 1864, 36; Letter of Rufus Saxton to Mr. George H. Lambert, January 13, 1864; Letter to Mr. Joseph Pettince, Brooklyn, NY, February 26, 1864, Saxton Papers, Yale University.

102. "There has been the most disgraceful squabbling among the tax commissioners, General Saxton . . . and other authorities. The people are the victims. At first most of the lands were to be sold at auction in large lots; that brought in white settlers—and only a little was for negro sales. Then one commissioner sends up to Washington, gets orders for a Western preemption system, and with a grand hurrah the negroes were told to go and grab the lands. The other commissioners then throw all possible obstacles in the way till they can get dispatches up to Washington too, and the answer comes back,—Preëmptions don't count, sell by auction." Letter from William C. Gannett, February 22, 1864, *Letters from Port Royal,* 254.

103. Letter of Rufus Saxton to Mr. C. C. Leigh, April 1, 1864, Saxton Papers, Yale University.

104. Letter of Rufus Saxton to Mr. C. C. Leigh, Saxton Papers.

105. Prices ranged from $5 to $20 per acre. See letter from William C. Gannett, *Letters from Port Royal,* 254.

106. Edward Magdol, *A Right to the Land: Essays on the Freedmen's Community* (Westport: Greenwood Publishing Group, 1977), 177.

107. Magdol, *A Right to the Land,* 156, 177.

108. Magdol, *A Right to the Land,* 177; Rose, *Rehearsal,* 287–90.

109. Letter of Rufus Saxton to Charles Sumner, December 6, 1863, Saxton Papers, Yale University.

110. Report from Saxton to Stanton, December 30, 1864, *War of the Rebellion*, vol. 4, no. 3, 1026; Rose, *Rehearsal*, 290.

111. Letter of M. French v. Hon. Mr. Lewis, February 23, 1864, General Correspondence, ser. 99, SC, Records of or Relating to Direct Tax Commissions in the Southern States, RG 58, reprinted in Berlin et al., *Freedom*, 291–92.

112. Report of Rufus Saxton to Edwin Stanton, December 30, 1864, *War of the Rebellion*, vol 4, no. 3, 1026.

113. William C. Gannett and E. E. Hale, "The Freedmen at Port Royal," *North American Review* 101, no. 2 (July 1865), 1, 24; see also, Letter from William C. Gannet, March 6, 1864, *Letters from Port Royal*, 255; "Three Years among the Freedmen: William C. Gannett and the Port Royal Experiment," *The Journal of Negro History* 42, no. 2 (1957), 108–9.

114. Letter of Rufus Saxton to Mr. C. C. Leigh, April 1, 1864, Saxton Papers, Yale University.

115. Letter of E. P. Hutchinson to Hon. J. B. Alley, March 2, 1864, reprinted in Berlin et al., *Freedom* 307.

116. McGuire, "Getting their Hands on the Land," 86; Letter from Lt. Col. Ed. W. Smith to Messrs. Brisbane, Wording, and Smith, February 25, 1864, and Letter from A. D. Smith to Edward W. Smith, late February, 1864, reprinted in Berlin et al., *Freedom*, 293–96.

117. Petition to his Excellency Abraham Lincoln from John H. Major and eighteen others, March 1, 1864, reprinted in Berlin et al., *Freedom*, 297–99

118. Austin Smith to Hon. S. P. Chase, May 15, 1864, reprinted in Berlin et al., *Freedom*, 299–307

119. Brig. General R. Saxton to Hon. Edward M. Stanton, December 30, 1864, RG 94, Letters Received, NA.

120. *New Orleans Tribune*, November 20, 1895; *New York Herald*, October 22, 1865; Magdol, *A Right to the Land*, 164–66; Joel Williamson, *After Slavery: The Negro in South Carolina During Reconstruction, 1861-1877* (New York: Norton, 1975), 63.

121. "On Christmas night seven hundred cold, shivering, and hungry

freedmen of all ages came into Beaufort . . . The homeless ones were 'in a state of misery which would have moved . . . a heart of stone,'" in Rose, *Rehearsal*, 321.

122. See Report Concerning Freedmen on Port Royal and Adjacent Lands, Agent H.G. Judd to Bvt. Maj. Gen. R. Saxton, August 1, 1865, "Reports of Conditions and Operations July 1865–Dec. 1866," Records of the Assistant Commission for the State of South Carolina, Bureau of Refugees, Freedmen and Abandoned Lands, 1865–1870, M869 Roll 34, NA.

123. Report of Brig. General Rufus Saxton to Major General O. O. Howard, December 6, 1865, Sen Exec. Docs. 27, 39th Congress. First Session. (1865-66), 141: "some forty thousand destitute freedmen, who followed in the wake of and came in with [Sherman's] army."

124. *War of the Rebellion*, Series I, vol. XLVII, 37–41 (January 12, 1865); Mary Frances Berry, *My Face Is Black Is True* (New York: Alfred A. Knopf, 2005), 11.

125. *Minutes Of An Interview Between The Colored Ministers And Church Officers At Savannah With The Secretary Of War And Major-Gen. Sherman*, Headquarters Of Major-Gen. Sherman, City Of Savannah, Ga., January 12, 1865–8 p.m., *New York Daily Tribune*, February 13, 1865, *Negroes of Savannah*, Consolidated Correspondence File, series 225, Central Records, Quartermaster General, RG 92, NA; Hoffman, "Slavery to Self-Reliance," 20. These demands were reflected in editorials in the *Anglo-African Magazine* on January 2, 1864; March 19, 1864; April 16, 1864 and June 4, 1864. Hoffman, "From Slavery to Self-Reliance," 20.

126. "The islands from Charleston, south, the abandoned rice fields along the rivers for thirty miles back from the sea, and the country bordering the St. Johns river, Florida, are reserved and set apart for the settlement of the negroes now made free by the acts of war and the proclamation of the President of the United States." *War of the Rebellion*, vol. 47, series 2, Part II (January 16, 1865), 60–62.

127. "At Beaufort, Hilton Head, Savannah, Fernandina, St. Augustine and Jacksonville, the blacks may remain in their chosen or accustomed vocations—but on the islands, and in the settlements

hereafter to be established, no white person whatever, unless military officers and soldiers detailed for duty, will be permitted to reside; and the sole and exclusive management of affairs will be left to the freed people themselves, subject only to the United States military authority and the acts of Congress. By the laws of war, and orders of the President of the United States, the negro is free and must be dealt with as such. He cannot be subjected to conscription or forced military service, save by the written orders of the highest military authority of the Department, under such regulations as the President or Congress may prescribe. Domestic servants, blacksmiths, carpenters and other mechanics, will be free to select their own work and residence, but the young and able-bodied negroes must be encouraged to enlist as soldiers in the service of the United States, to contribute their share towards maintaining their own freedom, and securing their rights as citizens of the United States." *War of the Rebellion*, vol. 47, no. 7 (January 16, 1865), 60–62 .

128. *War of the Rebellion*, 60–62.

129. "Whenever three respectable negroes, heads of families, shall desire to settle on land, and shall have selected for that purpose an island or a locality clearly defined, within the limits above designated, the Inspector of Settlements and Plantations will himself, or by such subordinate officer as he may appoint, give them a license to settle such island or district, and afford them such assistance as he can to enable them to establish a peaceable agricultural settlement. The three parties named will subdivide the land, under the supervision of the Inspector, among themselves and such others as may choose to settle near them, so that each family shall have a plot of not more than (40) forty acres of tillable ground, and when it borders on some water channel, with not more than 800 feet water front, in the possession of which land the military authorities will afford them protection, until such time as they can protect themselves, or until Congress shall regulate their title." *War of the Rebellion*, 60–62.

130. In July 1862, after the cotton crop was planted, the freedmen living on Edisto Island had been evacuated to other islands when the troops defending the island from rebel incursions had been

withdrawn to aid in the defense of Washington City. Edisto Island remained unsettled until the spring of 1865 when Saxton began relocating families there pursuant to Sherman's Field Order. Within a year, roughly 2,300 families had established Edisto homesteads, albeit with possessory titles. Records of the Assistant Commissioner for the State of South Carolina, BRFAL, M 869, Roll 34, NA.

131. Hoffman, *From Slavery to Self-Reliance*, 21.

132. "In order to carry out this system of settlement a general officer will be detailed as inspector of settlements and plantations, whose duty it shall be to visit the settlements, to regulate their police and general management, and who will furnish personally to each head of a family, subject to the approval of the President of the United States, a possessory title in writing, giving as near as possible the description of boundaries, and who shall adjust all claims or conflicts that may arise under the same, subject to the like approval, treating such titles altogether as possessory." Special Field Orders, No. 15, Part V; *War of the Rebellion*, vol. 47, no. 1, Part II (January 16, 1865), 62.

133. "Several occurrences had led them to doubt our good faith," he wrote Stanton on December 31, 1864, *War of the Rebellion*, vol. 4, no. 3, 1028.

134. Bt. Maj. Gen'l. R. K. Scott to Maj. Genl. O. O. Howard, 5 May 1866, vol. 11, Letters Sent, ser. 2916, SC Asst. Comr., RG 105 [A-7396], 111.

135. 38th Congress, Session II, Chapter 90, An Act to Establish a Bureau for the Relief of Freedmen and Refugees, Statutes At Large XIII, March 3, 1865.

136. LaWanda Cox provides a thorough reading of the integrity of the government's title to abandoned and confiscated lands, as well as to the legislative history of the land provisions of the first Freedmen's Bureau Act. Cox, "The Promise of Land," 413–440; see also, Paul A. Cimbala, "The Freedmen's Bureau, the Freedmen, and Sherman's Grant in Reconstruction Georgia, 1865–1867," *The Journal of Southern History* 55, no. 4 (1989), 597–632.

137. Letter from T. Edwin Ruggles to Charles P. Ware, May 6, 1865, *Letters from Port Royal*, 310–11.

138. "The South as It Is," *The Nation*, November 30, 1865, 682–83.

139. Report of Brev. Brig. General C. H. Howard to Maj. General O. O. Howard, December 30, 1865, Sen Exec. Docs. 27, 39th Cong. 1st Sess. (1865-66) at 125.

140. George R. Bentley, *A History of the Freedmen's Bureau* (Philadelphia: University of Pennsylvania, 1955), 93.

141. Bentley, *A History of the Freedmen's Bureau*, 95.

142. William S. McFeely, *Yankee Stepfather: General O.O. Howard and the Freedmen* (New Haven: Yale University Press, 1968), 133. The struggles in Washington between the various actors in the Congress and the Executive Branch, resulting in conflicting instructions to the officers in the field, in many cases never made their way to the field officers, many of whom held the belief that no policy was being set with respect to settling the land claims of either the freedmen or the returning white planters. See e.g. Report of Brev. Brig. General C. H. Howard to Maj. General O. O. Howard, December 30, 1865: "Now the old owners are returning and the freedmen are unwilling to give up the land; in fact. I am not aware that any order has been issued requiring them to relinquish it." 125.

143. Report of Brev. Brig. General C. H. Howard to Maj. General O. O. Howard, December 30, 1865 at 124; Report of General Rufus Saxton to Maj. General O. O. Howard, December 6, 1865, Sen Exec. Docs. 27, 39th Cong. 1st Sess. (1865-66) at 140-41.

144. Report of General Rufus Saxton to Maj. General O. O Howard, December 6, 1865.

145. William S. McFeely, *Yankee Stepfather: General O. O. Howard and the Freedmen* (W.W. Norton, 1994), 133.

146. Report of James C. Beecher to Capt. Hodges, December 1, 1865, RG 393, Part 1, entry 4112.

147. D. W. Whittemore to Capt A. P. Ketchum, January 30, 1866, enclosed in first Lt. Erastus W. Everson to Bvt. Lt. Col. H. W. Smith, May 30, 1866, E-48 1866, Registered Letters Received, ser. 2922, SC Asst. Comr., RG 105 [A-7393].

148. D. W. Whittlemore to Capt. A. P. Ketchum, January 30, 1866.

149. D. W. Whittlemore to Capt. A. P. Ketchum, January 30, 1866, 141.

150. D. W. Whittlemore to Capt. A. P. Ketchum, January 30, 1866.

151. Report of General Rufus Saxton to Maj. General O. O. Howard,

December 6, 1865, Sen Exec. Docs. 27, 39th Cong. First Sess. (1865-66) 141.

152. McFeely, *Yankee Stepfather*, 146.

153. Report of James C. Beecher to Capt. Hodges, December 1, 1865, RG 393, Part 1, entry 4112, at 143.

154. Bentley, *A History of the Freedmen's Bureau*, 393, 2016, 99–100.

155. An act to amend an act entitled "An act to establish a Bureau for the relief of Freedmen and Refugees," and for other purposes, December 4, 1865.

156. Ibid., 118–19.

157. President Andrew Johnson, Veto Message, Washington, D.C., February 19, 1866. Lillian Foster, *Andrew Johnson, His Life and Speeches*, (New York: Richardson & Co., 1866) available at: http://teachingamericanhistory.org/library/document/veto-of -the-freedmens-bureau-bill/.

158. Ibid.

159. Rosie Gray, "Trump Defends White-Nationalist Protesters: 'Some Very Fine People on Both Sides,'" *Atlantic*, August 15, 2017, available at: https://www.theatlantic.com/politics/archive /2017/08/trump-defends-white-nationalist-protesters-some -very-fine-people-on-both-sides/537012/.

160. Rose, *Rehearsal*, 357.

161. First Lt. Erastus W. Everson to Bvt. Lt. Col. H. W. Smith, May 30, 1866, E-48 1866, Registered Letters Received, ser. 2922, SC Asst. Comr., RG 105 [A-7393].

162. 39th Congress, 1st Session, Chapter 200, An Act to continue in force and to amend "An Act to establish a Bureau for the Relief of Freedmen and Refugees," and for other Purposes, *U.S. Statutes at Large*, vol. XIII, July 16, 1866.

163. 39th Congress, 1st Session, Chapter 127, An Act for the Disposal of the Public Lands for Homestead Actual Settlement in the States of Alabama, Mississippi, Louisiana, Arkansas, and Florida, *US Statutes at Large*, vol. XIV, June 21, 1866.

164. Ironically, many of the freedmen's farming implements had been confiscated or pillaged by Union soldiers as they moved through the South during the war. Dylan Penningroth has provided a careful account of the freedmen's efforts to receive

compensation from the Southern Claims Commission for their property stolen by Union troops. Dylan C. Penningroth, *The Claims of Kinfolk: African American Property and Community in the Nineteenth-Century South* (Chapel Hill: University of North Carolina Press, 2003).

165. W. E. B. Du Bois, *Black Reconstruction in America 1860-1880* (New York: Simon and Schuster, 1999), 538.

166. McFeely, *Yankee Stepfather*, 213; Du Bois, *Black Reconstruction*, 538.

167. Provost Court, Sea Islands, S. C. Edisto Island, November 28, 1866 (Morris and Finnick cases), Provost Court, Sea Islands, Charleston, S.C., December 22, 1866 (Clark case), RG 393, Entry 4257, Box 1, NA.

168. Report of M. R. Delany, Major, Military Inspector, Pt Royal to Bvt. Lt. Col. W. L. M. Burger, March 5, 1866, RG 393, Part 1, Entry 4112, NA.

169. Report of Delany to Burger.

170. Kerry S. Normand, "By Industry and Thrift: Landownership among the Freedpeople of St. Helena Parish, South Carolina, 1863-1870," Master's thesis, Hampshire College (1994), 74.

171. Saidiya V. Hartman, *Scenes of Subjection: Terror, Slavery, and Self-Making in Nineteenth-Century America* (New York: Oxford University Press, 1997), 117.

172. Malik Miah, "From Reform to Nonviolent Revolution: The New Poor People's Campaign," *Against the Current* 2, no.4 (Mar/Apr 2018), 33.

173. $66,770 for white households compared with $27,207 for African Americans. 2015 American Community Survey, S1903: Median Income in the Past 12 Months (in 2015 Inflation-Adjusted Dollars).

174. $59,698 median household income for white people nationally, and $36,544 for Black people. Ibid.

175. Robert B. Cuthbert and Stephen G. Hoffius, eds., *Northern Money, Southern Land: The Lowcountry Plantation Sketches of Chlotilde R. Martin* (Columbia, S.C: University South Carolina Press, 2009), 47.

176. "George McMillan, 74, Dead; Writer of Books and Articles,"

New York Times, September 4, 1987, https://www.nytimes.com /1987/09/04/obituaries/george-mcmillan-74-dead-writer-of -books-and-articles.html.

177. See generally, Rosengarten, *Tombee*, 218.

178. Movoto Real Estate (Website), property listing, http://www .movoto.com/beaufort-sc/21-whooping-crane-ln-beaufort -sc-29902-812_1013839/.

179. Zillow Real Estate (website), property listing, https://www.zillow .com/homedetails/601-Bay-St-Beaufort-SC-29902/2112110934 _zpid/

180. *A. R. and Sarah Chisolm v. Jane M. Chisolm and others*, South Carolina Appeals in Equity (February 1851); Slaves in the Estate of Alexander Robert Chisolm, Beaufort District, SC, 1827, https://www.fold3.com/page/283278484_slaves_in_the_estate_ of_alexander_robert_chisolm_sc_and_ga_ _ 1827#description.

181. "Sanford Family's Coosaw Plantation Protected with $2.5M Conservation Easement," *Beaufort Gazette*, May 11, 2011.

182. Cuthbert, *Northern Money, Southern Land*, 95.

183. "Tidalholm: One of Beaufort's many larger-than-life historic homes," Eat Stay Play Beaufort, available at: https:// eatsleepplaybeaufort.com/tidalholm-one-of-beauforts-many- larger-than-life-historic-homes/.

184 Cuthbert, *Northern Money, Southern Land*.

185. President Andrew Johnson, Veto Message, Washington, D.C., February 19, 1866. Lillian Foster, *Andrew Johnson, His Life and Speeches*, (New York: Richardson & Co., 1866), available at: http://teachingamericanhistory.org/library/document/veto-of -the-freedmens-bureau-bill/.

Chapter 2

1. Varina Davis, *Jefferson Davis, Ex-President of the Confederate States of America: A Memoir* (New York: Belford Co., 1890), 1, 49–50, 171–72.

2.   Davis, *Jefferson Davis*, 163.
3.   James T. Currie, *Enclave: Vicksburg and Her Plantations, 1863-1870* (Jackson: University Press of Mississippi, 1980), 85.
4.   Janet Sharp Hermann, *The Pursuit of a Dream* (Jackson: University Press of Mississippi, 1999), 6, 13.
5.   Janet Sharp Hermann, *Joseph E. Davis: Pioneer Patriarch* (Jackson: University Press of Mississippi, 1990), 54.
6.   Ralph Miliband, "The Politics of Robert Owen," *Journal of the History of Ideas* 15, no. 2 (1954), 233.
7.   Arthur Eugene Bestor, *Backwoods Utopias: The Sectarian and Owenite Phases of Communitarian Socialism in America, 1663-1829* (Philadelphia: University of Pennsylvania Press, 1950), 114–22, 160–201; Margaret Cole, *Robert Owen of New Lanark* (London: Batchworth Press, 1953), 144–60.
8.   "For nine long hours Joseph Davis had an opportunity to hear and argue [the advantages of cooperation for human productivity and happiness], and he was profoundly impressed with Owen's ideas." Hermann, *The Pursuit of a Dream*, 43. Davis, *Joseph E. Davis*, 49–50, 171–72. Davis was also interested in employing the most modern methods of production, and in the 1830s was one of the first people in Mississippi to purchase a steam engine, which he later used to power his mills. Hermann *The Pursuit of the Dream*, 11.
9.   Hermann, *The Pursuit of the Dream*, 55.
10. Davis, *Joseph E. Davis*, 174.
11. Hermann, *The Pursuit of the Dream*, 12–14. Kenneth Stampp documented how tooth decay was a constant problem for most enslaved people. Kenneth Stampp, *The Peculiar Institution: Slavery in the Ante-Bellum South* (New York: Vintage Books, 1956), 305.
12. Hermann, *The Pursuit of the Dream*, 14.
13. Hermann, *The Pursuit of the Dream*, 18–19.
14. Hermann, *The Pursuit of the Dream*, 19.
15. Frank Edgar Everett Jr., *Brierfield: Plantation Home of Jefferson Davis* (Jackson: University Press of Mississippi, 1971), 13.
16. He instituted trial by jury of their peers, and taught them the legal form of holding it. His only share in the jurisdiction was

the pardoning power," (Davis, *Jefferson Davis*, 174).

17. Hermann, *Joseph E. Davis*; Hermann, *The Pursuit of a Dream*, 12–13, 28.

18. Janet Hermann notes evidence of only one other planter who permitted his slaves a trial before punishing them. (Hermann, *The Pursuit of a Dream*, 14).

19. Hermann, *The Pursuit of a Dream*, 13–14

20. Hermann, *The Pursuit of a Dream*, 31–32

21. Hermann, *The Pursuit of a Dream*, 32.

22. Hermann, *The Pursuit of a Dream*, 40.

23. See "Interview with Isaiah Montgomery," Hermann, *The Pursuit of a Dream*, 89.

24. DuBois, *Black Reconstruction*, 62; see also W. E. Burghardt Du Bois, "The Freedmen's Bureau," *Atlantic Monthly*, 87, no. 519 (1901), 354–65.

25. James W. Garner, *Reconstruction in Mississippi* (Baton Rouge: Louisiana State University Press, 1968), 256.

26. John Eaton, *Grant, Lincoln and the Freedmen: Reminiscences of the Civil War with Special Reference to the Work for the Contrabands and Freedmen of the Mississippi Valley* (Lexington, KY: CreateSpace Independent Publishing Platform, 2012).

27. Grant's Special Order No. 15, November 15, 1862, 4–5.

28. Ibid., 24; Wharton, *The Negro in Mississippi*, 30.

29. United States American Freedmen's Inquiry Commission, *Preliminary Report Touching the Condition and Management of Emancipated Refugees* (J. F. Trow, printer, 1863), 14, supra n. 1.

30. General Lorenzo Thomas ordered that all of the "horses, mules, oxen, wagons and carts and farming implements" that the freedmen had in their possession be confiscated. John Eaton, Jr., *Report of the General Superintendent of Freedmen, Department of the Tennessee and State of Arkansas, for 1864* (The Superintendent, 1865), 39–40. "The government regularly seized all animals and tolls from contrabands who entered their lines on the assumption that they were stolen goods, since slaves could not legally own property; the army hoped thereby to secure more supplies for their own use and keep them from falling into enemy hands. This peremptory confiscation of their

property infuriated the Davis ex-slaves and left them unable to continue farming on their own," Hermann, *Joseph E. Davis*, 50.

31. Eaton, *Grant, Lincoln, and the Freedman*, 59–60

32. Wharton, *The Negro in Mississippi*, 33.

33. James E. Yeatman, *A Report on the Condition of the Freedmen of the Mississippi: Presented to The Western Sanitary Commission* (The Commission, 1864), 8.

34. Yeatman, *A Report on the Condition of the Freedmen*; James E. Yeatman, *Report to the Western Sanitary Commission in Regard to Leasing Abandoned Plantations: With Rules and Regulations Governing the Same* (Western Sanitary Commission Rooms, 1864); James E. Yeatman, *Suggestions of a Plan of Organization for Freed Labor: And the Leasing of Plantations Along the Mississippi River, under a Bureau Or Commission to Be Appointed by the Government* (Western Sanitary Commission, 1864).

35. Just as Port Royal had two Shermans, Davis Bend had two Thomases: Captain Samuel Thomas and General Lorenzo Thomas.

36. Eaton, *Grant, Lincoln, and the Freedmen*, 85-86, 165; John Townsend Trowbridge and Joe Henry Segars, *The South: A Tour of Its Battlefields and Ruined Cities, a Journey Through the Desolated States, and Talks with the People, 1867* (Macon: Mercer University Press, 2006); Steven Joseph Ross, "Freed Soil, Freed Labor, Freed Men: John Eaton and the Davis Bend Experiment," *The Journal of Southern History* 44, no. 2 (1978), 213, 214.

37. Hermann, *The Pursuit of a Dream*, 42.

38. *The New York Herald*, December 28, 1863.

39. Yeatman, *A Report on the Condition of the Freedmen of the Mississippi*, 13.

40. See e.g., Eaton, *Grant, Lincoln, and the Freedmen*, 163.

41. Such as James Yeatman, president of the Western Sanitary Commission.

42. See Hermann, *The Pursuit of a Dream*, 48–49.

43. Eaton, *Grant, Lincoln, and the Freedmen*, 190.

44. L. Thomas to Edwin Stanton, September 14, 1864, OR, Series III, vol. iv, p. v. 4, no. 3, 708.

45. Special Orders, No. 120, Lt. Col. T. H. Harris, By Order of Maj. Gen. N. J. T. Dana, November 5, 1864, OR, vol. 41, no.1, 437–38.

It is worth noting the serendipity that Sherman and Thomas both issued Special Orders No. 15 regarding the allocation of land to freedmen; quite a remarkable coincidence.

46. Special Orders, No. 120.

47. Special Orders, No. 120.

48. Recall that Congress did not allocate any funding for freedmen's affairs until the Second Freedmen's Bureau bill in 1868.

49. See Thomas to Stanton, September 11, 1864, 709.

50. Hermann, *The Pursuit of a Dream*, 46.

51. Report of Samuel R. Shipley, President of the Executive Board, of His Recent Visit to the Camps of the Freedmen On the Mississippi River, January 12, 1864, in *Statistics of the Operations of the Executive Board of Friends' Association of Philadelphia and its vicinity, for the Relief of Colored Freedmen* (January 19, 1864), 24.

52. "In the active aid of such association as our own, the true solution of this great problem may be found; and, as it seems to be a work of a kindred character with that in which we as a society have been so long engaged in behalf of the Indian Tribes, it ought to find special favor with us. It is believed that if an assignment of a plantation were made to one hundred laborers, and it were divided into tracts of five to ten acres each, to be under their individual care and management, subject in a measure to the director of a capable and faithful Friend who would assume the general oversight of all matters of interest for the plantation, it would prove a great success. Such a tract will be furnished by Colonel Eaton at Palmyra, Davis Bend, twenty miles below Vicksburg . . . If 1,000 acres were divided in the manner above stated, and a Friend could be found who would undertake the supervision of it, there would be no difficulty in at once procuring the necessary laborers and proceeding to work it . . . In short, it is proposed to enable these 100 laborers to become lessees on a small scale, by the disinterested aid of our Association." Report of Samuel R. Shipley, 24–25

53. Report of Samuel R. Shipley.

54. Colonel S. W. Preston to General Lorenzo Thomas, October 9, 1865, RG 105, M 826, Roll 8, NA.

55. "In 1864 the Home Farm [at Brierfield] accommodated some

955 people, according to a detailed record book. The vast majority of them were females of all ages. There were many male children and quite a few men over sixty; some were in their eighties, and one was age ninety-two. But there were only a handful of females in the eighteen-to-fifty age group, and most of those were labeled unfit for work. The typical family consisted of an adult female and her children, although there were some families with two adult females, either sisters or mother-daughter groups. The overwhelming majority were described as Black; there were three listed as yellow, one brown, and three white." Hermann, *The Pursuit of a Dream*, 53.

56. Report of Col. Samuel Thomas, Sen. Exec. Docs. 27, 39th Cong. First Sess. (1865-66), 39; James T. Currie, *Enclave: Vicksburg and Her Plantations, 1863–1870* (Jackson: University Press of Mississippi, 1980), 100.

57. Trowbridge, *The South*, 384.

58. "Visitors from the North often cited this court system as evidence of a unique experiment in self-government; few realized that it was simply a continuation of a tradition established by Joseph Davis more than a generation earlier. The ease with which the older residents, who may well have suggested and helped plan the court system, adopted this form of community control stemmed largely from their previous experience under Davis's tutelage." Hermann, *The Pursuit of a Dream*, 63–64.

59. Freedmen's Court, Davis Bend, Record Court of Freedmen, Davis Bend, Miss., RG 105, Entry 2153, NA.

60. Freedmen's Court, Davis Bend, Record Court of Freedmen.

61. Eaton, *Grant, Lincoln, and the Freedmen*, 165.

62. See Trowbridge, *The South*; "Record Court of Freedmen, Davis Bend."

63. Trowbridge, *The South*; "Record Court of Freedmen, Davis Bend."

64. Trowbridge, *The South*; "Record Court of Freedmen, Davis Bend."

65. Trowbridge, *The South*, 384–85

66. Eaton, *Grant, Lincoln, and the Freedmen*, 166.

67. Report of Col. Samuel Thomas, Sen. Exec. Docs. 27, 39th Cong. 1st Sess. (1865-66), 39; Wharton, *The Negro in Mississippi*, 41.

68. Hermann, *The Pursuit of a Dream*, 95–96.

69. James T. Currie, *Enclave: Vicksburg and Her Plantations, 1863-1870* (Jackson: University Press of Mississippi, 2007), 101.

70. Hermann, *The Pursuit of a Dream*, 83–84.

71. Hermann, *The Pursuit of a Dream*, 74.

72. Currie, *Enclave*, 121.

73. See *Vicksburg Daily Times*, November 21, 1866.

74. Isaiah Montgomery reported that they ranked third in the county in cotton production. George F. Porter, "Extracts from Newspapers and Magazines," *The Journal of Negro History* 8, no. 1 (1923), 89.

75. Benjamin Montgomery led the state in experimenting in diversifying cotton seed, and crop rotation. See Hermann, *The Pursuit of a Dream*, 153–54.

76. Wharton, *The Negro in Mississippi*, 44.

77. Porter, "Extracts from Newspapers and Magazines," 90.

78. Currie, *Enclave*, 126.

79. Currie, *Enclave*, 91.

80. Everett, *Brierfield*, 3–6.

Chapter 3

1. Eric Foner and Joshua Brown, *Forever Free: The Story of Emancipation and Reconstruction* (New York: Knopf, 2005); Elizabeth Hyde Botume, *First Days amongst the Contrabands* (New York: Arno Press, 1968), 74.

2. Foner and Brown, *Forever Free*.

3. In fact, the enslaved people at Port Royal had been legally emancipated twice prior to the enactment of the Emancipation Proclamation. On May 9, 1862, Major General David Hunter, Commander of the Department of the South, issued a general order declaring that "the persons in Georgia, Florida, and South

Carolina heretofore held as slaves, are . . . declared forever free."
President Lincoln quickly revoked Hunter's declaration just
as he had General Freemont's order emancipating enslaved
people in Missouri in August of 1861. (General Orders, No.
11, *Rebellion Records*: Volume 5. Doc. 28, vol. 5, no. 11 doc.
28). Then two months later, on July 17, 1862, Congress enacted
the Second Confiscation Act of 1862 in which, among other
things, it emancipated the slaves of any person in rebellion or
insurrection against the United States. (US, Statutes at Large,
Treaties, and Proclamations of the United States of America, vol.
12 [Boston, 1863], 589–92). Lincoln felt that he must do more
than rely upon the Confiscation Act to free the slaves in part
because of concerns about the Act's constitutionality but also
due to the difficulty in proving that a particular slave's master
was in rebellion or insurrection as defined by the Act.

4.   See Katherine Franke, *Wedlocked: The Perils of Marriage
Equality* (New York: NYU Press, 2015), 25.

5.   Elizabeth A. Povinelli, *The Cunning of Recognition: Indigenous
Alterities and the Making of Australian Multiculturalism*
(Durham, NC: Duke University Press Books, 2002), 56.

6.   Eric Foner, "Thaddeus Stevens and the Imperfect Republic,"
Pennsylvania History 60, no. 2 (April 1, 1999), 136–37.

7.   See Sally Engle Merry, *Colonizing Hawai'i: The Cultural Power
of Law* (Princeton: Princeton University Press, 2000), 26:
"Some New Englanders came to do good, others to do well for
themselves, and some to do both."

8.   Timothy C. Jacobson and George David Smith, *Cotton's
Renaissance: A Study in Market Innovation* (New York:
Cambridge University Press, 2001).

9.   In this argument you see a convergence of the interests of
Black people and capitalists that Derrick Bell later identified as
underlying the civil rights struggles of the 1950s. See: "Brown
v. Board of Education and the Interest-Convergence Dilemma,"
Harvard Law Review 93 no. 3 (January 1980), 518.

10.   Rose, *Rehearsal*, 227.

11.   Foner, "Thaddeus Stevens," 136.

12.   President Andrew Johnson, Veto Message, Washington, D.C.,

February 19, 1866, Lillian Foster, *Andrew Johnson, His Life and Speeches*, (New York: Richardson & Co., 1866), available at: http://teachingamericanhistory.org/library/document/veto-of-the-freedmens-bureau-bill/.

13. See the *Nation*, March 21, May 9, 16 1867.

14. See generally, Foner, "Thaddeus Stevens," 128–49.

15. See the *New York Times*, July 9, 1867.

16. Fifty-First Congress, Sess. 2, Chap. 469 Sec 4 An act to credit and pay to the several States and Territories and the District of Columbia all moneys collected under the direct tax levied by the act of Congress approved August fifth, eighteen hundred and sixty-one. (March 2, 1891): "To the owners of the lots in the town of Beaufort, one-half of the value assessed thereon for taxation by the United States direct-tax commissioners for South Carolina; to the owners of lands which were rated for taxation by the State of South Carolina as being usually cultivated, five dollars per acre for each acre thereof returned on the proper tax-book; to the owners of all other lands, one dollar per acre for each acre thereof returned on said tax-book."

17. See table of eligible claimants for compensation from confiscated land, Stephen R. Wise et al., *Rebellion, Reconstruction, and Redemption, 1861–1893: The History of Beaufort County, South Carolina, Volume 2* (Columbia: University of South Carolina Press, 2015), 466–471.

18. Carter Godwin Woodson, *The Mis-Education of the Negro* (CreateSpace Independent Publishing Platform, 2010), 20.

19. Frances Wright, *A Plan for the Gradual Abolition of Slavery in the United States, without Danger or Loss to the Citizens of the South* (Baltimore, 1825).

20. Jessica Gordon Nembhard, *Collective Courage: A History of African American Cooperative Economic Thought and Practice,* (University Park, Pennsylvania: Pennsylvania State University Press, 2014), 37–38; William Henry Pease and Jane H. Pease, *Black Utopia: Negro Communal Experiments in America* (Madison: State Historical Society of Wisconsin, 1963), 36–37.

21. Nembhard, *Collective Courage*, 38–39; Jacqueline Jones, *Labor of Love, Labor of Sorrow: Black Women, Work, and the Family, from*

Slavery to the Present (New York: Basic Books, 2009), 52; Pease, 160.

22. Nembhard, *Collective Courage*, 39.

23. Letter from Rufus Saxton to Hon. Edwin M. Stanton, Secretary of War, December 1862, Saxton Papers, Yale University.

24. Letter of Rufus Saxton to Prof. J. J. Child, March 15, 1865, Saxton Papers, Yale University.

25. The international community has fully embraced the notion that human slavery violates fundamental human rights. See Slavery Convention of 1926: "The High Contracting Parties undertake, each in respect of the territories placed under its sovereignty, jurisdiction, protection, suzerainty or tutelage, so far as they have not already taken the necessary steps: (a) To prevent and suppress the slave trade; (b) To bring about, progressively and as soon as possible, the complete abolition of slavery in all its forms."; Universal Declaration of Human Rights of 1948: "No one shall be held in slavery or servitude; slavery and the slave trade shall be prohibited in all their forms."

26. This notion is more fully elaborated in Katherine Franke, *Wedlocked: The Perils of Marriage Equality* (New York: NYU Press, 2015) chapter 3.

27. Rose, "Property as the Keystone Right?"

28. Arthur Lee, *An Appeal to the Justice and Interests of the People of Great Britain, in the Present Disputes with America* (New York: 1775), 14; James W. Ely, *The Guardian of Every Other Right: A Constitutional History of Property Rights*, 3rd ed. (New York: Oxford University Press, 2007).

29. Lee, *An Appeal*, 15 quoting John Locke.

30. Adam Smith, *Lectures on Jurisprudence*, eds. Ronald L. Meek, D. D. Raphael, and P. G. Stein, new ed. (Indianapolis: Liberty Fund Inc., 1982), 5.

31. Michel Foucault, *The History of Sexuality*, vol. 1 (New York: Vintage, 1990), 10: "It appears rather as an especially dense transfer point for relations of power."

32. Frantz Fanon, *The Wretched of the Earth* (New York: Grove Press, 1963), 40.

33. Quoted in Jeanette Davis-Adeshote, *Black Survival in White*

America (Orange, NJ: Bryant and Dillon, 1995), p. 87.

34. Foner (1988), 6–7; Donald (1995), 396; DuBois (1935), 150.
35. Frederick Douglass, quoted in Berry, *My Face is Black*, 39.
36. Frederick Douglass, "Celebrating the Past, Anticipating the Future," April 14, 1875, quoted in Peter C. Myers, *Frederick Douglass: Race and the Rebirth of American Liberalism* (Kansas City: University Press of Kansas, 2008), 143.
37. Browne (1972)
38. See Berry, *My Face is Black*.
39. Johnson v. McAdoo, 45 App. D.C. 440 (1916); aff'd, 37 S.Ct. 649 (1917).
40. Berry, 42, *My Face is Black*.
41. Kevin Samaita, "Zimbabwe to Pay White Farmers for Land Taken and Work with Them in Partnerships," *Business Live*, September 27, 2018, available at: https://www.businesslive.co.za/bd/world/africa/2018-09-27-zimbabwe-to-pay-white-farmers-for-land-taken-and-work-with-them-in-partnerships/.
42. Department of Rural Development and Land Reform, Republic of South Africa, *Land Audit Report 2017*, February 5, 2018, available at: http://www.ruraldevelopment.gov.za/publications/land-audit-report/file/6126.
43. World Bank, *An Incomplete Transition: Overcoming the Legacy of Exclusion in South Africa*, April 30, 2018, available at: https://openknowledge.worldbank.org/bitstream/handle/10986/29793/WBG-South-Africa-Systematic-Country-Diagnostic-FINAL-for-board-SECPO-Edit-05032018.pdf?sequence=1&isAllowed=y.
44. Report of the Secretary of the Interior, 1877, House Executive Docs. No. 1, Part 5, 45th Cong, 2d Sess., serial 1800, xi: "The enjoyment and pride of the individual ownership of property being one of the most effective civilizing agencies, allotments of small tracts of land should be made to the heads of families on all reservations, to be held in severalty under proper restrictions, so that they may have fixed homes. Indians who can furnish sufficient evidence that they have supported their families for a certain number of years should be admitted to the benefits of the homestead acts, and, if they are willing to

detach themselves from their tribal relations, to the privileges of citizenship."

45. Stuart Banner, *How the Indians Lost Their Land: Law and Power on the Frontier* (Cambridge: Belknap Press, 2005), 262.

46. Annual Report of the Commissioner of Indian Affairs to the Secretary of the Interior for the year 1878 (1878), viii; Banner (2005), 272.

47. Smith v. Stevens, 77 US 321 (1870).

48. Cobell v. Norton, 283 F. Supp. 2d 66, 75 (D.D.C. 2003).

49. Francis La Flesche, "An Indian Allotment," *The Independent* 52 (November 8, 1900), 2688, quoted in Benson Tong, "Allotment, Alcohol, and the Omahas," *Great Plains Quarterly* 17, no. 1 (Winter 1997), 22.

50. Banner, *How the Indians Lost Their Land* (2005), 285.

Chapter 4

1. Donna Owens, "Veteran Congressman Still Pushing for Reparations in a Divided America," NBC News, February 20, 2017.

2. The Movement for Black Lives, "Platform,"(website), https://policy.m4bl.org/platform/.

3. "Platform," The Movement for Black Lives (website), https://policy.m4bl.org/platform/.

4. Ta-Nehisi Coates, "The Case for Reparations," *The Atlantic*, "Platform," The Movement for Black Lives (website), https://policy.m4bl.org/platform/, June 2014.

5. "Statement to the media by the United Nations' Working Group of Experts on People of African Descent, on the conclusion of its official visit to USA, 19-29 January 2016," available at: http://www.ohchr.org/EN/NewsEvents/Pages/DisplayNews.aspx?NewsID=17000&LangID=E.

6. Coates, "The Case for Reparations."

7   Charles J. Ogletree, Jr., "Repairing the Past: New Efforts in the Reparations Debate in America," *Harvard Civil Rights-Civil*

Liberties Law Review 38 no. 2 (Summer 2003) 279.

8. Matthew Desmond, "How Homeownership Became the Engine of American Inequality," *New York Times*, May 9, 2017, https://www.nytimes.com/2017/05/09/magazine/how-homeownership-became-the-engine-of-american-inequality.html.

9. William Darity, Jr., Darrick Hamilton, Mark Paul, Alan Aja, Anne Price, Antonio Moore, and Caterina Chiopris, *What We Get Wrong About Closing the Racial Wealth Gap*, (Oakland: Center for Community Development, 2018).

10. Darity, Jr., et al., What We Get Wrong About Closing the Racial Wealth Gap, 4.

11. Richard A. Benton and Lisa A. Keister, "The Lasting Effect of Intergenerational Wealth Transfers: Human Capital, Family Formation, and Wealth," *Social Science Research*, vol. 68 (2017), 1–14.

12. Darity, Jr. et. al. *What We Get Wrong About Closing the Racial Wealth Gap*, 4.

13. For more information about these innovations, see *Community Control of Land & Housing, Exploring Strategies for Combating Displacement, Expanding Ownership, and Building Community Wealth*, (Washington, DC: The Democracy Collaborative, 2018), available at: https://democracycollaborative.org/content/community-control-land-and-housing-exploring-strategies-combating-displacement-expanding.

14. Letter of Rufus Saxton to Mr. C. C. Leigh, April 1, 1864, Saxton Papers, Yale University.

15. John Emmeus Davis, *Origins and Evolution of the Community Land Trust in the United States* (2010), available at http://cltnetwork.org/wp-content/uploads/2014/07/1-Origins, pdf.

16. See generally, Kali Akuno and Ajamu Nangwaya, eds., *Jackson Rising: The Struggle for Economic Democracy and Black Self-Determination in Jackson, Mississippi* (Montreal: Daraja Press, 2017).

17. The Baltimore Housing Roundtable, *Community + Land + Trust: Tools for Development Without Displacement*, available at: https://www.nesri.org/sites/default/files/C%2BL%2BT_web%20copy.pdf; Abigail Savitch-Lew, "The NYC Community Land

Trust Movement Wants to Go Big," *City Limits*, January 8, 2018.

18. Desiree Justina Fields, "From Property Abandonment to Predatory Equity: Writings on Financialization and Urban Space in New York City," PhD Dissertation, CUNY (2013).

19. Abigail Savitch-Lew, "The NYC Community Land Trust Movement Wants to Go Big"; The New Economy Project, https://www.neweconomynyc.org/our-work/campaigns/advancing-clts/.

20. Stephen Witt and Kelly Mena, "De Blasio Defends City Taking African American Properties," *Kings County Politics*, October 4, 2018.

21. "Platform, Invest/Divest" The Movement for Black Lives (website) (emphasis in original), https://policy.m4bl.org/invest-divest/.

22. Boston College Center on Wealth and Philanthropy, "New Report Predicts U.S. Wealth Transfer of $59 Trillion, With $6.3 Trillion in Charitable Bequests, from 2007–2061," news release, May 28, 2014, available at: http://www.bc.edu/content/dam/files/research_sites/cwp/pdf/Wealth%20Press%20Release%205.28-9.pdf; John J. Havens and Paul G. Schervish, *A Golden Age of Philanthropy Still Beckons: National Wealth Transfer and Potential for Philanthropy Technical Report*, (Boston, 2014, available at: http://www.bc.edu/content/dam/files/research_sites/cwp/pdf/A%20Golden%20Age%20of%20Philanthropy%20Still%20Bekons.pdf.

23. Sven Beckert and Seth Rockman, eds., *Slavery's Capitalism: A New History of American Economic Development* (Philadelphia: University of Pennsylvania Press, 2016), 1–2.

24. See Demos, *The Racial Wealth Gap: Why Policy Matters*, stating that lower homeownership rates among the roots of lower wealth of African Americans, ranging from lasting legacies of past policies to disparate access to real estate ownership.

25. See the Serviceman's Readjustment Act of 1944 (GI Bill of Rights), 58 Stat. 284 (1944); see also Ira Katznelson, *When Affirmative Action Was White* (New York: W. W. Norton, 2005), 115, 139–40.

26. Pew Research Center, *On Views of Race and Inequality, Blacks and Whites Are Worlds Apart,* (2016).

27.   See Tom Brokaw, *The Greatest Generation* (New York: Random House, 2005).

28.   Baldwin, "On Being White," 28.

29.   What does it mean to invoke the closet in both these contexts? Does Representative Moore mean to draw a similarity between the racism of white supremacists that deny the crime of slavery and the shame suffered by lesbians and gay men on account of systemic homophobia? What exactly does it mean to analogize the denial of responsibility for the enslavement, torture and murder of millions of Black people to the shame that gay and lesbian people have suffered by "closeting" themselves in dark, self-hateful and self-denying spaces?

30.   Maurice Halbwachs, *La Topographie Legendaire sitaires de France* (1941), 7, quoted in Barry Schwartz, "Iconography and Collective Memory: Lincoln's Image in the American Mind," *Sociology Quarterly* 32 no. 3 (Autumn 1991).

31.   "We preserve memories of each epoch in our lives, and these are continually reproduced; through them, as by a continual relationship, a sense of our identity is perpetuated," Halbwachs (1992), 47.

Index

About Haymarket Books

Haymarket Books is a radical, independent, nonprofit book publisher based in Chicago.

Our mission is to publish books that contribute to struggles for social and economic justice. We strive to make our books a vibrant and organic part of social movements and the education and development of a critical, engaged, international left.

We take inspiration and courage from our namesakes, the Haymarket martyrs, who gave their lives fighting for a better world. Their 1886 struggle for the eight-hour day—which gave us May Day, the international workers' holiday—reminds workers around the world that ordinary people can organize and struggle for their own liberation. These struggles continue today across the globe—struggles against oppression, exploitation, poverty, and war.

Since our founding in 2001, Haymarket Books has published more than five hundred titles. Radically independent, we seek to drive a wedge into the risk-averse world of corporate book publishing. Our authors include Noam Chomsky, Arundhati Roy, Rebecca Solnit, Angela Y. Davis, Howard Zinn, Amy Goodman, Wallace Shawn, Mike Davis, Winona LaDuke, Ilan Pappé, Richard Wolff, Dave Zirin, Keeanga-Yamahtta Taylor, Nick Turse, Dahr Jamail, David Barsamian, Elizabeth Laird, Amira Hass, Mark Steel, Avi Lewis, Naomi Klein, and Neil Davidson. We are also the trade publishers of the acclaimed Historical Materialism Book Series and of Dispatch Books.

Also Available from Haymarket Books

A Beautiful Ghetto
Devin Allen, Introduction by Keeanga-Yamahtta Taylor
and D. Watkins

Black Liberation and the American Dream:
The Struggle for Racial and Economic Justice
Edited by Paul Le Blanc

Class Struggle and the Color Line: American Socialism
and the Race Question, 1900-1930
Paul Heideman

Freedom Is a Constant Struggle: Ferguson, Palestine,
and the Foundations of a Movement
Angela Y. Davis, Edited by Frank Barat, Preface by Cornel West

From #BlackLivesMatter to Black Liberation
Keeanga-Yamahtta Taylor

How Capitalism Underdeveloped Black America:
Problems in Race, Political Economy, and Society
Manning Marable, Foreword by Leith Mullings

How We Get Free: Black Feminism and the Combahee River Collective
Edited by Keeanga-Yamahtta Taylor

Organized Labor and the Black Worker, 1619-1981
Philip S. Foner, Foreword by Robin D. G. Kelley